THE
CANNABIS
PREACHER

SERMON THREE

The Thrilling Hunt for a Ruthless Killer, the Uphill Battle to Rebrand a Company, and a Race Against Time to Eliminate Suspects in One Pulse-Pounding Financial Thriller

SABINE FRISCH

Publishing Services provided by Paper Raven Books LLC

Printed in the United States of America

First Printing, 2023

Hardcover ISBN: 978-0-9878580-9-2

Paperback ISBN: 978-0-9878580-8-5

PROLOGUE

"67-year-old local businessman Tadeo Ivers was found dead at his place of business Thursday night. First reports indicate that Ivers appears to have been shot at close range. Sources close to Ivers reveal that he never left his home or office without several armed security escorts, indicating the shooter must have been someone he trusted, but police and investigators are not prepared to make a statement at this point. Investigations continue, according to Detective Sergeant Robertson. Tadeo Ivers has long been an enigmatic persona in the business world."

"Enigmatic persona, there's a good one. Could just call a spade a spade and say criminal, period, and that he was found in the dingy diner he used for money-laundering purposes." The man reading the paper pushed it away from him and waved at a passing waitress for a coffee refill.

"Enigmatic, my ass." He shook his head. "The man was a nasty, mean criminal. That's all. I've done the world a huge favor."

He stopped as his waitress approached with the coffee. Of course, he had done the world a huge favor by shooting Ivers and ending his criminal career, but he wasn't naïve enough to expect any kind of thanks for it.

"Everything OK?" his waitress asked, nodding at the wadded-up newspaper beside him.

"All good, thanks, luv."

Just peachy, he thought, *I killed Tadeo Ivers, and the police are investigating every which way but mine—I'd call that better than good.*

ONE

"Barry J. Wentworth, I would like for you to accompany us down to the station and answer a few questions about the death of Tadeo Ivers."

Detective Sergeant Robertson stood calm and polite in the room, his hands relaxed by his side, eyes never leaving his person of interest. In his 40 years with the police service, he had seen almost everything, but anyone underestimating the grey curly hair, lined face, and slightly stooped posture would make a big mistake. Robertson missed nothing. He had not liked Wentworth on sight and would have loved nothing better than slapping some cuffs on the slimy bastard, dragging him out to the cruiser, kicking and screaming if needed. Fortunately, good manners and his detective shield prevented him from doing so. His instinctive dislike puzzled him, but Wentworth wasn't making it any easier on himself.

"I told you already," he snarled, "I did not kill Tadeo Ivers. Do us all a favor. Quit standing around questioning me and do your job. Go out there and find the real killer."

"Our investigation is ongoing, Mr. Wentworth. In the meantime, all we want to do is ask a few questions down at the station. Just to set the record straight. Please don't make this harder than it has to be, sir. If everything you tell us checks out, you'll be back in a few hours with your friend Mr. Covin here."

"Rafael—Rafael, a hand here please. I didn't kill Tadeo, and you know it."

"I…"

"Mr. Covin, there are a few questions we have for you as well. If you will kindly hold yourself available for a little chat."

"Wasn't planning on going anywhere, Detective, but you are making me want to call a lawyer."

"You're not considered a suspect at the moment, but that is of course your prerogative."

"Is this really necessary—I mean, dragging Barry to the station?"

"I'm afraid it is, Mr. Covin. We tried to speak to Mr. Wentworth about the death of Tadeo Ivers at his hotel room. His first reaction was to run from us, straight to your house. That's not a great look from where I'm sitting."

The man shrugged and nodded to the policemen he had brought with him.

"Go accompany him out to the car and take him downtown. Wait until I get there before anyone questions him. And for God's sake, keep an eye on him. Now…"

He turned back to Rafael and spread his hands. "Taking him downtown might be overkill. I don't think your friend…"

"Former friend," Rafael said, raising a forefinger.

"Interesting you should mention that. I do remember another occasion when I tried to ask a few questions of Mr. Wentworth, and he ran from us. Straight to the South Pacific, it appears. Perhaps that is a habit of his. Of course, that was a couple of years ago. He was calling himself Connor Beauregard back then, and you two were best friends."

"Yeah, I remember." Rafael Covin dropped and sat on the lowest step of the stairs leading to the upper floor of his house, weariness and exhaustion leaching from his body into the woodwork of the stairs. If you'd asked him to stand, he would have said *forget it*. The last two days had been one heck of a roller coaster of emotions and incidents, and his body was telling him *enough already.*

He'd gone straight from outright pride and joy in what he had accomplished at Perfect Cannabis Corporation, the company that would be the country's leading manufacturer of medical marijuana, to being fired by its major shareholder, Tadeo Ivers, to seeing Connor Beauregard return to the country as Barry J. Wentworth.

And while he was still trying to come to grips with the fact that a friend he considered gone and most likely dead stood in front of him, like some evil ghost from the past, the news broke that Tadeo Ivers had been shot. A mere few hours later, Barry J. Wentworth turned up on his doorstep claiming to be the one and only innocent party in this mess. Barry played innocent rather well, all while suspecting anyone and everyone around him of various nefarious misdeeds. He probably had a theory on the shooting already, but the detective here had interrupted the narration of it.

"You two have quite a bit of history together, don't you," Robertson said, sitting down beside him.

Careful now. A little red alarm signal went off in Rafael's head. *If a detective is trying to be chummy, he wants something, and that something is most likely information you shouldn't be giving him.*

He shrugged and managed a thin smile. "The story has been though all the major papers, Detective. Barry and I were the founders of Perfect Cannabis Corporation. I'm sure you remember it."

"Only too well. Show me somebody in this town who hasn't. Back when he was still called Beauregard. I was just a secondary investigator on that case, but I found it fascinating. A guy puts an illegal grow op into your factory building, right in the shadow of a legal one. The man has a talent of getting himself into tight spots now, doesn't he?"

"That he does," Rafael said, nodding. "You're not wrong there."

"And what about your—lady friend, Kayla Montecito?"

"If you are as well-informed as you claim, Detective Robertson, then surely you also know she used to be Barry's fiancée."

"And now she is yours."

"Whoa, easy." Rafael raised his hands and pushed back a little. "I mean—we hang out together…"

"I think you do more than hang out together, and I also think so does she."

"That's a lot of thinking. You want to know what I think? You are doing more than just shooting the breeze here, Detective. Is this an official questioning?"

"Just getting the lay of the land, Mr. Covin."

"I'm sure you are, Detective Robertson, and it's all quite harmless." He put his hands together, resting his fingers on his face. "Nevertheless, let me get back to my original question. Should I be calling my lawyer now?"

"I don't know, Mr. Covin, should you?"

"Far as I am concerned, I did not do anything a lawyer would have to help me explain."

"That there is an interesting way to put it, Mr. Covin."

Rafael sat up a bit straighter and managed the bright, charming smile that convinced many an investor who was just a bit hesitant about putting money into marijuana.

"Call me Rafael. And until a few days ago, I was running a company producing medical marijuana. I think putting things in an interesting way comes with the job."

"He fired you."

"Who—Wentworth, no? Tadeo Ivers did. And strictly speaking, he didn't have to fire me. The agreement made at the very beginning said that I was to be interim CEO of PerCan until such time…"

Robertson waved a hand and took off his glasses, letting them dangle from long, slender fingers. "What I'm interested in hearing is whether you were mad at the guy when he said you could go."

"I was not mad."

"Not mad? I would have been."

"Nope. I was steamed right up under my non-starched collar. I mean, come on, Detective. I'd done a good job for the man. Scratch that—I'd done a stellar job for him. The company was dead when he made me CEO, D-E-A-D. Bury the thing, put up a cross. I didn't want to be CEO. But fine, he had his methods."

"Methods?"

"Ways of convincing a person to do something for him, even if that someone didn't want to have anything to do with it."

"Another statement that sounds rather interesting, Rafael."

"That was number one. Number two, if there was a way in the world to make my job difficult, if not impossible some days, Tadeo Ivers would find it. The man put rocks into my path that would put anybody to shame."

"If you're trying to make this easy for yourself, you're failing," Robertson said with a raised eyebrow.

"I know that. But I'm not telling you anything you don't know. The next guy you interview is going to tell you Rafael Covin really had a bone to pick with Ivers, more than once. So, I'm going to tell you now, before you come around complaining, 'Why didn't you tell me this right away, Covin?' Doesn't make me look any more or less guilty than I am anyway."

"True."

"And when we have a serious, official-like chat in your office, darn straight, Harvey Finkelbein of Finkelbein and Harmon is going to be right there beside me."

"Long as you know. So, you were mad at Ivers."

"I was absolutely steamed at Ivers. But I didn't kill him—because I had another plan."

"Go on."

"Instead, I was going to go into business—the cannabis business, which I found out I was surprisingly good at. And I was going to bring with me all the good people he needed and didn't appreciate while he had a chance."

"So, you were going to ruin him."

"It would have taken a lot more than that to ruin Tadeo Ivers. No. Let's just say if he didn't think he needed any of us, I was going to let him try it, and that's all."

"Like I said, Rafael, you don't exactly make yourself look any better telling me all of this. But I still appreciate it. Anything else you want to tell me while you're at it?"

Rafael spread his legs out in front of him and folded his hands behind his head, leaning into them.

"Kayla," he merely said.

"The lovely gossip columnist, ah, yes. Now there is a lady with a temper."

Rafael actually laughed and shook his head with a knowing grin. "True enough. She does have the fire. But in this case, no, she had nothing to do with it."

"You're so sure about that?"

"Detective…" Rafael leaned back a little, staring at an unseen spot on the ceiling, thinking for a while before he spoke. "I believe I know what you're thinking. Maybe she killed Ivers, hoping to blame it on Beauregard—Barry Wentworth, silly bloody name."

"You're not wrong about that. No comment on what I might or might not be thinking."

"But, you see, Kayla was over Wentworth. Totally."

"I would expect you to say that."

"I mean it. He treated her badly, left all of us without giving it a second thought, and she went through a bad time. A very bad time. But we were building this company back up, we were succeeding, and she was just as excited as I was. Ivers—he scared her witless most of the time. Other times, she could get right up on her high horse about his morals and the way he treated women. In the end, she didn't want to be around him if she could avoid it."

6

"Well, Mr. Covin." Detective Robertson rose awkwardly from the step they had been sitting on and dusted off his pants. "Getting too old to be sitting down there on the stoop."

"You tell me." Rafael rose as well and offered a hand. "But the last few days have been crazier than most. Might as well go all in, don't you think?"

"You will come down to my office, for a nice little official chat then, with your lawyer Finkelstein?"

"If I can find one with a goofball name like that, I will set something up, sure enough. Take my word on Kayla, though."

"I never take anybody's word on anything. You ought to know that."

Robertson shook his hand a little stiffly and left, and once again, Rafael stood in the hallway of his own home, lost.

He had nowhere to go today and nothing to do. Tadeo had fired him, all but thrown him out of the building. By now, his son Al had probably taken over as CEO. Jesus—Al Ivers.

His father had been adamant about not giving him any kind of role at PerCan, but there he was, CEO. The one man who couldn't possibly have shot Tadeo Ivers, on account of being at a police station all night, dealing with a motor vehicle accident. Talk about luck.

And Al had been right to take over. A company manufacturing marijuana endured enough scrutiny on anything and everything. Having half of the board of executives under investigation for the murder of its biggest shareholder would, well, not look good, for starters. Hurt the company's share price, most likely, and potentially bring down a host of other investigations from any government body that felt like investigating them.

Still, Rafael wondered how Al was faring. Should he call him? Would it be appreciated? Or would Al feel he was intruding, checking up on him? They were friends after all.

Could be, had been, maybe still were. Who the heck knew on this roller coaster?

The last thing he remembered clearly, before all hell broke loose for the second time in just as many days, was that he had put together a business proposal for a consulting company serving the medical marijuana industry, just as he had told Robertson.

He was proud of it. It was a great idea, incredibly sneaky, and probably a little nasty to boot. He wanted his own team. If Ivers did not want to play ball, he could rot in hell. Nobody had cared to make them sign noncompetition clauses when they scraped the company back together from the broken pieces Connor left behind. HR? Not on anybody's mind.

Rafael Covin and Al Ivers for business development; Kayla Montecito for investment and public relations; Dante Ivers, the youngest Ivers son, and Nick Ambrose, Colorado's best weed grower, for biology and agronomy. They would have been one kickass team. World-class. Add his recent acquaintance Irving Moody for financing and they would have been unbeatable.

That's what he had told the group. *If Ivers doesn't want us, let's just strike out on our own. Marijuana is the hottest thing going right now. How many companies out there are in trouble already? How many startups are barely getting by looking for the knowledge, the know-how, and the financing to be a great, maybe even fabulous, company?*

These were all people who had worked at PerCan under him, Rafael Covin. He had picked them, hired them, and kept an eye on them. They had come to respect him and like his leadership style, and everyone was ready to sign on, even Dante Ivers.

He'd been worried a bit about Dante. Daddy had sent him into the ranks of Perfect Cannabis to spy on Rafael and Barry, to figure out what was going on and what he wasn't being told. What Tadeo Ivers hadn't counted on was that Dante got to like the business, working with Nick Ambrose to learn how to be a first-rate grower, and eventually, he even got to like Rafael.

All the people on his team respected each other's style and territory—quietly. Maybe even grudgingly some days, but they respected it. They learned how to disagree with one another and still get along and make PerCan the best it could be. Rafael sometimes wondered about Nick and Dante and how close the two of them were. When they thought nobody was looking, they sure acted like more than colleagues. There would be a touch and a look, a smile that said so much more than just ha-ha. But it wasn't any of his business. They did first-class work, and everybody got along. Until Tadeo waltzed in, with his harebrained decision to fire Rafael and put Dante into his place.

How could you not know your own son? How could you miss the fact that being CEO, sitting in an office all day long and talking to investors, business partners, and the press, would kill Dante? Ask him what a marijuana plant liked and be prepared for a three-hour discourse. Ask him about mergers and acquisitions and get a 30-second uncomprehending stare. That was the Dante Ivers Rafael knew.

So, when Rafael came up with the consulting company idea, all Dante asked was *where do I sign on?* Everybody else was with him anyway. And then the opposition came from the one place he didn't expect it: Al Ivers.

Al Ivers, a man he had grown used to calling his friend.

He didn't want to think about that right now. Rafael went into his kitchen and mechanically put coffee into his ancient wheezing machine. From the other side of the counter, it mocked him—the shiny, stainless-steel, pod-bearing coffee system Kayla had installed—but Rafael didn't trust the thing. Who knew what was going on behind its grinning façade and digital panel? How about putting six spoons of dark roast and a carafe of water into his machine and pushing go? That was a process he could understand.

Al... If he allowed himself to think back to the very beginning of Perfect Cannabis, to the time he and his friend Connor Beauregard had come up with the idea of becoming a manufacturer of medical marijuana, he automatically saw an image of Al.

Connor and Rafael had realized very quickly that they needed two things: knowledge and money. Knowledge was no problem. That's why God invented the internet and specialty consultants. Money was a little harder to come by. Connor could always raise funds like nobody's business, but he did so in style, an expensive, flashy style, and so Rafael had brought in Al…

Coming out of the construction business, Rafael knew Al as a man who owned nightclubs and strip joints and always had cash handy, looking for a place to go. Not until he brought Al into the company as an investor did he realize how large these available funds were, and that it was his father, the mysterious Tadeo Ivers, who owned everything and controlled everything—including Al.

Connor saw their money and took it. And immediately proceeded to plot a way to get rid of the entire Ivers clan.

God, where had those days gone?

His coffee finished, Rafael poured a cup and tasted the hot, bitter liquid just as his phone rang.

"Am I interrupting?" Kayla asked.

"Never you. Push me hard enough, I might go as far as to say you saved me."

"Oh?" Kayla had a way of making that one syllable an entire sentence. "If you tell me why, my love, I might take you out for lunch later."

"Just taking a long walk down memory lane. Not having any fun with it, that's all."

"Not the Hallmark-moment kind of memories, I would assume."

"No." Rafael sat, idly stirring his coffee, watching the liquid go around and around before continuing. "No, I was thinking back to the very beginning of this thing."

"You and Connor."

"Yup. Connor and me, the day of our great presentation."

"I was there."

"You were there, and so was Al."

"Al, who had more money than God, never carried a phone, and never made any notes," Kayla chuckled softly.

"And then," Rafael said, "he hands Connor half a million dollars and says, 'Get the company started, will you?'"

A silence spread between them, and he heard the clink of Kayla's gold earrings against the receiver of her phone.

"Why are you thinking about this now, Rafa? Today of all times?"

Because Connor made a mess of the company, left you and the country, and left me to clean up his mess? Because I did clean it up, only to have Tadeo fire me? Because I couldn't have done it without Al? Al, who had become my friend and then...

"Just an old man woolgathering, I suppose," he said, trying for a laugh and failing. He liked to refer to himself as 'an old man,' although his 50th birthday hadn't been all that long ago. Years in the construction business had kept him reasonably fit, and he looked it, but of late, he'd been exhausted. "The cops were here and took Barry downtown for questioning."

"I heard," Kayla said. "He ran from questioning at his hotel and straight to your house. It's the topic on social media just now. Looks like he's their favorite suspect in the 'who killed Tadeo Ivers' sweepstakes."

"Can't say I blame them. That Sergeant Robertson is pretty sharp, and he remembers Connor, not in the best way. He wants to talk to you, too."

"Rafael? You remember what I told you. Don't go chatting with a police detective just like that. Any time you speak to him, it would be better if you had..."

"A lawyer present? I didn't do anything, Kayla. Why would I need a lawyer?"

"Because you are smart and careful, and there's no such thing as a casual chat with a policeman. You know all of this. I write about this stuff. At the worst moment, you will say the wrong thing, or say the right thing and have it interpreted the wrong way. You run a large company..."

"Used to run a large company."

"Fine, used to. You still need to be careful about talking to police. Promise me you will not do so without a lawyer again. Besides, Al is just keeping the fires going for a while. You need to be ready to come back."

Rafael said nothing and stared down into the depths of his coffee once again.

"Rafael? You know that, right? The moment this whole thing is over, Al is going to step down and make you CEO again. He's only doing this for the company."

"Do I know that?"

"Dear Jesus, I really do have to go and save you, Rafa. Of course. Al never wanted the main seat at Perfect Cannabis. He said so a dozen times. All he wanted to be was a consultant, quietly helping you in the background. What in blazes is the matter with you?"

"And when I asked him if he wanted to come into our consulting company in preparation..."

"He said no because of family obligations. Christ, Rafael, you all but stood there and said, 'Decide, your father or me.' What did you expect from the man?"

I expected him to be on my side, Rafael thought, but said nothing and turned his spoon in a cup of coffee that contained neither cream nor sugar.

"You never wanted it either, remember... the main seat at Perfect Cannabis? Tadeo all but forced you to take it."

"He did force me. He threatened my sons and their inheritance."

"And you stepped up to save the company—and them."

She made sense, of course she did, in that way women always made sense when men were too stubborn to admit it. Still didn't explain why he felt a pain between his shoulder blades, like a knife had gone there just now.

"Al Ivers got thrown into this much the same way you did, Rafael. If you want to be of some use, why don't you go see if you can give him a hand with something? Instead of sitting at home spinning more conspiracy theories I mean."

"I'm sure the last thing Al is looking for at the moment is my advice," he said weakly, knowing he sounded defensive, like a stubborn old fool, potentially.

"Oh, well, why do I spend a small fortune on advisors then, if I could just ask you, Mister Know-It-All? Rafa, I have to go. There's an editorial meeting here, and I won't miss it to help you lick your wounds. Al is the only one person in this entire group who most definitely did not kill Tadeo Ivers and thus can run PerCan. Chew on that for a bit and talk to me later."

Or maybe that's what he wanted us to think, Rafael thought, stubbornly, and stared at the phone in his hand. Or she was right, and he was being a fool, pouting because Al now suddenly carried the title of CEO of the country's largest manufacturer of medical marijuana. Something he wanted so badly.

TWO

Their building. The building Barry J. Wentworth—né Connor Beauregard—had called the biggest and ugliest head office of a cannabis company in town. It was true that when he had purchased it, using money from a loan shark and duping the entire executive board into signing off on it, it had been seriously ugly.

Then Kayla had come in, prettied it up for a grand opening. It hadn't really done much but paint over the dirt, and after that, Rafael had taken charge.

Under his leadership, their ugly building had transformed into a super-modern, high-tech medical building of chrome, steel, and glass. Serious, modern, clinical, automated, and clean. Everything was measured, weighed, recorded, sterilized: just what you would expect to see if you were the representative from the Ministry of Health.

It was actually amazing how little even the people in the highest level of the ministry knew about a plant that had been around for centuries and was now being 'discovered' and hailed as the new wonder drug.

Did it cure cancer? No, but it certainly helped those afflicted to live a near normal life. Did it eradicate pain and suffering? No again, but it made them bearable. And once you explained to all of those anti-smoking warriors out there that the new cannabis, the pure medicinal drug, no longer had to be smoked, and it did not get you high anymore either, they were usually ready to sign on the dotted line. Even if the whole 'doesn't get you high anymore' thing was just the tiniest bit disappointing.

They were already talking recreational use now, and once that new regulation passed, Perfect Cannabis could really ramp up. He designed their grow rooms to handle massive capacities. And all of the other manufacturing areas were completely modular, able to be used for any of the multiple stages in the life of a cannabis plant within the next hour.

Rafael pushed through the huge double glass doors and stood in the reception area for a second, breathing past the lump in his chest. Last time, he'd stormed out of here without as much as a goodbye. He'd just been fired by Tadeo Ivers, and, before he could make a fuss about it, Barry Wentworth showed up in the middle of the boardroom, like an evil spirit resurrected from the dead.

"Rafael?"

He looked up at the group of ladies chatting by the reception desk.

"Rafael…"

His former personal assistant, Connie, abandoned any pretense of cool and rushed over to enfold him in a massive hug.

"You're back. I told them you would be—eventually."

"Thanks, Connie, but I am not actually, uh, back…"

"No?"

Her disappointment felt like a physical thing, and ironically, it made him feel better. Just a bit. Nice to be missed anyway.

"Nah, I thought I'd retire."

"Yeah right. Show me somebody who's going to buy that. Remember, I know you, Rafael. Better than yourself sometimes, it seems."

"OK, yeah. I came here to… well, I don't actually know."

"You couldn't stay away?"

"Maybe. How's Al doing up there?"

He pointed up toward the second floor, where the CEO's office was located behind a huge floor-to-ceiling glass wall that allowed him to keep the entire growing and manufacturing area in view.

"How? How do you think, Rafa? His father, the main shareholder of this company, has been murdered, and pretty much everyone on the executive board and the growing staff is under suspicion. He's struggling is what he is."

"Really?"

It was good to hear, and embarrassing that it should feel just a little good.

"Yes, really. Although with Al, erm, you never really know if he is struggling, or just hungry because he skipped breakfast. He doesn't ever show much, does he?"

"Not as long as I've known him, Connie. As for breakfast…"

"He's in the building before anyone else, and stays long past the last janitor leaves, I believe. At least it's usually him who sets the last-person alarm at night. Some days, I'm worried he actually sleeps in his office."

"It's what I used to do, sometimes." Rafael nodded, and the stab in the area where his heart should have been reminded him how much he missed those days.

It should have been him up there, feeling the pulse of this company, guiding it. He should be the one running this show.

"I think I'll go up and see him."

He had turned to go when one of the ladies at the reception desk called out and stopped him. "Wait—wait, Mr. Covin."

She waved a visitor's pass at him.

"I am—jeez, I'm sorry, but… Rules and regulations, you know."

Rafael stared at the visitor's pass in her hand. *You have got to be kidding me*, he thought. *Are you out of your ever-loving mind? A visitor's pass for Rafael Covin, the man who saved this company, who shaped it, resurrected it from the trash? A visitor's…*

"Sure," Connie said, swiped the pass out of the young girl's hand, and pinned it to his shirtfront. "If I know him, he'll forget why he's here, and we'll find him tonight, giving some poor sod a lecture about job performance, efficiency, and cleanliness. Here you go…"

She straightened the badge and winked at him.

"You're retiring, remember? And I know I won't have to give you an escort. You know the way."

He darted up the stairs and down the hall to the office that used to be his and opened the door without knocking.

Al stood at the window looking down over the manufacturing floor, his phone in his hand, finishing up a call. Much as he had, many, many times in the past. Rafael froze in the open doorway and simply stared. Tall, thin, and dark was how most people would describe Al. *Add precise and fussy*, Rafael thought, taking in the tailored suit and perfectly polished shoes on his friend.

"Rafael, if you're going to waltz in unannounced, you might as well come in all the way now, don't you think."

Rafael did just that, closing the door behind him.

"Sorry, I wasn't—thinking," he finally managed. "How are you doing?"

"Sit, take a load off." Al nodded at the very chair where he used to sit when he wandered into Rafael's office and dropped into the one behind the desk.

The big desk. Rafael's desk.

"How do you think? It's been a challenge, to put it in the words of the official press release. Unofficially? I can't hear myself think in this chaos. And you actually liked doing this? Every single day?"

"I loved every minute of it."

"Christ." Al pushed a pad away, covered in notes scribbled every which way in his precise, spidery script, and sighed.

"I don't know, Rafa. When did I ever think this was going to be easy?"

"It's not."

Al cocked his head and regarded Rafael for a long silent moment. "You're strangely monosyllabic today. What's going on?"

"Nothing. I mean, nothing, really. I just came—I wanted…"

He stopped and looked around, grasping for something, not finding it. Finally, he quit and shrugged. "Just like that."

Al raised an eyebrow until it all but disappeared into his hairline and stared, his eyes stopping at the visitor's badge on Rafael's shirt.

"Ah—there's the offensive item, I believe."

"It is not like that…"

"Rafael Covin, I know you."

"What, you and Connie swap notes this morning? I just wanted to come in and see how you are doing. Can a guy do that without being interrogated?"

Rafael rose and looked around. Alas, he had brought neither a briefcase nor his ubiquitous iPad or phone. He stood looking at the door, wanting to be anywhere but here right now.

"It's fine, Rafa. I know you to be the best CEO this company could ever have, and if it were not for the minor issue of a murder investigation, you would have to hold a gun to my head to accept the job."

"Didn't take much gun-holding to get you to do it," Rafael mumbled, and still, Al heard him. Not only did he hear him, he grinned broadly and leaned back in his chair, folding his hands behind his head.

"And it bothers the heck out of you, doesn't it? Well, rest assured, my friend, that all of this…" His hand swept around the executive office. "All of this is temporary."

"That's what your father said when he hired me."

"And you grew into the job. Nobody is arguing that fact."

"I was a slob who ran construction sites when Barry and I started this thing," Rafael said and dropped into the chair again. "Ask me how often I wanted to quit—ask Kayla how often I wanted to quit this job. She's the one who shook me out of it most of the time. And then…"

"Then we had the merger on the go and a real chance to make everything work."

"And I loved every minute of that. Darn right I did, and darn right I resent you sitting in my chair, Al Ivers."

There, it was out.

"You feel better now?" Al asked and took a couple of bottles of water from the fridge in his main cabinet.

"Yeah, not really—fuck. You got anything stronger than water in there?"

"Probably. You're the one who stocked it. But I refuse to look. We need to get through this, Rafa. We need to get over this dreadful moment in company history somehow and keep the confidence of investors, customers, and inspectors from the ministry up high. Frankly, I have no idea how we're going to do this, but we have no chance— zero—if the two of us are at each other's throats. I can only imagine how this must feel to you, but I really don't have the time for it."

"Makes sense," Rafael mumbled and looked for something on the floor close to his shoe.

"What did you say?"

"I said it makes fucking sense. Shit, don't enjoy this too much, will you?"

"Remember what you said to my father when he gave you a hard time about having me here in the company?"

"I don't. I'm sure I don't want to either."

"Well, I do. You said, 'Sir, I couldn't have done this without Al, and frankly, I don't want to do it without him, so one way or another, we'll be working together, whether you like it or not.'"

"I couldn't have. I would never have called Tadeo sir."

"Never you mind, Rafael Covin. I am slowly getting a little pissed off here. I assure you I did not stand in line for all of this..." He swiped at the papers on his desk again. "But at the moment, I'm the only one in our group who is not being questioned for Tadeo's murder and can therefore lead this company. Deal with it, please. And don't insult me by coming in here suggesting I had my father killed to take over the company."

"I never..."

"You never what, Rafael? You never put it into words like this? You didn't have to. Look at the face on you! You shuffle around miserably, you stir up our employees, you can't string a proper sentence together. Tell me what I am supposed to think, what our people will think? Get it together. We need a plan. And if you look at me and ask 'who is we,' so help me God, I'm going to slap you—hard."

Rafael opened his mouth and closed it again. Of all the possible scenarios he had been running through his mind, this was not the one he would have labeled as the 'most likely' a couple of hours ago.

"But…"

"Not the right answer, Rafael. Try again. I need your help as much as you needed mine, so please, if I can ask you for anything today: man up, deal with whatever resentment against my father still remains, and help me navigate this company through this…"

"Shitpile?"

"*Difficult situation* we find ourselves in, OK?"

Rafael forked both hands through his hair and blew out a big breath, blowing up his cheeks in doing so.

"What have we got so far?" Rafael finally asked, and Al sorted through a mess of papers on his desk. "We have every single government agency out there wanting to know what is going on," he said. "We have the Ministry of Health threatening our license, and, last but not least, we have the people from our brand-new merger partner wanting to bail on us."

"Thomas Donnelly? He and his Mariposa Industries would be dead in the water without us. They won't survive another day if they think this is the moment to pull out. The merger is a done deal; the agreements have been signed, good-faith payments have been made…"

"Mercy." Al threw up his hands, palms out. "Please. I don't think he wants to pull out. He and his people are confused, as are ours. We have just formally merged companies, not yet operations. It's difficult to know just where to put your hands first."

"Made more difficult by the fact that no matter where you do put them, they'll be coming up covered in shit." Rafael nodded. "OK then. I think the first thing you'll need is a working board."

"I suspect you are right. But I'm having a hard time visualizing that. I'm not exactly—a board kind of guy. I have always run my affairs my way. I'm sure you remember. I don't, uh, do group efforts."

"Then let me give it right back to you, buddy: man up and deal with it, Al, because this company and its fate depends on it. Last time I looked, we had just put the clones into growing medium. Somebody needs to check on them, make sure they're thriving. Which further means somebody needs to check that Nick and Dante are still on the job. Tadeo fired them—tell me you overruled that. Then I had hired a guy to put in a server system to track them, clone to leaf to customer. Somebody needs to check how far he got, and what the parameters of the system are. The security system ought to be all right. Simon Graff designed it, but you need to…"

"Stop, stop, stop…" Al stood up and took a number of giant steps toward the farthest wall of the giant office, holding his hands out in front of him. "Stop, you're making me dizzy."

"You see? That's why you have a board. Take some of the load off you, even if they don't do it your way."

Al sat back down. "Honest opinion? Can't I leave the board the way it was—before all of this happened? Just do nothing?"

"I think you're going to need Simon Graff and Josh Novak. They've been there from the very beginning. They had their run-ins with your father, but…" Rafael shrugged, "Heck—so has everybody. You're going to need Kayla."

"But she is…"

"A person of interest at the moment. Nobody is accusing her of anything. I'm pretty sure she'll be cleared ASAP."

"Your word to God's ear, Rafael. Let's hope so. People are going to dig up her old relationship with Connor, it will all come back, and she will need to be strong to weather this. If she chooses to come back, I'll need her to be 100 percent solid."

"She can, and she will be. I assure you. The authorities might not recognize the concept of innocence, but I do. Heck, she never did anything to that dickwad who really deserved it, the way he treated her."

"Your former friend Barry."

"Barry," Rafael spat and shook his head.

"Right then. Kayla. I think I can make it work with the rest of the board. Who else?"

"I'm burning to remain in the CEO chair. You're not wrong about that. I want it so bad I can taste it, but I also know nobody on this board is going to vote for me. I'm not even sure I ought to be in here. I got fired a few days ago. There is a half decent case against me, all circumstantial of course, but I suppose I am under pretty close scrutiny."

"You had arguments with Tadeo. So did others."

"A lot of others. Problem is, because of the firing and the way it was done, the cops are using the word *motive* a lot more than I like, no matter how many other men your father argued with."

The two men sat quietly across from each other for a long moment. Al wiped the rim of his water bottle with his handkerchief, over and over, and Rafael stared down on his splayed fingers on his thighs. They knew each other too well, so awfully well.

"So," Rafael finally said. "If you're not going to say it—I will. Who do you think did it?"

Al only shook his head and continued to run his finger around the top of his water bottle.

"You must have an idea. A suspicion at least," Rafael asked.

"Do you know how many men in this town had a beef with him? Hundreds. And that's just the folks he actually did business with."

"Is that why he sent you out to do his bidding?"

"I guess he thought I had better people skills," Al said wryly, and Rafael could only laugh.

"Sure you do. That's why we called you that weird dude back when you first invested in PerCan."

"The thing is," Al said, shaking his head, "one of these people hated him enough to want to murder him. And who was savvy enough to kill him the day he fired you and tried to make my little brother CEO?"

"And the day Barry Wentworth came back into town. The day your brother Roberto dismissed his bodyguards. Man, that is one hell of a coincidence, don't you think?"

Al looked down at his desk again and sorted the mess of paper into a number of piles. He didn't meet Rafael's eyes for a very long time.

"Doesn't matter what I think, it really does not. I have a company to run. I can't worry about who killed him at the moment."

Rafael said nothing and waited him out for a long heartbeat.

"And you are correct. I need a solid corporate structure and people who are behind me 100 percent. I also need competent advisors." He looked up and at Rafael again. "So, while I won't argue with you, most of them won't want you anywhere near the board of executives for the moment, never mind in the CEO seat—fact is, I still need you."

His eyes never left Rafael's, who chewed on a thumbnail, glowering. *Goddamn bloody idiots,* he wanted to say. *There is no one, no one who knows more about this company than I do. I lived and breathed PerCan. I gave up my life for PerCan. Literally. There is someone out there running my Covin Construction Company, while I was forced to straighten out PerCan.*

"Rafael Covin, you are being utterly stubborn."

"Didn't say I wasn't."

"Then please, tell me you will help me out here, even if I can't let you sit on the board right at the moment."

Rafael still said nothing, chewing the inside of his cheek, until Al slapped his hand down onto the table in front of him.

"Well?"

"Answer me this first. Why did you say no when I asked you about the consulting company?" Rafael asked, not meeting Al's eyes.

"The consulting company? Is that what this is all about? Because I didn't jump when you said, 'Hey, let's all leave Tadeo Ivers the idiot and PerCan and go out on our own?' Are you kidding me?"

"He fired me. After I gave up everything for him. My construction company, my family, my salary—my life. I gave it up, Al, to save his company, and he fired me."

"Yes, and it was wrong. Is that what you want to hear? It was wrong, Rafael, and I thought eventually I could make him see reason. If he forced Dante to be CEO and if he saw how unhappy and inefficient he was, maybe he would give in. Dante was the baby, his favorite. If he realized he had made him unhappy and he made a mess, well, eventually, Tadeo would have changed his mind, don't you think? I am well aware he would never have asked me to lead the company. He was jealous of my success. But just maybe, if we worked it right and let him come around on his own, he would have come back to you. That is why I did it. Trying to keep the peace and quietly working in the background, steering everyone to where they needed to be. Silly me, huh?"

He slapped down his hand on the desk again and refused to look at Rafael. This time, he pulled one of the neat stacks of paper toward himself and started reading the top piece. He made some notations in the margins in his neat spidery script and carefully placed it into a folder at his right. Then he pulled down the next one and repeated the process.

Rafael watched. He knew Al was the stronger man. Al was stubborn enough to sit there for the rest of the day pretending to go through his paperwork, pretending to ignore Rafael sitting there.

Rafael cleared his throat, but Al frowned at a set of figures and refused to look at him.

"Um—there's an easier way to do that."

Al did not reply, but repeated the procedure of looking at a document, making notes in the margins, and putting it into the folder at his left.

"Look, Al, there's an easier way to do this. You don't have to work over each and every one of these personally. Just…"

"Were you not leaving, Mr. Covin? Quite a while ago as a matter of fact?"

"I was. I'm not saying I was right."

"No kidding."

Al still didn't look up from his document and grabbed a highlighter, marking a particular passage in a document.

"Are you kidding me here? Securities lawyers? They charge a small fortune, it looks like, but one does appear to require their services."

"Necessary evil, always has been, but it saves you a lot of grief. I was in touch with a decent guy, easy to work with, open-minded. Harvey… something. I think you might have his letter right there. If I were you…"

Al raised his index fingers, both of them, and finally looked straight at Rafael.

"You are not me, and I am busy. I am trying to make sure this company survives this most recent crisis. So, if you don't mind letting me work in peace. I do believe you know where your construction people left an opening in the wall fit for a door."

"I know that. Christ, don't make it so hard on me, will you?"

"Make what hard on you, Rafael? There are a lot of things on my desk at the moment, and I'm in no mood to be guessing."

"Saying I—might have been…" Rafael rested his chin in his hand and mumbled into his palm. "Wrong. I might have been wrong."

"Speak up? I don't think I heard you."

"Al! OK—Ok. I wasn't exactly, uh, right. I was wrong, OK? Pissed off and angry because you turned me down."

"We went there. I explained my reasoning. In detail."

"Yes. And now it makes sense. Why didn't you say so instead of making me guess?"

"Who had the time? All of a sudden, Barry Wentworth is back, and I'm still getting my brain around that, wondering what this is going to do to the company, and how my father is going to react, and here

Barry is, storming into your house saying my father's been shot. And suddenly, I have a company to deal with."

"If you still want me to, I will help you in any way I can. Just— don't remind me of being wrong again. At least not more than absolutely necessary."

Al sat back and glowered. He looked at Rafael for a long, silent minute and finally pushed back from the table just a bit. The casters on his chair barely moved. Maybe Rafael imagined it, but Al seemed to create a bit of distance between them. He moved away just the tiniest bit. Finally, he sighed and put his palms together before his face.

"Everything happened so damn quick, Rafael."

"Tell me about it! But we can deal. Come on, we've done it before. You and I have been in a lot tighter spots than this one, remember."

"I do."

Al reached down into the old beat-up brown leather briefcase by his side and pulled out a plain manila folder. From it, he withdrew a number of sheets that appeared to be photocopies of a handwritten document.

Not many documents these days were still handwritten, Rafael thought. OK, Al and his family were particularly eccentric. Al himself didn't trust online security and made handwritten notes all the time. Look at him now. But this was different. The look on his friend's face told him it was different. The deliberate, almost reverent way he touched the pages and placed them on the table between them, smoothing out a nonexistent wrinkle in the paper. This was no grocery list. These were not his notes on things to do and problems to solve.

Rafael refused to look at the paper and instead held Al's eyes with his own. He had his own suspicions what sat on the table between them.

"You know what this is."

"Hell no, I don't, Al. And I am sure I don't want to know. You're going to have to explain."

"It's a copy."

"Nice, the photocopier works. You know, I was fighting that damned thing for the longest time. Connie was just about the only one who could…"

"Rafael…"

"Work the thing—you know."

"Rafael. This is a copy of Tadeo Ivers's will."

"Don't know why it…" Rafael stopped and automatically made a tight fist.

Where did that come from, a copy of Tadeo's will? And how did Al have it already?

"So," he finally said, hating the fact that his voice shook, knowing there was no other way. "So, where did you get it? What does it say?"

"I simply found it in Tadeo's safe, and it says a lot of things about family traditions and how his sons should get along and how he tried to be a role model."

"In other words, a whole load of   never mind. One should not speak ill of the deceased."

"No, you are probably right. I might go so far as to suspect he had someone write it for him, so it would sound deeply moving when—when the time was right."

"You might be right on that."

There was more; there was so much more. Rafael panicked, didn't know where to look, and didn't know how to interpret his friend's sad eyes.

"A few surprises, as you might have imagined," Al said darkly.

"Whatever he said, he wasn't always smart when it came to business—you know that."

"You might want to change your mind, Rafa." Al put his fingertips on the lowest edge of the photocopied document and pushed it a little bit closer to Rafael. "It seems he felt I was not as useless as he always pretended when it came to managing the business. At least I hope so because he left me all of his business interests."

"All of—holy—well, shit, Al, I don't…"

"Any time you regain the ability to form a complete sentence, Rafael."

"I know, it's like—hey, congratulations, man. What about Dante?"

"Dante will receive a very generous cash settlement—once it is determined that he had nothing to do with our father's shooting."

"Makes sense. And Roberto?"

"Roberto, the middle son. He and Father did not get along whatsoever. You might have surmised."

"Tadeo stood by while Roberto was going to jail without lifting a finger or sending in one of his famous defense attorneys. I can see how that might cause a little bit of friction around the family dinner table," Rafael said, trying in vain for a bit of levity.

"Roberto receives what might commonly be called a pittance. A few dollars so he can't sue the estate for cutting him out entirely. Not enough to let him get his life back together."

"He did cooperate with Barry Wentworth to take the company away from your father," Rafael reminded his friend. "In a way I don't feel sorry for him. I know he is your brother and all—but first, the trick with the illegal grow op in the building, then working with Barry. The man had it coming. Even if Tadeo couldn't have known any of this when he wrote the will."

Al nodded and said nothing for a moment.

"What is it with Tadeo and his three sons? He loves Dante, makes you his errand boy, and absolutely loathes Roberto."

"I think he knew I had a knack for business," Al said. "In a way he never did, so I could never have a position in his business. Roberto? He just openly defied him—on anything and everything."

"He's your brother, Al. That has to count for something, I understand that, but…"

"But he has no one but himself to blame," Al finished. "You see now why I need you, Rafa—desperately, even. More to the point, what does this mean to the company? As you might guess, Roberto will not take this without a fight."

"You inherited all of your father's business interests?"

Al only nodded.

"All of the shares?"

"That's the way I read it."

"Which makes you—shit—the majority shareholder. And CEO. You're large and in charge."

"Not quite, Rafa, not quite. I am majority shareholder of Perfect Cannabis at the moment, not the new company, post-merger."

"Mariposa brings with it their majority shareholder." Rafael whistled. "Ladies and gentlemen, Mr. Barry Wentworth. The man who founded Perfect Cannabis Corp, ran it into the ground, established an illegal grow op in the back, then ran from prosecution, then bought most of the shares in the new merger partner..." Rafael folded his hands in prayer. "Jesus II... I don't know what to say. Somebody should write a book, but no one would believe it!"

"Barry will fight me for the CEO position. You can bet on that," Al said, leaning back in his chair and moving it ever so slightly again. Another fraction of distance between him and Rafael.

"But here is the thing, Rafael: a few months ago, perhaps even a few weeks ago, I couldn't have cared less about a manufacturer of medical marijuana."

"Yeah, but I thought you and I..."

"Were in this together, correct. But it always was my father's company. He didn't want me anywhere near it, so consequently I didn't want any part of it, other than to thumb my nose at him by consulting for you. If you recall, the only thing he wanted me to do was look after his clubs."

"Strip joints... and you had to go round collecting cash. Nice work for someone of your education and talents."

Al rolled his eyes. "Suddenly, I inherited the lot. Most of it, for the moment, is mine, and I have no idea what to do with it."

"Good for you." Rafael shrugged and finally rose from his chair, taking a few steps to the large picture window. He used to do his best thinking over there, he remembered. Looking down at the beehive of activity below, the grow pods, the men and women in environmental suits as they dashed between the pods, the people who cleaned up, the people who ran around with orders, the people who checked irrigation and fertigation—anything and everything, to make sure the marijuana plants had exactly what they needed and wanted at any given time to make medicine. He'd designed the grow pods with maintenance hall-ways between them featuring access panels and monitors every so many feet, so no one had to enter the pods unless absolutely unavoidable. 'Humans are the filthiest things,' he used to joke, 'so we keep them out of the grow areas.' And it worked; his sterile environment had never been compromised, save when the fertilizer agent sent a dirty batch…

It worked, it ran like clockwork, and Rafael used to love taking a few minutes to just stand and look down on it.

Growing medicinal marijuana was miles away from throwing a few cannabis seeds into the soil and waiting for the plant to come for a cheap high. This was a science that started with cloning the most successful plants.

And he'd put it all together, from the facility design to the invest-ment and marketing side.

And he had loved it, not right away and not always. But in the end he had loved every minute of it. He couldn't wait to roll out of bed in the morning and stand at this window again, looking down. If it hadn't been for Kayla, and because it looked so damned pathetic, he would have slept here.

Suddenly, it all belonged to Al.

"It's still a public company, you know. It doesn't actually belong to me."

Rafael startled because the voice came from directly behind him. He had neither heard nor seen Al move. He managed a nod and swallowed past the tightness in his throat.

"Yeah."

"I'm still getting used to all of this as well, Rafa. It's barely been three days that Barry stormed into your house and said somebody killed Tadeo."

"And you didn't believe him."

"Of course I did not believe him right away. I don't like the man…"

"Hard to hide that fact, my friend."

"But now, by hook or by crook, we have to run this company. I have no intentions of giving it all up because Barry Wentworth is back in town and challenging us for it."

"At the moment, he is still the strongest suspect in Tadeo's murder. Right now, you have nothing to worry about."

"Maybe, maybe not. I'm sorry. I know you used to be friends, but I believe Wentworth is a fool who doesn't know what he's doing, just got lucky a few times. Do I believe he shot my father? No. He doesn't have the guts to pull the trigger."

"You so sure?" Rafael asked. There was no love lost between his former partner and his friend Al, he knew that. Calling Barry a fool was Al's way of trying to be polite. But he didn't think of him a murderer. Interesting. And possibly more embarrassingly, Al didn't think Barry was man enough to pull the trigger. Ouch!

"Have you ever shot a gun, Rafael?"

"Nope, and I don't intend to."

Now it was Al's turn to smile. He elbowed Rafael in the side and put a hand over his face.

"Remember a couple of years ago? Barry/Connor was in default with that loan shark?"

"Don't I ever," Rafael groaned and rolled his eyes. "Mirko What-shisname. Showed up at the grand opening, and Barry—Connor— offered him a check!"

Both men laughed now, and Al shook his head.

"Unmitigated gall. But before that, just before you found Mirko, Connor yelled something like, 'Didn't you bring a gun?' It's like he was offended by the fact that you indeed had not, and I've never been able to make sense of that."

"You remember all that? I guess he always saw himself as the great man, the big guy who had armed security people follow him around every step. Because he was that important. In his mind, he was always 10 feet tall and bulletproof. Long as somebody else brought the gun."

"Well, I'll let you in on a secret, Rafael, I have never shot a gun either. Even though it may ruin my badass reputation to admit it. But there are enough—individuals—in our organization, in our family even, who will tell you that holding a gun, aiming at a living being, and pulling the trigger requires a special kind of guts and mental strength. You are quite possibly ending a life."

"Right," Rafael said, all the mirth instantly gone from the conversation. "And Barry…"

"Barry doesn't have it. Oh, he would tell *you* to shoot, but he could never do it himself."

Rafael nodded and looked down at the manufacturing floor again. Much like staring at the ocean, the picture down there always changed, and yet it never did.

"And I think I've always known that," he said softly.

"Barry is many things, Rafael, but he is not innocent."

"Not guilty then?"

"Of shooting my father? I don't think he is, no. So here comes the question I've been tiptoeing around, and I need you to be completely honest."

"OK."

"100 percent honest, Rafael."

"Jesus, what? Yes, I will be honest with you." Rafael raised his hands.

"I can see a conflict," Al said. "A showdown between Barry Wentworth and myself, at some point in the not-too-distant future. He will want to go one way, and I will need to go the other. It's going to take everything we have to get this company through it and out the other end in one piece. It's not going to be pretty. I don't like to lose; he doesn't like to lose. We are two men who want to be in charge, who own just about an even number of shares. It's going to come down to the people on my board, people like you and Kayla, whether we stand or fall."

Rafael nodded and swallowed hard, his throat suddenly dry and tight again. Of course. Why had he not seen this before?

"I need to know where you stand, Rafael. I need to know if, given a choice, you will be able to put aside your 20-odd year friendship with Wentworth and look at whatever issues we're having and make the right decision for the company."

For the company. Not *for me*, not a plain "whose side are you on," but for the company. He finally sat down again and took off his glasses, rubbing his eyes as if he could squeeze out the sudden weariness that settled on him. The roller coaster he'd been on for the last three days or so showed no intentions of stopping anytime soon, and he was rapidly running out of strength and determination to hang on.

Had he not stomped around the house full of righteous anger just this morning, furious at Al Ivers in particular, and the world in general, because Al had turned down his consulting company idea? Had he not stormed in here to tell Al what a moron he was, and no, he would never help him run PerCan? Then in the space of 20 minutes or less, he'd had to go to understanding Al's motives, to admitting he was wrong, in order to end up offering any help he could.

"Jesus H," he groaned. "Could you let a guy get used to the starting game plan before you throw another curveball?"

"My apologies if I'm pressuring you."

"You're not. I just can't keep up here. I feel like I'm stumbling around blindfolded in a cage fight."

"Business changes…"

"Business changes at the speed of light. That's my own line, Al."

Again, he rubbed his face and shook his head to clear it.

"OK then. Next crisis, Barry and you. We both know what's at stake. And I can promise you, no matter what the issues are, I will come down on the side of whatever makes the most sense for the company at the time. That enough for you?"

"It'll do." Al nodded. "I'm not asking you to betray a friend…"

"Some friend."

"No matter what he may have done, or not… you two spent a lot of time together, put together a lot of deals in your time. You have about as much history as any divorced couple does. Don't kid yourself. This will not be easy."

"Nothing about this deal is simple any longer. If it ever was. If you need any kind of assurance, take a look at my track record. For the past two years, PerCan has been my life. Morning to night. Is it going to be tough? Yes. Can I handle deciding what's in the best interest of the company? You bet I can."

"Good enough." Al nodded. "That's all I can ask for. The media is going to love every single bit about this one."

"Kayla. I'm sure she hasn't thought of it in those terms. Be nice to give her a heads-up."

"Yes." Al drummed his fingers on the table top. "And the police are still quite interested in her. She'll have a lot of questions to answer about her history with dear Mr. Wentworth."

"She didn't do it, Al. I know she didn't. I'm as certain of that as the fact that I'm standing right here before you."

"You're sitting."

"Al!"

"No need to be a knight in shining armor. I'll do my best to support Kayla staying on in charge of promotions and communications. I don't think anyone will fight me on it too much because they feel the same way about her as you do. Kayla Montecito is one smart, tough lady. She took a lot of heat the first time around when Barry disappeared being wanted for questioning in connection with incidents at PerCan."

"I know, I just…"

"You have that defender syndrome. Go, be a knight then. I don't think Kayla will need or want our help. Worry about yourself instead."

"Myself?"

"I need you cleared of any suspicion so I can have you back on the board, helping me get through this all. A half hour ago, you were saying anything I need, any time. I'm hoping that wasn't just a line."

"Of course not, just give me a little bit of time to get my head above water."

"You've got five minutes. That's about all I have to give you."

Rafael stared at Al for a moment to see if he were joking, but his friend's expression never changed. No time for kidding around.

"I'm good," he finally said. "What do you need?"

"I need your advice on putting together a working board, I need you on it as soon as you possibly can, and I need you to be me in the meantime."

"You?"

"Me." Al rose from his chair again, rolled his shoulder, and stepped behind the window wall to look down. "To run this company the way it needs to be run, I need Kayla, I need Dante, and I need you—by my side, on my board, voting with me, advising me in important decisions. I can't do that while the three of you are still considered persons of interest in this investigation into my father's death."

"I understand that, but…"

"Let me finish, Rafa. You know I have connections. I know—people—who can, unofficially, help with this investigation. People I used to call on when we had trouble at the clubs."

"Unofficially help," Rafael said, letting the two words hang out there dripping with the indication of misconduct he felt about them. "Jesus."

"Right at the moment, Barry Wentworth is their favorite subject," Al continued, as if Rafael hadn't spoken. "And I don't really care, except for the fact that if he is indicted, he will assign somebody to represent his interests on the board. And it is very likely that somebody will be my brother Roberto."

"Roberto," Rafael sighed. "Who was in collusion with him."

"To put the very first illegal grow op into the building, as well as take over Mariposa and PerCan a little while later, exactly."

Rafael said nothing. He felt as if his mouth still hung open hearing everything Al had just said. How the heck had his friend made this leap so fast, going from hearing his father had been killed, to taking over the company, to planning who would substitute for whom if someone was convicted of the crime?

"I don't think I can run as fast as you're going," he said when the silence between them dragged on too long. "You're like—20 paces ahead of me."

"Well catch up here, Rafael, and catch up fast. I'm well aware of how much work you put in on this project when Barry ruined it the first time, but we're not done yet. I need everybody, and I need everybody at their best if we're going to save this company. So?"

"I said I would help you, didn't I?"

"Yes. I need you to help to prove the people on my board innocent and, if possible, find the guilty party."

Al turned around, and, backlit from the fluorescent light fixtures out in the great manufacturing hall, he looked larger than life, looming like some dark, avenging figure. Rafael folded his hands in his lap to hold them still and tried to push back the thought that wouldn't be put aside: *I would most certainly not want to be on the wrong side of this man.*

"Well?"

"OK. I assume you're going to tell me what I need to be doing?"

Al pulled a sheet of yellow legal paper from beneath a few folders on his desk.

"These are the names and contact information for three men I know can be helpful in clearing yours, Dante's, and Kayla's names. Contact them, pick one, get him or her up to speed, and make use of them in any way you can."

"But the police are already investigating," Rafael protested weakly. "Shouldn't we let them do their job?"

"We are, but that doesn't mean we can't look into things a little on our own. If we can't actually find whoever did it, then at least we need to prove that you three are not guilty, so we can concentrate on PerCan." Al stood perfectly straight and held Rafael's eyes with his own.

I should have stayed in construction, Rafael thought, taking the yellow sheet of paper from Al and folding it into his inside jacket pocket. *Two years ago, when Tadeo Ivers asked me to step in as interim CEO to rescue the company, I should have said no.*

As if he could have. Tadeo had all but threatened his children and his livelihood, if he didn't do as he was asked to do.

And he had. As often as he had wanted to give up, he had pulled another rabbit out of a previously undiscovered hat and kept going.

He looked back at Al's desk and chair and remembered putting it there, moving into the office that said 'CEO' in etched gold letters on the full glass door.

"I know this is a lot," Al said a little more softly. "And I also know you're probably pretty pissed off at having to vacate that seat over there." He nodded toward the desk and chair. "But this isn't final."

"You're pretty comfortable as CEO, I dare say."

"Not because I want to be. What would you have me do, abandon a multimillion-dollar company because somebody's feelings are hurt? That sounds as ridiculous as it actually is, Rafa."

"I get it."

"Then get going. The sooner we get this done, the sooner you can sit in that chair over there again. Does that put it into the right perspective for you?"

"It does." Rafael managed a thin smile. "And...?" His hand touched his jacket where he had just put the list of names he had received from Al.

"Oh, for crying out loud, they're just investigators, Rafael Covin. Do you think I would send you out there to deal with hardened criminals?"

"No. No, of course not," Rafael said and managed another thin smile. But his voice sounded as phony and off-key as it had when he told Al he really didn't have an issue with him being CEO and running the company.

***

Driving home, Rafael couldn't help but remember the image of Al at the picture windows, his tall figure, casting deep shadows on his face and eyes, one fist balled so tight the knuckles had turned snow white. Something fierce and relentless burned behind those eyes. Logically, Rafael knew this man was his friend. They had faced challenges together and fought more than one battle side by side. They were on the same team, but when he closed his eyes, that dark fire on Al's face sent a shiver down his back.

"Enough with the drama, Covin," he finally said out loud, hoping the sound of his voice would finally drive away the stray ghosts sitting in the car there with him. No surprise it failed to do so, and he flipped on the radio and turned it up way too loud.

THREE

Back home he arrived to another surprise, finding Barry Wentworth lounging in one of the chairs he had recently put out on the front porch for Kayla and himself.

"Barry, I see they let you out," he said, stopping with his hand on the door handle. "What are you doing on my front porch then at this hour?"

"Thank your friend Robertson. My hotel room was sealed to accommodate their ongoing investigation."

"No friend of mine, I assure you, but I heard Ivers had been shot at his diner?"

"He was," Barry said, rising to stand behind Rafael as he opened the door and stepping inside without asking.

"Why don't you go ahead and walk right on in," Rafael said, rolling his eyes. "Make yourself comfortable. Mi casa and all that."

"Shut up, Rafael, I need your help."

"There's a lot of that going around."

"What is that supposed to mean?"

"Nothing. Forget it."

Rafael nodded toward his living room and kicked off his shoes. For a moment, he was tempted to call out to Barry to see if he wanted a beer and thought better of it. The man wasn't staying, and he'd be damned if he made him comfortable after his uninvited appearance.

"Now then." He fished a bottle of water out of the fridge and came back to the den, dropping back into his old easy chair, leaving Barry to stand by the window like the uninvited guest he was. "Why don't you tell me why your hotel room would be considered part of their investigations and what you think I can do about it?"

"Don't act like you don't know the story. I've been their favorite suspect from the word go, perhaps even their only suspect. I get the feeling nobody is even looking for the real killer. Incompetence on all counts, if you ask me."

Actually, I'm not, Rafael thought, but said nothing and took a deep swig of water. Barry narrowed his eyes at the bottle in Rafael's hands and frowned. Not hard to know what he was thinking, but he only sighed and folded his hands behind his head, staring into the darkening yard beyond the window.

"It's early days," Rafael finally said, stretching his legs. "The news just got out. I'm sure as their investigation progresses, they will look in every direction."

"I might have—made a few notes they don't like."

"Oh, here we go. This is the point where it gets interesting. I should have known with you sitting at my doorstep. What did you write down, how to get away with murder? 1-800-I-KILL?"

"You're such an ass, Rafael. Of course I did not. I told you I have nothing to do with it. Not one thing, how often do I have to repeat it?"

"And yet…"

"And yet they are treating me as if they'd caught me standing over the body with a gun in my hand."

"Jesus, Con—Barry, this is just like the last time, isn't it," Rafael said, put down his water, and wiped his hands over his face. "Verbatim, like the last time." He raised his hands left and right of his face and screwed up his voice. "I had nothing to do with it, Rafael, really. And then there's a video of you making a deal with that Roberto character."

"And you still don't get it…" Barry took two giant strides toward the easy chair where Rafael sat, staring down at him, fire in his eyes. Rafael would have loved to back up a bit. Another guy with anger issues. But this was 100 percent Barry's problem, and he was not getting involved. Not again. Shit. Rafael counted to 10 silently, refusing to back down from Barry's stare, and finally shrugged.

"Suit yourself, Barry. You're the one who showed up saying you needed my help."

"You, of all people know…" Barry said slowly, enunciating every word. "You know that I am innocent."

"Do I? Do I, really? Oh, wait now, which crime are we talking about here? The first one, the illegal grow op? The second one, shooting Ivers? Or is there another one in between I don't know about yet? Sorry, I get a little confused."

Barry pushed back from Rafael's easy chair and paced the length of the living room. His hands had fisted in his pockets, and the fury held in under the surface made his movements quick and jerky.

"You and I built this company," he finally said, still speaking slowly as if he couldn't quite expect Rafael to follow. "It is ours. Do you think I would ever do anything to ruin it?"

"Deliberately, no."

"There—you—have—it."

"I was there when we founded this company, Barry. Or do you prefer being called Connor? Let me get past your new name first. It takes a bit of getting used to. If you remember, I stood by your side. I defended you to the board up and down. Right up to the end, I told you: answer those charges and we will sort it out."

"Sort it out! Listen to you. Just listen to yourself, Rafael. Even back then, I was everybody's favorite scapegoat. Connor didn't do this right. Beauregard fucked up that procedure. Everybody had something they wanted to blame on me, everybody. But let me ask you this—did any of you have the balls to start something this big?"

Rafael shrugged, and Barry shifted up a gear. "No, of course you didn't. You and all of your wonderful and amazing friends, and lawyers and consultants and regulators, none of you would have had the sheer guts to start this when it was all just a dream. None of you. You followed me like sheep throwing your money at me so I would multiply it. That's what it was like. Here you go, Connor, here's a few thousand dollars, now go make a million out of it. All just so you could sit back and get rich in this green rush without lifting a finger. And when that didn't work, it was, 'Hell, Connor fucked up.' Don't you find that a little convenient?"

"That's the business we chose, Barry. Startup companies, the territory comes with a set of responsibilities. If you didn't like it, nobody forced you to do it. Nice, by the way, to know how you feel about the rest of us in your group. Thanks."

"I wasn't talking about you personally."

"Yes, you were, Barry." Rafael slapped the armrests of his easy chair—hard. "You've been looking down your nose at all of us because we didn't have your guts or your talent at raising funds. And you know what? Maybe you're right. I ran a construction company and Kayla a magazine. And we were doing just fine. Maybe we didn't have the balls to bet everything on red, roll the dice, and start up something of this magnitude. But you know what? When Ivers all but put a gun to my head and told me to save his company or else—or else, Barry—I sure learned in a hurry."

Rafael re-capped his water bottle, plunking it down on the coffee table with a bang that startled both of them. He pushed back and rolled his shoulders, shrugging off the moment and the angry energy.

"Are we good now? You've said your piece? You were the only one in the group to have the guts to start this, noted. So now you're the only one being blamed for things—again. It sucks. That's life. And now I think it's time for you to leave."

Barry raised his eyes from the coffee table, staring at him for a long moment. Somewhere in those dark eyes, just behind the anger and the frustration, something new was forming there. Barry clearly didn't admire anyone, never had. The people around him were bit players in a film starring Barry J. Wentworth.

It took Rafael a moment to realize the sound he was hearing was Barry laughing. And he couldn't help but join in with a smirk.

"My man, Rafael. You've grown a pair while I've been gone."

He grabbed Rafael's right hand and shook it vigorously. "What happened to the guy I left behind, the one who said yes and OK to everything I suggested?"

Rafael shrugged again and pulled back his hand. "He left the building. And where did that get me anyway? Cleaning up one giant mess after another, not getting paid for any of it, and being fired quite unceremoniously as the crowning achievement. Some might say you got the better end of the bargain. And we still have to talk about the whole 'you left' bit. Don't forget that."

"Thank you. That is exactly my point, Rafael. All of the Ivers clan— Tadeo, Al, Roberto, and even Dante—they did nothing but bring this company down. Nothing. They have to go. That is precisely why I did all of this. That is why I spent all of my money buying up Mariposa, preventing one merger, supporting the next one, and finally coming back into town. So you and I can take back what is rightfully ours. Can you follow me that far?"

"Wait. Back up the cart for a moment. What?" Something buried in Barry's rant did not make any sense, but before Rafael could zero in on it, his front door flew open again with a crash, and, seconds before she stormed into his living room, he knew Kayla was in no mood for polite chitchat.

She wore the fluffy white fur stole that made her look like Elsa, the Snow Queen, and with one fluid shrug, she flung it off her shoulder and toward Rafael.

"Will you look what the cat dragged in. Can somebody call the Orkin man real quick?" she said and slowly lowered gigantic tortoise-shell sunglasses. The phrase "if looks could kill" came to mind, and just then, he didn't want to step between her and Barry, for fear of getting zapped by 5,000 volts or so.

"Thanks for visiting," she said. "We gave at the office. Now if you'd kindly go back to whatever dank hole you crawled out of, we'd be ever so grateful."

"Well, hello there. Good to see you too, dearest Kayla."

Barry didn't even blink. He had the chutzpah to take her hand and try to kiss it, a move Kayla answered smoothly by pulling her hand away and reaching for her phone.

"I dare say I think the police are looking for you, Barry. Personally, I think it would be smart to take a good lawyer and go answer their questions, but then again, running away is more your style, isn't it?"

"Ever the sharp-tongued shrew, aren't you? No, I'm not running from anyone. I've already answered all of their questions."

"Really." Kayla's eyebrow shot up to meet her hairline, and she put the phone away again. "Then you already explained why you had a note in your hotel room that detailed how to use those Vietnamese gangs to put a hit out on Ivers?"

"What?" Rafael asked at the same time as Barry, and this time he did get up and step between Barry and Kayla. "Is that what you...?"

"Calm down, Rafael, of course I did not."

"You didn't? Are you sure?" Kayla asked, going toe to toe with Barry. "Absolutely sure? Because my source at the police department, and this is a really good source, my source says that is exactly what they are investigating as we speak." She poked her polished red nail at Barry's chest with those last three words. "Indeed, that particular note is why you made the top of their list of suspects, even though they let you go. An error I am sure they will correct shortly."

"'I might have made a few notes they don't like,'" Rafael repeated. "When you came in, that's what you said—'a few notes they don't like.' I'm such an idiot. This is what you were referring to."

"Well yes, in a way, but that doesn't mean I did it," Barry said, spreading his arms like a preacher might in front of his congregation. "I was just trying to figure out what it would take to convince

Ivers to leave my company. I was brainstorming a few kooky ideas, nothing more."

"And you wrote them on a piece of paper and left it in your hotel room?"

"Exactly. I didn't know Ivers would actually be killed and anybody would come looking for a few silly notes made while I had a couple of drinks. Surely that proves it."

"Even you aren't that stupid," Rafael muttered and went to the kitchen to get himself a beer. The hell with what time it was. He uncapped it and drank a fair portion right there, without looking for a glass.

"Rafa, please tell me you don't actually believe him," Kayla asked, and he raised his free hand.

"People, for once, what I believe no longer matters, OK? I am not on the board of Perfect Cannabis any longer. Neither am I in charge of the investigation into the death of Tadeo Ivers. Personally, I had nothing to do with it, and I hope that will be settled before long. You..." He pointed at Barry. "You are on your own."

Kayla moved to stand with him, and he took her hand, giving it a quick squeeze. "I know you didn't kill him."

"Rafael, Kayla—friends. Come on. I'm standing here telling you that I did not do it either," Barry said in that convincing tone he did so well. "I'm asking that you help me rescue my company—our company—from the clutches of the Ivers family. We have but one shot to prevent one of them becoming CEO now."

"I think Al makes a capable leader for the company," Kayla said, studying her long red fingernails. "Not as good as Rafael, but in the interim... he is great. Once Rafael's innocence is proven..."

"Don't be so quick," Rafael said under his breath, but Barry had already caught it.

"If you think Ivers is going to give up the title of CEO, you are smoking something I want, dearest Kayla. He owns majority shares in

PerCan, and he is going to move mountains to splinter up our group. Divide and conquer, it's how they operate."

"Give it a rest, Barry," Rafael said. "They own majority shares, same way they always did, and nobody is taking sides here. This isn't a war."

"Yes, it is, and the prize is my company."

The two men stood, staring into each other's eyes until Kayla raised her hands, gently putting one on each of their chests, pushing ever so slightly.

"Not now, guys, not right now. This is pointless. Barry—Connor—whatever you prefer to be called now, please leave us alone. I need to discuss this with my fiancé in private. I sincerely hope you understand."

"Fiancé," Barry sneered. "Good luck, Rafael. I hope you like sloppy seconds."

"Out."

Rafael pointed, and Barry took the door, wisely closing it from the outside.

Mere hours had passed since his morning coffee, and already he felt as if a freight train had run over him, multiple times.

"He's just desperate for something that will get to you."

"I know," he said, running a hand through his hair for the umpteenth time, figuring by now he probably looked like one of his cleaning woman's floor mops. "I know that. You snuck the fiancé in there quick enough. When did that ever…."

"Sorry. I didn't want him to think—he was being so bloody damn stubborn and superior. Somebody needed to take him down a notch."

He put a finger over her lips and shook his head. "Not now. We'll talk about it. Right now…" He dropped back into his chair and pulled the hair back from his face with a bit more force. "Right now, if I were a computer, I would call stack overload."

"Did you eat anything today?"

"I don't remember," Rafael said and began some pacing of his own. "What's this about notes in his hotel room? About using the Vietnamese gangs to move in on Ivers?"

"So I hear. Nothing they can pin on him concretely, or they wouldn't have let him go. The way the story goes, there's a turf war among a few of the gangs in this town, and they were trying to move in on Ivers's club business before he was killed. Barry spun some fiction around it, how they'd make a handy scapegoat. That's all they have."

"Something he said, just as you came in…"

"Please, stop thinking about Barry for just one moment. Here…" She reached into her bag and brought out a package from a local sandwich shop. "I figured you'd be running on empty. Start by eating something. Then tell me how it went with Al and what we need to do next."

"He's not wrong, you know…." Rafael sat back down, unwrapped the sandwich, and took a generous bite. "Al has taken over completely."

"Another thing you should stop worrying about." Kayla shook her head.

"This is good. This is really good. Thanks," Rafael said.

He took a few more bites and almost magically felt his strength and determination returning. Darn it if it didn't take a woman to figure out that he had been beating his head into a very solid brick wall all day and probably wasn't about to stop until someone gently but firmly made him.

"Al told me," he finally said with his last bites, licking crumbs off his fingers and folding the wrapper carefully, "Al told me he would gladly put you back onto the executive board if everyone agrees."

"This is good news. Thank you. He still has to be careful, and that police officer still may have a few questions for me."

"But you didn't do it," Rafael finished.

"Neither did you. I think the man who just left your house might have, but that's another story."

"Him?" Rafael nodded toward his front door where Barry had disappeared. "Why would he?"

"Revenge? Because he's crazy? Because he thinks Ivers wanted to take his company?"

"Nobody took anything from him, Kayla. He made a massive mess, and rather than deal with it, he ran. Now that that particular case has finally been dropped, he wants it back, yes. But as a motive, that doesn't cut it."

"Fine, then let's not go there. Tell me how you see the company's future."

Fine. Rafael lifted his head and put his hands together. His father used to say, "Any time a woman says 'fine,' that is the furthest thing from her mind, son," and just then Kayla did not look fine.

"Well…"

"If you want the title of CEO and the company back, then let's work with Al to do that. I'm going to be right there with you. But I do not want to give everything we have worked for to that man." Her hand snapped out, and a long, manicured finger pointed toward the front door. "And just roll over."

"I already told Al I would work with him, as much as I can, while I am still being questioned, but…"

"Good. That won't last long, and then we will destroy Barry, so he can never, ever, come back into this company again."

"Hold on. Nobody is destroying anybody." Rafael rose and took a few steps away from her. "We've merged companies with Mariposa, and he owns a large portion thereof. Like it or not, we have to come to some sort of an arrangement that works for everybody, or we'll break this thing to pieces."

"There will be no arrangements with Barry Wentworth. Besides, he's going to jail."

"Somebody is, yes," Rafael said, taking yet another step back. "And that is one of the things Al asked me to help with." He took the note out of his portfolio and smoothed it out on the coffee table. "Apparently these are—private investigators of some type he knows. They might be of some assistance to figure out who actually did it."

"He would know the best." Kayla barely glanced at the note and finally smiled again. "Use them and find out."

As tiny as she was in stature, Kayla suddenly had an intensity about her that reminded Rafael of a massive, exploding force field. All of the gentle softness he loved about her had gone from her face, leaving a fierce, hard-edged anger. Barry had betrayed her, her along with everybody else, and left her behind without a word. It made sense that his return would be harder for her than everybody else. Rafael didn't have the words that would take the heaviness out of that moment, and he looked down at his hands and traced a scar on his finger. Finally, he nodded.

"I do intend to find out," he said gently. "For the good of all of us. But I can see this is getting to you. Take a step back. Let me handle it."

With a huge effort, she dragged herself back, softened her face, and forced a brittle smile.

"I know," she said. "Just promise me you won't let him win, Rafael, promise me."

Later, Rafael didn't know what he had said, or if he had promised anything, but he could still feel the fire of her intensity. *Don't let him win—whatever you do.* He prowled around the house, picking up things and putting them back down, still undecided whether he should call any of the names on Al's note now, or later, or ever, and finally, he made an excuse and left the house.

FOUR

Other men went jogging or fishing. Rafael didn't like fish, and he had proven to himself that he utterly hated running. Every time he tried it, he ended up sore and miserable, on top of the problem he'd been trying to run from, so he finally settled for a fast walk.

'What do you want?' Kayla had asked, and he'd skillfully avoided an answer. What did he want, indeed? A few days ago, the answer would have been simple: to run PerCan with his group of talented people and new merger partner.

Today, almost everyone in this group of talented people seemed to be a suspect in Tadeo's murder. And the merger partner was now controlled by a man he didn't really trust any longer. So where did that leave him?

Get out now? He'd wanted to walk away a dozen or more times, and he never had, so no, he wasn't doing so now. That only left one thing: finding some way for them all to work together at this company without actually killing one another.

Killing! Bad choice of words.

He looked up and noticed he had walked most of the way to his favorite watering hole, The Lighthouse Bar and Grill in the harbor.

He had the door already in hand when he paused.

Barry was back in town. This used to be their spot. Indeed, PerCan had been first thought of, drunk to, and put together in this very same bar. For the moment, there was another spot just down the road, an Irish pub.

He headed there, found a seat, and ordered a beer, stewing.

"Listen to the voice of experience. It tastes the same whether you're miserable or not, mate."

He looked up from his glass and into the eyes of his friend Irving Moody, retired millionaire and private pilot extraordinaire.

"Irv, fancy meeting you in this place. I thought The Lighthouse had a barstool with your ass imprinted, permanent-like."

"Might say the same of you friend. Bad day?"

"And then some."

Irv slid onto the barstool beside him and began to tick things off on his fingers. "You got fired from your CEO gig, your old partner is back after skipping town a few years ago, and your current boss has been shot. What did I miss?"

Rafael snorted and took a hefty swig of his beer. "What did you miss?" He began to tick off his own fingers. "Everybody on my former board of directors is on the suspect list, I'm still fired and under suspicion, and the company is splitting into two very unfriendly sides, Al's side and Barry's."

"That's more like war, not business."

"A war fought in the boardroom, and the weapons are being polished as we speak, my friend," Rafael confirmed. "Moreover, both parties are more or less subtly trying to make sure I'm on the correct side—their side, that is—and Al, my good buddy, wants me to help figure out who really killed Tadeo Ivers."

"Just to keep you busy, seeing as how you're out of work at the moment?"

"Not likely. Running this company is a tall order for anyone, and I don't see a way to put a cohesive management group together without trust. Trust is not going to happen in this ragtag group unless we find out what happened to Ivers and why. That's not the issue here."

"So, what is the issue?" Irv got comfortable, stretching his long legs under the table, and took a generous swig of his drink. "You know I call a spade a spade, Rafael. So let's have it. What is the real issue here?"

"Who killed Tadeo Ivers?"

"Not bad, but there is an 'and' at the end of that sentence. And…?"

"Where does that leave me, and what the hell am I supposed to do now?"

"That wasn't that hard. What do you want to do?"

"Kayla already asked me that."

"That woman of yours is smart. So what did you tell her?" Irv took another sip of his beer and looked at Rafael expectantly.

"I said I don't know. If I had my pick, I'd go back to running Per-Can in a minute. I enjoyed it, I was good at it, we were just getting into the flow of this whole thing. If I could—go back, you know…"

"Go back to where?"

"To before Barry came back into town, before Ivers was shot. Right there. That moment, when we had the merger all done, the license in hand, and the building properly renovated, the plants in their pods. Right there."

Rafael tapped his hand onto the table as if to mark a moment in time, that very spot before everything had gone to hell, before all of their solid foundations crumbled apart.

"Great. Now you have a goal. So, what's it going to take to get back there?"

"What's this, life coaching?" Rafael saluted Irv Moody with his glass. "You have a company that is a merged mess. One of the majority owners is Al Ivers, current CEO. The other majority owner is Barry Went-worth. Making peace is not a tall order—that's mission impossible."

"So, choose option three. Rafael Covin runs PerCan, keeps every-body in line."

"Good luck convincing those two of that," Rafael scoffed. "Besides, I can't be CEO right now anyway. This is a dicey industry still. Everyone on the board is expected, if not required, to have a squeaky-clean vest. Al barely qualifies. Barely. Wentworth? He would have had trouble—not insurmountable—but trouble."

Irv Moody sat there staring into his beverage for a long moment. Something worked behind those dark eyes. Some thoughts that were turning around and around going this way and that, and Rafael knew better than to ask.

"How many shares are outstanding just now?" Irv asked, that far-away look still in his eyes.

"Pardon?"

"Shares, in the new entity?"

"Perfect Cannabis Consolidated, why do you ask?"

"No reason."

Irv performed a conversational 180 and opened his wallet to show him a few pictures of his latest acquisition, yet another small airplane to add to the fleet he already owned. Some of them antiques, but this new one was little and, well, kind of pretty.

"You're certifiable, my man," Rafael laughed, thumbing through the pictures of the little ultralight that was supposed to be super easy to fly for anyone—anyone at all.

"I'll take you up anytime you want, Rafa. Anyone can fly this thing, I'm telling you."

"And if you think these two feet are leaving solid ground, you are crazier than even I thought, but thank you for your efforts distracting me."

Rafael laughed, ordered another round and happily turned to subjects of absolutely no importance: small aircraft, world politics, and local sports. Anything to get his mind off business and the murder investigation. Tomorrow was another day, and experience told him his problems would patiently wait for him.

FIVE

"Miss Montecito. First off, thank you for coming down to the station. I apologize if this is, uh, somewhat uncomfortable for you."

"Be a lot more uncomfortable in my offices with staff looking on, don't you think, Sergeant Robertson?"

Kayla flung her white fur stole off her shoulders and looked around the sergeant's tiny office for a place to put it. Every available surface held either file folders or boxes she did not want to think about, other than his desk, which was covered in paper. Her lawyer, Richard Marks, a short squat fellow who looked as if he had forgotten to retire a number of years ago, stood ramrod straight about a step behind her, his hand on her elbow in a gesture that was supposed to keep Robertson in check.

"Here, let me." Robertson rushed around from behind his desk, took the stole from her, and awkwardly draped it over a file cabinet. He was probably calculating how many months' worth of salary it would take to buy one of these beauties. Kayla couldn't help but smirk just a little, then sat, very prim, in the only other available chair and folded her hands in her lap.

"For the record," Marks said, "my client is here voluntarily to help your investigation in any way she may be able to. We would appreciate it if you kept this brief. Very brief in fact."

"Of course. So, you knew Tadeo Ivers?"

"I knew of him—who didn't at PerCan? He owned a large quantity of shares in the company. Although Rafael usually dealt with him. I've never actually met the man."

"Never?"

"Not in person, no. I saw his face on a screen during video conferencing on the occasion of board meetings. Rafael usually dealt with him personally."

"And you are currently..." Robertson leafed through his papers for a minute, and fine beads of sweat appeared on his forehead. "In a relationship with Mr. Covin."

"Correct."

She didn't elaborate, just as Marks had emphasized. *Yes or no answers, don't offer anything he's not asking about, don't fall for any fishing expeditions. You're not there to help him or make his job easier or, God forbid, make him like you. Yes or no answers.*

The journalist in her wanted to jump up and tell this little sergeant what a wonderful man Rafael was and how much crap he had had to take from Ivers during those personal meetings.

Yes or no answers. So she kept her hands primly folded in her lap and her eyes on her lawyer's face.

"Ivers wasn't exactly easy to deal with, was he?"

Kayla opened her mouth and closed it again. "I wouldn't know," she finally said. "Like I said, I really didn't know him."

"Did Rafael Covin ever tell you anything about Tadeo Ivers?"

"You're really going to have to ask Mr. Covin about that," the lawyer said and put his hand over Kayla's briefly. "I don't think secondhand opinions would be helpful."

"Right."

The detective sergeant made a face and kept leafing through his papers. If that was all he had on Tadeo Ivers's murder, it surely didn't amount to much, Kayla thought, and straightened her shoulders a little.

Common lore would say showing up with your lawyer and checking every statement with him/her would make one look guilty, but Kayla knew better. As she had told Rafael: never talk to the police, always bring a lawyer, don't offer anything. Those were the rules of life, and this wasn't the time to take chances.

Robertson batted a few more idle questions back and forth—had she heard anything about Ivers, did she know anyone who might have had it in for him, that kind of thing. And dutifully, she answered with a simple no every time. Richard, still smiling, started shifting in his chair a little.

"I don't see how Ms. Montecito can offer you anything else here, Sergeant. Do you think we are done?"

"One last thing." Sean Robertson looked up from the notes on his yellow legal pad. "Barry Wentworth."

"Oh, you save the interesting, juicy stuff for the end, don't you?"

Richard shot her a warning glance, but Kayla shook her head and smiled.

"No worries. It's been through all of the papers—at least it was, years ago. Yes, Sergeant, I am sure you know Barry Wentworth and I used to be what they call an item years ago."

"You were engaged."

"Also true."

"And he fled town rather than answering charges about an illegal grow op within the company building."

Richard already raised his hand, and Kayla spread her hands.

"Oh, but Sergeant, you already know I wouldn't know what was going through his head back then. He left town, the charges were dropped eventually, and we are no longer together. That just about sum it up for you?"

"You don't like him very much, do you?"

"Does it really matter whether I like Barry Wentworth or not?"

"You were together with him. He left you. You must have been pretty angry at him?"

"And Miss Montecito's relationship to Mr. Barry Wentworth is entirely unrelated to your investigation of the Tadeo Ivers shooting," Richard said and rose demonstratively. "If there is nothing else, Sergeant?"

"I would like to know where Miss Montecito was on Tuesday night, let's say around 11 o'clock p.m."

Richard sat again, and Kayla folded her hands, primly in her lap once again.

"At home, Sergeant," she finally said. "And before you ask, yes, I was all alone."

"There's nobody who might have been with you?"

"No. But I would assume the doorman at my building saw me come in. The electronic key system probably has a record of my car entering the underground garage. But as far spending the night goes, I was all alone, Sergeant."

"I suggest you check with Miss Montecito's doorman," Richard said, rising once again. "And if you look at the CCTV footage at her building, and the one across the road, you will find she spent all night at her home, not leaving until the next morning. Now if you have nothing further?"

"We will check all of it, to be sure. No, for the moment that would be it."

Kayla rose and waited for the sergeant to bring her fur stole again, wrapped herself into its white cloud, and put her sunglasses back on her face.

"Thank you."

"My pleasure. You don't have any immediate travel plans, Ms. Montecito, do you?"

"Any particular reason why you would like to know?"

"My client has been most cooperative." Richard pushed himself between her and the detective sergeant and actually became a little taller than his usual six-three. "For you to continue to stand in the way of her conducting her ongoing daily business…"

"Not doing any such thing. Take it easy. I mean—just in case I have any other questions."

"My client has answered…"

Kayla put her hand on Richard's arm and smiled graciously. "I run one of the largest publishing houses in the area, Detective Sergeant. Do you really think I will pack a bag and run away somewhere at this point?"

"I didn't really…"

"No, I do not have any immediate plans to travel outside the country," she sighed as if it were a burden to carry. "And if it helps you sleep at night, my secretary can let you know when I do."

When, not if.

"We don't really have to…"

"No, Richard, we do not, I understand. But the detective here looks capable enough. Shortly, he will indeed find out that I most certainly did not shoot Mr. Ivers, and then all of this nonsense will come to an end. Until then, I would not have a chance to pack a suitcase, never mind run away somewhere. Good day, Detective."

Kayla nodded briefly and swept out of the room, leaving Richard to follow her like an obedient puppy dog and Detective Robertson standing in his office scratching his head.

"Damn," he muttered softly and dropped into his well-worn chair again. His chair creaked in protest, and Robertson dug the heels of his hands into his eyes until the knock on his doorframe brought him back to reality.

"This a good time?" Chad, the young detective he'd asked to search Barry Wentworth's hotel room, asked.

"Good as any, bad as any. What's up?"

"Was that Kayla Montecito?"

"The one and only. And the lady has an edge that is sharp enough to cut your throat, my friend."

"What'd she ever see in Wentworth?"

"Don't ask. Now what've you got?"

Chad opened his cell phone to his electronic notes, a habit Robertson couldn't get into, being partial to good old handwritten notes himself, and cleared his throat.

"Wentworth—used to be called Connor Beauregard, founder of Perfect Cannabis Corporation..."

"I know all of that. Fast forward just a little please. I don't want to be sitting here forever rehashing history. Anything interesting in his hotel room?"

"Other than the notes we already found, no," Chad said, a little irritated. "I don't know why anybody would write that kind of thing down. Pretty stupid if you ask me."

"People do dumb things when they feel safe," Robertson answered and leaned back in his chair. "Wentworth strikes me as a guy who is anything but stupid. Anything on his whereabouts last night?"

"He claims he was out running."

"Running?"

"As in physical exercise?"

"I know what running means. Why not the hotel gym, I wonder? Seems to me a five-star hotel gym would have everything the stressed-out executive requires. And the weather wasn't exactly balmy Tuesday night."

"Raining cats and dogs, my mother would say," Chad said, grinning. "Wentworth, on the other hand, claims he desired some privacy, decided to run outside, but did not use the elevator or the hotel lobby to exit the building."

"Interesting."

"Instead, he says he went down the back stairs at the end of the hall and exited through the rear entrance into the alley behind the hotel."

"Indeed." Robertson rubbed his eyes again and folded his hands at chin level. "Let me see if I follow here. The guy pays big time for a hotel suite, feels the need to exercise a little. But instead of heading down a couple of floors into the climate-controlled gym where he's got everything at his fingertips, including a television with the latest news reports, a sauna, and massage therapist and a perky receptionist, he sneaks down the back stairs and runs along a dark alley in the rain? That's what he's asking us to believe?"

"That's just about it," Chad said, still grinning as if someone had told a silly joke.

"Well then, our dear reverend, Mr. Barry Wentworth, is getting interesting."

In one smooth motion Detective Sergeant Robertson rose to his feet again, stretching the tension out of his shoulders.

"If you ask me," Chad said, waving the phone with his notes in the air, "I don't think we're going to have to look very much further at all."

"Maybe, maybe not. But something isn't lining all of my ducks up yet. If being a creep were enough to put him away, I'd book him in a second and go for a beer. But then he'd have to share a jail with most celebrities, and quite a few politicians. It would be a bit crowded. He's a creep, and he acts more than a little off for my liking, so let's have another chat with our Mr. Wentworth and see if he can shed some more light on this."

SIX

Another one of those days where he should either have stayed in bed or gone on an extended vacation, Rafael thought, pulling out of the parking lot. His own, mind you, much like the building the lot served, and everything within it. Covin Construction Corp didn't look like much from the outside—certainly, it lacked the flash and sheer grandeur of PerCan—but he had literally built it, walls, roof, and all.

He'd dug the spade in over in that corner to lay the foundations, personally. So, was it any wonder he got irritated hearing his 'former' employees raving about what an excellent job Roger Carmichael was doing managing the company? Roger Carmichael, the man Tadeo Ivers had lured out of retirement to run Rafael's company while Rafael dragged PerCan out of the ditch Connor Beauregard had crashed it into.

It was still his company. His own company. Realistically, all he needed to do was tell Carmichael to move over. The boss was back in town.

Except from the moment he walked in, he could tell it wasn't his company any longer.

They had processes now and procedures. No longer could he run in, holler, 'I'm home,' and just wing it for the rest of the day. Oh no, there were plans, forecasts, budgets, execution models, deliverables, reporting procedures, and whatnot. And they liked it! His own people liked it!

And yet… He wasn't coming back to run it. It had taken him all of two hours to realize that, and he'd left before his mood could become truly foul and affect everyone around him.

As if he hadn't known this morning when he decided to drop by Covin Construction, as if he hadn't known then that there was no place for him here any longer.

He didn't really want to run a construction company any more either. He really wanted PerCan back, the company that had become his life over the last couple of years, the company he could not legally run at the moment. One, because he'd been fired and, two, because he still had to reassure everyone that he, Rafael Covin, had not fired the gun that shot Tadeo Ivers.

Swell.

Consequently, his mood bubbled just south of utterly foul, and he didn't care to share it with anyone. Not even Kayla, who'd gone to see the irritating detective sergeant this morning. They couldn't possibly still believe she had anything to do with this.

He found himself driving around aimlessly, breaking the speed limit as a matter of principle, voicing his displeasure with other drivers around him in colorful and sometimes newly invented terms, when his cell phone rang.

He'd flung it onto the passenger seat earlier. In spite of all the warnings and ads about it, he reached for it.

"What," he barked, not really caring who was at the other end, not really wanting to speak to whoever had made the mistake of dialing Rafael Covin's number.

"Rafa, well, hello to you too. Where are you? I need to speak to you like half an hour ago. Can we meet?"

"Barry," he sighed. "This isn't really…"

"You're busy? Doing what exactly?" Barry asked, and if he could have, Rafael would have slapped him.

"Driving right at the moment."

"Good. Then drive yourself to The Lighthouse. I had an idea."

I had an idea. The last time Barry used those words and asked for Rafael's assistance, PerCan had been founded.

"Rafa, hello. Are you still there?"

"Yeah, I'm just… Going through a bad area." He bought time.

One thing about Barry's ideas: they were generally fun. Outrageous, big-time fun. His mind generated ideas like nobody else he knew, and the only thing a man could do was buckle up and knuckle down—things were about to start flying.

"Great, half an hour then, at The Lighthouse. And Rafael? We're taking our company back."

"Hey, what—wait? Connor? Barry? I never said… Shit!"

Barry had hung up. Another one of his famous moves: *here's what we're going to do. Thanks. Bye.*

He promised himself to say no this time. Just one word, no. Damned man, he surely had the charisma of a preacher, and, somehow, some way, people always did his bidding. But not this time.

He spotted Barry the moment he walked in. If he could have, Rafael thought, walking up to the bar, if he could have, Barry J. Wentworth would have been bouncing up and down in his seat like an excited five-year-old. His dark eyes darted around the room, taking in this and that, and the moment the door opened and Rafael walked in, he waved—actually waved.

Under tension—seriously high voltage—and most likely on something, Rafael thought. He should have turned on his heel, and still he walked over, grinning, when he should have gone back through the door and left.

"Rafael."

"Barry," Rafael said and smiled. He slipped on to the barstool beside him and ordered a coffee, painfully aware of the last time he'd done this. Meeting Barry at The Lighthouse, finding him flying high on something or other already, ordering coffee for himself, and trying to talk sense into the man beside him. It hadn't worked back then either. The Lighthouse was just that—an old lighthouse building that had been converted into an exclusive bar, with dark wood, lots of brass, and a massive picture window overlooking the harbor. Gave you something to look at when conversation lagged.

"Find any interesting illegal grow ops lately?" Rafael asked, stirring his coffee when it arrived, and finally laughed. "You know, last time…"

"Never mind last time. This is now. You were saving him for when we needed him. I knew you wouldn't just roll over and let those damned Ivers stooges take our company. I knew it. Thanks, Rafa. I owe you huge."

"What?"

He stopped stirring and blinked. Once, twice, just to make sure he hadn't fallen through a black hole somewhere.

"Irv Moody, Rafael. Hello, wake up." Barry snapped his fingers a few times. "I know who he is, and I know you were talking to him. What I didn't know is just how chummy the two of you are now. Then it occurred to me. Of course. You were saving him—to take back the company. Brilliant, Rafael, absolutely brilliant. He has all the cash we need to do that. I should have known you knew what you were doing. And don't mind my bad manners with Kayla. I just didn't think she was your type. That's all in the past, no hard feelings, all good. Now we…"

"Stop, stop, just stop, Barry. What the actual fuck are you talking about?"

Rafael held out his palms, physically pushing back as if he could stop the tsunami of words spilling forth from his friend. Hopeless. When Barry was on a roll, he could go up against the Energizer bunny.

"The outstanding shares we need to buy up—all of them. Every last one. He has the means, and he likes hanging out with you. Brilliant. Bring him over. The three of us, we can…"

"Bring him over? What the hell?"

"I'm talking about you lining up the perfect investor with the deepest pockets to buy up all the outstanding shares of PerCan—for us."

"For us," Rafael repeated, still dumbfounded, feeling like the kid in third grade who repeated everything back to the teacher, just so he wouldn't look stupid. "For…?"

"And when we have all those shares, when we are back in the majority, we will simply vote out Ivers, any and all Ivers goons. And hallelujah, dickheads are gone, company is ours again."

"For starters, right now neither one of us can…"

"Be CEO, blah, blah, blah. That will clear up soon enough. I told you I didn't do it, and I am assuming you didn't."

"No," Rafael snorted, supporting his forehead with his hands. "You can't possibly be thinking about this."

"Oh, I am not thinking. I am doing. Here's the plan…" Barry took a napkin and drew two *x*'s on it. "You—me."

"Brilliant."

"Stop it. I control Mariposa, you know that."

"All too well."

"Irv Moody buys up every outstanding share there is. Then between my shares, yours, Kayla's, and his—really ours—we will control just over 50 percent of the merged company. I checked the numbers. We can do this if he gets on with it. Right now. Then we structure it the way we want. Say we make Kayla CEO for a little while."

"Kayla?"

"Yes, it's cleaner that way—neither one of us. And she's got a reputation in business. I would pick Moody, but I don't know how far you trust him. This is your call. But say we make her CEO, you COO or something similar. So now the control is back in our hands. We tell everybody with the last name of Ivers to vacate their position in the company, immediately. Don't need them any longer. You hired that grower fella I always wanted, from Colorado, what's-his-name?"

Barry snapped his fingers again, trying to remember, the glow in his eyes matching that of the glass in front of him. Rafael still scrambled to follow.

"Nick Ambrose? That who you're talking about?"

"Exactly. He's the best. That's why I wanted him in the first place. So, it will be you, me, and him, Kayla. Thomas Donnelly of Mariposa can be CFO if he wants. He seems like the type. Is that brilliant or what?"

What do you say? Rafael shook his head and took a deep draft of coffee that was way too hot, just to spare himself having to answer right then and there. He used a coughing fit to cover another few seconds and finally wiped his mouth with a snow-white napkin.

"And you think," he said, carefully and obsessively folding the napkin again. "You think everybody on this list is really just meekly going to go along with your plan?"

"Of course they will. Why wouldn't they? We get control back—did you not hear me? Control."

Barry seemed genuinely surprised. Couldn't figure why anyone would want to be careful after the events of the past few years, why anyone would have misgivings or, God help him, doubts about Barry J. Wentworth's ability to find more than one rabbit in his hat and to pull it out at a very convenient point in time.

"Why wouldn't they, Rafa? The Ivers idiots are finished. Together, we can outvote them any time we want to. Look at our track record—look at what we've done."

"Exactly, Barry!"

"I founded this company. I raised a small fortune for it—scratch that, a large fortune. You took it, built it into something magnificent, arranged for a brilliant merger…"

"Connor—Barry—slow down. I can't figure out if you're drunk, on drugs, or really believe what is coming out of your mouth just now."

"On drugs! That was a long time ago." Barry waved his hand as if chasing the thought away like a pesky mosquito. "Kayla never told you about the party drugs?"

"Oh, she did," Rafael said, rolling his eyes. "Biggest mistake she ever made, giving you what you wanted."

"That was a lifetime ago. I needed the energy, and I quit that stuff soon as I noticed it wasn't doing me any good. Kind of worried me that something would happen."

"God forbid," Rafael said, but the sarcasm completely passed over Barry's head.

"Wasn't fun quitting, but it had to be done. Never mind that either. This plan is brilliant, and you know it, so tell me why you look like somebody just stole your BMW."

"I never had one."

"Rafa. What's the matter with you?"

"For starters? Just for starters, how about loyalty?" Rafael pulled the hair back from his face and shook himself. "These are the people who stuck with me when I didn't have a clue, helped me save this company, when Ivers threatened me with literal bodily harm if I didn't get it done."

"Nobody says they didn't. But that was a long time ago. Things change, as I just told you."

"And now I'm just going to say bye, there's the door, see you?" Rafael asked, honestly trying to wrap his mind around what he was hearing.

"It's business, Rafael, follow me here. You always think everybody is your pal if you do one deal with them. They are not your pals. Al is not your friend. His brother is not your friend. These are people who are in this deal—until they are not any longer. Nothing personal. Christ, how often have we been there? Unicum Oil? Tech Innova? New Energy? Deals we were in, then somebody said, 'sorry, see you later.' It happens—shit happens. You move on."

"Sure, but…"

"And now it's going to happen to the Ivers family. Keep reminding yourself: you, me, Kayla. The three people who were there, right here in this bar actually, when we started it. We will run this thing together. You enjoyed it. Don't even try to deny it. I can see it in your face."

"Yeah, but—"

"No buts. Then we're going to get it back. With Irv Moody's help."

"If he'll do it," Rafael said, knowing that the idea wasn't even as outlandish as it sounded, and Irv Moody might see it the same way. He could be convinced, if Rafael laid it out right for him, to buy up those shares and be a player in the company. He might want to have a board position in exchange. For reasons he couldn't quite explain, Rafael knew that the cannabis industry had grabbed Irv Moody. He wanted in. And if this was the ticket, if buying shares was what would do it…

"If you explain it to him, he will," Barry said as if he were reading Rafael's mind. "Of course he will. He'd be stupid not to. This is the hottest industry of the century. Fuck Dot Scan Software—this is it. And if he wants in, he can be on the board. Some advisory role of one kind or another, just so he can fly around in his planes and tell people he is in cannabis."

"Possible…"

"Not 'possible,' stop dinking around, Rafa. For sure. Now promise me you'll get it together and guide him—gently."

"He asked me yesterday how many shares were outstanding," Rafael said without thinking. He'd wondered at the time where Irv was going with this question. Perhaps he was thinking along the same lines already…

"Brilliant. You see? He's opened the door already. This was always ours. You brought in Ivers…"

"I brought him in because we needed his money, or we wouldn't even be here. Don't forget that."

"I'm not criticizing you, Rafa, but it's time for them to go."

Dramatically, Barry reached over to snuff out the little candle burning in a glass votive on the bar. He wiped his fingers raised one eyebrow and shrugged. Done.

Without any more thought or explanations, he reached for the bill and put it back down with his credit card. Another change.

"Picking up the tab, old friend?"

"Don't I always?"

"I beg to differ!"

"Rafael, I've learned a few things while I was away. So have you. No harm in that."

"Hear, hear."

"This is exactly what I mean," Barry said. "Marijuana, at least the pharmaceutical side, is the industry of the future, the 'can't lose,' tech-bubble, golden goose of the century. You and I are going to rule the industry, Rafael, rule it. We just need to iron out a couple of wrinkles. And the Ivers goons are nothing but a wrinkle."

His eyes got that faraway look again, the one that said he'd spun a story in his head. Then and there, he'd arranged the facts in way that allowed Barry Wentworth to have everything he wanted, the way he wanted it, and when. And when the picture was complete, he would stand up and sell it to anyone who listened to him long enough as the pure and complete truth. Rafael looked away, shaking his head.

"So, a preacher, Barry—an honest-to-God preacher?"

Barry shrugged. "Nothing wrong with that. Never have there been so many believers as when I lived on Vaomar Island. Simple people, simple life, simple beliefs. It was a refreshing change from the race we're in every day on this continent."

"Believing in what, I wonder?" Rafael asked and took a sip of coffee. "I just bet your particular brand of religion…"

Barry's shoulder rolled just a bit. He straightened his back, and his voice suddenly dropped to an impressive baritone. "Just when you decided that you would have to live without your dream," he said, raising his left hand to Rafael with dramatic flair. "Just when you decided that you would serve other people, and what God promised you might never happen, and you would make do with your situation. Just then, God rose and said, as you were taking care of my business, I am going to take care of yours. And everything that you ever wanted, all the riches, everything that looked like it got away—I am going to give it to you."

His left hand reached high up into the air, grabbing and holding something unseen but nevertheless real. Then he took both towards Rafael in a silent offering. Rafael felt a shiver crawling down his back and rubbed the gooseflesh on his arms.

"All right, all right, I see it. Your dad's gift for preaching."

"And the Lord…" Barry thundered, but Rafael raised a hand to stop him.

"And the Lord is a little disturbing at the bar here, Barry. Down, boy, I believe you."

Barry blinked, and for a second, Rafael almost had the feeling that there was another personality in there. Sure, they said this whole split personality thing was extremely rare and mostly fake. But man…

"Speak to Irv, please. For your future and mine," Barry said quite abruptly, in his normal voice again, and he paid the bill, clapped Rafael on the shoulder, and disappeared.

SEVEN

Al walked the length of the aisles between the individual growing pods, flowering pods, and vegetation pods, trying to keep all of the minute details that went into a grow in his head.

"At present there are 113 different strains of cannabinoids," the lab technician walking with him said. "And we're discovering new ones every single day. Well, on a regular basis, anyway."

"I understand," Al said.

"Cannabidiol being one of them," Paul said, cupping his right hand, "and over here, of course, you have THC, the hallucinogenic ingredient." Now the left hand. "It makes sense to think you should use one or the other."

"It's what I assumed," Al said cautiously. Never admit that you had no clue whatsoever. Never reveal anything that could be used against you.

"You don't. The true secret to medical applications lies in the combination," Paul finally said, putting both of his hands together. "The magic formulation of how much of which strain of the cannabinoids and THC, that is what we are perfecting. That is the key to the therapeutic area where the final product will be used."

He looked at Al, expecting praise, confirmation, criticism, or plain old agreement with the wisdom he had just shared, and Al nodded sagely. Looking around, he leaned a little closer to the environmental control panel outside one of the grow pods.

"Fascinating," he said, because most people loved to hear that whatever they did fascinated someone, that it was the most gripping topic encountered in the past several years. "Truly fascinating."

"Research and development are working full speed on this subject. What's possible, what is desirable, and how to have both. It changes every day. Every single day."

The man looked at his watch to underscore how quickly science was proceeding.

"Wonderful, Paul. Marvelous. Now if you could have a report on my desk by end of day about what everyone is working on and what your immediate targets are, I would appreciate it very much."

"Sure." The man nodded with a little smirk. "My name's Jason. Paul is not in our department any longer."

"Sorry—Jason, of course. I have a meeting with Paul in a little while. My mistake." Al's turn to look down at his watch. And he prayed to God Paul wasn't the janitor in this outfit, or he'd really embarrass himself.

"Right then. Tell him I said hello and I'm waiting for his report when you see him, would you please, Mr. Ivers? And I will be working on your reports immediately."

Immediately. Sarcasm, or did he truly mean it?

Al forced a smile and walked on, looking down at the clipboard he held before him like a shield. How did Rafael do this, he wondered. Rafael built things. He knew steel rebar, concrete, and brick. So how the heck had he managed to get all of the people in this never-ending anthill of a building to like him, to offer him their explanations, theories, and secrets and, most of all, to back him up?

It had become an effort for him to walk in here every day and pretend he was up to the job.

Straighten up, Ivers. Now who's making excuses?

"Something to smile about, Al?"

He looked up at Thomas Donnelly and offered a handshake. "Thomas, just a brief trip down memory lane as it were."

"Well, trip's over." Thomas didn't take the offered hand. "People are getting restless. We need a proper corporate structure that works for everyone. Not an hour goes by someone doesn't ask me about Barry Wentworth."

"Ah. The legendary Barry J. Wentworth, aka Connor Beauregard."

"It appears you know the chap. And if you do, then you know all of the rumors floating around about him. Not the least of which, that he shot your father."

"I believe I have heard that one a time or two, yes."

"Al, you're a little too laid-back for my taste at the moment. If I tell you we need structure, I'm not doing it for my own amusement."

"Neither did I assume you were."

Al straightened up a little at Thomas's tone of voice and looked down at his clipboard again. Embarrassingly few of today's tasks looked as if they had been accomplished.

"Pardon me if I don't instantly jump at your sense of urgency. Let me assure you I am well aware of the confusion within the staff regarding Barry's involvement in my father's..."

"Murder," Thomas suggested, and his shoulders slumped a little. "I realize this is a difficult time for you. If you would rather not..."

"I am more than capable of attending to my duties, Thomas." Al cut him off, a little sharper than he had intended.

"Hey, no offense. This is all new to us, all of us. I'm merely suggesting we could get some help if we need it. Outside help if required, help without..."

"So much baggage?"

Thomas nodded. "It might be a good thing. And it couldn't hurt, considering most everyone on the former board is under suspicion."

"Let's not bat about words like suspicion, Thomas. Our friends at the police department call it interest. Person of interest. So much more polite than plain old suspect."

"Rhetoric." Thomas forked a hand through his dark, unruly mop of hair. "Seems to me we'd all have an easier time running this company if this case were solved—and quickly."

Al squared his shoulders a little. "It appears you and I will have to do our best to navigate this perfect storm we find ourselves in."

Thomas spread his hands, and Al could almost hear his thoughts. *Rhetoric! What we need are real-time solutions.*

"At present, we don't know who killed Tadeo Ivers," Al said. "Neither is it our job to find out. What is our job is to take the resources we have, to get this first batch through its critical time, followed by harvesting, portioning, packaging, and sales. All due respect, but you have the experience of a COO there, I would expect you to pitch in with both hands. And yes, Barry is back, and, if I know him, he is here to stay until and unless they drag him off in handcuffs."

"I dream of that moment," Thomas said, rolling his eyes.

"And I wholeheartedly hope this is not going to happen here, at PerCan. So, with all due respect, let's all attend to our immediate tasks and worry about Barry Wentworth later."

"Nice speech, Al. You're missing the point. What exactly is his role in this company going to be?"

Al sighed and lowered his clipboard. "Honestly, I don't know. Yet. My—our—plan foresaw one set of executives from Mariposa and one set from PerCan, without an extra person thrown in. Rafael was to be CEO, which I stepped into temporarily, and you, quite rightly, COO. I don't…"

"Well, figure it out, will you? What is his role going to be? Who reports to him? Who does he report to? People want to know—people need to know, or they'll wander around on tiptoes all day long worrying about offending the wrong person instead of doing their jobs properly."

"Point taken."

Al raised his clipboard shield once again, making a mental note to speak to Barry.

Reasonably.

If such a thing could indeed take place. A reasonable conversation with Barry Wentworth. More likely, the man would spout a lot of nonsense about this being his company...

"Well, that's why you're CEO, then, Al, to solve problems such as this one." Thomas gave him the thumbs up and walked away before Al could say, 'thanks for nothing,' which wasn't strictly necessary anyway.

He wrote *asshole* on his clipboard, taking some juvenile satisfaction in the act, then scratched out the neat straight lettering and read the next item on his list. This was going to be a long day, like the chain of days before, and likely the ones after.

EIGHT

Rafael stared at his computer screen without really seeing anything. His thoughts kept circling the same subject. Perfect Cannabis Corporation: trading symbol PFCC; 63,250,697 outstanding shares; currently trading at $0.75; trading volume 130,000; average 83,722.

Not much going on. They had a brief spike after they announced the merger, but investors were still cautious. It was time to deliver on promises made, and to show them where the company was headed. Meanwhile, no one knew what the death of Tadeo Ivers was going to do to the company or the stock and, most importantly, who had shot him. A few crazy cowboys were buying, throwing money at the cheap share value. A few were selling, running for the hills because the sky was falling—and somebody had killed Tadeo Ivers. But who?

Who had pulled the trigger?

A mystery novel Kayla had read last year at the beach and needed to recount to him in great detail as she was reading came to mind. Some cockamamie tale about a guy who'd bump off CEOs and buy up all the available shares during the resulting share price dip. Of course he was caught. The bad guys always went away in books. In reality? For starters, that kind of stuff did not happen in real life, at least not in his life.

In his reality, dead people and gunshots were the stuff of primetime and the latest bestsellers, not day-to-day business. And still, suddenly he found himself in the middle of such an unlikely yarn, trying to keep it together. If it were a bestseller, he would have put the book down by now.

He shook his head, turning back to Yahoo Finance. The shares were available; he could buy as many as he could afford if he chose to do so. A lot less than Irv Moody would be able to buy, but still.

He would still need Irv to make sure their combined voting power would be enough to…

Enough to do what exactly? He forced himself to spell it out so he could look at it clearly in the light of day.

He needed Irv Moody's help if he wanted to buy up enough shares so their combined share votes would serve to remove Al Ivers from the post of CEO and Dante Ivers as Director of Agronomy and Operations.

There, he'd said it.

Rafael bit down on his thumbnail and blew out a breath. He had founded this company, with his friend and partner Connor, a man he knew well. Could he trust him?

He knew Connor well enough to know he needed to keep an eye on him—at all times. He and Barry. They'd run a dozen deals together, and then some. Had the idea, created the company, perfected the pitch, and raised the funds. Rinse and redo from start. It was a game, and they loved the rush of it all.

And along came Perfect Cannabis. Connor attempting to bribe a government official, taking off with a bunch of shares, making a deal with a loan shark… And finally—finally—an illegal grow op in a hidden part of the building. To say Rafael needed to keep a close eye on Barry was like suggesting a bit of adult supervision might be recommended for a convicted serial killer.

On the other side, there was Al. Did he really know Al?

Nobody would come out to say they knew Al well, though everybody seemed to know of him or at least have a cousin who knew a guy who…

A private person, his mother would have called him. But if there was something about Al you could count on, it was this: if he said a thing was such, you could darn well believe it without giving it a second thought.

Barry, he lived in Barry-land, where the sky was whatever color Barry decided it to be that day and things moved to the tune of his own drum and no one else's.

In all this he couldn't forget Al's father, who had forced him to resurrect the company, then turned right around and fired him, without so much as a thank you. The sins of the father…

Al Ivers and Barry Wentworth. If there ever had been two more diametrically opposite men in this world, Rafael didn't want to know them. Black-and-white, yin and yang.

It all came down to that one night, drinks at a bar and conceiving this company with Barry.

Was he even still considered an insider, after he'd been fired from the CEO seat? Would this kind of purchase dump him into another mess of hot water he didn't care to be in?

Rafael sighed and leaned back. Ever so slowly, he picked up his phone, scrolling down to the W section, where he found the number of his stockbroker, Jeff Warner.

NINE

"Mr. Covin, how are you? Thanks for coming in today." Detective Robertson shook Rafael's hand and nodded toward a chair in his office.

"Reasonably well, I'd say, considering…"

"Understood. And you and Miss Montecito appear to have engaged the same lawyer."

Rafael grinned broadly and dropped into the detective's visitor's chair with a heck of a lot more bravado than he actually felt, nodding to Richard Marks with a little smile.

"Well, you know what they say. Why break in a new one?"

Detective Robertson raised a single eyebrow and failed to laugh at the feeble joke. "Er—yes, of course."

"Once again, Detective, my client is here voluntarily to answer a few questions which may be helpful in your search for the actual killer. He is in no way considered to be under suspicion."

"We have not progressed far enough to name anyone as a prime suspect, sir. Right now, we're just asking a few questions, trying to piece together what actually happened that night. So why don't you go ahead and tell me…"

"That is a bit of a fishing expedition, don't you think, Detective?" Richard Marks broke in, and Rafael, who'd been about to open his mouth, deferred to the lawyer.

"Can we narrow it a bit there?"

"Just trying to establish what everyone around Mr. Ivers was doing that night, that's all. I've heard a few different accounts by now that there was a meeting going on at your house that night, is that correct?"

"That's correct."

"And what was said meeting all about?"

"Business matters." Rafael shrugged. "Things were—changing."

"Exactly." Robertson flipped over a page in his notebook as if he had to look it up. "Ivers had fired you that afternoon."

"It was a contract position to start with—and the contract was over. Finished."

"Just like that?" Robertson asked, and Rafael only spread his hands. No need to remind the man he'd been mad as hell.

"I also heard a few comments that you were quite angry at Ivers, and I quote, 'I saved his bloody company, and he repays the favor by firing my ass without as much as acknowledging the impossible task.' Seems to me it wasn't quite 'just like that,' Mr. Covin. Sounds like there were a few hard feelings, wouldn't you say?"

"Well…"

Rafael stretched his long legs and picked on the fabric of his trousers for a minute.

"You ever had a job you really liked, Detective? Something you suddenly found out you were good at, and you never knew it? To tell you the truth, I enjoyed running PerCan. It was exciting, it was new, it was cool. Why shouldn't I be just a bit peeved when he let me go?"

"In favor of his son. A son you did not feel was capable of running the company."

"Now wait just a…"

"I don't think Mr. Covin's opinions regarding the company's CEO have any place in this discussion, Detective," Richard Marks cut in.

"Oh, I think they do, Counselor. Rafael Covin is one of the founders of the company. He saves it, brings it back to life, and then Tadeo Ivers wants to hand it over to his son, a young man, a kid basically, who has no prior experience, and no business being CEO, doesn't even want to be there—hell, he had every right to be angry. I would be steamed if it happened to me."

The detective looked at Rafael and opened his hands. "It's completely understandable. Who wants their time and effort wasted in favor of a green kid?"

"Yes and no," Rafael said. "Yes, I was angry, very. Yes, I thought he was out of his mind. And no, there was no reason to be violent. Dante Ivers himself told me on several occasions he didn't want to be CEO. He would never accept that position, under any circumstances. Unless Tadeo Ivers hired a complete stranger to run the company, sooner or later, he would have to come back to me."

"You're so sure about that? Everything you had worked for and never got paid for, you would just hand it over, hoping they'd come back to you one day? That's a mite charitable."

"Maybe. And maybe people who can step in at a moment's notice to run an operation of PerCan's size and complexity grow on trees, and all you have to do is go out and pluck one. Could happen."

"Let's remember to stay with straight facts," Richard said and put a hand on his shoulder.

"So, tell me what that business meeting was all about then. The one that happened at your house that night. You'd been fired that day. Odd time to have a business meeting. At a private residence, no less, rather than a proper boardroom."

"Because," Rafael said carefully, glancing left at Richard Marks. "Because we were all planning to get into business together. A consulting firm."

"Without Tadeo Ivers?"

"He was not part of the arrangement, no."

"I'm not up on corporate law, but isn't that at least a little—crooked?"

"Let's not go calling something crooked and please leave my client's business deals to me, shall we, Detective? There was nothing illegal about the group opening a consulting firm together, period. That is what their meeting was all about. A new start for all of them."

"A new start—then…" Detective Sergeant Robertson shuffled a few papers on his desk and rubbed his hands together, never looking up. "According to our other witnesses, the meeting broke up around nine p.m."

"Correct," Rafael answered, nodding.

"And then…"

"And then I went to bed, Detective. I don't know about you, but that day had been what you would commonly call a doozy. A firing, a new business idea, a final board meeting, a man reappearing you thought dead and gone from your life. Yup—my body called curtains, and I answered."

"You went to bed?" Robertson asked, eyes lasering in on Rafael's face.

"I went to bed," Rafael confirmed. "Straight and without passing go or collecting $100."

"Had you had anything to drink? Anything alcoholic?"

"Enough to know I shouldn't have any more."

"Detective…" Richard raised a hand and snapped his fingers, and Rafael almost laughed. The image of an elderly schoolmarm came to mind and was dismissed just as quickly.

"I am not trying to paint your client as a drunk. I'm trying to establish his frame of mind."

"Exhausted, confused, and unable to take another step," Rafael answered. "So much so that even Kayla went to her own home, after the rest of them had gone on their way, and we agreed to regroup in the morning."

The detective rubbed his hands again and finally made a face.

"Not exactly what I would call a lot."

"No, Detective, as an alibi it probably sucks, but I can assure you it is the truth, and as far as I understand these here proceedings, unless you have a way to prove otherwise…"

The detective sighed and nodded again.

"I don't have to tell you, Mr. Covin, stay available. Let me know if you make any—big plans, will you."

"About Kayla…"

"Yes, I know. Your protective sense is still trying to remind me that she had nothing to do with the murder."

"Well, she didn't."

"I will get to that conclusion on my own—in due time and without your help, Mr. Covin."

"Thanks."

Rafael didn't know if the meeting had gone well or not, or what he should have expected in the first place, but his newly minted lawyer appeared satisfied.

Rafael didn't do it—he wouldn't, he couldn't—but other than his word, he really had nothing to offer. Just like every other suspect, or 'person of interest,' as they were called nowadays, who walked into the detective's office and said, 'I didn't do it.' Likely a courtesy on the detective's part to invite them in at their leisure to have a little chat.

Rafael had never been this close to an investigation before, but he had a suspicion if he wanted to, the detective might have been a lot less courteous. This much he told Kayla, who met him downtown for a quick coffee between meetings.

"The bright side would be Robertson going so far as to say he didn't really think you had anything to do with it, even if he didn't come right out and say so."

"And you did not either, Rafael. I know that, you know that, and he does." She put her hand over his and tried to smile as brightly as she could manage. "It is too bad you don't have a doorman and security systems in all of the hallways at your house."

"Any other situation I would say that kind of surveillance drives me insane. I had just hoped…"

"You hoped for a convenient suspect whom we could dispatch in a hurry and move on. Especially if he stood up and said, 'Yes, I did it.'"

"That would be something to celebrate. I hate the thought that one of us…"

One of us. He let the thought dangle and thought of the little group at his house that night for the thousandth time. Kayla—Al—Nick. All talking about what had happened at the board meeting. Barry's return from the dead, all worried about Dante Ivers, the youngest Ivers son who did not want to be CEO.

"You heard anything from Dante?"

"Briefly. He had a rough time watching you get fired and seeing Barry walk in. Then his father was shot. I imagine he is feeling pretty crappy right about now."

"I need to go talk to him. What about his worthless brother?"

"The erstwhile drug-dealing Roberto? Interesting you should ask. Barry wanted to make Roberto Ivers director in charge of horticulture."

"Oh, that's a really good look on an application to the licensing board and the Ministry of Health." Rafael shook his head and grinned. "We have an ex-drug dealer with a criminal record in charge of growing medical marijuana. Don't worry. It'll be fine. Talk about turning the goat into the gardener."

"Exactly why that plan went nowhere. It's one of the most key positions, and it requires someone solid and above reproach. I heard Al is planning to put a fellow from Mariposa in, with Thomas Donnelly overseeing the procedures." Kayla gave his hand a little squeeze. "I can stop talking about the company if it bothers you. I know you miss it, much as you stand there being flippant telling me you couldn't care less."

Rafael shrugged and folded his empty sugar package again and again this way and that. What was there to say anyway? *Yeah, I miss it, the company and the people.*

"This will be over soon. It's just this little bit right here…" she wagged her fingers in front of his eyes, "right here, right now. And then we will start over, and we will kick…" She smiled a little. "God, I wish I had called you that night, like I wanted to. Then it would be over already."

"I doubt our detective sergeant would have let that ride as an alibi, but thanks. Right now, they have little more than suspicion and rumor, and they won't move on that. Good attorney would sweep it out of the courthouse with a few words. Whether or not the Ministry of Health is going to take this lightly, though…"

"And that's why Al is here. To keep things on an even keel until you return."

Rafael worried his lower lip between his thumb and forefinger, weighing in his mind whether he should tell her about Barry's latest plan involving Irv's investment. Would she go for it? Could she? She'd be key to making it work, if he chose to go that way.

As if he didn't know that she would hit the roof the moment he mentioned Barry and getting rid of the Ivers clan. As if he didn't know right there, if he told her, he would have to make a decision: Kayla or Barry. Add that to his long list of deep thoughts.

Shit! Why did things always have to be this complicated?

"Rafael? You look like a man with the world on his mind. Their case against you amounts to nothing. What's going on?"

"Nothing, just…" He finally crumpled the abused sugar package and made to rise in order to pay their bill, but Kayla's hand clamped around his wrist, pulling him back down. His butt sank back onto the chair obediently.

"Hold it. The way you say nothing, I know something is going on. Something I am not going to like. And in this case especially. Call me suspicious, but why do I think your friend Barry has something to do with it?"

"Well—it's not—I mean… What I mean is…"

"I am listening…"

Her eyes narrowed and held his, and Rafael pushed back a little.

"You were there, at the beginning, with me—and—and him."

"Yes? And look where that landed me."

"Except—it was our company, our idea, our work."

"And Barry's carelessness and shady deals and underhanded moves that almost destroyed it. Let's not forget that while we're reminiscing."

"We were all there, Kayla. We let him do what he wanted and looked away when it got uncomfortable. None of us was dragged into it kicking and screaming. None of us said wait, you can't do that."

"Granted." Kayla nodded and settled back into her chair a bit. Getting comfortable now, too comfortable. He shouldn't have said anything at all. "We could have spoken up, and we didn't," she said. "Our mistake. So what's his plan now? The way you're sitting there, avoiding the mere act of telling me, is enough reason to believe there is something at least marginally wrong with it."

"Well…"

"And it's not hard to guess that Barry wants what he has always wanted, which is to get rid of the Ivers family and their involvement in this company. Which he considers his company. And most likely, he has you convinced that when he says 'mine,' he is graciously including you."

Rafael looked down at his hands and said nothing. She was right. It scared him the way she could look right through him, and his mind could not come up with one thing he might say to counter her argument.

"That silence right there, that tells me all I need to know, Rafael." She put her hand over his again and blew out a breath. "And now I am going to ask something of you. Don't even tell me what he has asked you to do. Don't think of all the ways that make it OK. Unless you can march right back into that detective's office and tell him about this plan, and nobody would raise an eyebrow. Unless that is the case, I don't want to know about it. If you're seriously planning on going there, I can't go with you."

She withdrew her hand and settled into her chair, reaching for her purse. Drawing back from him and from the thing he was wanting to do so badly.

Rafael had opened his mouth to answer when his phone chimed for an incoming message. It sat between them on the table, and Rafael looked down to glance at the screen.

"Thanks, knew you'd come through—B."

Kayla looked at it as well, and he didn't even have to wonder whether she could read upside down. He knew—and he knew another thing: he was done.

TEN

Al, meanwhile, realized he was the last person inside the building. Oh, a few security guards patrolled the area, on schedule and according to plan. And all the areas where cannabis was growing, stored, or just transiting were locked up tighter than a bank vault; he knew that as well. But the silence of the building around him was anything but comforting.

It had become oppressive, accusatory almost. As if the building itself were telling him it ought to be teeming with life that wasn't there. Money was tight until their issues were resolved, and he had to run short shifts and stretch his available manpower to the max. Once this next harvest came in, he'd be good for a while. If no other crises happened and he could get product sold right away. If. Right at the moment, it felt as if he were cursed in some way.

"Nonsense," he muttered and straightened out the lamp on his desk so the glowing pool of yellow became a little wider. No point sitting in the dark.

Yesterday, he heard somebody had been caught in a darkened washroom because the person had been sitting there without moving for too long, and the motion-sensing lights had gone off. That thought, at least, made him grin. *Please keep moving at all times to avoid being trapped in dark rooms, including toilets.*

Rafael would have made a joke out of it and been the first one to laugh it off with his people.

Right, Rafael.

Rafael, whom he had had to delete from the list of authorized personnel to comply with ministry regulations. The deletion had been overdue too long. After all, Rafael had been fired several weeks ago and had no business on the premises any longer. Specifically, not in the secured areas. It made perfect sense; it was required by law to keep visitors out of specific areas.

And nobody mentioned how much it would become a thorn in your side to delete your friend's name from such a list. How it would feel like betrayal when you actually went into the file and did so. Nobody ever mentioned that when they drew up said regulations.

Well, now he knew. It was a bastard of a task.

Carefully, he took the keycard Rafael had left behind, with a red stripe and a letter 'A' announcing to any and all it would grant access into all areas of the building. Al slipped it into an envelope, and the envelope beneath a number of small items in his desk drawer. He'd activate this card again someday, and then Rafael would be grateful to have it back.

Enough woolgathering for now. There was work waiting for him, or, more precisely, it wasn't exactly waiting for him.

He swiped a long finger over the touchpad of his laptop, bringing it back to life, and glanced at the square in the top right of the screen, the one displaying a direct linkup to Yahoo Finance and the latest trading data for Perfect Cannabis Consolidated.

There had been plenty of trading activity today, unusual amounts, as a matter of fact. Interesting too that every large block of shares that had been offered out there had been snapped up by a hungry, share-buying wolf almost instantly. The trading graphs showed a number of little spikes for today, as opposed to the flat graphs of the previous days.

Interesting, and a little worrisome perhaps. A public company, some changes in management—no surprise that there should be more trading activity. Meanwhile, staring at trading graphs only kept him from the real business of running a company.

He blanked out the little square and brought up a form the Ministry of Health was requiring him to fill in and certify in his capacity as CEO. One of many. And even Rafael's trusted executive assistant Connie hadn't been able to take care of the lion's share, as she usually did. Too many of the answers were to be filled in by the CEO himself. Another way official regulations strived to make his life overly complicated.

Al pinched his glasses a little tighter on his nose and squinted at the government jargon, reading it, then again, and a third time before it made sense. Who in his right mind came up with these questions and expected a logical and truthful answer?

Before he could clamp down on it, a memory came up, of him and Rafael sitting across from one another at this desk, making derisive comments about government paperwork. With an effort, he read the offending paragraph again. Christ, he needed someone to do all of this for him, so he could concentrate on building the company, but while money was tight…

There was a board meeting scheduled for the following day, and he needed to read his notes again. He had a feeling something was brewing just beneath the surface. That tingling feeling in his neck, that untouchable, unknowable, "right there in your gut" kind of feeling that something was wrong. And along with that feeling came the conviction that he was not going to like it. Not at all.

For what had to be the tenth or twentieth time that day, he went over the upcoming meeting in his mind and tried to put his finger on a sore spot, and again, he found nothing. A few things had to be cleared up; that was it.

Thank God Kayla appeared to be in the clear as far as the murder of his father was concerned, and he would have one solid ally. His younger brother Dante had disappeared in a huff after Barry dismissed him, Barry himself would fight him at every turn just for the sake of fighting, and then there was Thomas Donnelly.

Thomas didn't miss an opportunity to mention he didn't think much of the way Al was running this company, and Al was certainly not doing as good a job as Rafael had.

That last one could be a bit of spite, but he was getting a little bit tired of hearing, 'Rafael would have.' Had he asked for this job? He had not. Had he ever even applied or mentioned he would like to try out for the CEO seat? He had not. So why was everyone busy telling him he was unsuited to the position?

Al blew out a breath and pulled his notebook a little closer.

Then there was still the small matter of the million dollars they had given as a good-faith payment when they contemplated the merger with Green Technologies. Before Mariposa. His father had insisted they choose Greg Turner and Green Technologies as a merger partner, likely in part because he knew that Rafael and Al favored Mariposa.

They had given in—he and Rafael. At the time, it hadn't been worth another fight with Ivers Senior. They'd had a meeting and finally decided that it didn't really matter one heck of a lot which merger partner they choose, as long as they stayed in control of the company. They needed a merger partner with a license to grow, as their own chances of receiving one had kept dwindling. So as long as that partner had a license in good standing, what did it matter?

They had decided to forgo this one argument, and Tadeo Ivers had personally come up with a million dollars as a good-faith payment to Greg Turner to secure their upcoming merger.

A million dollars, gone like that when Turner made a decidedly indecent offer to all the executives and talent at Perfect Cannabis: to leave both companies dying with the accumulated debt and start over in another project, with that million dollars as seed money and another large investor in the person of Irv Moody.

Remembering the day it had happened made Al's skin crawl, and he consciously relaxed his right hand when he realized he had made an impossibly tight fist. That man…

If he remembered correctly, Rafael had disliked Turner on sight. Greg Turner, he would say, 'gave him the creeps.'

Turner had as much as given the kill shot to his own company. Rumor on the street had it they were all but gone now, hanging on with spit and baling wire until one of their big lenders pulled the plug. Still, Al wanted his million dollars back, and he wouldn't take no for an answer.

It was likely going to be an uphill battle to collect even a portion thereof, but Al Ivers was a man of infinite patience where revenge and getting his way was involved. Al Ivers might give in on the surface, but he always played five moves ahead. His father had made a feeble attempt to play chess with Al when he was very, very young. Even Tadeo had to give up on the game when he realized that he would never beat his seven-year-old son, not after the first three games and, most certainly, not a few years in. Perhaps that was where his intense jealousy of his oldest son had come from.

The promise of a long and difficult fight didn't bother Al. Even the possibility that, after paying lawyer's fees and other contingent expenses, he would walk away with little more than a pittance didn't bother him. Not nearly as much as the fact that somewhere on this planet, in this town, there existed a man who had taken money from him and thought he could just walk away.

That man must be found and taught differently.

Al dialed the number of their security lawyer Gregory D. Johnson and settled into his chair a little deeper. This one would take a lot of explaining. And it was not about to be easy either.

ELEVEN

"Let me get this straight," Sandro, the young man across from him, said, as he took off his narrow, wire-rimmed glasses. "Al Ivers sent you to me to clear up the mystery around his father's death?"

"Yes, he did," Rafael answered, trying to get comfortable on a plain white plastic chair, the kind found in every church basement. He couldn't help feeling as if he were sitting on hot coals.

Nothing wrong with the chair, he suspected; it was this whole situation. He thought Sandro's wire-rimmed glasses were purely decorative, there to make him look bookish, non-threatening, and at home in an office such as this. An office that read CDC Consulting on the door. *Consulting what?* Rafael wondered.

"He did."

"The police are looking at the case pretty thoroughly, are they not?" Sandro asked.

"They are."

"And he sent you to me. If I did not already know, I would guess they have asked you a few uncomfortable questions."

Rafael only nodded.

"Now then, if Al Ivers recommended you come to see me, then the issue—or you, or both—are quite important to him."

"He's CEO of Perfect Cannabis in the interim," Rafael attempted. "He needs this cleared up as soon as possible. For the good of the company. And you seem…"

"Like the kind of fixer who can make that happen, any way needed." Sandro suggested.

"No offense intended. Sorry, you see…"

"Don't bother." Sandro waved a hand. "You all but carry a sign on your back that says you'd rather be anywhere but here."

"I guess I'm not accustomed to being in the middle of a murder investigation," Rafael salvaged and pressed on. "The last few weeks have been a nightmare. If I seem on edge, let me assure you I am. And Al needs his executive board working again. So, he suggested…"

"Me. That's why you're here. Understood. What I don't understand is why you're sitting there acting as if you are in fact the guy who is guilty."

"Guilty? Now you just wait for one goddamned minute." Rafael half rose out of his chair. "Al and I are friends as well as business associates, and there is no way, no way in hell, I had anything to do with the murder of his father. If you are suggesting otherwise…"

"Save it." Sandro waved a hand again, smiling. "Just trying to get a rise out of you, seeing how you reacted. I find it helps."

"Well, you got your reaction."

Another wave—Sandro seemed to do that a lot—and he leaned forward, studying the rough outline of the case Rafael had brought with him.

"That's quite a mess of suspects you've got here."

"The police are…"

"Going to have a hard time finding their own asses with both hands," Sandro said, and Rafael smiled for the first time.

"Indeed."

"I also understand Al seems convinced none of the people on this list of suspects is the actual killer."

"The k…" Rafael had a bit of a problem with the word. It rolled so easily off that man's tongue. "No, we don't," he finally said with an effort. "We've all been working together for a while now. We were actually going to get into another business…"

"That doesn't have to mean anything."

"Maybe not, but none of these people, not myself, Kayla Montecito, Nick Ambrose, or Dante Ivers, could have done it." Rafael let a moment pass and finally said, "I guess Barry Wentworth is out too. Al doesn't think he would have the guts, and I'd have to agree."

Now it was Sandro's' turn to smile, and he nodded softly.

"It does take a certain fortitude to point a gun at someone and pull the trigger. Not as easy as it looks on TV. Roberto Ivers?"

"Yes?"

"Roberto Ivers is on the police department's list of suspects as well. Your take on him?"

"You're asking me?" Rafael scratched his head. "I don't trust him as far as I can throw him."

Another faint smile from Sandro.

"He cheated me—us—during the early days of PerCan, so I'm going to reserve judgment on the man for the moment, all right?"

"Al didn't think we should include him," Sandro said thoughtfully and looked down at the list. "He's a screwball character, but I'm willing to go with Al's insights on this one."

"How do you know how Al feels about all of these anyway?" Rafael asked, and Sandro leaned back in his chair a little.

"He did send me a message, Rafael, told me I should work on this thing with you… and gave me his insights at the same time."

"Why am I here then, if he told you everything?"

"As you said, Al is busy with that company you all started. And while it may not be a good look for the CEO of said company to go see a private eye—his trusted friend can."

"So, you're really just a private investigator?"

"I don't want to know what you thought, Rafael, but yes, I really am just a plain old private investigator. License is hanging out there in the foyer. I will help any way I can."

"Hmm, sorry." Rafael tried to hide his embarrassment. What was he thinking? His overactive imagination had had Al send him out to see some sort of 'fixer,' who would make everything all right, any way possible. Paranoia mixing into everything else now, not a good sign.

"Back to Tadeo," Sandro said as if nothing had happened. "Somebody breaks into that grubby little diner late at night, tasers the waitress and one security guard, and shoots Tadeo. Guy came prepared—knew what to do and where to go. That's pretty personal. That feels like revenge that's been simmering for a long, long time. Not a quick, nasty business dispute that came up yesterday."

"Roberto did have a beef with his father. And it was pretty common knowledge, too. I think that could serve as a motive if you wanted."

"Maybe not," Sandro said with a shake of his head. "The revenge angle would suit Roberto, but I'm pretty sure it wasn't him. If he wanted to get to his father, he would probably do something a little more spectacular. No, my money is on someone else."

"I beg to differ," Rafael said. "True, I don't like Roberto, but I wouldn't write him off that quick."

Sandro settled back, resting his hands on his stomach.

"Sorry, Rafael, I left out another important bit here. Roberto has a rather nasty drug habit, reacquired just recently, when he got back into town. I spoke to his dealer already. Now his dealer is an interesting guy…"

"No doubt," Rafael said dryly, trying to wrap his mind around the image of an interesting drug dealer, as opposed to the regular kind.

"Our dear Roberto has a very large tab with this man, who for a drug dealer is actually quite generous."

"Do tell."

"Indeed. The night his father got shot, Roberto was out delivering drugs for this man, in order to, uh, reduce said tab a little."

"So, he'd rather go to jail for murder instead of saying he was running errands for a drug dealer? That doesn't even make sense."

"Oh, Roberto wants to stay out of jail entirely. Been there, done that. Not an experience he is eager to repeat. Our dear Roberto wants justice just as much as you do."

"I don't follow."

Sandro looked down at the papers on his desk. "He too expressed his interest in finding the real killer to me. And it is worth quite a bit to him."

"Oh." Rafael pushed his fingers against his eyebrows when the penny dropped. "He hired you too. Do they get a family discount?" Rafael did settle back into his chair this time and folded his hands and continued. "Well then, Sandro. There goes my well-rehearsed theory. Which means we're back to ground zero. We have nothing. Other than this list of suspects, and I'm still convinced none of us did it."

"Right." Sandro studied his fingernails for a long moment. "Tadeo and his unorthodox lifestyle do present us with a rather large number of suspects."

Rafael snorted assent.

"So, where do we start?"

"What do you mean we? I thought you were the consultant."

"I am. And you're going to help me."

"I'm not really sure I'm the guy for that," Rafael said slowly. "I really am not…"

"For what I need, you are just the guy. Trust me."

"How so, exactly?"

"We're going to make a comprehensive list of suspects and eliminate them one by one by one, until we are left only with the actual murderer."

"You're kidding me? This is what Al pays you for?"

"I need input from you. This cannabis business, aside from being new, interesting, and a blow-your-mind moneymaker, it attracts some, shall we say, colorful people."

"No shit, Sherlock."

"What I heard is that Tadeo was pulling out of the club and skin trade. Word on the street is he was moments away from retiring officially. The Vietnamese only came in to deliver the final blow. That's what makes me believe the killer is found somewhere amongst the cannabis, if you will."

"One of us."

Rafael didn't want it to be one of them. He didn't want the killer to be from the medical marijuana trade, maybe even someone he knew, someone he had dealt with before, sat with for negotiations, perhaps even a meal. He'd desperately convinced himself that it was only Tadeo's business and milieu that had led to his murder, nothing to do with cannabis. Not because he knew, not because he had seen or heard anything, but because instinctively, he didn't want it to be someone in his sphere of business associates.

"You have a problem with that," Sandro interrupted softly.

"I do." Rafael nodded and clenched and unclenched his fingers. "I guess I just—assumed it was because of these gangs Kayla mentioned, or a business dispute in one of his clubs."

"Let me ask you this, Rafa—you don't mind if I call you Rafa? Let me ask you this. Tadeo has been running strip clubs and bars for the last 40 years. He's had a couple of dustups with people who disagreed with him, sure. It's the nature of the business. You understand."

"Much like construction." Rafael nodded. "Always one problem or another."

"Right. But for the last 40 years, he didn't get killed over it. Obviously."

"Yeah, but…"

"He was ready to sell the last of the clubs to a conglomerate. One of the Vietnamese groups. There were contracts to that effect in his desk drawer for crying out loud, agreements, legally drawn up. It was a done deal. Actually a good one. For a little while, Al was going to be there as a kind of facilitator, make sure everything got handed over and wrapped up correctly, and that was that. Done. Tadeo Ivers is out of the skin trade. Retired. So why would he get killed over it?"

Rafael shrugged. On the one hand, Sandro made sense, once he had his mind past the image of the so-called gangs walking in with a lawyer and drawing up legal contracts. On the other, well, he really didn't want to follow that thought down the rabbit hole. Sandro did it for him.

"The only thing that makes sense here is that our shooter comes out of the cannabis group."

"Or it was personal."

"Personal," Sandro snorted. "Personal. Do you know how many personal friends Tadeo Ivers had?"

"No."

"None. That's how many. The people around him were either his sons or people he had hired. End of story. Nothing personal to be found."

"That's damned sad," Rafael said.

"It is at that. Now back to our suspects."

Back and forth they went, for almost an hour. Rafael felt his head spinning as he finally sat back and slapped the desk in front of him with his flat hand. None of it made any sense. Nobody was a suspect, and everybody was. The people with the strongest motive were the people that could be excluded right off the top. They were going in circles. And yet somebody had gone out to the diner a few weeks ago, taken a gun, and shot Tadeo Ivers.

"I'm exhausted," Rafael finally said, digging the heels of his hands into his eye sockets. "I don't think we're getting anywhere."

"On the contrary." Sandro looked quite as exhausted as Rafael felt, but the desk in front of him was covered in handwritten notes. "You've given me a ton of stuff to follow up on. Business deals, disputes… This is good stuff." He swept his notes into a neat pile. "I'll have someone follow up with each and every one of these people. See what shakes loose. You…" He paused, shaking his head. "You look like a wet rag. Go home, rest, talk to your woman, do whatever. Keep thinking about the business deals of the last few months. Anything that might have gone wrong. And if something sticks out, tell me about it."

Rafael only nodded. Just then he couldn't have said what business deal went wrong and which one went right. He couldn't name a single agreement or instance. His brain had turned off for now.

"Go home, Rafael."

He grabbed his portfolio and rose. At the door he paused, hand on the handle, but Sandro already had his head down, staring at the papers in front of him. *Go home, Rafael.* Without another word, he closed the door behind him and did just that.

TWELVE

That morning the glass wall that overlooked the production floor from above had been automatically blanked by a plain white specialty screen, and the group in the conference room stared at a projection of the Perfect Cannabis logo. Reminiscent of a hand scooping up a fresh green leaf, Rafael thought morosely, remembering when he had ordered it. Worked with the designer actually, put his hand and pencil to paper, and made it happen from a bunch of sketches on a yellow legal pad. It had turned out well.

Like so many things he had put into place for PerCan, this too had turned out rather well. He liked looking at it, and usually, it gave him a bit of pride to do so. This was something he had built. One of those things he had dragged out of the misery it had fallen into, cleaned up, polished, and made to shine. He liked those things.

Not today. Today, the logo irritated him, the canvas drape irritated him, and the people in the conference room, above all, irritated him. And Al—the fact that Al was late to his own board meeting irritated him beyond all get-out. That was a no-go. What the hell?

Barry wasn't here yet either. Barry was all about appearances. So why was he late? And did it have anything to do with why Al wasn't here yet too? Were the two of them…?

Rafael folded his hands in his lap under the table, forcing himself to sit still. Why couldn't Al have left the glass wall open, so the board members could at least look at the comings and goings down on the production floor? Why? What was the point in isolating them up here?

He turned to whisper to Kayla and air his grievance, when he realized she had turned away and was whispering with the man at her right, Thomas Donnelly. Right, Kayla was mad at him—still. Get in line, Kayla!

And then there were those shares. Trying to be inconspicuous, he tapped a few keys on his phone to look at the latest quotes, but no matter how much he stared, the results wouldn't change.

Almost every free trading share in Perfect Cannabis Corp had been purchased in the last couple of days. Some of them well over recent prices. A few sellers out there would be laughing all the way to the bank.

Rafael had to work to suppress a little grin.

Voting power—expressed in dollars and whoever had…

His head snapped up when Al's quick entry interrupted his woolgathering and staring at share quotes, and quickly, he put the phone away again before Al called him on it.

Look at who the cat dragged in, he thought morosely and barely cut back the words leaving his mouth. Al indeed looked as if he had been dragged in—by the hair. Rumpled, disheveled, unkempt. The power seat did not seem comfortable to his former friend.

"Sorry, folks," he said a little out of breath. "I did not mean to be late for this very important meeting."

"Then maybe you shouldn't have been."

Dante, loudmouthed and sullen as he had been when he first started at PerCan. Somewhere between those first few months and now, Dante had turned into a knowledgeable and responsible grower who enjoyed what he was doing and couldn't wait to do his job every morning, just as much as Rafael had. What had happened to them—what had happened to all of them?

Al merely nodded at his younger brother.

"Apologies, Dante, there was an emergency in our shipping department that required me to…"

"Well, you know what, Al, Dante is quite right," Thomas groused. "Why are you personally attending to the shipping department? Perhaps you need to start delegating and concentrating on the stuff that is really important and really in your wheelhouse right now. The days where everyone could simply do what he or she wanted are gone. Maybe you used to run your dad's company like this, and that worked, but it is not working any longer."

Whoa. Rafael cleared his throat, if only because of the 'maybe you used to run your dad's company like that' comment, but Al raised his hand to chest level.

"Thank you, Thomas. No need to get upset. I am well aware of the trouble this company is facing. When you get to know me, you will find out that when a man gets injured on my watch, I drop everything else to make sure he is OK. If you have an issue with that, I'm sorry to tell you I have no intention of changing. We did have a physical injury on the loading dock—the man involved is OK and on his way to the hospital as we speak."

He let his hands slowly sink down to waist level again and carefully took a seat.

"Now then, is there anyone else with a comment about leadership, leadership style, or work ethic?"

"I think we all just need some clear guidance, structure, and ground rules," Kayla said softly. "Right at the moment—I don't even know who does what around here."

"Correct. I have a suspicion many of us feel this way. Creating a cohesive whole is of paramount importance right now. Hence, it is the only topic and the agenda of today's meeting—logical task distribution according to talent, experience, and leanings. Is everyone on board with this?"

"You forgot to add, 'lack of criminal record,'" some smartass Rafael had never met piped up.

Must be one of the guys who had come over from Mariposa, Rafael thought, and, not entirely unexpectedly, Al did not take kindly to the remark.

"Now that I've been reminded that the murderer of my father is still at large and on the loose, why don't you remind me who you are, young man?"

"He's my assistant and intern," Thomas said and had the good grace to look away. "Brent Loge."

"Brent."

Al looked at the young man as a snake might, contemplating its dinner, finally pulling a stack of papers out of his portfolio.

"Pay attention in these meetings and you might perhaps learn something. First and foremost, when to keep your mouth shut."

"You cannot deny the fact that a startling number of people in this room are still on the police's wanted list."

"Wrong, Thomas," Al corrected without looking up. "There are a few who are still considered persons of interest, as they have information to add to the proceedings, but nobody is on any wanted list, or even an official suspect. Let's make that clear right off the top."

"Then where is he—the famous and colorful Mr. Barry Wentworth? Or should I say infamous? Should he not be here? Does he not have an interest in what keeps happening to this company, now that he all but bought my company out from under my ass and is doing the same thing to yours? Don't tell me you're not watching what's going on with free trading shares at the moment."

Al distributed papers around the table, and the room became so quiet that the soft sighing of paper on the pristine, white boardroom table actually became audible. Al, unlike others, could handle silent gaps like this one without missing a beat.

"Mr. Wentworth said he would be here when he was invited to the meeting," he finally said after everyone else was already shuffling uncomfortably in their seats. "He will join us shortly, I presume. We will give him a few minutes. If he does not appear, we will start the meeting without him."

"You sure you can do that?"

"Why wouldn't I, Thomas? I admit I am only acting CEO at the moment, having stepped into voting and executive power through my father's shares after his death."

"Oh, don't bullshit me, Ivers."

Al straightened a little in his chair and fixed Thomas Donnelly in a long unmoving stare. Neither good nor ill will, neither anger nor joy lay in that look. Only a curious and cool detachment.

"You know as well as I do that Wentworth is buying all of the free trading shares available to buy himself into your seat. He'll outvote all of us, send us home, and put a bunch of criminals into these here board-room seats," Thomas said with a furious snap of his meeting agenda.

"Interesting," Al finally said. "Not sure where you are getting your news, but they seem to have left me off the distribution list. I must remedy that."

"Ivers—stop the smartass comments and help us do something about him. This is our company he is taking. It was your father's. It was your partner's." A quick nod toward Rafael. "That is if you're still partners. Who the fuck knows around here? Kayla is right."

"She is right—correct—outspoken and eloquent as you, no."

Kayla shook her head and smiled, not like she had not heard that kind of language before. Used it just as often.

"Ivers—"

"Thomas, before you explode in your seat, yes, I have been keeping an eye on the interesting developments on the stock market. As has everybody around this table, I presume. Shares have been purchased, sometimes at a multiple of their actual value."

"So, what are you going to do to prevent Wentworth from acquiring enough to boot all of us out of here?" Thomas's voice had become almost shrill.

Silence.

Kayla looked down at her feet and picked on her perfectly manicured thumbnail. Rafael felt his throat constrict and his mouth go dry, as if he had swallowed a huge chunk of cardboard, and even Dante and Nick Ambrose had stopped fiddling with pens and paper and stared at the two men, who sat squaring off like prizefighters.

"Well?"

"I will do—exactly nothing, Thomas," Al said. "Nothing whatsoever."

Thomas Donnelly jumped to his feet, flinging his PerCan branded pen into a corner. Standing six foot four, he'd always had a hard time containing the raw energy inside him. Something about him always stayed in motion. In a boardroom, he looked out of place.

Now he paced the lengths of the boardroom and finally stood in front of Al, who had not moved a muscle for the past few moments.

"Nothing?"

"Nothing."

"You are just going to sit there, wait for him to walk all over you and let him take everything? Everything I have worked for, for the past five years, everything you and Rafael have worked for, and Kayla? All for nothing, down the crapper, see you later, because you don't feel like it?"

"No."

"Ivers, if it's the last thing I do in this boardroom—open your damned mouth and tell us what you're doing about it, or I swear to God I am going to…"

The company's anti-violence policy probably prevented him from finishing the sentence. It might have been a reflection of the light, or the way he finally looked down at his portfolio and back up again, but a very tiny smile formed on Al Ivers's face.

"No need, Thomas," he said. "No need to do anything. Mr. Barry Wentworth did not purchase all of those free trading shares, even though I am quite certain he moved heaven and earth to do so."

If one could have heard the sighing of paper on a table earlier, now the world stood still.

Kayla turned ever so slowly and looked at Rafael. Her mouth formed one soundless *who?* Dante raised his hands, looking confused, and Thomas Donnelly seemed to deflate all of a sudden, as if Al had taken a pin and poked him, letting out all the anger and frustration.

"But if he…"

He didn't finish the sentence, but dropped heavily into his chair again, looking around the table from one person to the next, halting briefly at Kayla and stopping at Rafael.

"Covin?"

Rafael shook his head, still in shock that Barry's oh-so-secret plan appeared to be the worst-kept secret of the century. How the heck did everyone here know?

He looked back at Al and put his hands together.

"And just how do you know he didn't?" Rafael asked the question everyone wanted to know, and for the moment, he even ignored Kayla's confusion and her attempts to catch his eye.

"How do you know," he asked, "that Barry Wentworth didn't buy all of those shares? Because as much as everyone suspects me around here, and despite some temptation, I can tell you I sure as hell didn't."

The heck with language just now.

"No, you didn't, Rafael. And thank you for that. I wasn't sure what I would do if I had found you buying up all of those shares. The reason I know that Barry didn't buy those shares is that I did. All of them."

He'd done a superb job soundproofing the boardroom, Rafael thought irrationally. His ears felt as if they needed to pop from the silence. And then he thought that the world actually hadn't stood still, and the thought of Al buying all of those shares sank in all the way.

"How?" he asked almost soundlessly, although it hardly mattered right then.

"How? You want to know how I bought those shares? They represent most of what I own. Does it really matter right now?"

Rafael shook his head. "Irv?" he asked, and Al nodded.

"Some."

That was all the two men wanted to say about Irv Moody's involvement in the operation in front of the others. At least for now. They well remembered what the involvement of a large-scale personal investor had done last time.

"Now wait just one goddamn minute," Thomas thundered and rose again, both hands flat on the boardroom table, his massive body leaning across into Al's face. "Do you mean to tell me you own this company now? You?"

"Not personally, no. It is still a…"

"Publicly traded company," Kayla finished and finally caught Rafael's eye. "You didn't. You really did not."

Rafael waved his hands and turned back to Thomas and Al.

"No, Thomas, I don't own the company," Al said quietly. "I own a huge block of shares, and I am in a reasonably good position to gather support on this board and—shall we say—make my point if required. I bought those shares to minimize the influence of large blocks of votes in the hands of people who would use them to get their way."

"Instead, you will get your way. Geez—pot, kettle, black?"

Donnelly seemed thunderstruck just then and unsure if he was hearing good news or bad news. He wanted to say more, but Al finally cut him off.

"I'm not going to argue any further about this," he said, folding his hands on the table before him. "Call it what you will. We have a job to do here, and I would like to get on with it now."

"A job which is going to be done exactly the way you want it done or move on out, is that what I am hearing? You will run this company the way Wentworth did?"

"Thomas." Al, the man who usually didn't show a shred of emotion, now slowly teetered toward exasperation. "What is it you want to hear? Without PerCan, your company would have gone under. Now you have Barry Wentworth to contend with. For better or worse, our companies are linked by the merger agreement. Unless you wish to break it, which will cost more money and frustration than any of us in this room has available right now, I suggest you sit down again and we will work something out that has an actual chance of functioning."

Thomas sat. Heavily. He had nothing else to say or to do.

Rafael took a breath to say something when Al zeroed in on him.

"Rafael, before you say anything—you and I both know that I have to take the CEO seat. You can't."

"I was going to…"

"There's going to be a firestorm coming over this company, with Tadeo's death and Con—Barry Wentworth's return. I am firmly convinced that I am the best man to handle it and to steer the company through it. No offense."

"None taken," Rafael said and blinked once or twice. "I wasn't going to argue with you."

Yes, you were, the little voice in his head said, and he conveniently chose to ignore it. Hell with that voice…

"Rafael needs to have a say in the company," Kayla objected. "He is the one who brought us all this far. He is the only one who knows all the ins and outs. He is one of the founding members."

"Rafael will have a voice, Kayla, and so will everyone else." Al looked up and included everyone in one long look. "Rafael Covin will stay on as an advisor—my advisor, if he chooses to accept that role. And when the situation with Tadeo Ivers's death is dealt with, we will revisit the issue."

"The 'situation'—guess it's not like you were close or anything," Thomas muttered and shifted the papers in front of him with violent, jerky movements.

Al did not respond. He sat perfectly still and fixed Thomas with one of his unnerving, cool, quiet looks for several minutes.

"This would be my cue to leave," Rafael said, breaking the spell, and half rose from his chair.

"You don't have to leave, Rafael. I appreciate your presence. I just can't give you a vote on the board at this time."

"Understood."

His butt hit the chair again, and for the first time this morning, his eyes met Kayla's. She had the good graces to look away with something akin to embarrassment.

"We here in this room, ladies and gentlemen, need to have a united vision and direction for this company, and I intend to get all of us on the same page this morning and moving forward—together. Anyone who has misgivings about it, please speak up now."

Dante glowered at his brother, and Thomas abused the stack of papers in front of him again, but no one said a word.

"Then, if you will, look at the proposed slate of officers I have taken the liberty to draft. Page two in your package. Thomas, if you would prefer a clean copy…"

Al waved a new set of documents at him.

"I am good."

"Great. Then let's get down to the nuts and bolts, have a roundtable discussion about the officers I am suggesting, and get to a vote."

In the end, the 'roundtable discussion' had its moments. Thomas Donnelly seemed happy enough and satisfied to see his name on the COO line, Dante, on the other hand, expressed some misgivings about having to report to the man, and his own 'demotion' to a mere team leader—Operations. Newly minted Senior Director of Operations, Nick Ambrose, managed to calm him somewhat, but couldn't do anything about the man from Mariposa they found themselves having to contend with.

Yes, rumor had it Jason knew his stuff, but they'd been fine until now, hadn't they? Why bring in somebody new at this point in the game? Did he not trust them any longer? Did Thomas Donnelly not trust them and want to put someone in their midst who would be reporting to him? Directly.

Al kept his cool and refused to get into an argument with anyone. No, he trusted Nick, and especially Dante, implicitly—but yes, he wanted a man from Mariposa in the growing side of things. It had nothing to do with trust, everything with teambuilding and community.

"Come on, people," he finally said, "this is PerCan Consolidated now. We are one company. This is not about old loyalties or 'guys from over there.' We are building the one company, and we have to work together, or we might as well not start."

Rafael nodded, knowing that Al was right, painfully remembering that only days ago they had been planning a consulting firm that would have undermined everything here. Et tu?

All of these guys had been ready to sign on the dotted line—all of them. Except perhaps for Al. Al, the one guy who stuck to his guns and wanted to save PerCan. Rafael sighed and raised his hand.

"Many of you know," he said softly, "that I founded this company together with Barry Wentworth, who was back then Connor Beauregard... Let's not get into it. It's too confusing unless you know the story. When it was in shambles, I picked up the pieces and made it work. And then I got fired."

He chuckled and shook his head. "Not saying everything Tadeo did made sense."

"Hear, hear."

This from Dante, and Rafael shot him a grin.

"Tadeo fired my ass, sorry, Kayla. And I was going to show him—big time. I was going to build my own consulting team and take everybody in here who was worth his salt in the company. Everybody. Don't look so embarrassed now, especially not the people who were more than ready to sign on with me. It was a good plan. It was a great plan—and let me tell you something. We, this group right here," he vaguely swept his hand around the conference room, "we would have rocked this business. Big time. We would have been awesome."

He paused, folded his hands, and looked around, grinning. "Oh yeah. But then there was this one man who refused to commit to me. He was right there, thinking only of saving this company."

"Rafa, don't bring that up now."

"Why not? It was you, Al—you who said no to me because you wanted to make this company work. Now that, ladies and gentlemen, is what he is talking about. Building a great company that everyone is going to want to stand up for. That is what we need to be doing."

"Are you almost done swinging great monologues, Rafael Covin?" Al shuffled the papers in front of him, and Rafael grinned when he saw a faint blush on his friend's cheeks. Not so detached and cool as he would have them believe, now was he?

Rafael opened his mouth to say more and closed it again. He shrugged and sat back down.

"Yes, I am," he said. "And just for the record, I know I can't be CEO at the moment, and that bothers me like crazy, but if you're serious about wanting me to be an advisor, get ready for one hell—heck of a lot of good advice."

Nick looked at Jason and shrugged. Jason grinned and finally took the first step. He rolled his shoulders, relaxed in his seat, and stuck his hand out first to Dante, then to Nick.

"Guess we need all the good men we can get down on the floor. I did hear good stuff about the two of you."

"You too."

Dante didn't quite like it yet. He'd been at the top of the heap for too long, and an Ivers to boot—but he managed a thin little smile and shook Jason's hand. A truce perhaps, though if the two would ever be friends was questionable. And wasn't that what they had said about the dynamic duo of Nick and Dante during the very first days of their cooperation?

A little piece of paper appeared right by Rafael's hand, and he realized Al had pushed it there discreetly while all eyes were on Dante, Nick, and Jason. Rafael covered it with his hand and unfolded it in his lap.

'Where is Barry?' the note said, and Rafael shook his head. Good question. There was no way—no way on earth—that Barry Wentworth would have missed this meeting. He would have wanted to spike the board with people whose loyalty he could buy if he couldn't count on it. Even yesterday, he'd been going on about it. He wanted the CEO seat badly enough to go after every rogue available share out there. So what happened?

Did he figure out that Al had bought all of the available shares to stop him from doing just that?

How would he? He still thought Rafael had purchased those shares—at least he had when he sent that text that infuriated Kayla. Where was he then?

No idea. Bad? He wrote on a piece of paper and shifted it back to Al in the same manner, but the love fest across the table was over by now, and all eyes returned to them.

Al covered the piece of paper with his hand and folded it away, looking around the table with a smile.

"Progress. I like it. Kayla—promotions, as always. Temporarily, I would like you to work together with Thomas's sales team, until we get an executive in charge of sales in here. Are you OK with that?"

"OK and ready," Kayla said. "About time we get a decent sales and marketing department, I would say. I'd like to interview your sales manager Thomas, see if he has any suggestions, any ideas."

"Cool, set it up."

Rafael saw Al exhaling. Not visibly enough for everyone around the table to notice his relief, but still obvious to someone who had known him for a while and considered him a friend.

He said a silent thank you to whatever stray guardian angel had prevented him from buying those shares yesterday. Had to be one—and sure and enough it was someone else's because he, Rafael Covin, had been all set to buy every share he could and commit to the remainder in the hopes that Irv Moody would come through. The only thing that saved his tush was a failure to reach his broker on the phone.

Guardian angel, maybe—stray, for sure.

Opened the door for Al to come in and spend a small fortune to prevent a war in the boardroom. So far, at least. Did anybody really know Al? Hell yes, he thought he did—and what he knew of him made him a damn fine human being.

So where in three blazes was Barry Wentworth?

Rafael swallowed hard and fought the hollow feeling down there in his stomach that had nothing to do with the fancy coffee Al served in the boardroom or those pastries they wisely kept at the other end of the table. Barry should have been here, and he would have been unless something serious happened to him—like being dead or in jail.

This company was Barry's child. He had thought of it, dreamed of it, brought it to life, fled the country for it, and now likely bankrupted himself for it... There was no way he was missing a board meeting where its next leader was chosen. He should be standing right in that boardroom convincing everyone within earshot that the one and only true leader of Perfect Cannabis Corporation stood right before them.

Rafael inched over closer to Kayla, who seemed to have forgotten about being mad at him and gave him a warm smile.

"Thank God you did not buy those…"

"Have you heard from Barry?" he asked under his breath and watched one eyebrow crawl up all the way to her hairline, before she shook her head and leaned in closer.

"Not a word. I thought you knew where he was."

"I don't."

"Then what's going on? There is no way…"

"He would miss this," Rafael finished. "Are you sure you haven't heard anything…"

"I haven't. Until a minute ago, I thought you—and he—and those shares…"

Al glared at both of them and cleared his throat. Whispering in a board meeting was still not among the acceptable things to do.

"Anything you have to add?" he asked pointedly, and Rafa and Kayla shook their heads.

"No, just some…"

"Scheduling issues," Kayla said, smiling brightly. "Just a minor appointment I forgot to tell Rafael about—carry on."

Carry on. As if.

Al was no fool. And Al knew Barry. He had to be wondering the same thing—where the heck was he, and why was he not interrupting this meeting, which would have entirely been his style?

It turned into one of the longest board meetings of Rafael's life. His mind kept straying to Barry's conspicuous absence. Where the heck was the guy?

And why should it matter? He had more than enough on his plate with convincing the police he had no involvement with a certain murder, keeping his newly minted advisor's post at PerCan, making up with Kayla, and carefully toeing the lines of office and company politics around here, all at the same time.

Another note appeared under his hand, and he unfolded it cautiously on his knees under the table.

'Do you think something serious happened?'

Well, duh! Rafael felt like rolling his eyes at Kayla, but he merely shrugged. No, he didn't think—he knew.

Two hours later, Al finally called a halt to the meeting. Most of the junior people disbanded for lunch or to find their new offices. Rafael fidgeted with his phone, waiting to get out of this meeting to figure out what Barry's no-show meant.

THIRTEEN

Al was giving directions to a younger team member when Thomas approached Rafael's seat.

"So what happened to your friend today? He chicken out?"

"I assume you refer to Mr. Barry Wentworth."

"One and only. I was sure he would be here today raising holy hell. Instead, he sent you."

"Nobody sends me, Thomas," Rafael said mildly and stuffed down an angry and bristly retort at the thought of being someone's errand boy. Last time he looked, he had run this company.

"I was sure you and he…"

"He and I founded this company, correct. Anything else that's bothering you today? Any questions?"

"No, but…"

"You and everybody else in this room is wondering why he didn't show up today. Join the club. It's a big one."

His phone vibrated in his pocket, and Rafael took a quick glance. Detective Sergeant Robertson, the last person he wanted to speak to at that very moment. He pushed decline and put the phone back into his pocket.

"And now, Thomas, I have…"

Work to do, he meant to say, when Al materialized by his side as if by magic and took his elbow.

"Thomas, I am afraid I have to interrupt this chat—I have a few questions for Rafael. It can't really wait."

"Anything I need to know about? Like what's happened to our former fearless and fugitive leader, Mr. Wentworth?"

"Mr. Wentworth did not show up for the meeting. Too sad for him. If he needs help keeping his schedule, I can recommend someone. Now, if you don't mind."

Keeping his hand on Rafael's elbow, he led him away, leaving Thomas and Kayla behind to discuss whatever came to mind. Kayla would handle it.

"Not that I want to involve Thomas into this, Rafael," he said with some urgency. "But I really do need to know for myself. What the heck is Barry up to? Does he have an endgame here? Why not show up?"

"Your guess, Al. Do I look like I know?"

"You look like the man who has been closest to Wentworth of everyone here in this room. Since you didn't make a move on the shares…" Al paused for a moment and released Rafael's elbow. Rafael did not speak; he merely held Al's look with one of his own. "I wanted to thank you. Since you did not make a move on the shares, I am assuming you still wish to work with me to get this company where it deserves to be—the top. I appreciate how difficult this is for you."

Rafael said nothing for a long moment, battling thoughts, emotions, silly ones and serious ones, and finally, he nodded.

"You and I can make this work, Al."

"You can, and don't forget that. Being CEO of this company in the state it is right now is much like herding a large number of cats."

"Cats don't really herd well."

"Don't I know it? This is not for me, Rafa."

"You're doing pretty well from where I am sitting."

"That only means all the bullshit is working. There are only two things here I want—one is to hand this position back to you as quickly as I ended up in it, and two is to figure out what in blazes Wentworth is up to. Because this smells like trouble from a mile away."

"Robertson just tried to call me."

"Great! Any idea what it is all about this time?"

"No. I declined the call. Let him think what he wants. I wasn't going to carry on a conversation with him in the middle of a board meeting."

"The end—we are adjourned."

"I know that, but I still don't need Donnelly and all of his people to listen in on what's going on between you, me, and Barry. That's personal. Last thing we need to do is add fuel to this barely concealed animosity."

Al shook his head, walked away a few steps, and came back again.

"The moment it started impacting this company, it quit being personal, Rafael. Your friendship aside—but if there's even a chance of a hidden landmine here, I need to know where it is and what it is so I can control it."

"You're in full CEO mode now, aren't you?"

Rafael elbowed Al in the side and tried for a bit of levity, but Al only narrowed a cool stare at him.

"Fine," Rafael said with a shrug. "I will go find out."

"Do that. And report…"

"Back to you as soon as I have something—yes, sir."

Rafael mock-saluted and went to look for Kayla. Before he went searching for trouble, aka Barry, he had some serious making up to do. He turned away when Al grabbed his elbow once again, stopping him in his tracks.

"What?"

"Mirko," Al said, as if the word would explain everything. "I forgot his last name."

"Huh?"

"Barry—Connor borrowed money from him, a lot of money, and he came after you at the grand opening, remember? It's a long shot, but I am concerned Mirko might be the reason Barry didn't show up today."

"Shit, yeah." Rafael dropped heavily into the nearest chair and forked his fingers through his hair once, then again, and again.

"Gaah, Mirko—I haven't…"

"Worried about him?"

"No. Not since the grand opening, when he threatened to shut us all down because Barry had missed a payment."

"Or two or more," Al said and put his hands together as if in prayer. Hell, they all ought to be praying if what he was thinking was true.

"Mirko the loan—moneylender," Rafael said and blew out a breath. "But you paid him back that night, with a huge wad of cash if I remember right."

"Correct, but that wasn't everything that was owed. Not by a long shot and I knew it. I gave him enough to keep him from doing something stupid to the main power switch of the building or to wave a gun around any of our guests."

"If he had one."

"If he had one?" Al turned around and only stared at Rafael. "He might have been joking that day because you and Barry had the stupidest ever conversation about not bringing a gun to a grand opening—but believe me, he was not in a fun kind of mood."

"No, no, you're right, just remembering."

"I am almost certain Barry still owes him a huge amount of money."

"And if he realizes Connor came back as Barry, and he is in town, and he is going to be part of this company again…"

"Yes, Rafael?"

"Trouble—big time. Damn, this just keeps getting worse every time I turn around."

"Correct."

Al sat on a chair beside him while the huge conference room emptied, and finally, someone knocked at the frame of the open door.

"Interrupting?"

"Well, actually, we're in a… Oh—hi, Irv." Al waved in Irving Moody and motioned for him to close the door behind him. "Sorry, we're kind of—having a war counsel here."

"That bad, huh?"

"Worse." Rafael never looked up and settled heavily into the back of his chair. He had no desire explaining things to Irv just then, when he hadn't make sense of it in his own head yet.

"Did Wentworth cause a massive stir here?"

"Not at all. Exactly the opposite, matter of fact."

Irv sat across from them, spinning his finger in a large circle, encouraging them to get on with the story.

"I don't know," Al said slowly, his voice completely colorless, "if I should."

"Well." Irv folded his arms. "It's like that is it? Don't fall over yourself treating me like a guy who cares about this outfit, who owns quite a bit of it after he helped you buy up an outrageous amount of shares. All I wanted was an update on how this first board meeting actually went down. But it couldn't have gone well, to go by your faces."

"Irv—take it down a notch." Rafael waggled his fingers toward the ground. "We're a bit fried because we think Barry Wentworth is actually missing." He blew out a breath and forked his hands through his hair.

"You think or you know?"

"We think we know," Al supplied helpfully. "He didn't show up for the board meeting—no apologies, nothing."

"Strange as that might be, people, it's not exactly a disaster."

"No, no, no, Irv, that's not strange—that's a disaster," Rafael said, jumping to his feet. Restless energy drove him around the boardroom once, and he stopped in front of Irv Moody. "Don't you see? Barry moved heaven and earth to get control of this company. He bankrupted himself buying Mariposa, knowing that Al and I would have to enter into a merger with his company if we wanted to survive. He took a massive chance and almost missed. Almost. But in the end… here he is."

"And then he doesn't show up."

"That's not Barry. Barry does a lot of things—but he never just 'doesn't show up.' He'll fight. In this case, he will fight to get Al and anyone else from the Ivers family out of this business. It's what he has always wanted."

"I am aware of that. But from the way you were talking, I assumed you and he were… You know…" Irving grinned. "In bed together—on board to get this done."

Rafael squeezed his eyes shut and made a fist. *Now of all times*, he thought, *now you have to mention that idle pub chatter about buying shares. Your timing sucks.* When he opened his eyes again, Al looked straight at him, unblinking and cold.

"I am no altar boy," he said. "Barry came to me, said, 'You and Irv buy those shares, and the three of us will run PerCan. Forget about the Ivers clan.'"

"Interesting," Al said stiffly and folded his arms. "Now I find out."

"I didn't go through with it, Al. I—just…" Rafael took off his glasses and flung them onto the table. "It was just talk. Except Barry thought I did."

Both men now looked at him as if he spoke in tongues until he took out his phone and showed them Barry's text.

I knew you'd come through for me. "He saw that the free trading shares were gone, and he assumed I had purchased them. He assumed you and I had done as he said, and the three of us would march into this meeting and take over."

"Nice plan." Al sounded bitter.

"To him it was a done deal, and then he doesn't show up. That's not normal."

"And did you tell him that you changed your mind?" Irv asked, leaning in closer.

"No, I did not tell him. I was a little busy trying to prove I didn't shoot Al's father, and Kayla saw that text and was ready to string me up. With all that, I haven't seen Barry in days. He's like a ghost... And what about you? You went and bought those shares, whether it was Al or I asking, so clean your own house first."

"Wait just one minute, both of you. This isn't helping," Al said, raising his hands, creating distance between them. "The moment we fight with one another, bad things happen. We need a plan—to protect the company and to figure out what this means."

"Perhaps before we go making a plan, we need to know what in fact happened to him," Irv suggested. "What if he just—had an accident or something? In a hospital somewhere, injured, fell off a bike. I don't know. It's possible, right?"

"Awfully convenient."

"It happened to you, Ivers, or you would be on the suspect list just like everybody else."

"Right." Al shrugged. "First order of business will be to find out what happened to Barry Wentworth."

"I would like an answer to that as well if you please."

Three heads snapped up and turned to see Detective Sergeant Robertson strolling into the boardroom as if he were coming to a tea party.

"Well?"

"With all due respect, Sergeant, this is a private and closed board meeting."

"With all due respect, Mr. Ivers, where Barry Wentworth is concerned, private and closed meetings are off the table. This is a murder investigation I am running here. Your company secrets are of no interest to me. Barry Wentworth is. So I ask you again—where is Barry Wentworth, and what happened to him?"

Rafael could feel the detective's stare boring into him and walked away a few paces. Where was Barry, and what would his disappearance do to him and his own case?

"As the CEO of Perfect Cannabis Consolidated, Sergeant, I am a bit disturbed by your lack of respect for what is protected company internal… Be that as it may, I am happy to tell you that we are just as confused as you are by Mr. Wentworth's sudden absence. We fully expected him to attend the board meeting this morning."

"You haven't seen him or heard from him?"

"No."

"What about you?" Robertson turned fully toward Rafael, allowing no escape, while at the same time taking in Irv Moody, probably trying to assess his role in this drama, and the potential of information from that side.

"I have not," Rafael said curtly.

"Are you sure? You two are best buddies and sometime partners in crime from what I heard."

"I don't know where you heard what, Detective. Nor do I really care at this point. I am telling you that a) I have not heard from Mr. Barry Wentworth, and b) I have not been in touch with him. I have no idea where he may be located at this point. Is that specific enough for you? And you still have not told us why you are barging into this meeting."

"And I am fully aware of what I have or have not told you, Rafael." Robertson physically stepped close and into Rafael's face, so close indeed he could have smelled him should he have chosen to do so. Rafael planted his feet and stood his ground. He couldn't stand the old detective who thought he may have shot Tadeo, but he wasn't going to give him the satisfaction of making Rafael Covin back down.

"I am going to give you one more chance to tell me if you know anything, and I am also going to tell you that during this active murder investigation, I can easily obtain a warrant for your cell phone records and see for myself who you called or texted, WhatsApped or instant messaged, and vice versa. Now did you want to change your statement or not?"

Rafael looked down at his hands and made a face. "Rafael?"

Al and the detective almost asked at the same time. "Rafa?"

"I sent him a text, OK? When he didn't show for the meeting, I wanted to know where he was. Here, you can check for yourself."

He took out his phone, unlocked it with a quick touch, and found the texting app.

Where the hell r u? Meeting is starting

"That was it. Then the meeting began, and I became a little—preoccupied."

"It was nothing. Yet you felt the need to lie to me."

"Strictly speaking, we were not 'in touch,' Detective. I am well aware of your theory, that Barry had something to do with Tadeo Ivers's shooting, but I do not and cannot believe he did."

"That's the thing with beliefs, isn't it, Mr. Covin?" Robertson refused to back down just as much as Rafael did. "You're just never sure."

"Hold on, both of you." Al stepped in once again and hushed Rafael with a raised hand. "Back up for just a moment, Detective. Back up... Why are you so interested in Barry Wentworth's whereabouts and our board meeting?"

The detective seemed to grow a little, and the smirk on his face became a little broader.

"Look who's interested in talking all of a sudden."

"Detective," Al said, his face very carefully composed. "We are not your favorite people—it does not take any detective skills to see that. Be that as it may, I would really appreciate if you told me. If not for our sake, please consider this company, its employees and investors, and any damage control I have to do. I would be personally grateful to you."

That much politeness when he had expected a gruff 'what the fuck is going on' or a more heavy-handed 'do you have any idea who I am' took a little of the bluster out of Robertson. He still held the trump card, and he was going to enjoy playing it. Rafael could see him relishing that moment.

The moment stretched, with the four men facing off on opposite sides of the conference table, Al and Rafael on one side, the detective on the other, and Irv Moody at the head end, as if he couldn't decide where he belonged just now. The detective reached into his portfolio and produced a completely unrelated piece of paper, looked at it, and pushed it back into the portfolio. Irv hushed his phone when it chirped, and finally, the detective spoke.

"Well, Mr. Ivers, this will be in your interest and in the company's interest then. My detectives discovered something rather interesting this morning."

The air conditioning kicked in with a loud hum it didn't usually make; somewhere outside the room, two people were discussing something in raised voices. Or perhaps they hadn't raised their voices at all, but the silence within the boardroom had become overwhelming.

Al didn't move a muscle, and finally, Detective Sergeant Robertson cleared his throat.

"This morning," he continued, relishing every moment, just as Rafael had expected, "one of my junior officers spoke to a witness who sold a 9-millimeter hand gun to a man who not only looked like your former partner, but also called himself Barry. Barry Wentworth to be exact."

Rafael brought his hand to his mouth, shoving back the expletive that wanted to come out at that moment. He took a huge breath and tried again.

"Lots of nine-millimeters out there," he said tonelessly, missing the casual comment he tried for by a mile.

"You're sure about that, Mr. Covin?"

"Pretty sure. How the hell should I know?"

"Correct. You don't carry a gun yourself, do you?"

"Of course not. I am a builder. Most recently a CEO of a publicly traded company. Why would I carry a gun?"

"Then you also wouldn't know that the Smith and Wesson M&P9 your friend bought is one of the most sought-after concealed-carry firearms available today. Reliable, durable, accurate, and very, very compact. They are so tiny your wife could carry one in her evening purse. And when things go really bad, it is what I would want to have at hand to make it home safely."

"Thank you for the lesson, Detective. Do they pay you a commission?"

"No, Mr. Covin, they do not. It's my job to know weapons, and I do know that Tadeo Ivers was shot with a nine-millimeter. So, I would like to speak to your friend Barry Wentworth to ask him just why he would buy exactly such a weapon. On the black market. Without going through the administrative hassle of registering it. Why do you think that is?"

Rafael shook his head and looked at Al. Even Irv had found a chair and covered his mouth with a fist. None of them spoke.

"But he was—no—no way." Rafael convinced no one. "He wouldn't have bought that thing over here. Barry wouldn't carry a gun. He'd probably shoot himself in the foot with the damn thing. Your witness is wrong. Or making a deal," he added a moment later.

"Rafael, number one, our witness is positive it was Barry J. Wentworth he sold the firearm to. Number two, there was no deal made with him or anyone." Detective Robertson pointed at his own chest. "He came to us with this information—we didn't go looking."

"But, but—wait."

"I think what Rafael is trying to express is that it is awfully convenient for this evidence to show up right at this moment." Al put his hand on Rafael's shoulder and literally took some of the pressure off him. "You have no suspects to speak of, and all of a sudden, out of the blue, this evidence appears? That is just a very odd coincidence."

"You are discussing police procedure without knowing the first thing about it. Police work isn't a science. Mostly, it consists of being thorough, waiting and hoping to catch a break. And we just caught such a break."

"How would this witness even know to identify Barry Wentworth, know what he looks like?" Irv asked and moved a little closer to the crowd. This was getting rather interesting now.

"Newscasts, where else? The return of Connor Beauregard, aka Barry J. Wentworth, was in a lot of papers. Not all of them, and not on the front page—but the financial pages had some fun with it. Surely you didn't miss it, Mr. Moody?"

Irv laughed and shrugged, pushing his hands into his pockets. "I spend a lot of time in the air, not reading the paper."

"What's your interest and role in all of this, if you don't mind my asking? I know who you are, Mr. Moody, at least by reputation. I have seen you with these gentlemen before, but what's the sudden interest in this case and Barry Wentworth all about?"

"Before you ask me to leave because it's none of my business, you mean?" Irv laughed and moved closer, in that confident way that said he knew Robertson couldn't make him do anything. "If you really need to know, as a major shareholder, I have a keen interest in situations that might impact my business interests, Detective. Does that do it for you?"

"Nevertheless, you are not directly involved?"

"A man's life was taken. I do understand the weight and importance of your task, Detective. I am not going to try to make you understand how much money I have invested into this company. I am sure that would be overwhelming. Anything that concerns Barry Wentworth has the potential to affect this company and thereby my investment... sir."

Irv could be charming, Rafael thought, the smiling fellow who flew planes a lot. At the same time, he could throw his weight around and let you know that with his kind of money came a lot of influence and power, all while still smiling and being charming. Finally, the detective relented and nodded.

"Now then, Detective, do you mind telling me, your confidential informant..."

"Small-time—nothing major. A crook we've had in our sights for a while, but left in place so we could keep an eye on him."

"And this small-time crook, he saw Barry Wentworth's picture in the financial pages, and he felt the need to come to you and tell you, 'Hey—I've sold a gun to this man... just in case you needed to lock me up for that.' Is that what I'm hearing?"

"No need for sarcasm, Mr. Moody, even if I still don't quite grasp your interest here—but essentially, yes, he came to us. Now what I have is a man who sold a weapon to Barry Wentworth. The same type of weapon used to shoot Tadeo Ivers. What I don't have is a permit to carry such a weapon issued to Barry Wentworth, or the man himself so he could explain to me why he carries it without a permit, or if he could kindly show it to us so our ballistics experts can determine whether or not it was indeed used to shoot Ivers. Are we all done with the politeness now? I am asking you for the last time if you are aware of the whereabouts of Wentworth. And if I find out later on you didn't tell me…"

No need to finish. It didn't look good if you were Barry Wentworth. Regardless of his reasons or motives for buying a gun, not showing up when the police wanted answers did not generally work in your favor. It hadn't last time either, when he had run. Run. Rafael felt a deep pit opening up in the area of his stomach, and it grew quickly.

Irv looked at Al and Rafael, and the same light bulb moment occurred in all three men. Run!

Al recovered first and cleared his throat.

"As I mentioned, we expected Barry to attend this morning's board meeting. He was keen on being appointed to the board," he said.

"But Wentworth did not show?"

"No." Al shook his head. "When you walked in here, we were discussing how strange that was."

"So none of you—not one of you…" The detective looked from one to the other, settling on Rafael in the end. "Knows where Barry Wentworth might be at this moment?"

Rafael only shook his head, fighting the sick feeling in his stomach. "I told you everything I know, Detective. I texted him to see where he was at and why he was late—that is it. Then the meeting started, and there were quite a few agenda items, and I lost track."

"So you just thought—what? That he had skipped another boring board meeting?"

"No, Detective. I knew this was important to him. I actually thought something might have happened to him. An accident of some sort…"

"An accident—that's convenient."

The detective didn't even bother to hide how little he thought of the group of three who stood before him. He reached into his portfolio and pulled out a couple of pages of tightly spaced typed material, boasting a number of official stamps and signatures.

"This is an official warrant for Mr. Barry Wentworth for questioning in conjunction with the shooting of Tadeo Ivers. I will find him, and I will arrest him. I would appreciate it if you did not interfere. I don't have to tell you the implications of interfering with a police investigation. At the moment Barry Wentworth is considered a suspect. As of this moment, he is also considered a fugitive."

Rafael shook his head and fought a growing wave of nausea, Al merely looked stunned, and Irv had taken a step back as if he needed to distance himself from what was going on. Robertson enjoyed his moment.

"Gentlemen, I will most definitely see you shortly," he said. "Make yourselves available please."

He stalked out of the boardroom without a backward glance, and Rafael finally exhaled in one huge whoosh.

"Shit," he said, voicing their collective sentiment.

"Dear God, Barry and a gun," Al said softly, and Rafael squeezed his eyes shut. "He might be the shooter."

"He's not, Al. I know him, and I am convinced he did not shoot Tadeo."

"This witness? He has to be solid, or no judge would issue an arrest order. What possessed Barry to purchase a gun—on the black market no less?"

Rafael pulled his hair back with both hands and began pacing.

"I don't know," he repeated. "No idea. Something must have gone on in his head and…"

"Rafael, you and I are friends, and I have trusted you every step of the way with this company, but right now, right at this moment, you need to make a choice…"

"Hold on here," Irv said, stepping between them. "Nobody is making choices, Al. Nobody is picking sides. Right now, all we have is a story this detective has told us."

"Do you need any more?"

"Frankly, I need to understand what the fuck just happened, Al. Yes, I need a little more than the detective saying, 'Woohoo, now we have somebody who sold a gun to Barry, let's haul him off to jail, and case closed.'"

"You don't even know Barry."

"I don't. But I know this detective, and I don't like him, and I don't want us three to start fighting over something he said, OK?"

"Barry sometimes does things when they occur to him because they occur to him," Rafael said softly. "Thinking things through from A to Z is not exactly his favorite thing to do. I can believe that he bought a gun—just because, but..."

His pacing became more urgent, his hands making erratic motions in the air as he tried to get a handle on what he had heard, groping for anything that would help him understand. Except there was nothing. Motive, means, opportunity? They were all there, staring him in the face.

"I guess—he could have..."

"Yesterday, you told me flat-out Barry didn't have the guts to pull the trigger."

"And he doesn't. I don't think he does, but he's been gone for a while. Who knows what happened to him on that island? Who knows who he turned into? What if he felt cornered? Maybe pulling the trigger is something that makes sense to him now. Shit, Irv—I just don't know any longer."

"He bought a gun," Al repeated, a stoic counterpoint to Rafael's erratic movement. "He went out and purchased a gun—choosing to do so in an illegal and furtive manner. What does that tell you?"

"Even when we were facing a mad-as-a-snake loan shark, it never occurred to him to use a gun, Al. You remember, he asked me." Rafael stopped short and suddenly snapped his fingers a couple of times. "That loan shark? Mirko. Remember him? We were just talking about him moments ago. What if he is involved in this situation—somehow?"

"You're reaching." Al shook his head and turned away. "Moreover, you are looking for excuses."

"Mirko? Who is he?" Irv asked, stepping in again. "Another player I don't know?"

"Loan shark," Rafael said, shaking his head. "Barry borrowed money from him when things weren't going so well, and kind of—fell behind on the payments."

"Oh yes." Irv nodded. "That kind of thing usually goes over well with moneylenders."

"It did. Guy came in and threatened to shut down our grand opening. And here's Barry. 'Didn't you bring a gun?' he asks me. Didn't you bring a gun?" Rafael grinned with the memory and shook his head again. "Crazier than a loon, Barry, but guns were never his thing. Now, if he felt threatened by Mirko, maybe."

"Be that as it may, folks." Al spread his hands and flexed his fingers, as if that would allow him to grasp what was going on just then. "The way I see it—this is not all bad."

"How can you say that?"

"Quite easily, Rafael. Call me self-serving, but while they are investigating Barry, hopefully, they will leave you be and drop whatever they have going on against you."

Rafael turned in his pacing and stood before Al. "They have nothing going on against me—nothing, because I didn't do anything, Al."

"Exactly. And when the news about Barry hits the newswires, it will take a load off everyone else. I can safely bring you back on the board without worrying that our shareholders will crucify us, and we can finally concentrate on getting this company moving in the right direction."

"But it doesn't get you anywhere, Al." Rafael grabbed an abandoned pack of meeting notes and snapped them in his hand. "Personally, I don't think Barry shot your father. And if Robertson and his people are any good at their jobs, it won't take them very long to figure this out. Which brings us back to square one—whodunit?"

"We can deal with that when the time comes." Al swiped the paper out of Rafael's hands. "Meanwhile…"

"Meanwhile, you look like fools if it turns out Wentworth is not guilty," Irv said. "All at a time when you need to build up investor confidence and trust. You can't do that willy-nilly, blaming people, hoping you won't have to say, 'Oops, wrong guy, sorry,' later on."

Al walked away from Irv and Rafael, and for a moment, he looked as if he wanted to strike the far wall of the boardroom. His sharp sudden turn made his shoe soles squeak on the polished floor, and he stalked back toward them, rolling his shoulders and shaking his head.

"So you're telling me to do nothing? That's your advice?"

"No, we're not doing nothing. We sit tight and wait, and we gather more facts." Irv sat again and nodded at Rafael. "This is going to shake out within days. You're sure you have no idea where Barry might have gone?"

Rafael rolled his eyes because everyone felt the need to ask that. As tempting as it was to accept Al's solution because it was the one thing he wanted, Irv had a point.

"None. He hasn't lived in this town for a couple of years."

"And you have no idea where he might hide out?"

"Where is this leading, Irv? You suggesting I am hiding him in my basement? Is that it?"

"You had better get used to those questions, Rafael," Irv said. "You will hear them—a lot. What do you think will happen when the police can't find him in a reasonable amount of time? They will come to you and ask you, over and over. You were the last man to speak to him."

"I didn't speak to Barry."

"Texted him. Tomato, tomahto. He trusts you and vice versa."

"Please don't issue orders around here, Irv." Rafael shook his head. "I know you have invested money in this company."

"A rather large investment."

"A rather large investment—fine. But when did you become our official advisor here?"

"When you and Mr. CEO over there in the corner started treading water. There is a billion-dollar company at stake here, and if there is something that will help find Tadeo Ivers's killer, then we need to do it so the turmoil around this company stops. I don't want to flush all of the money I just invested."

"Hear, hear." Al raised his hands again as if he wanted to shake Irv, which might have been a pretty good guess right then. "Didn't I say that—like, oh, let's say five minutes ago."

"No, you said let's just let Barry take the fall and pretend nothing happened."

"This is nuts." Al dropped into the nearest chair with a heavy thud and rubbed both hands over his face. "I just can't…"

"Regroup," Irv said quickly. "Let's find Barry first and see if we can control this thing. Wherever he is hiding, the smartest thing is to go to the police, explain—whatever he has to explain and take it from there. Make him see that. I'm just an investor, but I think this is our best option."

Rafael and Al looked at one another for a long moment, and finally, Rafael shrugged.

"I hear you. But I still have no idea where the heck he would go. Guys." Rafael spread his arms. "I don't know what to tell you. I don't know him anymore."

"Then we go about it logically," Irv said. "Does he know people in town still?"

"Probably."

"Anybody who would hide him?"

"No clue." Rafael shrugged again. "This wasn't a topic that came up when we hung out at The Lighthouse."

"Then we need to use our resources. There is a private guy you hired, isn't there, Al?"

Running and controlling meetings and large groups of people came naturally to Irv. He took charge by default, and Al and Rafael let him do so. Rafael still wrestled with the image of Barry with a gun, perhaps lining up the sights. Al looked plain worn-out, deep lines carving his face. It had been too long, this nightmare. Too damn long and he still couldn't see the end from here.

"Sandro." Rafael shook his head to clear it. "Sandro whatever-the-heck his last name is. Can he help us find Barry?"

"Probably," Al said. "It is what he does for a living after all. It may be a moot point, but this is the worst thing Barry could have done in this situation, to run from the police once again."

"Maybe he wasn't running from the police," Rafael tried again, if only because he thought he should.

"And maybe the sky is green—could happen," Irv said and took a few steps away. "Give your head a shake, Rafael, and stop coming up with excuses. You can be certain he owes money. Barry was running from the law. The last thing you do is stop to pay off old debts."

"And you know this how, Irv? Experience perhaps?"

"No. From what I heard about him, I don't think he would have, that's all. Which means we may now be adding a pissed-off loan shark into the mix. Nice."

Rafael said nothing, but drew lines and arrows on a piece of paper in front of him.

"Barry?" Irv asked. "Barry knows the police want to talk to him and possibly a loan shark. Where does he go?"

"I don't know, Irv."

"Think, Rafael. Parents? Siblings? Lovers? Former lovers?"

"None. His father ran an evangelical church out in Dunnville, but they fell out a long time ago. No love lost there. Then, of course, he was gone for a long time."

Just as Rafael's patience with those kinds of questions ran out, Irv's phone rang again, a different, more insistent ringtone this time, and Irv glanced at it and rose.

"People, I really have to go," he said. "I have to hangar the plane and take care of a few things at the airstrip. Let's all agree here that finding Barry is top priority. Text him, call him. Send a personal messenger—whatever. Just make sure he doesn't go on the run again. If he hasn't already."

He rapped his knuckles on the polished walnut conference table and disappeared, leaving Al and Rafael behind.

"I," Rafael began slowly, "don't know what to say."

"Welcome to our nightmare." Al shook his head. "Although I really don't appreciate Irving Moody coming in here to run the show all of a sudden."

"We both let him waltz in and play chief honcho—never mind. What I want to know is…"

"What the heck happened," Al murmured, and Rafael raised an eyebrow.

"One word, yes."

Rafael looked down at his phone and texted Barry yet again—the fifth or sixth notice his friend was ignoring in a row. Former friend. And still he kept trying. *Come on, Barry, where are you? There's some heat developing here, and you need to face it.*

No answer. Although Barry's phone must still be connected and on, or the messages would have remained undelivered. So where the hell…

"Nothing again?" Al asked, and Rafael let his finger slide down the list of calls that had gone unanswered before he put his phone back into his pocket. "Did you really expect him to answer?"

"Call me crazy," Rafael said, "but yes, yes, I did."

"Then you are naïve. Connor runs. He did the first time around."

"But he wanted this; he wanted this company. He wanted the CEO seat so badly—why would he run?"

"Because he may have shot my father."

There it stood in the middle of the room. The statement, the suspicion. Rafael took a deep breath and let it out again, settled back into his chair, and let his eyes rest on Al. So long, in fact, that his friend had to look away.

"Do you really believe that, Al? Can you look at me and say, 'I do indeed believe that Barry J. Wentworth shot my father?' If that's the case…" He folded his hands and rested his face on them. "Hey—if that's the case, just tell me now, before I get any deeper into this."

Al sat back too, hands folded, eyes turned down so no one could read his expression, and he thought. He thought long and hard. The silence in the room became so oppressive, the hum of the air ventilation system so loud, Rafael thought he might have to jump up and yell something loud and inappropriate, just to break the spell. Then, ever so slowly, Al shook his head.

"Hell if I know. I still don't think he has the guts. It's just… He makes a great suspect."

Al continued, "Motive, means, probably opportunity." Al ticked them off on his fingers. "And let's not forget running from questioning is a pattern with him."

"Maybe he is—afraid," Rafael let that sentence hang in the air for a long moment and got to his feet again. "Of someone or something."

"Then find him. And make him explain."

"I'll try. And God help him, it had better be good."

Rafael turned and grabbed his portfolio off the conference table and nodded a brief greeting at Al. In the space of a couple of hours, his priorities had shuffled once again, from guiding this company to finding Barry and, once he did, making him explain why he owned a gun, had run, and should still be considered innocent after all.

Goddammit, Covin, he scolded himself, taking the stairs two at a time, *you don't set easy goals, do you?*

FOURTEEN

Rafael realized what he was doing could best be described as driving recklessly—speeding, forcing others out of the way, but today, he'd chance a ticket. He had a job to do.

He flew past the girls at Reception with a nod and a smile, as if he had good reason to be pushy, and pushed into Kayla's office into the middle of a meeting.

"Excuse me, gentlemen," he said, catching himself against the doorframe. "This is important—do you mind?"

Four pairs of eyes regarded him with a certain amount of suspicion, until Kayla raised a hand.

"It's fine, folks. We're done here anyway."

Rafael fell hard into the white, comfortable visitor's chair across from her desk and shook his head.

"Before you start—"

"I wasn't going to."

"Kayla—I need your help."

She put away the file she had been working on and handed him a bottle of water from a small fridge built into her desk.

"Go on. All I have to do is look at you to know you do."

Rafael drank some of the water and tried to fill her in on everything that had happened after she left the meeting with Thomas, as quickly as he could. When he got to the detective barging in on them and the part where Barry bought a black-market gun, the silver pen dropped from her fingers, and her hands flew to her mouth.

"Dear God…"

Rafael didn't answer. Instead, he drank most of the water.

"The same gun that was used… So, he might have…" Kayla groped for words, searching his face, but Rafael only shrugged and fired the empty bottle at the waste basket.

"Honestly—I don't know what to think," he finally said. "This is going to come down like a shit storm."

He looked up, but Kayla didn't even blink at the phrasing.

"Guess now we know why he was a no-show for the meeting. He is on the run again."

"I thought—maybe that loan shark."

Kayla closed her eyes, her fingers tapping a light rhythm on her desktop. Likely counting to 10, Rafael thought. When she opened her eyes again, he saw the cold edge of determination.

"Unless Barry can come up with an explanation of why he had this gun in his possession, the public, the police, and I are going to assume he is the shooter," she said softly.

"That is about what Irving said. He needs to explain."

"But instead…" She pointed out the window at the traffic down below. "Instead, he is out there somewhere."

"Yes."

"Do you want to know what I would do in your place?" Kayla asked, and Rafael nodded.

"Find him, if you have any idea where he might be, ask him to give up this running and speak to the investigators, and let the dice fall where they may," she said, with more emphasis than he would have liked. "And then you figure out a way to make peace within the company. The company isn't going to survive if we don't all find a way to work together, and from where I am sitting—you'll be CEO before long anyway."

Rafael thought for a moment and narrowed his eyes at the wall behind her. He had some ideas about bringing the two companies together, about bringing the people together. It had come to him while contemplating the utter shambles his life was just then. His life and his company both were a mess—but they were parts of the same mess.

Clean up one, perhaps he could clean up the other. The idea got a little bigger as he allowed it to get comfortable, and it reminded him of something he'd been doing just recently, just before everything had gone to hell in a handbasket. Kayla still said nothing, leveling a cool, dark stare at him.

"I'm trying here," he finally said. "But I have no clue where to start looking. I can hardly wander the streets until I trip over him. I think I'm better off to leave Sandro to do the searching."

"Fine. As long as somebody does. And you?"

Rafael got to his feet and paced, teasing away at the edges of that idea he knew was there, if he could just make it come out.

"Until we have something concrete on Barry, I think I should work on the company instead. That's where I am needed."

"Glad to hear it."

"You see, Sandro feels the killer could be found in the cannabis business," Rafael said. "I hate the thought—but he's convinced. That's one puzzle. At the same time, we have to piece together a company from a giant set of pieces of two formerly separate companies. Coincidentally, they are the same puzzle pieces. The cannabis company. While we are looking at all of those individual pieces and people of PerCan and explaining them to the Mariposa folks, we might just stumble across something that would help."

"It sounds a little farfetched if you are hoping it will point you to the shooter."

"Possibly." Rafael made a face. "But it has to be done anyway, and right now, I don't know where else to start but in the company history and structure."

"Worst-case scenario, it will give you something constructive to do, and it will make PerCan Consolidated a better company." Kayla smiled. "Best-case scenario, you will discover something helpful. So, what are you waiting for?"

Rafael grinned, rolled his shoulders, and limbered his arms, the paralyzing exhaustion gone all of a sudden, with the promise of a new task ahead of him.

"I think I have a plan," he said and grinned broadly. "I think…"

Just at that moment, his phone announced itself with the deafening noise of an alarm klaxon, his ringtone for Irving Moody, and he rose as he checked his phone.

"It's Irv. He could help me with this thing. Hold on. Hey, Irv. Great timing. Listen, I am working on a fantastic idea…"

He never got to finish the sentence. Irv's irate voice spilled forth from the phone, words tumbling over one another in the haste to get them out, and Rafael sat back down hard. He only heard and understood the first few sentences. After that, his brain went into blackout mode, refusing to take in any more.

"Rafael?" Kayla took the phone from his hand before it dropped to the ground and gently took hold of his shoulder. "What's going on here? Irv? Hello?"

Without taking her eyes off Rafael, she reached down and toggled speaker mode on his phone. "What's happening, Irving? Whatever you just told Rafa—he almost passed out."

"Barry is gone."

"We know that. Did they find him?"

"My plane—the new ultralight. It's gone too."

"And you're thinking…?"

"I am not thinking, Kayla. I know. I'd parked it at the aeroclub intending to come back to do some minor work on it, clean it, and hangar it tonight. He took it, Kayla. Goddamn Barry Wentworth grabbed my plane and took off." Irv almost spat with anger.

"Jesus, Irv, Barry is no pilot. He took a few flying lessons when we had the helicopter, never applied for his license. I know it's convenient, but how do you know it was Barry who took your plane?"

"Because the bastard asked somebody to gas it up not more than an hour ago. I showed them a picture. There's no doubt—it was him."

"But... but..." Kayla stammered all of a sudden. "OK, focus, these things can be located, can't they?"

"A plane? Hell yes. Unless he turns off the transponder, which is highly illegal. Goddamn that man. When I find him, I'm going to strangle him with my own hands."

"Irving..."

"If he puts as much as a scratch on that plane—"

"Let me call you back, Irv. Don't go anywhere. Don't do anything."

Kayla hung up on Irv Moody and slowly turned back to Rafael. Neither one of them could say anything to help wrap their minds around what had just happened.

Barry Wentworth had stolen a small ultralight plane and taken off for parts unknown. If anybody had the sheer gall to steal an airplane, despite knowing very little about operating it, never mind doing it safely, without a thought as to who else might be injured in the process—it would be Barry.

And the clock on being discovered started running the moment he took off, which made it a desperation move.

What did that mean for the case, for them, for the company?

Thoughts were assaulting him hard and fast, and Rafael brought his hands to his head.

"Who—steals—a plane?" he said slowly and deliberately. "Who the hell goes out and steals a—pardon my French—fucking airplane, lacking any knowledge on how to fly it? Has he gone insane?"

"There is a warrant out for his arrest. You need to tell the detective."

"The hell if I do. This is Irving's plane. He can go tell the detective. I barely know what the thing looks like. Why would Barry do something so utterly stupid? Why not just take a nice anonymous minivan and drive?"

He didn't wait for an answer; none was required anyway. Kayla nodded and sat back down behind her desk.

"That foolish man actually did it again. Did he think he was going all the way back to the South Pacific?"

"Rafael, you're going to give yourself a heart attack."

"He ran last time, and he's running this time. Last time, he left me to hold the bag and to straighten out a company he messed up so completely…"

"This time, we are ahead of the game," Kayla said, determination in her words. "He's all but confessed by running. This team-building plan you were talking about, I like it. And when PerCan is running the way it should, we will all have the freedom to decide what we want to do."

Rafael held his head in his hands. "Yes, and a very large holding of shares will be owned by a man who is currently on the run. In an airplane. Which does not belong to him. What happens if he evades justice again? Can you tell me that?"

"Don't know, don't care. All I am interested in is, hopefully, he will not be back. And you—square this thing with the detective. Call him. Show good faith, and it will all be over soon."

Rafael's phone rang again, and he checked the screen with a quick, jerky motion. "Al," he said curtly, accepting the call. "You heard."

"I heard," Al snapped. "My office—now. Do you know where Kayla is?"

"With me."

"Bring her along. You, me, Kayla, Irv, and Dante. We're going to figure this out."

"What about…"

"Never mind what about, Rafael. Get your ass back to my office, now."

Rafael hung up again. Al very rarely cussed. Matter of fact, in all the time he had known him, he had heard him use foul language only on the rarest of occasions. Like the time when Greg had blown up the merger. When all of their finely laid plans went down the toilet. It was happening again. This time, he wouldn't allow it.

He nodded to Kayla, and without another word, they packed their respective portfolios and rushed out of Montecito Publishing, leaving behind a number of bewildered employees of Kayla's. They both looked and acted as if the world had come to an end. Rafael couldn't be bothered to wait for Kayla's driver and herded them toward his new silver Mercedes, parked in the 'strictly no parking' zone in front of the building. Neither one of them had spoken by the time they pulled up in front of Perfect Cannabis Consolidated.

Right away, Kayla took charge, still being a board member and all. There would be questions and requests for comments and confusion, among their own and former Mariposa employees soon enough. They would have a few hours at best, before the news hit the streets. If it was not on Twitter already. In this day and age, everyone would know shortly, and it was her job as Director of PR and Promotions to prevent the worst.

She merely nodded at the girls at the front desk and at Rafael.

"He's with me. Where is Al?"

"I'm not sure, Ms. Montecito."

"Page him. Find us a private room somewhere. Not the boardroom. And then no interruptions—none whatsoever, unless the building is on fire, understood?"

"Understood. There's a large office in section two, by the labs, that's…"

"Ours now," Kayla said and moved on, Rafael in tow.

"But it's empty," the receptionist called after them, which didn't stop Kayla.

On the way to the empty room, which had been designed as an extra office for senior laboratory staff to gather and exchange information, Kayla called Connie, Rafael's former PA, and had her bring some chairs down there. Personally. No one else was to be involved—they didn't need any tables or other equipment.

Al messaged them shortly. He was on his way, bringing Dante and Nick Ambrose with him. The old group was back together.

Short hours after the company's first formal board meeting, they stood in the bare room awkwardly, not knowing where to turn. No one dared sit on one of the five chairs Connie had dragged in, although Al must have briefed Dante and Nick on the way. Shock and disbelief stood visibly on their faces.

Dante wanted to speak, but Al raised his hand to silence him and went to close the door with exaggerated care, avoiding even the slight snap of the door closure.

Finally, he turned and faced the group.

"This is a disaster," he said, "and we need to figure out how to keep the company safe and out of the media storm that's about to descend. Within this group," he spun his finger once around the room, including them all, "we need to be on the same page before I inform Thomas of this latest."

"Do we know that he's actually done it?" Dante asked, and Al raised an eyebrow.

"He ran from the police, he owns a gun of the type used in the murder, he hated our father, and he has no alibi." He ticked off on his fingers. "For good measure, he stole Irving Moody's airplane to get away. That looks like the desperate act of a guilty man. Anyone care to disagree?"

Al spun around, but no one answered.

"I don't care about his guilt or degree thereof. What I do care about is that he is one of the major shareholders and founder of this company. When the press gets wind of this in, oh, about 20 minutes, we need to know what to tell them. And we need to have a united front, distancing ourselves from anything and everything that Barry J. Wentworth may or may not have done with or to this company at any point in time, is that understood?"

That last bit was directed straight at Rafael, who could only nod. Shock colored his expression. He had founded this company with this man. Barry took shortcuts, and he would say anything if it got him what he wanted right then and there—but murder? Murder?

He straightened his shoulders a bit and sighed. "I have to agree with Al," he said. "First priority is to make sure the company does not get dragged into this. Thomas is a very astute and forceful man, and he's already unhappy with the direction of this merger and recent, uhh, developments. Let's not give him any reason to do something rash."

He chewed on his thumb for a moment and turned to Kayla. "We will—you and Al will—have to make a statement."

"Saying he is just a shareholder now, nothing to do with the company any longer. Not even on the board." Kayla nodded. "People will remember him as the founder, though. They will want to see the next chapter in this drama. He is—entertaining if nothing else."

Rafael smiled, thinking of the many times Barry had done something outrageous to attract media interest. He just couldn't help it. Whenever he did something, he did it with flair. He did things in ways no one else did them, and in the end that was what made him so magical and charismatic—and dangerous.

"Nothing to grin about," Dante grumbled. "If he really did shoot our father…"

"Then he will be brought to justice, Dan. That's not what had me smile. I was remembering…"

"Never mind your memories just now, Rafael. We don't have time. We need a plan," Al said, turning to Kayla.

Kayla propped her notebook up on a ledge and began typing furiously. "We'll issue a statement, Al, saying that Barry has no role within this company save that of a shareholder, and has not for the past two years. That ought to do for the moment. Then…"

"Then it would be best if he were found and the investigation closed," Al said with a finality that said he was done with the subject, and the group fell silent for a long moment.

Everyone in the room likely tried to wrap their mind around the question of if Barry Wentworth really had done it. Nobody wanted to ask, and yet everybody wanted an answer.

"But we don't know, and we can't afford to guess," Al finally said. "We're turning in circles. I say we forget about Barry as of right now. He and his issues don't exist. We run this company, end of story."

"Indeed, Rafael has a couple of ideas about that," Kayla said and quickly outlined what he had told her earlier.

"That'll work," Al said. "I like it—that way all of you are still going to be here where I need you most, giving me advice, helping me run this thing, connecting people." He nodded and gave Rafael a tired but hopeful high five. "Great idea, thanks."

Rafael let out a massive breath. He gathered what was left of his energy today, smiled at Kayla, and put his hand on her shoulder.

"Thanks. For everything. And I know nobody has asked you this, but how are you dealing with all of this?"

"Same as everybody else, Rafa. I am—coping. Barely some days, but coping. You're right. We stood by and let him run everything without saying a word. It was all good and all forgiven because he could present and raise funds like no other man on the planet. Not this time. This time, he has gone one too far."

FIFTEEN

Walking out of the building, Rafael once again felt a deep and heavy exhaustion creep into every bone of his body. It was a feeling he had become used to over the short span of a couple of weeks, something he dragged around like a heavy piece of luggage wherever he went. He put one foot in front of the other because it was expected of him, and because he might have fallen over if he did not, but if he looked for drive and ambition, he came up empty.

Kayla, on the other hand, had become stronger under the outside pressure, leading and taking charge, where she had been content to let the boys do their thing while acting as their mouthpiece.

"Have you registered a consulting company to be the official advising entity to PerCan? No? Then do it now. It will act as a barrier between you and the board of directors, in case anyone asks or has an issue with this arrangement. Not likely, but we need you there without any questions."

"I'll get to it."

"Now. Next, you will need to prepare for the questions Robertson is going to ask of you. What did you know, when, and where did you find out? He will be nasty, and he will be thorough. Talk to Martin. Get some advice and coaching on what could get you in trouble. Be prepared for everything, Rafa. Absolutely everything."

"Got it, everything."

"You look…"

"Like crap?"

Rafael forked his hands through his hair for the thousandth time that day and managed a thin smile. They had driven to Kayla's house, and she had taken him straight to the rooftop lounge to sit in a secluded corner amongst potted palms and ferns with a view of the city skyline and the lake beyond. A cold northerly wind whistled up here, and they were huddled in their parkas, but far from prying ears and eyes.

Life should have been great right now—more than great, awesome. He should have time with this amazing woman who adored him for some strange reason and the enjoyment of a job well done at PerCan every day.

"What do you think?" he finally asked Kayla.

"What do I think of what—Barry? I think I can't afford to have an opinion either way. I was engaged to the man, for God's sake. To find out that he is capable…"

Her voice trailed off, and Rafael only nodded. Capable of murder. Jesus. Her cell phone chirped, and Kayla looked down at it.

"Doorman," she said by way of explanation and walked off a few steps to speak.

"Well, well—as if this day couldn't get any stranger," she said, coming back to his side. "Tessa is down at the door, wishing to speak with you. Urgently."

"Tessa Goodwin? Our Tessa? Former assistant to Barry and me?"

"One and only. Do you want to let her up here and speak to her? You don't have to."

"I…" Rafael shook his head and raised his hands. "Christ, I haven't talked to her in ages, although we always got along. Why not? The news must have got out. This day has gone to hell already. How much stranger could it get?"

He sat back down and closed his eyes for a minute, remembering the old days. The really old days. When Barry was still called Connor, and they ran any old deal together that offered itself. Oil and gas, liquor, software… It didn't really matter. If there was an idea and a way to make a public company out of it, raise funds, find a shell, and issue shares, then Barry was all over it. This was what he did.

With the charisma of his preacher-man father, he would promise you the moon and the stars, anything you wanted, and get you to pick up the check for it at the same time.

Heaven on earth, all expenses paid with no possibility of failure. He could sell it to you. Issue the shares, grab the money, get rich. Rinse, repeat. Sometimes it worked, sometimes it didn't, or at least not the way he had promised. Hey, that's the life of startup companies, he would say, shrug, and walk away. Either that or someone was at fault who had screwed up badly. There was never any shortage of scapegoats. Perhaps the lawyers had made a mess and overcharged, one of Barry's favorites. Or a partner had reneged on a deal, or he had been given erroneous information. Sorry, couldn't be helped. On to the next deal.

And through all of it, they had stuck together. Rafael, Connor, and only one other person, Tessa Goodwin. Not exactly fresh out of school, not exactly ambitious or driven, but smart and loyal to Barry and Rafael. Or so they thought. She'd run their back office with perfection and efficiency—although the dyed, raven-black hair, tattoos, and piercings did take some getting used to.

Didn't really matter either because, if you gave her a computer and a keyboard, there was nothing Tessa Goodwin couldn't find, figure out, or manipulate. She was scary that way. Really scary. And in the end, the person who actually recognized that had been Tadeo Ivers, when he snapped her up and gave her enough money to roll on Barry and Rafael to give him all the little secrets he needed to take on PerCan.

Nothing serious to be had on Rafael. He hadn't really committed any sins worse than cussing a lot, being slovenly, and standing behind Barry. But Barry—Barry needed to pay. And with the balls Tessa Goodwin played to Tadeo Ivers, it was a done deal.

The potted palms up there on the rooftop terrace had been placed in such a way as to create little pockets of privacy to sit and chat, or simply enjoy the view. Rafael opened his eyes again when he heard the palm leaves rustle, and there she stood. She looked a little older than the last time he had seen her, a couple of the piercings had been removed, and the black hair—the shiny black hair was gone, replaced by a standard, run-of-the-mill brunette.

He pushed up his sunglasses and nodded toward a chair.

"Look who the cat dragged in. Take a load off."

"Rafael, thanks for seeing me. I am so sorry."

I am sorry, no hello, no preamble. *I'm sorry*. Rafael blinked and sat up a little straighter.

"Define sorry. Sorry about what? Selling out to Tadeo Ivers, throwing your lot in with a criminal, or getting rid of the black? I like it by the way. Suits you."

Self-consciously, she touched her hair and looked down. "Rafael, I…"

"Unless there is something recent you did and need to be sorry for, it's all ancient history, and not worth finding excuses for. I'm too old for excuses anyway. If I was gonna take a guess, it is you probably needed money back then."

Tessa nodded. "And…"

"And Ivers offered you gobs of it, so you sold out Barry and me."

"Rafael, I never meant…"

"Save it." Rafael swished his hand in between them, as if chasing a pesky mosquito, and settled further back into his parka and his chair. No, he really didn't feel like rehashing the past. What for? Why even think about it? Barry J. Wentworth right here, right now gave a man enough things to worry and think about, without dragging up past sins.

"Ancient history and not worth my time. So why are you here now?"

"I think I can help you, Rafael. I never meant for you to get into any trouble, never. You said it yourself. I needed money, and Connor—Barry—hadn't paid me for a while, and…"

"Get to the point, sweetheart, I'm not getting any younger here."

"I think I can help you find Barry."

"Was that on the news, seeing how everybody is talking about it? You think or you know?"

"I think… I mean—it shouldn't be too hard."

"The police are working on that part of it, Tessa. They will get to him soon enough. First thing I thought too. I should go and find him—but really, it's not my job."

"Wouldn't it be easier if you spoke to him first?"

Maybe it would be. Except that too was a classic Barry Wentworth move in some ways. *Let's get together first and talk, make sure our stories match. This is what we will tell them, this is what it will mean, and this is what we will make of it.*

Now, all of it just felt like too much work. Having to work out a 'story,' having to make sure it made sense and it matched.

"Let the police deal with him, Tess. This is not a game of secret agents and finding missing people. There's no movie trailer here, no treasure to be found, nothing. Barry stole Moody's plane, and he disappeared—end of story."

"Connor can be an ass sometimes."

"It's Barry now, and yes, Tess, he can be an ass—a lot of times. We've all noticed that. And he plays hard and fast with the truth and the rules, he always thinks of himself first, and he has no respect for other people's money. What else is new?"

"Nothing—that's the point. Whatever he is, Barry is not the kind of guy who will shoot a man. Oh, he will cheat him out of his money, sure, and then he will walk away with that money and have a good believable story why the deal didn't work out. But he would never shoot a guy. You know that, Rafael."

"I thought I did."

Tessa was getting more animated now, jumping to her feet and pacing on the rooftop patio—a few steps away from Rafael and back to stand square before him. She shook her head and spread her arms, as if that much stupidity were just too much to handle for her.

"Really, Rafa? That's the best you can do? Give it another shot. Barry—does—not—shoot—people. He doesn't. For one he would be too concerned about getting blood on those Ferragamo loafers and that fancy Valentino gear he carries. No, he would not. Dammit. He is not a violent guy. A total mess, yes. Violent? No."

She kicked at one of the fancy planters holding potted palms and other greenery and winced, despite the heavy motorcycle boots.

Rafael merely shrugged.

"And what would you suggest instead? Some cloak-and-dagger, 'find him and hide him from the police' kind of thing? That's not going to work, and this isn't the movie screen. He's flying around out there, with a gun, remember."

"Then somebody is setting him up, Rafael. I've worked for him…"

"Do you really think you know what he's all about? I've been his friend for well over 20 years. You went over to Tadeo's when the going got tough. Don't forget that." Rafael was losing patience with her now.

"I regret that more than…"

"Forget it, Tess. Tell the police if you like, that you don't think Barry Wentworth could ever shoot somebody—I tried that already. Robertson is the man in charge, Detective Robertson. See what he has to say."

"If I can find Barry—will you talk to him? Will you convince him to go work with the police to clear this all up?"

"For God's sake."

"Rafael!"

Kayla called his name across the expanse of the rooftop—and not the way she usually called him. This time it was a scream, an expression of such utter terror it made his heart stop.

Rafael jumped to his feet, roughly pushed a planter out of his way, and all but sprinted to the exit stairwell.

"Kayla? Are you all right?"

She had run all the way up the stairs instead of opting for the comfort of the elevator. Comfort that took a few extra minutes, and no makeup in the world could have made her look anything but ghostly white. One hand rested on the doorframe, the other over her heart. Her eyes went from Tessa to Rafael and back, as if trying to decide, and finally, she made a fist.

"They found him. Rafa—they found Barry."

"Thank the good Lord. Did he give himself up? Is he in custody? Speak, woman, for crying out loud—and why do you look like somebody... Like a... like something happened."

Rafael tripped over the last few sentences, and all of sudden, Kayla really didn't have to continue. He already knew. As if he had read it in a paper or seen it on the news somewhere.

"Irving Moody's ultralight crashed," Kayla said, her voice flat and devoid of any color. "Somewhere—up north. In the wilderness."

They stood as stone statues for a moment. The spell that had been cast over them kept them rooted in place. As if somehow, if they all stood like that for the end of their days, no one would ask the question they all needed answered, no one would answer it, and they could just...

Somewhere, a door slammed, voices rose on the other end of the rooftop terrace, someone laughed, and Rafael blinked, shook his head, and cleared his mind.

"Is he—in custody?" he finally asked. His way of asking the same thing, and still not using the words.

Kayla shook her head and reached for his elbow to steady herself. In that one moment, she had become small and helpless.

"He—is in pretty bad shape. They took him to the nearest hospital at Silver Lake."

"But he is all right? He is going to make it? I mean—he's fine, right? They must have told you..."

Tessa's voice had become shrill with panic, and Rafael used his free arm to steady her as well. He shook his head gently—don't ask now—but Kayla managed to continue with a deep clearing breath.

"It was Irving who called me. He is furious that his plane is in pieces, and he wants to break every bone in Barry's body that's not already broken. But even he thought—he may not get to do that after all."

"How did he find out first?" Rafael asked, and Kayla shook her head, letting go of his arm and dropping into a chair.

"Transportation Safety Authority, maybe. It is his plane after all—or was, anyway. Why does it matter?"

"I'm assuming then that detective was informed," Tessa said, grabbing Rafael's arm in a hard grip. "They are likely already on their way—you have to go talk to Barry. You have to."

"Number one, Tessa, if he's in bad shape, then they won't let me go near him in the ICU. Number two, I still don't understand why you want me to go talk to Barry Wentworth so badly. Did you not have a falling out with his former partner in crime, Roberto Ivers? Roberto and you were an item for a while, if I remember correctly."

"I know." Tessa's hand fell from his arm. "Roberto was a mistake, and he got me to spill everything there was to know about PerCan and that merger."

"Allowing them to complete their little takeover scheme," Rafael finished. "Pardon me if I'm a little confused here why you are suddenly standing on our patio, demanding I do something for Barry. What is it you know or want, and does it have anything to do with Roberto?"

Slowly, Tessa shook her head. "I don't even know myself, Rafael, and I told you—I regret turning on you and going over to Ivers originally."

Rafael waved his hand in front of his face as if to shoo a pesky fly and spun an index finger in the air. Enough of the drama—continue already.

"I don't know for sure, except—guns…"

"Yes?"

"Guns are more Roberto's style. He's not afraid of them, and—he has a number of guns. I think." Tessa swallowed hard.

"You think?"

"I know—I know. In his bedroom. I saw… One. Once."

"Interesting company you keep." Rafael's eyebrow shot up to his hairline, and again he shook his head.

"And where is this going then? So, Roberto plays rough. We already knew that. He's been to jail. He owns guns, although he probably should not. So what?"

"He was furious with Barry. They had some sort of a deal on the go while Barry was still away. Roberto helped him with something over here Barry couldn't do, and in exchange, Roberto would be a part of the company. He would get an executive role."

Rafael laughed and pushed back from her.

"Forget about it. Holding a license to grow and having an executive with a criminal record—a drug-related criminal record, no less—are basically mutually exclusive. No matter who promised what. Sorry, Tessa. That just won't fly."

"I know," she said, furiously jamming her hands into the pockets of her parka. "I know, and I think Roberto at least suspected. Tadco tried to give him a position in the company at one point, and his lawyer said forget it. But Barry promised he would make it happen—somehow."

"That sounds like our Barry," Rafael said. "But still—assuming that Roberto would go after Barry because he was out of an executive position? Nah, that's too farfetched even for me."

"He was in a bad place, Rafael. His father had used him to get rid of Barry, Barry used him to make some sort of deal to get back into the company. And when it was all done, everyone said thanks but no thanks. He became convinced this was Barry's fault."

"Or maybe it's just what happens when you move on the criminal edge of things, Tessa." Rafael opened his arms wide. "Look, I appreciate you coming out here, but I think you've got a suspicion and nothing else. You don't want Barry to be guilty. I've been there." Rafael forked 10 fingers through his hair and held his palms pressed to either side of his head. "Far too long. I don't think there's anything I can do for Barry, or for you."

"I know Roberto has access to and an ownership share in the off-shore company Barry uses to hold his PerCan shares."

"Why the hell would he have done that?"

"In case something happened. Who knows—he probably meant to clean it up and didn't get to it."

"So you kill a man for a holding company? That's insane, Tessa!"

"Perhaps not insane in the eyes of a desperate man with nothing to lose," Kayla suddenly threw in. "Roberto got played by both parties. His father is dead. So he is going to use Barry's shares to make the rest of his life rather comfortable, while Barry rots in jail. It's twisted, but it makes sense."

Rafael felt like sitting back down. Instead he walked to the edge of the rooftop terrace, leaned against the parapet, and stared down at the sidewalk below.

He wrapped his fingers around the edge of the railing, clinging to the one bit of solidity around him. Al needed him here. PerCan needed him here to make a coherent whole out of a company in pieces.

"Can you put the information groups together I was planning?" he asked of Kayla. "With Tessa's help, perhaps? Organize those of us who cannot serve on the board just now, pair them with the Mariposa employees to make sure information is shared properly and the company comes together?"

"If you need me to."

"I do. I trust you to set this up properly. I will go to…" He looked at Kayla for help.

"Silver Lake."

"Silver Lake and try to speak to Barry before the detective does and get some information out of him. But I won't promise anything."

"Be careful," Kayla said, unnecessarily, and he nodded.

"You can damn well trust me on that one. You please update me if you see or hear anything from our friend Roberto Ivers?"

"Wouldn't Al…"

"I don't want to put this on Al. If you guys are right, and somebody is trying to frame Barry, maybe that somebody is going after the company. The best thing we can do is make sure PerCan is going to function as a whole, and Al will have his hands full with that."

He pushed away from the edge of the rooftop and put his hands together. "I will talk to Al from the car. Meantime, I have to run. You understand."

He kissed Kayla on the cheek and headed for the exit door. Mid-stride, he turned around once more.

"Tess, I'm trusting you one last time with this. I probably shouldn't, but what the heck. You came to me. Betray me again…"

"I won't, Rafael. I swear to you."

"Don't swear. Just help Kayla any way you can. And if you can use your—specialized talent—to figure out what Roberto is up to, go ahead."

"I'll do everything I can. Rafael—I am so…"

"Sorry. I heard that." Rafael shook his head and kept walking. "Just help Kayla, will you?"

He grabbed the door and took the stairway as well, two at a time, his head still spinning. Barry had stolen a plane, run from the police—again—crashed the plane, and put himself into the hospital. And now it looked like Barry's former partner might not be playing on the same side with him at all.

Fun and games. He still couldn't believe Barry would shoot anyone—and Tessa had just confirmed it. Something bigger had to be going on here.

In his car, he oriented himself on the GPS and dialed Al's personal number the moment he knew where he was going.

"You heard?" he asked by way of greeting, and he really didn't have to.

Al's voice bled stress all the way through the phone line, so presumably the news had made its way.

"What do you think, Rafael? Of course I've heard. I have to tell you… I really don't know what I have to tell you. I don't even know what to think. I'm just—I don't know, that's all."

He sounded defeated, and Rafael could just see him dropping heavily into his chair, rubbing his eyes.

"I'm on my way to Silver Lake. I'm going to see him in the hospital, try to get some answers."

"Is there any point? I mean—can the guy even talk? You know if he's…"

Al's voice trailed off, and Rafael couldn't blame him. Crashing a plane. That part was survivable—apparently—but what state would Barry Wentworth be in when he found him? Would he be able to speak to Rafael? Would they even let him? Did this trip make any sense at all?

Presumably, their detective was even now on the way to Silver Lake, perhaps hours ahead of Rafael. He might well be wasting his time on the road here. Hell, he knew that, had known it from the moment they told him Barry had crashed a plane. And still he had to try.

"I don't know, Al. Heck, I don't know much, other than he crashed but he's alive. That's it. What I do know is I have to try to find out what really happened, for the company's sake—and for our sake, or Irv's plane won't be the only thing to crash and burn."

"All right."

Al sighed deeply and shifted back in his chair, eliciting a protesting squeak from the abused piece of furniture.

"Hurry up, will you, Rafael? I need you here, more than ever before."

"Oh, I hear you. But listen—I am sending you Tessa."

"Tessa? The goth girl who used to work for you? Then by some sleight of hand and financial magic ended up in my father's back pocket? I'm pretty sure she slept with Roberto, too, although I couldn't swear to it. You sure that's a good idea?"

"Probably not, no." Rafael laughed and pulled out to pass a couple of particularly slow-moving tourists. "It might be a stupid idea at that,

Al, but the woman has magic when it comes to computers, and she's worked for us for a long time. Before she listened to the call of your dad's money, that is."

"Still…" Al dragged out that one word.

"Yup—still. I'm not saying let her run wild without supervision, but use her, get her to help you put those working groups together we were talking about, suss out information, and make sense of it all. She'll be good at that."

"But keep an eye on her."

"Keep a wary eye on her, my friend. I'll call you the moment I know something new."

SIXTEEN

HQ. Head office. The new home of PerCan. Tessa took a deep breath and paused just a little, pulling in through the double front doors. Last time she'd been here for more than a minute had been at the grand opening. The whole place had still looked like crap, garbage stuffed into bins quickly and covered up, and the front area dressed up, construction scaffolding holding up dividing walls, and outside—outside stood Connor's helicopter.

She smiled at the memory and pushed through the doors. Connor. Connor Beauregard, now Barry J. Wentworth, didn't do anything on a small scale. Connor didn't know the meaning of the word *understated*. Anywhere he went, he went with flair, trumpets, and fanfares. And Kayla Montecito, his fiancé. Behold Kayla and Connor, king and queen. The fairy tale with an abrupt ending. She'd hardly recognized Kayla. That's how much she had changed in the intervening time—but hell, they all had.

The day of the grand opening, Kayla had gifted Connor with a helicopter. A helicopter for God's sake. It had landed right there in the back lot and stood for all to admire, in the gleam of hastily rigged landing lights. Getting a landing permit in the middle of the city had required a small fortune in bribes dressed up as fees, and likewise finding a pilot available on a couple of hours' notice, but they'd done it. And through it all, all of them truly thought it would keep going like this forever. She should have known. Connor always told her to make hay when the making was good *because it wouldn't last.*

That night, no one cared to think about that. The building had been dressed up like Snow White for the ball. Form over function, make it look pretty. Hide the unmentionable stuff. Another one of Connor's one-liners.

Rafael, on the other hand, had done real work here, she realized. Rafael, the guy who had always been happy to follow around behind Connor, to shake hands, smile, and nod. He had dug in here and made something of the place. More than she had ever dared dream of, more possibly than even Connor had thought of.

Two ladies sat at Reception, one speaking intently into her headset, making notes, the other smiling with the kind of encouragement designed to take the weirdness out of visiting a manufacturing plant for medical marijuana for the first time.

The generous entrance area looked more like an exclusive medical clinic and spa than a manufacturing facility of any type, and doors, frames, and even the floors gleamed and sparkled in white, stainless steel, and chrome. A cheerful green carpet runner snaked around to indicate the shape of a leaf and led the way right up to the front of the reception desk. Somewhere in the background, soothing mellow music played; a fountain set into a little alcove burbled away merrily. No expense had been spared to make the visitor more comfortable. Less aware that they were standing in the foyer of a major pharmaceutical manufacturer.

If you looked closely—and Tessa always looked—you could spot the little security cameras that kept an invisible eye on everything and anything and the electronic access pads next to every door leading out of the foyer. A person who didn't have business here would never get any further than this charming front hall. And somewhere at hand, she suspected a well-trained group of security personnel would deal with them, quickly, efficiently—quietly. *Well as they should,* she thought and shuddered a little.

Roberto had lost sight of where the fine line was. If something were possible, he was ready to give it a shot, and never mind the legalities. Quickest way to lose your growing license, but Roberto didn't really think that far. No further than the money a little illegal side grow would provide him with anyway. Connor, Rafael, or Al could deal with the government and its endless rules, requirements, and forms.

But you executed, Rafael, Tess thought, still looking around taking in the entire place. *You really executed this time.* Of all the startup businesses Barry, Rafael, and she had been in together, all the IPOs they had done—and this one had made it. Execution and a functioning, ongoing business concern.

She took a deep breath, straightened her shoulders, and slowly walked toward the reception counter when one of the doors to the manufacturing floor opened, and Al Ivers emerged.

She had known Al mostly as an investor—a decidedly strange person, shrouded in stories and myths, who came in with a wad of cash to invest, signed some papers, and left again—but he too had changed.

Gone were the odd affectations that were designed to keep him in the shadows and apart from everyone else. This Al, she realized, didn't need the myth of being a man who never used a computer or cell phone, and never wrote anything down for fear of being tracked. This Al Ivers naturally commanded authority and respect.

He signaled briefly to the ladies at the Reception and came out to meet her. "Tessa Goodwin," he said by way of greeting. "I didn't think I'd see the day…"

"It's been a long time, Al." She reached out to shake his hand, and it took him just the barest of moments to accept.

"A lot of time and a lot of history," he said, nodding. "Rafael recommended I work with you, although…"

You're not sure, she wanted to say. *You know where I've been and who I've spoken to,* she wanted to say, but for once, she held her usually quick tongue.

"I have a few reservations," Al finally finished. "Roberto…"

"Your brother is incredibly charming and equally convincing when he wants to be," Tessa said, feeling her cheeks flush just a little. "And right up until that board meeting, I didn't actually realize he was your brother."

Al waved a hand, wiping away her comment, and forced a smile.

"Others have fallen for his act, and I know it's a convincing one. He's quick and well-spoken. Now, Rafael appears to trust you. So, much as I am somewhat reluctant, I'll go along. To a certain extent, mind you. Right at the moment, we could use you and your experience. The house is on fire, so to speak."

Tessa nodded. "I'm sorry about your father."

Another waggle of the hand, as he put his hand behind her and lightly guided her toward the back of the building, through the security doors.

"Thanks. I'm sure at some point, I will actually be able to think about it. Right now…"

"You have a company that's in tatters once again, and you need to put it back together. Understood."

"No, actually," Al said with a tiny smile, "I have two companies, both somewhat tattered, which need to be married into a seamless whole, despite the fact that no one trusts the other guy, a handful of important people are still considered persons of interest in a murder investigation, and then there is Barry…"

"Oh, there always is Barry." Tessa smiled at his phrase.

People had been using words to that effect for as long as she could remember. Whether he called himself Connor or Barry, the man had a singular talent to get into situations—cause situations, quite frequently—that resulted in a huge mess. A mess others would need to clean up, and it was inevitably bound to take more time and energy than anyone had assumed.

"Are you sure you're comfortable with this situation? I understand you and Connor were—close at some point."

"At some point. But, no, it wasn't like that, and I will be just fine."

The moment between them stretched, silent and deep until it was almost uncomfortable, and then another few heartbeats, and Al finally nodded.

"I will keep a close eye on you, you know that, right? First sign I get of trouble..." He cocked his head toward the door they had just passed.

"Didn't expect anything else," Tessa confirmed.

"Just tell me this one thing. After you'd been working with Rafael and Barry for years and years—at least that's what I've heard—suddenly, you just turn on them and throw your lot in with my father? Explain that one to me. I just want to understand."

"There is nothing to understand, Al. OK if I call you Al?"

"It is my name."

"There's nothing to understand," Tess said, bristling a little. She took a step back to put some distance between her and Al and raised her hands beside her head. "Maybe you don't get it because you can't. You were born into money. You don't know what it's like, living paycheck to paycheck—and startup businesses..." She laughed bitterly. "Startup businesses are great when they start up. Then you hit tight spots, and tight spots grow into dry spells, and suddenly, there is no money. Anywhere. I was about ready to live on the street, and there comes your father, offering me what I needed most—money. He gave me more money than I had ever seen before, and I took it. It was dirty, and I knew that. But I did what I had to do to survive, and I stick to it. Is that OK with you?"

Al nodded slowly and closed the distance between them again, standing squarely before her for a long moment. Finally, he smiled and offered a hand.

"Excuses I wouldn't have been able to handle. Same goes for betrayal. You gave me what I needed to hear—the truth."

"Such as it is."

"The truth and a reason. Don't assume I don't know what economic need is all about, Tessa. There are things no one knows and won't ever know. Now I need you to get a temporary badge at HR because you can't come in here without one, and I'm not picking you up every time. Tell them I will send a consulting agreement to back everything up. Then come back to see me. I need you to start working this minute, if you're up for it."

"I am."

Tessa nodded and spread her hands, spinning a half-circle in the hallway. "Where do I go?"

***

"I think the growers, chemists, and geneticists are going to be OK for a little bit," Al said a good half hour later in his office overlooking the manufacturing floor. "The plants are growing, and for the rest they can compare notes—Dante and Nick are down there. It's not perfect, but it works. Here is where I need you…"

He opened the door to the office next to his and pointed to a large folding table covered in binders. Rows of binders stacked three deep and four across. Beside that, there were a few little stacks and towers and a trolley full of folders and bound documents.

"Welcome to Financial and Admin."

"All—hard copy?" Tessa asked, blanching a bit. "You ever hear of the digital age? Putting this stuff on servers everyone who needs it can access, search if needed?"

"We have, but this is two companies' worth of documentation. PerCan and Mariposa. We need to find a way to integrate the whole mess and we need to do it quickly. If you need 17 people to scan all of this in, let me know. I need a road map, and I need it yesterday."

"Sh… Shoot. This is going to take a while." Tessa advanced on the binders and opened a few in the top row. She read the titles, tried to make sense and order of what she was seeing, moved one to the side, and opened the one below.

"I need time, Al."

"We don't have time," he said, suddenly closer behind her than he had been before. "That is one luxury we don't have, Tessa. What I need are people to help me make sense of this. Rafael says I can trust you. What do you think?"

"I think—aw, man, Al." Tessa wheeled away from the binders and ran her hands through her hair. "You don't ask the easy shit, do you? First of all—first of all, I need a few high-speed, double-sided scanners. The good ones. Then I need a few kids to work 'em. Preferably the kind who don't ask any questions, just take orders."

Al chuckled and rubbed his hands.

"You got it."

"Then I need somebody to go to my apartment, get my computer rig, and set it up in here. I'm going to start going through this sh… uh, stuff."

"We are in the process of setting up the IT department. I can easily have someone assign a laptop or workstation to you."

"I know." Tessa shrugged. "But that's not going to do it. To analyze all of this…" Her finger spun around all of the binders in various stacks and piles. "I need a very specialized software setup. One I already have because I know the guy who developed it."

"IT will want to strangle me for bringing in an outside computer that hasn't been checked."

"And it won't be. Hacking into your system is the last thing I want to spend 10 minutes on right now."

Al's eyes flashed just a little, and she grinned.

"Joking, just joking, OK? IT will just have to un-bunch their panties here."

"I have a feeling it will take—a bit of time to get used to you," Al said just a little stiffly, and this time, Tessa grinned broadly.

"I get that a lot. But I finally get a chance to make things up to Rafael, so let's get to it—boss."

She offered her hand to Al, and her face fell when he refused to take it. A moment passed and another, and a faint smile spread on Al's face.

Finally, he raised his hand and offered it to her, and Tessa took it in a hard grip.

"This is what we do, Al. So hang on to your hat, and hang on tight, 'cause it's going to get a bit intense in here."

"Scan it if you must, but go over this material, understand it, and divide it into work groups. While you're at it, check every document, for nothing necessarily specific, but anything that 'doesn't look right' or 'might be wrong.' Then help me assign working groups with people from each company, who will study it again, fix what needs fixing, and generate one unified whole. Sounds easy?"

"Sounds like a party all day long. Now let me crack into it."

They shook hands, and Al turned for the door. He had no doubt that Tessa could handle what he had given her. After all, this was what she had been doing for years upon years for Rafael and Barry, organizing their companies, their papers, and sometimes even their lives. He opened the door to issue the orders that would get her the equipment and people she needed, then turned around again for a moment.

"While you're at it," he said almost too casually, "going through this mess in there. Somewhere in that pile, there is an agreement whereby my father, on behalf of this company, paid a million dollars for a merger that never happened to a fella by the name of Greg Turner, Green Technologies. When you find it, drop everything and come running. I want it, and I want that money back."

"You got it, du…"

167

Al raised two index fingers. "Before you call me dude, just stop. Nobody ever calls me dude, and that's final."

He left the room followed by Tessa's raucous laughter, and when the door slammed behind him, Tessa finally yelled, "Dude. You got it, dude." Then she turned onto the stacks of paper in front of her and slapped her palms on top of them, flat.

"You are going to be gone, all of you," she said with an evil grin. "And if somewhere in here a million dollars are hiding? Guess what? I am gonna find you."

SEVENTEEN

Was he in darkness or in light? Were his eyes merely closed, or were they open, and he had gone blind? Could he move? Could he move if he wanted to? Did he want to move? Barry Wentworth allowed himself to drift a little—through clouds, big puffy white clouds that carried him safely, off to nowhere. He heard voices now and then, and he heard the shrieking sound of rending metal again, the one that told him he was going down. Down much faster than he had planned, faster and faster, spinning around and around on the way.

Wait—shouldn't he be…? The clouds came back, and a moment later, he didn't hear any sounds anymore.

It might have been seconds, hours, or days before he asked himself those very same questions again. This time, he tried to force at least one eye open, and daylight rewarded him with a piercing stab of brightness. *Check one*, he thought, closing his eyes again. He hadn't gone blind. He told himself to wiggle a toe, and his blanket moved awkwardly. *Check two.* He kept his eyes closed and forced himself to listen, really listen, with the attention of one who truly was blind.

He heard the sound of machinery behind him, clicking and beeping away, the far-off sounds of people coming and going, a chemical smell he knew. Conclusion: he was probably in a hospital. No surprise there. He did remember crashing a plane.

That thought almost made him chuckle. Almost, because the simple act of breathing rewarded him with a hard stab in the side, which likely meant he had broken a couple of ribs. Ribs healed. Depending on how much other damage he had done, internally or externally…

He wiggled his eyebrows a few times and moved his head back and forth on the pillow, ascertaining that someone had placed a massive bandage on his head. So, he had bashed his head up fairly well, too. Voices, voices reasonably close. So he lay perfectly still again, resisting the urge to open his eyes when he heard the sound of an opening door.

Too soon, his cautious side screamed. Too soon to tip his hand and let them know he was back amongst the living again, whatever that meant. *Assess the situation and find a way out first.* He made himself melt back into the pillows and breathe evenly, deeply, like he had as a kid, pretending to be asleep when there were chores to be done.

"He's still out of it," a man said.

That voice, he'd spoken to him before, and he knew he didn't like him. Robertson. Detective Robertson. Whatever else he had done to himself, his brain still worked.

Of course the good detective would be sniffing around here, and the moment Barry opened his eyes, he'd likely want to arrest him. Another reason to keep his eyes shut, at least for now.

"He shouldn't be." A slightly concerned voice.

A woman this one. Likely the nurse. Soft-soled steps came closer, and with a rustle of clothing and a tap on what had to be the instruments above his head, she checked on him.

"I was expecting him to be conscious, wanting to know what was going on. I am not sure why…"

"I'll just wait here."

The scrape of a chair.

No, not right here, he thought. *I need to figure out a few things before I can deal with you. Do not sit your fat ass there on that chair in my room.*

Something above him beeped, and Concerned Voice Nurse came a step closer again.

"I don't think that's a good idea. His vitals are all over the place all of a sudden. Whatever is going on inside his head, he needs a bit more time—alone time. It would be best if you waited outside."

That's right, make the little ass wait outside. Away from me—far away. Until I figure out what's what.

"I can't just…"

"There's a waiting room just down the hall, Detective, and he is not going to get out of this bed and disappear on you. That kind of stuff only happens in the movies. Besides, with several broken ribs and broken legs, he wouldn't get all that far, now would he?"

She had a damn good point. Whatever figuring out he had to do, he had better do it right here in this bed and be ready when they called his bluff with the closed eyes.

Fact one: this detective thought he had killed Tadeo Ivers, and he had some dumbass evidence to support his demented conclusion. Like Barry was the only man to carry a gun in this city. Fact two: he had tried to get away and failed miserably. Crashed Moody's plane.

If that idiot Moody hadn't put more bells and whistles on that plane than a high school marching band, a man might actually have been able to fly the thing—but no. Somewhere along the line, all the beeps and tweets from the cockpit had irritated him to the point that he slapped and turned buttons and dials just to shut it up. Wrong move. Wrong move if you insisted on faulting him for something. After that, the ground had come up at him hard and fast, and he couldn't right the plane again, no matter how hard he tried.

He would, however, take credit for spotting a cornfield while all of this panic was going on and dropping Moody's plane in there instead of on the highway. He didn't think he would have survived that! What he should have done was ignore the sound, keep his hands on the steering column, and fly the damn plane, and he'd have been well on his way to a safe hideout by now.

If he could have, he would have reached out and slapped himself. His company was being taken away from him for the second time while he sat there not being able to do one damn thing about it.

Last time, misleading evidence and dumb conclusions. This time? Guess what—same thing, history repeating itself in all its glory. Goddammit, how was he getting out of this one? He needed a story, and it needed to be good.

Number one: the gun. *Mr. Wentworth, how do you explain the illegal handgun you purchased from a street dealer?* he imagined a judge asking of him. How? Give them a good answer. *Because I am surrounded by assholes, and I needed some backup?* Dismiss that. *Security—because my so-called partner, the victim's son, was running amok? Because I needed that gun to hang on to in case Roberto did something totally stupid, just because I didn't make him an executive?* Scratch that, too. He could almost hear his hypocritical, hard-nosed, imaginary judge dismissing that particular excuse. So, what could serve as a decent excusable reason for owning a gun then? One no one could argue with? Being afraid for your life cut it, right? After all, he was working in a dangerous business and with dangerous people. Hmm, that got a bit closer. Hard to argue with that.

What a dumb idea, buying that gun in the first place, he thought, remembering the slimy little street dealer. It had a 100 percent chance of going sideways. *You just don't learn,* he lectured himself, bitterly realizing that he sounded like his own father.

You are incapable of learning, my son, which means I have to teach you. Usually followed by some type of corporal punishment.

One needed protection—at all times—but there were smarter ways than buying a gun from a shady dealer who would have reason to cut a deal on the inside of 24 hours flat.

Could he say someone had threatened him, anonymous phone calls, maybe? Letters that threatened his life? If he could get his hands on a threatening letter, he'd be in business. Yes. Hard to argue with that, right? Oh, sure, they could tell him to go to the authorities—but hey, he was a man just about to take over one of the biggest manufacturers of medical marijuana in the country. If someone threatened him... In that case, it only made sense to take steps to protect himself.

Barry allowed himself to relax a little. Closer to an explanation now. Good. Someone had threatened his life, and that was why he had purchased protection. Could have gone the legal route and purchased from an official store and acquired a license, but time was of the essence. The threats were getting worse. That was good. Now to fill in the little details that made his story believable. Little details that most people missed or ignored, but Barry Wentworth did not. Most importantly, the police detective did not. Letters, he needed letters—he needed someone to make up a few threatening letters for him and put them into his hotel room. Who? Who would do it for him? Who to ask?

His brain clicked through his mental rolodex when he heard the door open once again.

"Don't worry, Nurse. I'll just stay a moment. I won't upset the patient."

Barry Wentworth had to fight the shit-eating grin that wanted to bloom on his face. Oh, yes. He had a friend who would do anything for him, correct. And Heaven had sent him just in the nick of time. *Thank you, Lord.*

A chair scraping close by and the rustle of fabric. A man settling in, a deep sigh. "You do have a talent for getting yourself into tight spots, my friend."

"What fun would playing it safe be?"

The searing brightness almost blinding him was still worth seeing the stunned look on Rafael's face.

"Don't worry, not dead."

"Well, I—wow, they said you weren't… You couldn't—didn't…"

Same old Rafael. Throw him an unexpected curve ball and he would fumble. Every. Time. Still, you couldn't ask for a better wingman. One who'd have your back and save your life if needed.

"Relax, just woke up."

Bit of a white lie, but worth it. Besides, the rough and raspy sound of his voice would make anybody believe.

"I need you."

"I'll say. Barry, I'm not even going to ask what you were thinking—taking off in Irv's plane, never mind that whole business about you buying a gun. Do you know how guilty that makes you look?"

"I didn't do it."

He struggled to sit up, fighting against blankets, tubes, wires, and not to mention his miscellaneous pains, splints, and bandages.

"Good one. I didn't do it, your honor." Rafael rolled his eyes. "For what it's worth, I neither thought nor suggested you did. But to anyone else, this just looks bad. Real bad. And the moment he realizes you're awake, that detective is going to come running in here…"

"Moron."

Barry coughed heavily and let his body sink back into the supporting pillows.

"Moron or not, he found a dealer who supposedly sold you a gun, and then you went on the run. I am fast running out of ways to explain things to him, if I ever could."

Barry closed his eyes, took a deep and theatrical breath, and waved his right hand before his face, fighting emotion, pain.

"You OK? Want me to call the nurse?"

"No, I'm good." He opened his eyes again, forcing a smile. "After all, I did buy that gun, Rafa."

"Why in God's name? There was only one way this was going to look."

Rafael sat straight back in the chair and cocked his head to one side. Barry knew, in his world, people didn't buy a gun just because,

because they felt better having it, because it might be a good idea, because maybe—just maybe—down the road, there might be a reason to use it. No. In Rafael's world, if you bought a gun, you had every intention of using it on your fellow man or woman. *Careful, careful now*, Barry thought, *make him believe. Spin it just right.*

"I know," he said, and closed his eyes just long enough. "I know it looks bad. But there were—people…"

Think of something, something a little better.

"I had a suspicion that little prick Mirko would come out of the woodwork at some point. Look, you're just going to have to…"

The rest of Rafael's sentence trailed off as Barry's mind raced through his memories until he placed the name. Mirko! Bingo. Thank you, God.

He had not heard of, thought of, or mentioned the creepy little loan shark in years. Mirko Rabino-something. Whatever. The best bad guy borrowed-and-never-paid-back money could buy. Of course, Mirko. He was owed money, he had shown up threatening havoc before, and, best of all, he was never coming out of the woodwork to claim otherwise.

Mirko, welcome to my story. You've just been upgraded to gun-toting blackmailer. Don't mind if I do.

He groaned deeply and shook his head a bit, just enough to make the starched white linen crackle.

"I know," he said softly. "I shouldn't…"

"We've been there. You shouldn't have borrowed money from a loan shark. Yada, yada. Yesterday's news. What made him waltz on in here and threaten you again anyway?"

"I do—still owe him."

"No, as a matter of fact, the company does. If at all. If there was a proper loan contract and agreements and…"

No, actually, I secretly gave him an equity position in your building. Wonder whatever happened to that, Barry thought. *I guess old Ivers took care of it, his way. Do I care? No.* Barry shivered at the concept of Ivers taking care of things. If that indeed were the case, one wouldn't have to worry about Mirko Whatshisbucket any longer, but then he would hardly make such a perfect villain here. And he needed a villain. Again, he smiled weakly and waved a hand.

"I guess he wanted his money, and I can't blame him. He is owed."

"There are proper channels to deal with that."

For a loan shark? Right. "Maybe."

"Not maybe. But no matter. That Detective Robertson wanted to know why you bought a gun and left town, here you go. That's why."

"I'm afraid it's not that easy, Rafael."

"Didn't say it was easy. You just show him… Show him… Er, you don't have anything but this story, do you?"

You catch on quickly, Rafael. And you know me only too well. No, I don't have anything but this story. But since when have I ever needed more than the story? Since when was the story not enough? He closed his eyes and shook his head softly.

"I don't have anything…"

"What exactly happened then?"

"There were a couple of guys who came to me, late at night… and… You know what, Rafael? I wasn't really in a position to ask them to document their demands."

"Just relax, relax, Barry. We'll fix this."

Barry sighed and waited. Thank heavens for the guardian spirit that had sent Rafael in here today. If there was one thing Rafael was good at, it was fixing things. Maybe he secretly enjoyed it, cleaning up a mess, setting it straight again. Who knew? Everybody had these secret little things they enjoyed, right? And Rafael just couldn't help himself. Even when he, Barry, didn't even ask him to, he would always step in, shake his head, and roll up his sleeves to fix things, grousing all the way. You needed those kinds of people.

"Mirko threatened us at the grand opening. I guess I should have expected it," he said softly. "But now you understand why I got a gun and got the hell out of Dodge."

Rafael got to his feet now, taking a few steps back on forth in the tiny space. His mind was likely churning and running through the story Barry had constructed for him—just like old times. Rafael did make a good follower, always had.

"But the question is—why is there no evidence?"

"That's a good question and one I would like to hear an answer to, Mr. Covin. Nice to see you awake, Mr. Wentworth."

Shit, shit, triple shit. Of all the bad moments in the world, this one had to be the worst for Detective Robertson to come marching into his room. He had him—he'd almost had Rafael where he needed him. If he could have made Rafael believe, he would have been halfway home.

"Detective," he managed to croak while his mind clocked away at 100 miles an hour looking for the way out. "Long time."

"Not long enough, Mr. Wentworth. I know I don't have to tell you why I am here." Barry shook his head.

"I am here to arrest you and take you in when you are well enough to be moved, so we can take our time figuring out why you were wandering around town with a gun the day Tadeo Ivers was shot and why you felt you had to steal an airplane trying to evade questioning and eventual prosecution. I am going to have a detective stationed outside your room at all times. I am sure you understand that. As for you…" He turned on Rafael, who raised his hands, palms out.

"I came here to visit a friend who has been through a plane crash, that's all."

"A plane crash he caused while flying without permission and without a license. Let's add that to his list of offenses."

Rafael shrugged. "These little things are dangerous. I don't know how often I've told Irv Moody that."

"And that is the only reason you are here?" Detective Robertson closed in on Rafael a little.

"Do I need a lawyer?"

"Smart answer, wrong way to put it," Barry muttered, and both the detective and Rafael turned back to him. "It's true. You don't ask if you need a lawyer. You always need one where the police are involved. Period."

"Especially when there are guns in play, right, Mr. Wentworth?"

The detective stepped a little closer and looked down at Barry. "Now, I am sure you have an interesting story to tell me about that gun. Because that is what you do, tell stories, is it not?"

"I think this is going a bit far," Rafael said, quickly stepping forward a bit as well. "Certainly, you're not calling him a liar, are you?"

"Not outright, but..."

Barry waggled his fingers, calming down Rafael, and smiled as brightly as he could.

"It's all easily explained, Detective, no need to get excited. PerCan is doing reasonably well right now, but there was a time when it did not, and we were in dire need of funds..."

"A time when you were in charge."

Another bright smile and a half shrug. "Startup companies—that's life, no matter who is in charge, Detective. Only a small percentage of them make it. That's a well-known fact."

"Back to PerCan?"

"Back to PerCan. We needed funds—desperately. It was that or go under, so we borrowed some money from some, shall we say, less-than-reputable characters?"

"A loan shark. You went to a loan shark. Is that what you're telling me?"

"Tomato, tomahto." Again, Barry smiled. "We had no other choice. Yes, it was a Hail Mary pass. Most likely, it was unwise, but there you have it. We did. How could I know that upon my return, those people would—let's say—pay me a visit? And mention there was an unpaid balance?"

"One that I am sure you were completely unaware of," the detective said, folding his hands with a smile. "I have to say..." He shook his head.

"Careful, Detective, you have a bit of sarcasm on your chin there." Barry sat up a little straighter, and so did Rafael.

"Well then, there you are, Detective. We had a loan shark after us, hence the protection. And while it was probably equally unadvised for Barry to run, you don't exactly have a reputation for believing him."

"The two of you." The detective took a small step back to keep them both in view and shook his head. "Like a lousy two-man comedy routine. Do people actually fall for this and give you money?"

"Detective…"

"Mr. Covin, number one, as you so succinctly mentioned when I walked in, there is absolutely no evidence to back up this yarn about a rogue loan shark threatening you, or you would have handed it to me on a silver platter right now. Number two, explain to me why a creditor who is owed money wouldn't simply knock at the door of PerCan, where there are actual assets, show a letter of demand, and ask to be paid."

"Comedy routine," Rafael scoffed and looked at Barry for help that was not forthcoming. "And you didn't let us finish," he finished weakly. "There's more."

"There always is more, Rafael, and I will hear it, but why don't we get back to your involvement then?"

"I don't have any involvement here."

"No? Well, for starters, if this unidentified loan shark who loaned money to the company, not you personally, was really such a fearsome character you had to arm yourself in secret, why is this the first time I hear of him? One thinks you might have mentioned him before now. And number two—and this one really is a biggie, so watch out. Number two, you claim you never left the house the night Tadeo Ivers was shot."

Rafael physically pushed back, palms out. "I did not," he said, frowning. "It might be a feeble excuse, but I think I was far too drunk to go anywhere that night."

"Really?"

The detective suddenly smiled with smugness neither one of them liked. He had something up his sleeve, and whatever it was, it was big. Scratch that. It was massive, or he wouldn't make such a big deal out of it. Rafael felt a cold fist clench around his gut and a shiver pass down his spine. What had he got himself into now? Goddammit, if he only had listened to Kayla and kept his mouth wide shut unless that lawyer fellow was close by.

Or maybe stayed home in the first place—too late now. This detective here had a way of weaseling things out of you. Stuff you never meant to say in the first place. *He is a moron*, Barry had said, dismissing the man, but at the moment, he was a moron holding some information they had seriously underestimated.

"It's a little too late to add a DUI here now, but I'm sure we will manage without it just fine, don't you think?"

He reached into his portfolio and pulled out a single printed sheet. Forcing himself to breathe and acting as if he couldn't care less, Rafael glanced down at it. And he had been right. This was going to be bad.

"Rafael?"

Finally, he looked down at the sheet again and covered his mouth. Barry didn't bother. He'd leaned back in his pillows, eyes closed, and shook his head.

Right there in the detective's hands was a picture. A printout of a photo, to be exact, but there it was in grainy black-and-white. Rafael's Mercedes, the one with the ding in the fender. Some lousy parking job at some construction site he didn't remember. But that stupid ding mocked him now because the Merc was standing right there in the middle of the parking lot of Ivers's diner, and the time stamp in the lower right-hand corner showed a time of 10 p.m. A time he didn't remember clearly, although he'd been pretty sure he'd been in bed back then, passed out from exhaustion and alcohol.

"Where did you get this?" he asked, marveling at how damn guilty and frightened he sounded all of a sudden. This wasn't him. This just so wasn't him, dammit. *Straighten your shoulders, Covin.*

"I don't know where you got this picture," he finally said with as much conviction as he could muster. "But that's got to be either a fake, or somebody grabbed my car and put it there."

"Indeed. While you were sleeping? Without you noticing or saying anything about it? And when that great unknown person was done with your car, he—what? Just put it back into your driveway? Broke back into your house and put the keys in your pocket? Is that what happened?"

"Rafael never puts car keys into his pocket," Barry defended him. "He loses them, so they're always under the mat of the front seat."

"How convenient. I'll remember that next time I need a set of wheels."

The detective wasn't buying any of it, and Rafael still stared down at the picture. That was his car all right, no point in denying that one. That was Tadeo's old "family diner," no point in denying that either.

"You still haven't told me where you got this picture," he heard himself say. All of the bravado had gone out of his voice, and damn if he didn't sound defensive as shit, but what he was feeling was none of this man's business. *Matter of fact, why don't we stop cheerfully cooperating right now?* Rafael tapped the picture in the detective's hand.

"I have a niece who can turn you into Captain Kirk from the Starship *Enterprise* on Photoshop, so I'm pretty sure whoever did this is good. Great even. But it has got to be a fake."

"Nice try, Rafael. But this one is from the security camera from a warehouse directly across the street."

Rafael stared down at the picture, trying to make his brain snap into gear. This couldn't be, right? Any minute now, any second, as a matter of fact, he would hit upon that one reason why it couldn't be.

"We've been canvassing the area for any business that might have a security camera trained on that lot, Rafael. So, before you tell me this is a fake…"

"Wait, and this comes out now?" Barry jumped in. "Nobody keeps security footage longer than a day or so." He sat up as much as his various bandages and supply lines would let him and shook his head. "That's a little weak, don't you think?"

"Not really, Barry, not really. What's weak are the excuses the two of you are making. So, with all due respect, I am going to take Rafael here with me right now, and you will just follow when you are well enough to be transported. We'll keep you in custody for the moment, just until we get this all sorted out."

EIGHTEEN

Kayla Montecito prided herself on being calm and collected most of the time. Even though she ran a magazine most would describe as a gossip rag, even though many of her contributing writers and photographers were of the variety best described as slimy or even smarmy, Kayla stayed on top of it and kept them all in line. She made sure the magazine never printed anything that was blatantly wrong or hurtful to someone, she worked to keep things tantalizing and interesting while staying in good taste, and she did not lose her temper. Never. Ever.

Enough books and articles had been written about women in the publishing industry who were all but toxic that she had sworn not to fall into this very trap. Kayla Montecito stayed above all of that. Tasteful, classy, and always calm.

Until somebody actually arrested her partner. Then all bets went out the window, and Kayla became a force of nature that no one had counted on.

"I want Rafael out," she said, carefully enunciating every single word. "Do you understand me, Richard?"

"Yes, I do—but there's evidence…"

"Undermine it. It's false or fake. I know they think he did it." Her voice was so deceptively soft and gentle, if one missed the clenched fist.

"And I also don't care. You're our lawyer. Make it happen."

"Miss Montecito."

"I also don't care what it costs. I don't care what I have to sign or sell. Just get him out of lockup. Do you understand?"

"I will do my best," her lawyer said with a careless nod, as he already groped for his paperwork.

"Wrong, Richard. Dead wrong." Her lawyer's head snapped up. "You will do your best—then you will go back, find a few things you haven't done yet, and do those. And when you are done with that…"

"I understand, Kayla. You want Rafael out, but it is not going to be easy."

"Then work harder. If it were easy, I would be a damned fool for paying for the best legal advice in the county."

Richard Marks's hands stuffed paperwork into a folder with quick and jerky movements.

"Let me get to work on this."

"And when you have Rafael out of there," she continued, not taking her eyes off him, "then I need you to work on his defense. Full time. To the exclusion of everything else. You will put together the best team my money can buy. Is that understood?"

"Understood."

"I also want you to collaborate with a young lady over at Perfect Cannabis. Her name is Tess Goodwin. I am told she can work miracles on a computer."

"But…" Kayla's forefinger came up, silencing any objection he might have had.

"OK—yes."

"I am told the picture came from a surveillance camera somewhere on the street. Find out who. Find out what their game is."

"Their game?"

"Richard, catch up with me here, will you? Obviously, this picture is a fake. It isn't Rafael. You know that, and I know that. Ergo, someone faked it. Ergo, that person has a game plan. I want to know who, and I want to know what that game plan is. And if there's any money to be paid…"

"As your attorney, I can't be hearing this," Richard said quickly and put his hands over his ears.

"Understood. Just make it clear that money isn't the obstacle most people will think it is."

"OK."

Again, he rose and reached for his briefcase.

"Furthermore, I need you to cooperate with a man by the name of Sandro."

"Sandro?"

"He is a private investigator who works for Al Ivers, also at Perfect Cannabis. Get in touch with him, find out what he's got. Make sure he shares it with us."

"OK."

He looked as if he might be quite ill in a moment. Working together with a computer hacker and a private investigator on a murder charge. This was not really what he had envisioned when he became the lawyer in charge of Montecito Publishing.

"Is this a problem for you, Richard? You are a corporate lawyer, not a criminal defense attorney. Perhaps I should assign co-counsel..."

"Our law firm is big enough," he assured her. "You're coming at me pretty hard, and criminal law is not my specialty, but we'll handle it."

He straightened up a bit more and managed a smile again.

Sure you can, Kayla thought. He probably counted on all of the publicity this case had already gathered and would gather as it went forward. Who killed Tadeo Ivers? A whole city wanted to know—the entire cannabis community wanted to know—and Michael would be there. Best advertising you could find. Unless he failed, of course.

"We'll handle it," he said quickly. "Don't you worry. I will work with the best criminal defense guy our firm has on the masthead. I have to go."

"You do that, Richard. And keep me updated—about everything! I am going to go home and order dinner. For two people. Make sure there will be two consuming it."

***

On the other end of town, Al finally battled his way through the building to the tiny little supply office where Tess had barricaded herself, analyzing mountains of data. Tess didn't want any help, any company, or anyone to know where she was to be found, and that sat just fine with Al. What he needed from her were results—no matter how she got there.

No matter how she got there. Why was that normal all of a sudden? Wasn't that what had started the trouble with his father in the first place? He well remembered the look of triumph on the old man's face when he bragged how he'd managed to pay off Connor Beauregard's controller, and she'd given him all the secrets money could buy, and then some. *I won*, he'd said. *I won, and they will never know what hit them.*

Al had always wondered what it was in the end that made her turn on her bosses, although money was usually a good guess.

They had all worked together in that tiny office downtown, Connor, Rafael, and Tess. And as far as anyone could tell, those two rooms were it. The entire compact operation. Who did what—who knew? Who kept control on anything? Nobody? He had scared the pants off Tess when he had delivered their investment money to her at the beginning. In cash. In a brown envelope, just for the fun of it.

Al slowed down and allowed the memory to have one moment. He'd walked into her office and delivered half a million dollars to her, 'to get the company started.' How naïve they had all been back then. Medical marijuana—that seemed like such a fantastic business to get into.

Sure, let's all be drug dealers.

He'd known Rafael, and Rafa had talked him into it easily enough. He, Al, hadn't really wanted to invest, but his father—oh, Tadeo was all over that one. He'd been sick and tired of bars and strip clubs then. Gangs were moving in on him. Quick pivot, let's be drug dealers.

Besides, every biker in a 100-mile radius was somehow or other indebted to Tadeo, and somebody had to keep the bikers out of the legal marijuana business, right?

And then…

And then Connor had lost all reasonable perspective, and Rafael had finally become serious and started to run the company. He fought it in the beginning, but Tadeo didn't really leave him a choice, so he sat down and learned how to run a marijuana manufacturer.

Rafael, a man who came out of the construction business. Nobody thought it would last, but Rafael had done it, and he'd done it well. Somewhere along the line, he and Al had become friends while trying to put things right, only to see it all go down the drain again.

Al pushed open the door to Tessa's little domain and entered without pausing.

"You know what I need, right?"

"Oh, hello, Al. Nice to see you, why don't you come in—sit down while you're at it."

Tessa never looked up from the computer screen she stared at, one of three clustered around her, all running, all busy doing something or other, impossible for him to tell what it was other than lines of code spooling slowly downward.

"No sarcasm, Tess, please." This time she did look up.

"Did the great Al Ivers just say please to me?"

"Tess…"

"I know, OK?" She sliced her hand through the air, cutting off any reply. "You don't have to spell it out. It is not Rafael—it can't be Rafael. This is complete bullshit, and there has to be some evidence out there."

"Well?"

"What do I look like, Houdini?"

"Houdini was an escape artist."

"Pick another magician then—anyone. Not me." She leaned back in her chair and whipped black, heavy-rimmed reading glasses off her face. "Anybody but me. I don't know, Al. These…" She pointed at the grainy pictures of Rafael's vehicle in the diner's parking lot. "These look pretty goddamn real to me. If somebody messed with them, even I can't tell."

"That's not what I want to hear."

"Tell me something I don't know."

Tessa put her hands behind her back to stretch out a kink and shook her head.

"Rafael did not shoot Tadeo," Al said, his eyes flashing. "I know this as well as I know my own name."

"Ivers? Funny that, same as the victim, your father."

"And he and Rafael had their differences. But he didn't shoot him, end of story. Now prove it."

"Then give me something, Al. Help me come up with an explanation for why his car is there in the diner parking lot, in the middle of the night." Tessa stabbed a finger at one of the screens in front of her and the security camera footage. "Anything, Al, I'll take it."

"He's been there before. Plenty of times. In the middle of the night. Maybe the time stamp is wrong, faked somehow—I don't know. You're the computer expert. Rafael said…"

"Rafael said I could do just about everything with a computer. He does that. He counts on me. You don't think that bothers me?" Tess punched her desk, making it rattle, hard. "The one time he needs for me to be there for him, I strike out. You don't think it pisses me the hell off?"

She pushed pack from her desk violently and spread her hands.

"It fucking drives me insane, but if there's something there, I haven't found it yet, OK? And I can't make up something just because you and I think—know."

"Easy, easy, Tess. We can stand in this room swearing at one another and fighting all day long. It won't get us results any quicker."

"Then get off my case and don't stand there telling me you need results."

Al said nothing, just sat silently with his hands folded while the minutes ticked by.

"There are a couple analyses I can do," Tessa finally said, peering at the screens again.

"Good... But?"

"But here's the thing. If this is that well done... right? So well that my best software is having trouble finding the tiniest little flaw...?"

"Yes?"

"Then somebody spent one hell of a lot of money on this. I mean real money. I mean a luxury car or a small house kind of money."

"And?"

"For what, Al—three pictures? I don't get it."

"I think we can safely worry about the reasons behind why it was done once we find out that indeed it was done, and perhaps by whom."

"I know." Tess rolled back slowly until she sat straight in front of her terminals again and dragged 10 fingers through her hair. "I know—just keep trying, right, keep showing up until you wrestle the bastard down?"

"As long as there are still a few things you can do to find out what happened—yes, just keep trying. If you're out of options..."

"What then? What if I am out of options, Al? What happens then? What happens to Rafael?"

"Then you come to me," Al said softly. "That's what happens. There's always something else. There's always a solution."

"Hallmark card philosophy, Al. Somebody is trying to frame Rafael. Why? Barry? Damn straight. Barry has pissed off more people than I can count. It's a given. But Rafael? He's the sunny guy, the teddy bear, the friendly one. Why him?"

"Then perhaps that's the reason, Tess. People like Rafael. They trust him. They do things for him. Look at you sitting in this cell of a room, trying to find out what's going on with these pictures and… And whatever that is." Al pointed to an untidy stack of binders and folders, which had gotten only untidier by being pushed aside crudely, likely when the security camera emergency happened.

"Oh, that." Tess barely looked up to see where he was pointing. "That's the million dollars you were looking for earlier."

"Indeed? This I want to hear." His interest piqued, he sat back down and attempted to straighten the mess on the desk with his hands.

"Not now, Al. Now I have to…"

"Yes, now. A million dollars rolls off the tongue rather quickly, Tess. Doesn't even take a second to say it. But in reality—in reality, a million dollars can make a man do things he wouldn't ordinarily do."

That got her for a moment. She pulled her hands off the keyboard and sat back up straight. "But the two issues…"

"Don't look connected, aren't likely connected, could have some strange connection—who knows, Tess? If there is one thing I know… a million dollars has made men do stranger things."

"And women," she admitted a bit sheepishly.

"He didn't…"

"No, he didn't. Your father was strange but not crazy. I am just agreeing with you. Money sometimes makes you do things you wouldn't ordinarily do, and probably know better as well."

Al nodded went to the door to close it and came back around to her desk.

"Now there is a subject on which we can spend weeks in discussion, when this is all done and over with. In the meantime, I need the two-minute download on what you found about Green Technologies and the million dollars they owe us."

"Won't need two minutes." Tessa shrugged and rifled through the folders in the closest stack, finally pulling out one, a suspiciously slim one with no label on it whatsoever.

"All I found on GT were a number of versions of the LOI you and Rafael passed on to him, refinements, descriptions, etcetera."

"Yes?"

"Nobody really bothered documenting this transaction in detail, did they?" she asked, raising an eyebrow. "What there was, I had to dig up from miscellaneous sources and scrap piles."

"Yes, yes." Al said and spun his right hand. *Get on with it.* "Where's the million?"

"In fact there were no accounting records concerning the good-faith payment whatsoever. Not even a note in accounting. You'd think they would had—never mind. The money didn't come out or go into PerCan accounts, so nobody recorded it. I thought we were screwed. Until."

"Until?"

"Until I found an old notebook your controller had left behind in his office. And tucked in the back, almost like an afterthought—a receipt from Greg Turner. $1 million received from Mr. Tadco Ivers, as a good-faith payment for the signing of the LOI and merging of the two companies. I guess he was the only one who felt he needed to anchor that in real time with a piece of paper. But that's it. That is basically everything that exists on this transaction."

"Oh, there was a whole lot more," Al said, remembering. "We wanted this merger—we needed this merger. Rafael and I had gone over every possible scenario, and without a license to grow, we were essentially sunk. No bureaucrat in his right mind would issue a license to a cannabis company with our history and our problems for a long time to come."

"So you tried to purchase a license. I mean—essentially."

Al cocked his head lightly and smiled. "You're right. Essentially, we did. We were planning to take over another company that was in trouble and had a license already."

"Green Technologies—your father asked me to do some research on them at the time."

"Did he now? Correct. We were all set for the merger. Then Greg Turner went ahead and imploded the entire thing, by suggesting to Rafael and Nick Ambrose, Kayla, and a couple of other directors that they should just abandon both companies and start over elsewhere, without all the baggage."

"And without you," Tess said dryly.

"Without us—correct."

"And now this dude has your million dollars, he thinks he has the key people from PerCan, and he wants to start over."

"There was a bit more," Al said, remembering, "but essentially, yes."

"In the end it didn't work."

"No, it didn't work. Rafael told him to go to hell. And now." Al held out his hand for the folder and its meager contents. "Now I am going to get that million dollars back—any which way I can."

"Jeez—wouldn't want to be on your bad side." Tess shuddered and brought her hands together, palms flat. "Look, I want to get back to those damn pictures and finding something that will help Rafael, but if you want my opinion… something about this whole deal just doesn't make any damn sense."

"How so?" Al asked and sat back down.

Time was burning a hole in his pocket, but something about this young lady intrigued him. Perhaps it was her complete lack of pretense and her straightforward manner. On any given day, if she found a spade on the ground, she would open her mouth and call it a spade, no matter who might be offended. At the same time, she could drill into data and files and find the smallest detail, make sense of numbers and paragraphs and spot an error a mile away. *She takes some getting used to*, Rafael had said, and he was finding himself getting used to her and hearing what she thought. Double fool on his father for not involving her more in his business affairs.

"Why does it not make sense?"

"It makes no sense because Turner was hanging on by a thread when your father asked me to look into the company. Surviving from one day to the next, no more." Tessa narrowed her eyes and shook her head. "If they didn't find someone like your father and PerCan, someone to inject some quick cash into the company, they would have to close up shop. Nobody was going to lend them a dime."

"Cannabis companies." Al nodded. "It's notoriously hard to find a lender. Nothing new there or unusual about it. So?"

"But why torpedo the deal? That's the part that makes no sense. Greg Turner signed his own death warrant by blowing up that merger. He is done. He could never expect that you wouldn't go after the million. He knows he owes it, and the moment you ask—boom."

She drew her flat hand across her throat. Done.

"Made no sense," Al said. "It looked like a done deal, and suddenly, he pulls out—in the worst possible way. Best I could figure was that he saw we had a pretty big investor lined up, with the kind of money that could buy a new start. Minus all of the problems that existed in both companies."

"Just screw the shareholders and creditors? And he thought…"

"And he thought it would be a clean start," Al finished. "Back then, it happened more often than you think, especially with cannabis companies. Take what you learned, leave the problems behind, start over. Except Rafael would never play along, and we wanted to get the million back. The day it happened, I wanted it back personally. But between orchestrating a new merger, Tadeo firing Rafael and then getting shot, it fell between the cracks."

"Pretty big cracks."

"True. But here we are." Al waggled the file in front of her. "I am going to set our securities lawyer after them. He and our new CFO can have some fun with this. Thank you very much for digging this out. Meantime." He pointed back at the screen.

"Business at hand, young lady. Find me something so we can challenge these images. Better yet, prove beyond the shadow of a doubt that they are an outright manufacture. That would be great."

NINETEEN

The door opened, and Kayla threw her arms around him, all in the same nanosecond.

Rafael, tired from his trip and ill-tempered because of his stay at the police station, and just plain bone-weary, took a step back and steadied himself against the doorframe.

"I am all for hearty greetings, Kayla, but…"

"You don't know how glad I am to see you home. Richard has been fighting for the better part of the day to get you out of that place."

Rafael stepped into his hallway and dropped the plastic sack containing his wallet, watch, and belt onto the hall table. He'd been in a similar hurry to get the heck out of Dodge that he hadn't taken the time to unpack it at the police station.

"I appreciate it. In the end, it came down to the fact that there's no identifiable face in any of those pictures. It's my car; that's it. Everybody who's ever worked a construction site with me has probably driven it at some point. Capable defense lawyer would have a field day."

"Didn't Richard…"

"Richard Marks was fine." Rafael waved her off. "He did his best, and in the end they had to let me go. But add to my long list of newly acquired chores: choose a highly skilled criminal defense lawyer. The poor man was sweating bullets right up to the end."

He lifted the hem of his shirt, inspected it, wrinkled his nose, and nodded his head up the stairs.

"Never needed a criminal defense lawyer," he groused. "This shirt is fit to be a cleaning rag by now. I'm going up to change."

"This is beyond ridiculous. Who would even think you would shoot Ivers?"

"I don't know. I don't know what to believe any longer." Rafael looked at the stairs and dropped into a chair in his living room instead of going up. "And Barry—what a mess..."

"They let him go too?"

Rafael shook his head. "Unlike me, he doesn't have a house to go to, a business he owns, or what they commonly refer to as ties to the community. He's considered a very high flight risk. No pun intended."

"Good—very good."

"We've had this fight before, Kayla, and I promised I would drop it, but I don't think he did it either."

"Oh, come off it. You said you wouldn't..."

"This isn't about friendship." Rafael rubbed the side of his head with the heels of his hands, wishing he could get the bone-weary tiredness out of his brain. "I just know he wouldn't shoot a man—just as I know you or I wouldn't do it."

"You keep saying that."

Kayla walked to the sideboard and poured him a glass of wine, handing it to him silently before she massaged his tight neck and shoulders.

"Oh, that feels good." Rafael closed his eyes and took a sip of wine. "Don't ever stop."

"I'll try not to. In the meantime, since you are freshly out on bail now..."

"Don't remind me."

"Somebody has to. And in case nobody else is reminding you, it would be a heck of a lot better to figure out who actually did shoot Tadeo, which means figuring out who framed you and why."

"Before all of this happened," Rafael mused and stared down into the bottom of his wine glass, "I would have laughed and said let the

THE CANNABIS PREACHER : SERMON THREE

police take care of this kind of stuff, keep your nose out of it and clean. And I would actually have believed they'd work on getting to the truth."

"Well, wake up," she said bitterly. "And understand that you are a very handy suspect, unless we personally do the research into who framed you. I don't want to imagine what happens if we can't find anything."

"And who sent that dealer with the gun Barry's way? If you ask me, that wasn't an accident either."

"Just convenient."

"But who, Kayla, who?" Rafael put his empty wine glass down beside him, hard. "And why? Originally, I thought Tadeo's killing had to be gang-related, but it seems he had made his own deal and his own peace with them. He was selling his clubs and getting into the marijuana business. Sandro was convinced that's where the shooter would be found. Our business, Kayla."

Kayla folded her hands before her and rocked back and forth a little, deep in thought.

"I had a story on gangs in the paper a while ago," she finally said, eyes unfocused on some spot in the middle of the living room that wasn't there. "It was kind of tough to get anyone to do the research on that particular subject."

"No shit. For love and good money, I wouldn't want to deal with some of these people." Rafael opened his eyes again and rolled his shoulders, the weariness and defeat finally letting go of him a little.

"The thing is, Rafa, these gangs… eventually, somebody always talks. Why? Because they need to brag. They need the other guy to know. Look at what I did, look who I killed—better don't mess with me."

"Look at the size of my stick and be afraid of me," Rafael muttered.

"Correct. If one of the biker gangs or Asians had killed Tadeo, there would be talk. There would be bragging. Someone would want to move into Tadeo's territory and hang his head on the wall as a trophy."

"Should you be having this kind of in-depth experience with the subject matter?"

Kayla only snorted. "Watch yourself. Before I married Howard Montecito, and then a few years later became a widow and magazine publisher, I had—some experience in this particular field."

Barry had always hinted that Kayla came up from the wrong side of town and clawed her way out of the dirt until she finally married into money, Rafael remembered. He had always said that this woman could hit back and hit back hard when required. He opened his mouth, but one look at Kayla and the dark shadows around her eyes made him change his mind about delving into that particular part of her past.

"So how does this help me?" he finally asked. "You agree with Sandro?"

"I agree with Sandro in that, if the shooter came out of the gang milieu, there would be chatter—bragging—and my researchers would have picked up on something. For sure. They don't miss stuff like this. Not when I specifically asked for it."

"OK." Rafael had this mental image of a horde of Kayla's researchers sitting in a dim and smoky room behind a bank of computer monitors, probing the deep web, although in this day and age, he reminded himself, they were most likely ordinary folks who hung around bars in the city and earned a bit of coin passing classified information her way. How else to run one of the most successful gossip magazines in the country?

"Back to the cannabis world, then. And the question I asked about half an hour ago, why?"

"The money," Kayla said softly. "Usually, the reason is money. I don't see anything else."

"Love, power, greed, revenge—nothing?"

"The only thing Tadeo, you, and Barry have in common is Perfect Cannabis. So if the person who shot him is the same one who framed you and Barry…"

"I'm just sick of it, and I am sick of trying to figure it out," Rafael said, feeling an irrational surge of anger. "Maybe I did do it—who the hell knows?"

"Go have a shower, come down and eat something, and we'll figure it out."

"As I meant to do half an hour ago and ran out of steam."

Rafael picked up his meager little sack of belongings again and weighed it in his hand.

"Maybe just for a few hours, can we not talk about or think about who shot somebody and who framed somebody else around here? Is that possible?"

Kayla nodded and forced a smile, but deep down, they both knew that it would be the only thing either one of them would think about. No matter what harmless subject they chose to converse on, it wouldn't take more than a few minutes for them to return to the one at the front of their minds again: Who had shot Tadeo Ivers?

She wouldn't be a successful publisher if she didn't realize and capitalize on the fact that this very question was the one being asked all over town, in the bars and back alleys: who the heck finally got to Ivers? Never mind why. There were enough good reasons, and just as many bad reasons—but who had done it?

TWENTY

He really had enough on his plate right now, Al thought. Rumors, innuendo, a broken board, suspicion within the company, a million dollars he had to collect.

He dropped into his chair in his office, grateful for a few minutes' worth of peace, and opened his laptop. Maybe he could just sit here and stare at the screen for a while, recovering. His thoughts bounced this way and that, and he pressed his hands into his temples to hang on to his sanity. Except there was a message on his desk. Clint, the CFO who had come over from Mariposa and taken the executive position, needed to see him urgently—first chance he got.

Al kept massaging his temple. He didn't know Clint all that well. He was a name on an executive roster, nothing else, but he was friends with Thomas Donnelly and likely not impressed with Al's leadership. Clint might have been a banker at any of the large institutions—he looked the part. Everything about the man was grey, from his perfectly pressed suits to the hair that never had one bit out of place. He personified the word *correctness* and tried to stay out of Al and Rafael's way as much as he could.

"Well, you can take it or leave it," Al said softly and sent a text to Clint to come and see him. The man didn't waste any time.

***

"You appear to have a bunch of short sellers out there," he said, settling into Al's visitor's chair, only moments later. "You are aware what that is, correct?"

"Indeed I am." Al worked to keep his features neutral. Did everybody around here assume he had no clue and no business running this company? "People whose brokers allow them to borrow shares from the brokerage's holdings and sell them now, hoping our stock price will go down by the time they have to pay up."

"Essentially, correct. There are a few versions of that, but essentially, that's it." Clint pulled out a high-tech little silver tablet that might have been a cross between a phone and an iPad and began to scroll through pages.

"These guys are real sharks. If I had my way, short selling would be made illegal. Oh, I know, I know…" He raised his hands when he saw Al opening his mouth for a reply. "It's a trading strategy, and there are moments when a company's share price is overvalued, but usually these sharks are only out for profits. There is something sick about betting on a company's demise."

Demise. Al did not like hearing that word. Demise, what demise, he wanted to ask, but Clint was still searching.

"I'm not arguing the point," Al said, trying to click through his memories of recent large stock transactions, valuations, prices. He had taken his eyes off the stock market in the last few days, what with everything else that had been going on. "I was under the impression that short sellers are just one of those things one has to contend with. In this industry, potentially more so."

"Again, not arguing with you." Clint had finally found the page he'd been looking for and passed the tablet over to Al.

"This, on the other hand, is very, very close to illegal. I think our lawyer can make a case for a cease and desist, but I wanted to show you first."

Al reached out his hand and took the compact little tablet, turning so he could read, and immediately, he wished he hadn't.

"The fox is running the henhouse, criminals in charge of pharmaceuticals manufacturing."

"How did anybody in their right mind issue a license to these people?"

"How many bribes were paid?"

"Did Beauregard succeed?"

Al didn't need to read more. He turned off the screen and ground his teeth to contain his anger.

"What is this?"

"It's a website that 'supposedly,'" Clint made air quotes around the word, "supposedly informs investors."

"None of this is true. This is pure and simple defamation. Have they got any idea…"

"Of course it's not true, Al." His CFO swept the tablet back into his portfolio. "If it's not outright lies, they are fantasies, and erroneous conclusions drawn between unconnected events, old facts, and personalities. It's ridiculous."

"Then why are you sitting here? Stop it. And stop it now. I don't want that out there. What if the investigators stumble over this nonsense?"

"Calm down, Al, I am on it." Clint tried to raise his hands to do just that. He probably looked a fright, Al thought, half out of his chair, his hands poised to grab somebody and—make them stop. With an effort he settled back.

"Who is spreading this garbage?"

"Remember the short sellers I mentioned a minute ago? Those people."

"Making other investors nervous, causing panic selling. And those leeches profit from the price drop they caused. I will not stand by to watch this. Not with my company."

"Not much we can do about it, unless this…" Clint pointed at his portfolio where he had just put the slim, silver tablet, "contains outright lies."

"I assure you it does."

Al reached his hand out again for the tablet. "I am going through this garbage right here, right now, and show you…"

"Al, leave it with our lawyer, please. Reading all of it will only upset you, and I don't want you to do something rash. All I wanted was show it to you and tell you we are dealing with it. It will be in the news…"

"Oh, I'll do something rash all right."

"No, you won't. Whoever is behind this short selling just put a whole lot of unrelated facts together to make it look like you, Rafael, Barry, and possibly Dante are the worst kinds of criminals. With Roberto, they didn't have to go far. His entire criminal record is hanging out there. The investigation into your father's death is discussed in great detail. Blowing up at somebody will only serve to confirm this nonsense."

Al heard the grinding noise, and his jaw ached from clenching his teeth. With an effort he relaxed his face and hands and counted to 10.

"Fine. Have somebody check this—this so-called investor website," he said.

"Already on it."

"If you find the slightest—the most minute piece—of wrong information, even if it is just a wrong date somewhere—"

"We are moving on it, Al. You got it. But in the meantime, nothing can come out of this company or out of this investigation that feeds their storyline. Investors are a paranoid bunch. You know that."

Al only nodded.

"With everything in this company's history, if there's a panic selling that starts, God help us all. If the stock price falls too low, we may not be able to raise capital or meet our debt obligations, and then…"

He drew his fingers across his neck, and Al did not need any more explanations.

He waited until he had his voice and his reaction completely under control again and rose from his chair.

"Proceed as you see fit," he said tonelessly and watched Clint go from his office again.

He sat and stared into space for a moment.

We may not be able to meet our obligations, and then… Add another thing to his list of concerns: short sellers who might bankrupt them all, even if he did everything right.

Clint supposedly 'had it in hand,' but he sat down anyway, opened his laptop and started searching. He'd find that website, and the person responsible for it, and then…

Then his phone chirped.

"Need 10 minutes from you. I've made progress of some sort."

Al stared down at the text he had just received from Tess and resisted an impulse to text back, 'Be right there.' If she had made progress? If so, he wanted to be the first person who heard about it, evaluated the progress, and decided on next steps to take. Naturally. But he still had a company to run, and he couldn't drop everything and attend to a side project. Even if that side project involved getting Rafael out of trouble.

Tessa should know that. She had, however, come through for him on the million dollars his father had paid to Green Technologies and one Greg Turner.

He closed the search bar on the browser he had kept busy for the last half hour and considered demanding Clint give him that website. If anybody were spreading rumors about him, his family and friends… Alas, that was why Clint had not given it to him.

'In a little while,' he texted back to Tessa and asked Connie to put him through to their securities lawyer, Raymond.

"Al, how nice to hear from you again. How are you doing?"

"About as expected, Raymond," Al said, shaking his head. What exactly was expected when a family member was shot, most of the company executive under suspicion, and the press going mad? "A few issues and a lot of nervous investors, but I'm coping."

"Good, good—how can I help you?"

Al leaned back, squeezed his eyes shut, and pinched the spot at the bridge of his nose.

"Remember the merger we almost entered into a few months back?" he asked without opening his eyes again.

"Green Technologies, Greg Turner—how could I forget? He made an indecent offer to the entire…"

"To the entire board of directors—well, most of them," Al said. "With the exception of me, my father, and anyone else who happened to carry Ivers as a last name."

"Um—yeah—some hard feelings there," Raymond said, and Al opened his eyes again.

"Far as I know, he didn't know any of us, but be that as it may, my father issued a check to the man in the amount of $1 million. I want it back."

Raymond said nothing for a moment, and Al pushed on.

"My—one of my people has been going through every piece of records we have here at the office, in preparation of the merger we are currently completing, and she found it. A receipt signed by Mr. Turner himself."

"I didn't realize we had any documentation at all," Raymond said, and Al could almost hear how he sat up a little straighter. And he probably calculated in his little lawyer mind just how much he could charge for suing Green Technologies.

"We can do that," Raymond finally said. "We can go about getting a judgment against GT. I just need to warn you that it may not amount to much. From what I hear, they are done over there. Finished—stick a fork in it. We could start proceedings, and before we file, he might go into bankruptcy and…"

"And it will cost time and money—I am well aware of that, Raymond. And even if I do get a judgment, there are no guarantees that we will ever collect a single cent. Noted as well. But here's the thing. I am not going to let anyone get away with taking a million dollars from me and just keeping it. That's not going to happen, do you understand?"

He punctuated every word of his final sentence, and it only took a moment for Raymond to respond.

"Understood."

"Wonderful. So I am going to have someone copy the receipt and whatever little there is of an actual file and deliver it to your office. I want you to start proceeding toward a claim. You follow thus far?"

"Yes, Al, I follow. I am just pointing out…"

"You are merely pointing out that I might be wasting my time and money, understood and noted. It's mine to waste."

"I just wanted to point out our chances to you," Raymond said quickly. "With a signed receipt, we won't have any trouble getting a judgment and getting on a list of creditors. But you'll be at the bottom. Collecting the money, that's on another page entirely."

"Understood."

"Then again, perhaps you have—well—ways to convince people that they ought to pay up?"

This time Al actually laughed out loud. Indeed, it was a well-known story cultivated by Tadeo. *The Ivers clan has ways to make you do what they want.*

He had spent years polishing and refining that image, with the help of his father and his strong-arm adjutants. Yes. But to be confronted with it now, at this particular time, was worth a laugh.

"Raymond, you must have been reading the website of those short sellers who are waiting for us to fail. Don't lie awake at night and think about how I am going to collect, or if. I can be a patient man—and at some point, who knows? We might get our chance."

"We might—OK."

Al could almost hear the sarcasm dripping off those words. Raymond really didn't think there was any *might* about it. Anything but filing the debt and taking a place on the creditor list was a waste of time and a fool's errand.

"I won't hold my breath. Now please. Prepare a case and send it to me for a signature. Can you do that?"

"Yes, of course, as long as you are aware of your chances. I will have it over to you as soon as possible."

Al sat back and pinched the bridge of his nose again. When had he ever thought that running this company together with Rafael and Kayla and his younger brother would be fun? And what had he been drinking at that moment?

He rose and walked over to the glass front, looking down over the production below. People scurried to and fro, and the smell, the smell just never went away. That faint sickly-sweet smell of marijuana that hung in the air, no matter how many carbon air filters he had them install. For some reason, it just never went away.

We got into this business because we thought it would be fun. Rafael's exact words. *We thought it would be fun.*

Straighten up, carry on, and stop complaining. Nobody is going to do it for you anyway. That was what Tadeo Ivers would have said. *Carry on.* There was still Tessa and whatever it was she had discovered.

***

"You took your sweet time," she said when he walked into the little room he now thought of as her office, even though it looked nothing like a conventional office. On one end of the room she had installed three long collapsible tables, and four computer monitors faced him. On two other tables, left and right, stacks of papers had been organized neatly by some pattern that still escaped him.

"Hello to you too, Tessa. You said you had discovered something? Something that would help Rafael, I presume."

"That depends…"

"Depends? Depends is not the answer I was looking for. Depends on what?"

"Depends on how you see it," she said and keyed up something on the PC in the center.

A security video started playing, typical security video, Al thought. Black-and-white, grainy, mediocre quality. He watched Rafael's Mercedes pull into the parking lot of Tadeo's dingy diner. Not exactly what he wanted to be looking at right now.

"Forgive my lack of patience or desire to watch this thing again, Tessa. Kindly use as few words as possible to tell me what you found and how it can help us, if at all, and I'll take it from there."

He sat in a chair, still staring at the monitor she had indicated, and felt his body sink a little deeper than it used to. Weight, perhaps, the weight of all of these decisions, problems, and issues he was facing. To-do lists, requests for interviews, contracts, and letters of intent he had to prepare, review, and sign when ready. Deadlines he had to keep in mind, investors and traders he had to deal with.

He reached up, took the reading glasses off his nose, and rubbed his eyes with the thumb and forefinger of his left hand. One second of weariness was all he would let himself have. After that…

"So…? Do I understand you to tell me that this video is it—the end of the road? We might as well assume Rafael Covin shot and killed Tadeo Ivers?"

"Not at all."

He spread his hands and lowered his head just a little, looking up at her since she was still standing before him.

"You see how this security video is really perfect?"

"That's what I would call bad news, Tessa. We are trying to prove someone did this to Rafael."

"Correct. So I got real frustrated with this thing."

"You and others."

"Threw it against the wall…" Tessa's fist flew out to demonstrate.

"You'd be alone here."

"Then I thought… Wait—these people didn't hand over their security video until a couple of weeks after the incident, right?"

"Correct."

"Why?"

"What do you mean why?" Al asked, blinking a few times.

"Just that—why? I mean, a man gets shot, police are coming around, asking if anyone has security footage of the night in question. If you have the kind of system installed that will take this kind of video in this kind of quality, you're going to say, 'Why, yes, Officer, matter of fact, I do. Here it is.' Most people actually only retain their footage for a few days, if that, and then they erase it. Why hang on to mountains of security videos unless you have to? It just takes space and time to organize. Does that make sense?"

Al nodded. "It's—thin… But it makes some sense. Carry on."

"And I said I was struggling. The kind of system that will produce that kind of high quality," her arm snapped out, and a sharp finger pointed at the monitor in front of him, "that's a couple hundred thou…"

"As in thousand?"

"Yup."

"That company was empty warehousing storage," Al said, wrinkling his forehead. For the first time since they had shown him the security video of Rafael's Mercedes, a little spot of light appeared in that dark tunnel he found himself in. Why indeed would a warehousing company have a video surveillance system to rival his own, that of a pharmaceutical manufacturer? And on an empty building, no less.

"Here's another question for you, Al. What if they didn't? What if they had an ordinary, run-of-the-mill system, or maybe none at all, and the reason it took them a couple of days is because they had to make this thing up?"

"I thought you said you couldn't detect any manipulations in the video."

"Manipulations, no. It's about as perfect as perfect can get."

"So?"

"So I'm saying what if they made the whole thing up?"

"That's Rafael's Mercedes there in the video, unless somebody stole it, drove it around to make this video, and put it back again. I don't see how you could. And that—even to me, who wants to believe—is a bit of a stretch."

"Would be to anybody."

"So?"

"So… Rafael's been there tons of times, early morning, late at night, whatever," Tessa said. "He's been there. Parked that clunker of his and had one discussion or another with you… With Tadeo. They didn't reinvent the wheel. They had to find an old video showing Rafael driving into the lot there at night."

"And the time stamp?"

"Manipulating a single one, tough. Overlaying the whole video with a new one, not so tough. And it would be consistent."

"I don't know, Tessa… I will admit that I only understand a portion of what you are saying. What I do understand is this country's legal system. And I need something rock solid to take to our lawyer to get Rafael out. I need evidence."

"Like solid evidence?"

"Like solid evidence, yes," Al said, losing patience already. As far as he was concerned, they still had nothing.

"Like a garbage bin kind of evidence?"

Al blinked and shook his head. Even on a good day, much of what Tessa was saying sounded like a foreign language, and as long as he grasped the gist of what she tried to tell him, he didn't get hung up on the details. Best to let an expert do what he was good at and not interfere, Rafael would tell him. As long as you got the result you were looking for, you could make a face like you understood what he's talking about. Much of his time on the production floor, he made that face. But garbage-bin evidence?

"Pray tell, what is garbage-bin evidence?"

"You know I worked for your—for Tadeo, right?"

"You can call him my father," Al sighed. "If you're going to stumble over the term every time. Yes, you worked for him. I remember."

Oh, and he remembered all of Barry's secrets she had given his father, and every single weak spot for him to uncover, make public, and drive a knife into. But that was ancient history now.

"He had me coming to that old diner on a regular basis. I think he wanted me to work there, hack into his employees' electronics or something to see what I could find, but I wouldn't. It just didn't feel right."

"Perish the thought. Carry on."

"And the food they served in that diner…" Tessa physically shuddered. "I don't know if you've ever tried it."

"No, thank you. Except for Dinah's apple pie. That is divine."

"Hate to tell you, Al, but she bought it at a pastry place downtown for you and your father and told everybody she made it. Never mind. Suffice it to say most of what came out of that kitchen went straight into that big yellow dumpster right here."

With a long manicured finger, she tapped a vaguely rectangular shape around the left side of the diner on the screen, just captured by the cone of Rafael's headlights.

"Matter of fact, before I went home, usually, I would dump anything from the diner into that bin and stop by at the nearest Starbucks."

"Sound advice and I'm sure we've all done it, but I still don't see how this helps Rafael in any way."

"Because about three months ago, there were rats in that dumpster. And you know if there was one thing Tadeo was more scared of than rats… Well, there was no one thing."

"He did hate the little critters, but…"

"So he told the dumpster company from now on, they had to park that yellow dumpster at the back, 50 feet away from the building, which pissed off all of the employees because now they had to walk across the lot to get rid of all of this shit."

"Aside from your language…" Al, suddenly energized, rose to his feet, and took two steps closer to the computer monitor, where Rafael's car still stood frozen in time, about to make a turn into a marked parking spot. And just by chance, in the sweep of the headlights, barely visible, he saw the shadow of said yellow garbage bin.

"Garbage-bin evidence," he said softly and tapped the screen himself. "That bin ought not to be there. Hence its shadow ought not to be there in Rafael's headlights."

"Somebody could make a point and say maybe it had been put back there accidentally or it's a shadow of something else."

"But that's not our job. Innocent until proven guilty—that is how the law reads, or at least is supposed to! So, if our lawyers can poke a couple of holes here, they'll be scrambling to have anything on Rafael. Great job, Tess. Outstanding."

"Thanks."

"Even if it took you half an hour to explain."

He turned just in time and spotted Tessa's shit-eating grin just as she tried to hide with a fake cough into her elbow.

"I wanted you to have the whole picture."

"So you did. But who the heck went through all of this trouble to make it look like Rafael's car is sighted at the scene? And somehow or other, they had to have access to old security footage from the diner? This took some doing. And likely also quite a bit of funds. Who and why?"

Tessa shrugged and said nothing, and Al paced up and down in her tiny space, worrying his right thumbnail between his teeth. He didn't chew nails—he never chewed nails—but this…

"Sandro told Rafael to look for the shooter in our own ranks, the cannabis business," he said to no one specifically. "He was so sure. Supposing he is…"

He turned on his heel and took four steps into the other direction. "Supposing he does—come out of this business, one of our own—why would he do it?"

"He?"

"Or she." Al brought his palms flat together and rested his chin on them. "We are not suggesting Kayla…."

"Not suggesting, Al, just keeping an open, gender-unspecific mind. Assuming the shooter is a man just eliminates too many people."

"People who should not be eliminated as of yet. Correct. So once again, assuming the shooter, the person who framed Rafael, and the person who set up Barry, are one and the same, and further assuming this person is one of us, comes out of the cannabis business—then why do they do it?"

"Get control of the company—of PerCan?"

"But they don't get PerCan. I am in control here. At least mostly," he added, glancing down at his phone, which chose that particular moment to chime and remind him of a prior appointment.

"Tadeo—Rafael—Barry. What is to be gained by eliminating the three?"

"And you. Maybe you are still on the list, so to speak."

"Thanks, Tessa, that really warms my heart," Al said, rolling his shoulders. "And maybe all of those are completely unrelated. I have a conference call to attend. Make an appointment with the detective sergeant please, and show him what you've discovered. If he has any issues with it, have him speak to me directly. We need to get Rafael out. I need his help here. ASAP."

"Yes, boss," Tessa muttered, but he had already gone. "And thanks for not suggesting that 'she' might also be my insignificant person."

She turned around and stared at the frozen image of Rafael's Mercedes in the lot of Tadeo's family diner again. Pure coincidence that she had discovered the shadow of the old yellow dumpster where it should not have been—pure coincidence. Whoever had made this had to have known someone like herself would be looking at that video, with a magnifying glass, for hours on end. So they took the time to create a whole new video, took a chance that the delay in getting it to the police would raise a few red flags.

Why go through all of it? Just for control of the company? She did indeed know someone who would do almost anything to get his hands on the company—and with it, the big money.

But shooting Tadeo? Would he really go so far as to shoot Tadeo, or set someone up to shoot Tadeo?

Damn.

Tessa dug around in a box under her computer desk until she found the object she needed, an old scuffed tennis ball she kept around for situations like this one. With an angry flick of her wrist, she fired it at the wall of her little office and caught it again just as quick, returning it to the wall in one smooth motion. Whap, whap. Did she dare tell Al Ivers about her suspicions? Whap, whap. Did she dare not to? Whap, whap. But what if she was correct, and it was…? Whap, whap. It couldn't be. Whap, whap. Under no circumstances could it be. Well, then, there was no harm telling Al either, was there? Whap—whap—whap.

TWENTY-ONE

"Mr. Covin? Some new evidence came to light recently. We officially don't believe you were at Tadeo Ivers's family diner the night in question. Continue to keep yourself available please."

Rafael scanned through his messages listlessly while he sat in his favorite chair, feet up, staring at the ceiling, trying to think of nothing. Or not trying to think of a specific thing—both impossible.

Several people had messaged him or called and left some encouraging words, and still, he had no desire to speak to anyone. Somebody tried to frame him for murder, and that kind of realization just shut down everything. Boom.

Al called, and he'd meant to ignore the call but accidentally found himself answering.

"Rafael," Al said, exhaustion bleeding out of every word. "I need you here. I don't care if the media goes crazy, but I need you."

"Al—I…"

"You've run this place. You understand it, and you understand the people. I feel as if I'm playing squash with three people at the same time. I need you here, and that's final."

Rafael said nothing. Even thinking about going back to work was too much at that moment.

"Quit messing around, Rafael. Are you coming back, or do I have to drive to your house and convince you the ugly way?"

"It's like that, is it?"

"Quite."

The moment stretched over the phone, and Rafael sighed. "Al, if you're trying to wait me out…"

"I'm on hands-free, and you're a hothead. Who's it going to be giving in first?"

"Fine."

"Come again?"

"Fine. I said fine, Al. For God's sake. At least listen while you're badgering me. What do you need me to do?"

"I'm not badgering you. I am merely stating a fact. This company is drowning in uncertainty, debt, and suspicion. And I have damned short sellers taking advantage of that. I need you to help me stop that."

"Well—if it's nothing else…"

***

They had put fresh flowers onto the second desk in Al's office. Somebody had managed to find a box of the kind of coffee he liked, and Connie had found the picture. The one where he wore a hard had that said 'da boss.'

"Hung that in my first PerCan office—right after Connor…" he said and looked away because there was no way to finish the sentence gracefully.

"Well, don't put it away. You'll be putting it up again soon enough."

Al dumped a stack of files onto the desk that measured, conservatively speaking, a foot and a half high.

"What the… Are you kidding me?"

"I told you I need the help! I have customer complaints about a bad taste in the cannabis oil, the labels won't stay on the bottles properly and get greasy and unreadable too soon, the loose flowers fall to dust in the bottom of the jar, and somebody likened our packaging to a Granny Apple jar."

"That it?" Rafael asked and blinked rapidly.

"No. I also have problems with plant fertilization, the server keeps crashing, and three of my senior growing staff just quit. Besides that, I am bleeding cash on a daily basis at insane rates, I'm not sure what my salespeople are doing all day long—and, oh, I still need to collect $1 million off Greg Turner and shut down the internet sharks."

"Greg, Green Technologies, Turner," Rafael whistled. "Nice job finding the contract."

"Tessa did that. And a receipt acknowledging the million handed over to Turner by Tadeo. And I want it back."

"I wouldn't hold my breath on collecting."

"So says Raymond Hargrave. I hired him for securities matters."

"Talented man, large firm—not cheap." Rafael abandoned the files on his desk and leaned back in his chair, looking up at Al, standing before him like a schoolboy with his report card. "And you think you have a chance with Turner?"

"I don't know. Maybe I'm throwing away $800 an hour on a securities lawyer to get absolutely nothing—but this one time, just where Greg Turner is concerned, it's principles before practicality."

"Principles before practicality." Rafael nodded. "Rolls off the tongue nice."

"Go ahead. Tell me I'm a fool for throwing good money after bad."

"You are. But that's not the point. You already know that. Better settle in for a good, long fight." Rafael shook his head. "If I'm correct, Turner is going to drag this out as long as he can. He's broke, meaning he's got nothing to lose."

"You know I don't invoke the name Tadeo very often," Al said, looking down his nose and flexing his fingers as if he were trying to get rid of something sticky. "But times used to be when people realized they couldn't just take something that belonged to him and get away with it."

"Flow with that thought for a minute, Al."

"Why?"

"Your reputation—your family's reputation. Use it and get that money back. People may be just a tad afraid of owing to the company, to Al Ivers, you reckon?"

"Absolutely not." Al took his own files and plunked them down at his desk harder than he needed to.

"I said think about it, Al, that's all."

"And I said I'm going to at least try to get this money back the proper way—not by sending some knee-breakers out to Greg Turner's house demanding he pay us back."

Rafael suddenly broke into a grin and then outright laughter, and Al straightened his shoulders and walked back to his own side of the office.

"Are you quite done? This isn't funny, you know."

"Oh, yes it is. The way you say 'knee-breakers,' one would never remember that you used to be your father's strong-arm man, going around the various clubs, collecting money, making sure nobody skimmed."

"I never threatened to break anyone's knees, if that is what you are referring to. It was all in the—persona."

"Right, the one where you walked around like Al Capone's double, and people believed you were a tough guy who shot first and asked questions later. Most of them were too scared to even think about trying anything."

Al raised an eyebrow and brushed an invisible speck of dust off his lapel and off his pant leg.

"With—very few notable exceptions."

"Oh, I knew who you were and what you were. That's not the point. Others didn't. Point is it worked. Most people had no clue it was just an act. And if Turner would buy into it…"

"We're not going there, Rafael. Have you read the internet rumors on just this subject lately? They are going insane, and so are our share-holders. I would appreciate it if you didn't mention it again."

Al sat heavily in his chair and opened his daily planner, studying today's date as if it held all of the answers in the world.

"Well then…"

Rafael pulled the first file off his stack, flipped it open with too many jerky, ground-covering moves, and studied the first piece of paper inside.

"Bottle design. For God's sake, why didn't we hire the guy Nick Armstrong recommended about six months ago? They did a top-shelf design for the guys at Be-leaf. Does anybody ever listen to my suggestions? This here? This is a nightmare."

Al stared at him for a moment, but Rafael only continued to skim over the pages in the slim file, muttering to himself and making notes in the narrow margins of the pages. After a moment, he reached for his phone, stared at the screen for a moment, and put it down.

"Ah—Connie. Guess I can't page her from this… Well, needed to move anyway."

He rose and took the four steps through the office before Al stopped him with a raised palm and a shake of his head.

"I'm not saying you don't have a point," he said softly.

"Wha?" Rafael rubbed his ear with a finger. "I don't think…"

"You heard me. You might have a point, and there might come a time when it would be—useful—for Turner to believe I am given to drastic measures."

"Drastic measures. Uh-huh. Can you page Connie for me? I want to ask her about these cannabis oil bottles. Ours are terrible."

"Rafael!"

"Yes. You would rather forget that the name Ivers was connected to various types of criminal activity previously," Rafael said.

"Suspected criminal activity."

"Fine. You're cleaning up the family rep. Good on you. I'm all for it. But if it makes Turner pay up—all bets are off."

Al stood still for a second and finally looked away.

"Maybe."

"I got you all the way to maybe," Rafael went back and dropped into his chair. "And that only took—what—half an hour? This is going to be one heck of a long day."

He leaned back, took off his reading glasses, and massaged tired eyes.

"Turner is a creep, and he torpedoed the merger you and I had worked on for months for nothing. I've been waiting for a while to stick it to him. I want that money back for PerCan and everything we can do with it."

Squaring his shoulders, he lifted the file on his desk an inch and let it drop back down onto the desk top. "Like fixing our bottle design. Really? Just look at it. This is awful. We look like amateurs."

"They were available in a hurry."

"That's what they look like, Al. You need me."

"I told you that."

"Yeah, well..." Rafael turned away, trying to hide his grin, unsuccessfully so. "Tell our detective to quit creeping around and get on with finding the real shooter. That would help out a lot too."

TWENTY-TWO

The halls and growing areas, the trimming, cutting, storage, and packaging departments were abuzz with the news of Rafael's return. Suddenly, everyone seemed to walk a little straighter, have a bit more swing in their gait, and a ready smile for a fellow employee.

If he didn't like Rafael, if they weren't friends, if he hadn't been the one to call him back here, then he would have to resent it, Al thought. But he'd known quite well what he was doing. He knew he made a good analyst, planner, and producer of paperwork and reports. Leading people, not his favorite task. Nor was he very good at it, while it just came naturally to Rafael. How often had he asked any of the workers about their ideas on alternate bottling solutions? It boggled the mind.

Rafael? Snapped his fingers and ideas, sketches, and contact files came torrenting in. You'd really have to resent him if he were not such a nice guy. Which was of course why everyone followed him so willingly.

And here they were…

Al silently looked out over the production area and sighed. Yes, he did need Rafael. They complemented each other well. But there was another magical ingredient he hadn't even thought about when he stepped forward and said he would run Tadeo Ivers's cannabis empire.

They would need money. Soon. Lots of money. Jesus, the production standards for medicinal cannabis alone required nothing short of a small fortune to abide by. And he still had to tackle security. Their standards were barely adequate, and they'd had a few warnings from the Ministry of Health. And if he didn't want to stick to peddling cannabis oils and flowers on the internet, one customer at a time, he had to get into some serious distribution agreements with big corporations. Drugstore corporations, preferably.

Jesus.

He needed another player up here on the executive floor along with him and Rafael. Rafael alone had dragged this company out of a ditch, but watching him down there with the greenhouse workers, explaining some abstract concept with lots of ground-eating gestures, laughs, and smiles, he saw a man in his element. No, until he made him a director again, Rafael would be the perfect liaison between the workers and the executive level. They'd follow him without question, and they'd bring their A-game. Better than their A-game, even.

Which still left him needing some sort of corporate business development man—and a fundraiser. Preferably before his institutional investors pulled out of the game because they decided it was all over.

Thomas? Maybe, but he didn't fully trust the man as of yet. And Thomas was somewhere right down there with Rafael, getting his boots dirty checking those plants.

27,000 as of last count. Who would have thought you'd count cannabis plants individually and carry them as inventory?

With another shake of his head, he turned away and back to his desk. Work was still piling up there for him. And in that pile on the left—bills. Lots and lots of bills. Payroll above all of them. Jesus, how many people worked for him now, over 100? Al let the breath he'd been holding out with a whoosh and sat a little straighter. He just needed a plan. A good one. And he needed help.

***

"You ever get used to the smell?" Detective Sergeant Robertson asked, sniffing the air like a hound, and Rafael laughed.

"You don't notice it after a while. It's just there. But newcomers and visitors—gets them every time. It's fun to watch their eyes bug out the first time they smell it."

"Thank you for meeting me here."

Rafael shrugged. "Better than down at the station any time. The last week is not one I want to repeat any time soon."

"I don't blame you. And seeing how much trouble someone went through to make us think you were at the diner the night in question, that tends to divert my suspicions away from you."

"Glad to hear it, Detective. Although you don't mind my asking what you're doing here, if your suspicions are diverted elsewhere?"

"Somebody went through a lot of trouble to make us look at you as a suspect. Don't you want to know who?"

Rafael shrugged and rested his face on his hand, covering his mouth. *Yeah,* he wanted to say, *I want to know, and I want to beat the living lights out of him or her. And I want to know if it's the same someone who framed Barry, and why the hell he wants to destroy PerCan.*

"I do," he finally said. "I very much do. But it does fall in the category of 'your job,' while mine..." He swept his hands left and right, encompassing the mess on his desk, the floor, and Al's desk for good measure.

"Let me ask you a question then, Rafael. Do you think Mr. Wentworth might have his hands in there somewhere?"

"Barry? You're barking up the wrong tree, Detective. I told you that before. Sure, Barry can be a sleazeball, and there hasn't been a cookie jar invented that he hasn't figured out how to put his hand in and take a great big scoop of what wasn't actually meant for him. You got him on all of those accounts. And if the charge is being a blockhead rather frequently, you got him there too."

"But? Without considering your previous friendship now."

"But Barry, even when he was still Connor, would stop short of doing things that might actually land him in jail if discovered. Jail—that's a no-go for him."

"Even in the early days, when you started this thing? I seem to remember some wild and crazy tales from those days, and Mr. Beauregard was up on some pretty serious charges."

Rafael dropped back in his chair, leaned his head way back, and let his eyes travel to the ceiling, remembering. "He did some pretty slick and sleazy things back then."

"Bribing government officials? Misappropriating shareholder's funds? Not to forget the mother of them all—illegally growing drugs."

"You see, that's the thing with tales. They can be pretty tall, and Connor-slash-Barry—he was never convicted of any of those."

"Lack of evidence."

"Precisely, a serious lack of evidence. I just love our judicial system." Rafael stopped to inspect a notation on a clipboard he'd been brought and nodded at the worker carrying it. "There are so many different ways of looking at the old case—it's crazy. And no, I really don't think any longer he was growing the drugs in the backroom."

"Really? Even at two o'clock in the morning, when it is just you and the shaving mirror? You can be totally honest and say you don't believe it?"

Rafael laughed and slapped the detective on the back.

"You're being dramatic, Detective. I mean, sure, I had my doubts in the beginning, when it was all happening, and Ivers's son Roberto went on TV saying Connor made him do it."

"But? Be honest now."

Rafael remembered all of his internal struggles, trying to figure out Barry's involvement. Especially when he stole Irv's plane and took off with it.

"You know who Barry is, Detective? He's a storyteller. And he has a near eidetic memory to retain facts and figures to rattle off at will in said storytelling. If there's money in your bank account, you better sit on it because he is going to sell you something to get at it. And he will promise the moon and the stars, with no possibility of failing. Might it be a load of bull? Yup—be warned. But I just don't see him with the kind of criminal energy, determination, and patience to pull this off. Especially not the patience part."

"He is your friend."

"Was my friend. He's done a lot of damage to this company, and I happen to care about this company and the people who work here. Trust comes on foot and leaves on horseback, my grandma would say. Barry has a lot of ground to cover before anyone will trust him again. But the question is not, 'could he have done it?' It's who benefits by removing Tadeo, Barry, and myself from the game, all at the same time."

"Al Ivers." The detective tried shrugging his shoulders.

"Nice try, Detective, an obvious one to boot, but no. Look around you." Again, he pointed at his desk, the floor around it, and the mess encroaching on Al's own desk, pristine and tidy. "Al is hopelessly out of his league running a company this size. And he knows it, and so does everybody else."

"Ouch. Remind me not to get into business with you."

"He makes no secret of his issues with the CEO seat. He all but threatened me with physical harm if I didn't come back and help him. Just a figure of speech." Rafael threw up his hands quickly. "No, Detective, Al realizes that together we can do this and make the company successful. On his own, he gets sidetracked. Lost in the art of creating the perfect financial report and management discussion and analysis. It's a thing of beauty, I tell you, but he wouldn't last long."

"And exactly how does that take him off your suspect list?"

"Because he's always known it, Detective. He never wanted to be CEO while I was in charge, so he sure as hell wouldn't commit murder to make it his own. Make sense?"

"Some." The detective rose and reached for his jacket, shrugging into it. "You certainly know all of the players in this drama."

"No shi… No kidding."

"So please think about it, who in this whole cast of players sticks out to you as being capable of this kind of—what did you call it, criminal energy?"

"Greg Turner, look at that," Rafael said, flipping a file close to him open.

"Who?"

"Unrelated. I'm just reading this file here. Greg was a business partner—former business partner—we're having trouble with. Somewhat surprised to see his name here, that's all."

"I see. Well, thank you for your time, Rafael. I hope you don't mind if I pick your brains about the people involved here and there."

"Not crazy about it, but pick away."

"Then I'll be on my way. And good luck with that business partner there." Detective Robertson turned at the door and nodded at the paperwork in Rafael's hand. "Sounds like a real winner."

"Blockhead—like too many of them."

TWENTY-THREE

Rafael plowed through the files on his desk and the list of problems he was to deal with with dogged determination. Without looking up or breaking for lunch or coffee, he would take down one of the file folders, read through the issue, and fire off emails, phone calls, memos, and, in one case, an order for a new labeling machine.

He loved Al dearly, but the man got sidetracked in a forest of his own unnecessary minor details.

And that was a good thing, or he and Tess would never have spotted that bloody yellow garbage container that ended up saving his freedom.

A few hours of dogged determination later, he finally reached the lower end of his to-do pile, and the photocopy of the note regarding GT turned up again.

"Received from Tadeo Ivers on behalf of Perfect Cannabis Corporation," he read, "in consideration of and with the intent to amalgamate two corporations, namely blah blah blah…" On the following page, he found what he was looking for. "$1 million. You damned bastard…"

He stared at Greg Turner's signature on the page and remembered the desperation he and Al had gone through at the time. They were out of money. They were working with, and for, an unreasonable despot, with their chances at receiving a license dwindling like soft ice cream dropped on the sidewalk. It wasn't happening for them.

They needed money, and the investors who had the kind of money they needed all showed them the door. Too many startups like them had come and gone without leaving a trace, and even men with a fortune like Tadeo Ivers would have to give up unless they found a way to start growing and selling an actual product. For that they needed a license, and to get a license, they needed a partner.

Enter Greg Turner.

Greg Turner, who had made a mess out of Green Technologies, like so many other small-time growers before him. Fortunately for him, he had made it to the licensing stage before he mismanaged his own company into a manure pile. Together, they could have saved both companies. Until Greg imploded in a shower of sparks. Why did he have to blow up their deal—why?

Rafael leaned back and dug the balls of his hands into his tired eyes. Money, most likely. Turner had got wind of a real heavy investor interested in PerCan, and he thought, "Why not?" Why not ditch all of the old problems and creditors, unpaid bills, and unhappy people that belonged to the past and take the combined brain trust of both companies, add Irving Moody's money, and start fresh?

Take what you learned, hit the reset button, and start again. Didn't everybody deserve a second chance?

He'd blown up any chance his struggling company might have had—and for what? $1 million. $1 million, even though he had to know they would come after it. And if Rafael remembered correctly, once Turner found out the Ivers family was involved in the deal, he didn't want to have anything to do with them. Hated Tadeo Ivers from the get-go without ever meeting him, so why piss the man off and make sure he would come after him? If you knew you were destroying your own company and calling down the wrath of a man with a reputation for rash acts, well, was a million enough to make you do it? The only way he would have had a minute chance to get away with it was if he had packed up that cash in a suitcase and hauled ass for the Caribbean, and he hadn't. He'd stayed right here in town watching his company disintegrate, knowing he owed Ivers a million dollars—why?

It didn't make any kind of goddamned sense.

Rafael was still staring at the copy of the receipt when Kayla walked into his office and put a hand on his shoulder.

"I think you've probably put far too much time into whatever it is you are staring at. Your eyes are about to turn square. How about you call it and follow me home, soldier?"

"Hmmmm."

He put down his papers and looked up at her. "I am still trying to figure out why…"

"Enough figuring out for now, Rafa. Al said you've been at this all blasted day, without so much as stepping out of this room."

"Probably, there are a lot of problems right here." He tapped the untidy pile of paperwork on his desk and leaned back in his chair with a deep sigh.

"And they will not be solved right this minute, most certainly not by beating your head into them, no matter how hardheaded you may be. Come on."

Rafael cast one last look at the files and the receipt on his desk and finally pushed it back into the folder it had come out of, sliding the folder to the bottom of the pile.

"Right you are. Especially not this particular one. I'm going to let Raymond handle this one. That's why we give a fortune to the goddamn lawyers anyway."

"Rafael…"

"Sorry for the language."

"What I started to say was—you're starting to sound like Connor used to, back in the day."

"Oh."

"There wasn't a lawyer's bill written that he didn't want to argue over on sight. It was compulsive with him."

"I well remember," he said with a wan smile.

"You hear anything from him?"

"Nope." Rafael shook his head and tried to arrange the papers on his desk into some sort of order or a resemblance thereof. He failed, gave up, and finally shook his head again.

"Yes and no. For the moment, he's in jail, and they are not going to let him go. Bail denied, flight risk and all that."

Kayla tilted her head and lifted an eyebrow.

"That can't be a surprise, considering he actually stole and crashed an airplane to avoid having to answer questions."

"I still don't..."

"I'm giving up. You still believe he's innocent." Kayla advanced on the desk a little and smiled at Rafael, a bright little beacon in the midst of all the problems he'd had to deal with over the last little while. Make that a long while. "Your loyalty is humbling. How many people would have thrown the book at him long before this?"

"Aw, shucks." Rafael managed to smile back. "And a book wouldn't be enough. I don't think it's loyalty. More like wanting to find the blockhead who caused this mess." His hand swept around the room, generously encompassing the stacks of—issues, around them.

"Which brings us right back to the moment I stepped into this roomy but messy office of yours, Rafael. These problems have spent months growing to where they are, and they will not be solved in one day, no matter how hard you try. So please, leave it be for now and let's go home."

She stretched out a hand for him, and when he did rise and put his arm around her, she felt so good against him, so trusting, soft, and wonderful, that he forgot why he had ever wanted to be in an office wanting to solve problems all day anyway.

TWENTY-FOUR

One problem at a time, he did end up hearing that particular piece of advice from a number of different people over the next few days. *Slow down, Rafael. Don't try to fix the world in three days—solve one issue at a time.* And he might have listened, if he were not usually in too much of a hurry to get somewhere to fix something or solve a crisis of some type.

He had missed it, he realized. He had missed the stress and the hurry and all the little fires he had to put out on a daily basis. His life had really lacked something without them. If anyone asked, he would launch into a tirade about how he was getting too old for this, and how it was time for him to retire, let his sons take over the construction company and let Al deal with PerCan while Rafael Covin relaxed on a beach in the Caribbean. He'd send them postcards. In his heart he knew he walked around with a stupid grin on his face all day long, and he also knew the beach in the Caribbean had about a 0.1 percent chance of happening. And the 0.1 percent only existed because Kayla surreptitiously mentioned holidays here and there.

Not that she had any plans to leave Montecito Publishing while she was still breathing.

Rafael had no need for an alarm clock. He couldn't wait to jump out of bed in the morning and get back at it—every single morning. To him, it had become something of a game. Look at a problem, figure out a creative and workable solution, find the right people to implement it, and set them loose. Just so he could sit back, smile, and look at another problem.

Rinse and repeat.

He'd run PerCan like this back when he was in charge, and he had dropped straight into his old patterns as if he had not been away for a single day. The employees—his people—all pretended not to notice, but they were there when he needed them, gave him the advice he had always relied upon, and told him to back off when he was wrong, just as they always had. They called him first when they had a question, and they waited for his opinion before going ahead. Matter of fact, things were just like they used to be, except he didn't carry the letters CEO after his name.

He considered that a tiny price to pay. He'd never cared in the first place what they called him, as long as they listened and everyone pulled on the same string. This right here was what lit him up when he came to work. Solving issues, making things work, watching something turn from a problem to a working practice.

The stacks of 'issues' files on and around his desk became smaller bit by bit, and the day came when he didn't need the floor space around him any longer. Al remarked that he hadn't seen that floor in weeks and how he would now have to pay extra to have all of that floor space cleaned once again, and Rafael called him a moron. But in a nice way.

Al himself smiled more often, had a kind word for everyone, and finally managed to tackle the 'CEO' issues he had so long ignored and neglected.

Rafael was back. Title or no title, he was doing what he loved, with the people he loved and respected. And, like a chain reaction, the people around him suddenly were more productive, happier, and just nicer to one another. Could have been an accident, or it could have been that no one managed to escape from his good-natured humor and booming voice for very long. He thought himself unstoppable.

Thus, he literally barreled into the production office on a full charge of steam one morning, holding a new glass bottle design he wanted to show to Nick. Dosing cannabis oil was a delicate thing in the first place, and a matter of counting drops most often. This delicate process wasn't helped when the bottle containing said oil was awkwardly shaped, the inserted eye dropper leaking, and the content labels wearing off from spilled oil. Rafael had read through a stack of customer complaints mentioning this very thing.

For a few weeks now, he had insisted that there had to be a better way. He'd made drawings of different jars and bottles, downloaded every design other pharmaceuticals used, and gone on a tour of glass manufacturers. Armed with all of this, he'd set up a dozen tests down in the labs, asked anyone who could be bothered to help out, and collected all of his data in a massive spreadsheet.

He remembered discussing this problem with Nick what seemed like a lifetime ago—well before everything went pear-shaped. They'd agreed then that something needed be done right away, and still, their customers reported issues.

"Hey, Nick, can I bother you for a minute? I thought we had…"

It all came out in one long stream without pause or comma, and then he stopped. There in the office by Nick Ambrose's desk stood Dante. Dante Ivers, the young man who had come to be a competent and caring agronomist and cannabis grower under Nick's tutelage, who had been hit hard by his father's death and hadn't been here, except for required executive meetings.

"Dan…"

He never believed in calling him Dante.

"Rafael, I never thought I'd be so happy to see your ugly mug."

"Same here."

Two steps brought them closer and into an awkward man-hug.

"Where the hell have you been?" Rafael asked and slapped the younger man's back. "Don't you see when you're needed? Things are going to hell in a handbasket around here, and pretty damn quick…"

"Hey, Rafael, do you mind? I'm standing right here. What am I, chopped liver?" Nick groused, but there was only humor in his voice.

"No offense, Nick, but you gotta admit—we missed this guy." Another affectionate punch in the arm.

"That I have to, and that we did."

"I needed some time," Dante said, passing over the issue of his whereabouts. "Took my motorcycle, drove around every day until I could feel my head again. Hey, I heard about some dickhead trying to frame you for—for the shooting. Did they ever figure who that was?"

"Not yet." Rafael shook his head. "In the meantime, the detective thought if somebody went through that much trouble to make me look guilty, there was probably a half decent chance I was innocent."

"Innocent—listen to you. Are you trying to make me laugh, Covin?"

"Not guilty then, and don't give me that kind of grief when you've been back for all of five minutes. What about you?"

Dante shrugged. "You know… Hired a good lawyer, made them check every goddamn traffic camera from the night in question. I guess I'm on quite a few of them. I was mad—had issues with speed limits and red lights. Never thought that would be a good thing." Another shrug and he looked away. "Cost me enough money hiring people to look through them all. Sorry if that made them look at you real close."

"Are you kidding me? I told everybody who would listen you weren't involved. Why are you even standing here apologizing? Would have done the same thing for myself if I thought it would help any."

"Well, I knew you couldn't have done it either."

"Guys, if we're all done assuring each other that we didn't, and wouldn't, shoot Tadeo, can we get back to the business at hand then?" Nick asked, pointedly looking down at his phone. "I'm drowning in requests for status updates on plants, strains, genetics… You know— that marijuana growing stuff. What we do here to make money."

"Yeah, that's kind of why I am here." Rafael waved the sheaf of papers in his hand. "I wanted to talk to you about the bottles our oil comes in. We've got a wagon load of customer complaints here, and I thought…"

"Wait, now that both of you are back," Nick said, raising his hands, "I'm going to deputize Dante here to deal with that—with an assist from you, Rafa. I'm up to my eyeballs in testing our high-CBD strains, and it can't wait."

"Test away, good man. Dante and I have got it covered. You are still on the payroll around here, aren't you?"

Dante only nodded, and Rafael couldn't have been more pleased to have the old gang back together—almost. Shit they'd created magic way back when, and he told Dante so. Time to produce a miracle again.

***

"Whatever happened to Roberto, by the way?" he asked a little while later, when he and Dante had grabbed an available office, and kicked around bottle and label designs until they were tired, finally sending out for some sandwiches. "Last I saw him was—well, at the board meeting immediately before…"

"When my father foolishly fired you, even more foolishly wanted to make me CEO, and was subsequently found shot dead, you mean?"

"I wouldn't have put it quite that bluntly."

"No other way to put it, Rafa. It is exactly what happened."

"And Roberto?"

Dante took an enormous bite from his sandwich and chewed and swallowed at his leisure, buying time.

"I don't know," he said. "For the longest time, I thought maybe he had something to do with the shooting. Now, I'm not so sure anymore."

"Do I take this to mean you haven't spoken to him since then?"

"Nobody has spoken to him. He had grand plans where PerCan was concerned. And when he heard Father wanted me to be CEO—hell, he just about exploded. Said Barry Wentworth promised and Dad promised, and if they wanted to make him a director, nobody could

235

stop them. They still said no, not going to happen, and he wanted nothing to do with our father any longer."

"Some family reunion. And Roberto's history."

"Yup—sounds like a ready-made motive and handy suspect, no? But mad as he was, Roberto didn't do it either."

"Agree, I knew that."

"Back up the truck. How did you know?"

"The cops were looking at me for the shooting—and they were looking really closely, believe me. So, Al hired somebody to help me out sorting through the suspicions, figuring out what was real and was not."

"Let me guess, his old buddy Sandro?"

"The very same one, so you know him too." Rafael laughed. "Sandro creeps me out. But it turns out Roberto had the same idea and went to see Sandro—too. I'm surprised we didn't run into one another."

Dante laughed. "Heck, I was thinking about it as well."

"Turns out what really happened was Roberto was out committing another crime that night."

"I don't even want to guess."

Rafael shrugged. "Making a few deliveries you don't want to hand over to FedEx and UPS, that was all. Looks like he had a bit of a tab to work off. He disappeared for a bit."

"So much for the happy family business growing cannabis together."

Now it was Rafael's turn to buy some time eating.

"Not like I didn't say right at the beginning it wasn't any of us. For a case that was chock-full of suspects at the start, it's drying out in a hurry. Pretty soon, I'm going to have to worry again—being the only guy without a solid alibi."

"They'll find him before that happens. Something will shake lose, has to."

"I hope you're right. I want this thing to go away and to concentrate on making this one heck of a great company. It's getting a little tiring tiptoeing around the issue of who killed Tadeo, waiting for somebody to point at me again."

Dante nodded and wadded up his sandwich wrapper, aiming for a garbage can at the far end of the room and missing by a mile.

"My sentiments exactly. I'd never thought I'd wish for the day when things were 'normal.'" His fingers made air quotes around the word. "The production floor feels kind of weird now."

"Weird how?"

"Eyes on you all the time." He pointed between his and Rafael's eyes. "There are two teams on the ice, and each is watching the other one in the hopes they will make a mistake, so I am told."

"Shit."

"Not fun," Dante sighed and shook his head. "When I walked down here to see Nick, every time I turned a corner, there was a bunch of people whispering. Except then they saw me, and all of a sudden, everybody shut up and checked some paperwork in their hands."

"Are you kidding me?" Rafael was already half out of his chair. Surely 'his people' did not act like this.

"Probably not when you're around." Dante shook his head and took the few steps to the other side of the room to dispose of his wrapper properly. "Everybody likes you. At least everybody who was around during PerCan times. Most rumors concerning you end in, 'well, he probably did not do it.'"

"Gee thanks."

"Fact of life." Another shrug. "The new people, they don't really know what to make of you yet—genius or goofball. They are split down the middle, usually. Oh, and there are a bunch of internet rumors going around, along with a weird one that somebody owes you a million dollars and you and Al are going to break legs for it. You can see why people tread lightly."

"Oh, for fuck's sake—pardon my language."

Dante shrugged silently while Rafael stomped away a few steps, turned, and came back around.

"Where is all of this coming from? Who is spreading this stuff around?"

"Couple of weird internet chat sites—you know better than to ask. Then it goes around the breakrooms."

"I know that when I find whoever is spreading this nonsense…"

"People don't usually make stuff up out of thin air. Somewhere somebody heard something they shouldn't have."

"And made up a cockamamie story around it. Damn!"

Rafael had to stop himself from hitting something and worked to contain his temper. Wasn't it enough that they faced a huge set of problems in a recently amalgamated company? Wasn't it enough that that they had to battle for every crop and every cannabis flower because something somewhere always went wrong if two teams weren't communicating openly? No? It really wasn't enough? Now somebody had to spread rumors, making the divide worse? Did they want this company to fail? Rafael sighed and put his hands together.

"Remember Greg Turner—Green Technologies?"

"Vaguely." Dante nodded and looked around for a chair. Finally, he dumped a load of papers on the ground and sat in a grey rolling chair. "First merger partner you guys contemplated when Tadeo was still alive. Something didn't go as planned and the deal was called off."

"So reads the news release. Turner was just about finished. This deal would have saved him—and us."

Dante remained silent, and Rafael resumed his pacing up and down, dragging his fingers through his hair as he went.

"Until he tried to do an end-run around shareholders and creditors, take most of the money in the company and a big investor who was poking around the corners, and start over fresh. Leave PerCan and GT to the vultures."

Dante screwed up his face trying to remember those days, what they had done, and the rumors in the company, in the growing areas.

"Not cool. I knew there was trouble, but I was still new to the whole business, and I wasn't paying much attention at the time, I confess."

"Not cool? Dante, that is not only not cool—it is illegal as hell. You don't cherry-pick the valuable bits of the company and take off, leaving shareholders and creditors behind. The only reason he tried it was because he thought Irv Moody would invest big, and he didn't want to have to share. But before any of this happened, your father gave him a million dollars to cement the deal. That's that million dollars you're hearing about."

Dante popped back upright from a slouch, and his eyes widened as if Rafael had slapped him just now.

"So why didn't you guys bother to get it back? Why is it only now that we are dealing with rumors and whispered stories? No wonder…"

"You know, Dante…" Rafael stopped before him, hands spread as if ready to catch a football. Or strangle someone. He was getting pretty darn tired of people asking why he hadn't done this or that before now, why things had been allowed to slide into this much disarray, and why, for crying out loud, there didn't seem to be any decent cohesive management strategy.

"I've been a little busy. All of us have been a little busy—what with your father getting shot, most of us being suspects, and some of us spending time in jail for something we didn't do. So, pardon me if a few things have ended up on a 'deal with this when you find the time' list, OK?"

"I am not criticizing you, Rafael."

"Good. Because as you mentioned there is a lot of dissent in the company, and I really don't need anyone to make it harder. I'm getting out of here."

Rafael turned around and left the production office, slamming the door behind him. Oh, he knew he was stomping off like a teenager with a tantrum, but it was cool off and get some space or say and do things he couldn't take back. He knew without being told that he'd let things slide at PerCan. He'd done the best he could, for God's sake.

And how could he forget a million dollars? He hadn't thought about it since the GT deal exploded. He'd been fired, planned to become a consultant, and suddenly was a murder suspect.

Until Tessa found the receipt, that million really only existed in rumors and stories, and now they had a leg-breaking rumor to go with this mess. Al or Rafael would go and break somebody's legs for taking off with that money. Rafael stopped his headlong rush through the corridors of PerCan and slowed when he reached the courtyard.

He remembered the courtyard! Back when he was still in construction, back when Barry was still Connor and they had vivid dreams and a bright future as a company. Back then, he had conceived a garden-like space in the center of the building, covered by a retractable glass roof. Sort of an interior winter garden, a place for employees to gather and take a break, a place to have small intimate meetings in a green space, surrounded by grass and live trees.

In the meantime, this garden space had fallen into disarray, like many other areas in the building, while other things took precedence, like surviving. Weeds now grew and poked through the erstwhile, perfect, stamped concrete floor, and dead leaves littered the ground. One of the trees had died as well, either from lack of water or light, the dead skeleton a chilling reminder of what was wrong still with the company.

Growing plants, having a green space in the center of the building… When they just started out, this had sounded so beautiful. Rafael shoved at a piece of litter with his shoe and sat on a small concrete bench. Out of habit, he tapped his pockets, even though he hadn't smoked in years, and finally sagged and leaned back against the wall.

"Fuck," he muttered, folded his hands between his knees, and let his head drop. "Another thing gone to waste."

This—garden—and all of the plans he'd had for it. This company and the money they were going to make, building a great reputation as one of the country's best and most promising…

"You know, this space could be something great given a bit of TLC."

Someone slid onto the bench beside him, and Rafael strained his eyes sideways without lifting his head. Dante, sure, he would follow him here.

"Hmmm…"

"Storming off in a pout doesn't really suit you, Rafael."

"I don't want to talk about it anymore," Rafael finally said and sat up straight again. "I know there is some—history with your family."

"Perceived history."

"Perceived history—fine. What I have no use for is people running around on the production floor talking about leg breaking and large sums of money. It's ridiculous and has no place in business. It makes us sound like a backyard gangster outfit, not a serious pharmaceutical company. And if our employees are doing it, I don't have to wonder why the internet is ablaze with lurid stories."

"It's not a bad idea, Rafael."

"Excuse me? Please tell me that you are kidding me because what I do not want to believe is that you just told me it's not a bad idea."

Dante shrugged casually. "I won't tell you."

"You're not serious."

"Why? Our old man built his own fantasy character. He watched too many bad movies. Even Al used that image when it suited what he was doing."

"He told me," Rafael muttered, only a little pacified. "But…"

"But use it, man. You're telling me there's a million dollars out there for us, that's going to be hard to collect—use it. Make the guy believe that you really are going to break his legs. A few of us dress up, break into his office late one day, wave around a few clubs, talk some nonsense, maybe that's all it would take. Maybe he'd just send the money back."

"I will not."

"You don't have to. Go hire someone to scare him a bit. Come on. Do you know what Nick and I could do out there in Production with a mil? What they could do in Sales, in Marketing? You want this company to be a large pharmaceutical player, but you don't want to get a little serious?"

"I want PerCan to be a large serious pharmaceutical corporation. Last time I looked, nobody at Bayer or Sandoz was going around pretending to be a gangster."

"Probably not, but these are desperate times, and desperate times…"

"Call for desperate measures." Rafael sighed. "Can we at least try the legal way first? The way where there aren't any physical threats being uttered, or even thought about?"

Dante shrugged. "If we survive that long without needing the cash. Fine, do it your way, but…"

"If it doesn't work, we can still talk about other options."

"Have it your way. I won't be able to convince you…" Dante left again, but Rafael sagged back into the bench for a spell.

10 minutes later, he found a broom in a corner and began to clean up the courtyard. No good reason, other than he didn't want to see another brilliant plan shattered by time, adverse circumstances and sheer bad luck. Not like he hadn't known that starting a cannabis company would be difficult, heartbreaking, expensive. All of the above. So, he would clean up. Pick up a broom and clean up.

When he met Al, too many years ago to remember, well before they became friends, everyone referred to him just as some weird guy. The weird guy who had his eyes everywhere and who was completely unpredictable. You avoided things that would make him mad. And Dante thought they should resurrect him.

Except for the fact that a few years had passed now, he and Al had become friends, the nightclubs had been taken over by whomever, and they had to run a clean, serious business here.

"I'm not going there," he said out loud and continued sweeping, a little more vigorously. "Not my place anyway."

The money was likely gone anyway, disappeared into the black hole that was GT, unless Tadeo Ivers had insisted on escrow. Would he? As if, Rafael thought, as if.

For a moment he stopped sweeping and leaned on his broom. He really hadn't looked into things very thoroughly from the moment he discovered the receipt. Much like Dante, first thing that came to mind was what a million would do for the company. The receipt itself was just an odd piece of paper. It just said *received*. He had to assume even Ivers wouldn't be dumb enough to hand over money just like that. You went to a lawyer, you put the funds into escrow, that's how it was done. Except for the Ivers factor.

"I know we have to save money where we can, but this is ridiculous." Rafael looked up and found Al had stepped into the courtyard.

"I seem to remember I have a number of janitors on the payroll, Rafael. Although…" He looked around and shook his head. "Not like anybody has been in here for a while."

"Covin's folly, a green space within the company. Nobody has used it since things started going sideways."

"And today you just decided to come down here and play janitor? Is everything all right, Rafael? Nick and Dante are very cross, you're in a mood…"

"Tell me something." Rafael put down the broom and folded his hands before his face. "Could your father have been—how should I put this—stupid enough to hand funds over to Turner without going through escrow?"

"That's where you're coming from." Al sighed. "Like everybody else."

"No, I mean…"

"That receipt is strange, our securities lawyer knows nothing of the payment, Tess discovered it by accident…"

"Like that…"

"It doesn't look good. So much was going on back then, and Tadeo did not do things the same way everyone else did."

"Wow."

"Pardon me."

"You phrased that real nice-like. He could be a moron about business."

"That too." Al chuckled and put a hand on Rafael's shoulders. "Our chances at getting that back…" He let the sentence trail off and looked at the dead tree.

"Certainly, Raymond must be working on it."

"As we speak," Al confirmed. "But you are correct. If Tadeo handed the funds over without any kind of strings attached, any kind of guarantees, safe harbors or the like, then…"

"Then Turner has likely spent it by now, and you know what they say."

"No. What do they say, Rafael?"

"Can't reach into a naked man's pocket."

A faint shadow crossed Al's face, almost as if he were trying to smile in the midst of chaos and difficulty.

"That is—interesting, to say the least."

"It also sucks, Al. That means, if anything at all, we're going to have to fight hard and long to get anything back, while he shrugs and claims he's broke. And if he is not totally broke, then he will fuss and fight until all of us are tired of trying to get that goddamned money out of him."

"Correct. May I assume this is why you, Dante, and Nick are so cross today?"

"You may go straight to assuming that because," Rafael picked up his broom again and gave some serious, violent sweeps to a pile of dirt, "just because—it ain't right."

"No, Cowboy Jim, it isn't."

"Quit messing with me. You of all people, Al Ivers, know how hard we worked on this, how hard we fought Tadeo to be able to do this. You know what a million means to us, to this company—to our investors."

Al said nothing, and Rafael broom-kicked the rubbish again.

"We worked our asses off. We bled for this. And now you're going to shrug and say if Raymond can't get the money out of them with his lawsuit, then we're not going to get anything? Is that what I am hearing?"

"I am open to any suggestion that does not involve threatening or harming the man in any way, Rafael." Al's voice became brittle, icy even. "I would not expect a man who has just spent a few days in jail to resort to violence."

"I have no intention of going back to jail. But I also have no intention of letting that weasel Turner walk away with our money. Our money, Al. PerCan money. Damn."

He flung the broom away, hearing it clatter to the ground somewhere behind him, and paced.

"Don't you want it back?"

"And now," Al said, "you're suggesting what has been suggested before—that I dress up as the old Ivers gangster and shake down Turner."

He sounded bitter, Rafael thought, extremely bitter—and offended. So he stopped before his friend and looked at him for a long, silent moment before he spoke again.

"No—yes—hell if I know, Al. listen…"

"There are no guarantees, Rafael. Even if I did go and threaten the man, there are no guarantees he will pay, or that he has any money left to pay. What there are, however, are a number of vile websites, designed by a number of ruthless short sellers, dealing in just that kind of gossip, hoping to cause panic mass-selling so they can make money. Do you want to feed into that? Because if we do and our share price plummets even more, even a million dollars will not help."

Again, Rafael said nothing. Then he put his hand on his friend's shoulder.

"I hear you. But help me out here—help us out. How do we do this? We need this money so badly here."

"Raymond…"

"Raymond is a good guy and a good securities lawyer, I'm sure. But he may not be up to this fight."

"Then let him try, Rafael. That is all I ask. He will start proceedings shortly, and if he does indeed not come up with anything, then… Then we can have a conversation about alternate plans."

"Alternate plans," Rafael chuckled and clapped Al's shoulder again. "You know it is going to add months before we see anything, if it even happens, right?"

"I am well aware of this." Al picked up the discarded broom and passed it from one hand to the other, as if to decide what was to be done with this instrument. "In the meantime, it's not as if we were lacking for tasks to occupy our free time. And if we should find ourselves idle after all…" He passed the broom to Rafael.

Rafael snatched it out of his hand and launched another offensive against the rubbish on the floor.

"I got it."

"And I mean it. There are enough janitors on the payroll around here, so you don't have to…"

"Well, maybe I want to."

"You're still angry."

Rafael managed to scatter and disturb more debris he had already swept up and finally gave up on the task, still unhappy, still in a mood.

"Wrong. I am livid. Mostly…" He spun his hand around in a circle for a while and shook his head. "Mostly also at us. At me. I should have paid attention back then. I should have…"

"Should have, could have, would have. Rafael, what good does it do?"

"Nothing. Just like my sweeping up in here, not a damn thing. That's why I'm pissed."

"We were agreed on that. Now come on out of this hole and help me draft a memo to our employees. I need to quash these rumors, and I need to create some community, if I can."

"And while you're at it, you need to turn iron into gold, right?"

"Why do you think I need your help?"

Al didn't wait to see if Rafael followed. He strode out of the courtyard, head up, and left Rafael scrambling behind him. They should come back to this, Rafael thought on the way out. They should do something with this courtyard again, even if they just put their damned lunch room in here, to give people a bit of a break. They should…

Then again, if they didn't manage to come up with a serious load of investor money soon, something to tide them over until funds from their next harvests and sales came, it wouldn't matter anyway. This building would belong to someone else.

TWENTY-FIVE

Kayla had not been this close to Barry since he snuck out of his office using the back door, as the police were gathering at the front to take him downtown for a few questions. How many years did that make?

'Connor Beauregard, charismatic founder of Perfect Cannabis Inc....'

Dozens of news releases started this way—news releases she had written, had published. And she'd been there, right by the side of the charismatic founder, sharing his life, with a hand on his arm.

She closed her eyes for just a moment and let out the breath she'd been holding. They had been the power couple of the year during those heady times. Money, luxury, success—excess—everywhere, all the time. Any time you opened your mouth and said *cannabis,* someone was throwing money at Connor, and he had spent it only too willingly. None of them had said anything back then, no matter what they claimed now.

Then the illegal grow op, and a statement from Roberto Ivers that Connor had been in on it all along.

Connor had made himself too big a target. And he left—ran, really. When the news hit the wires, he slipped quietly through the back door. That was it. Until Barry J. Wentworth appeared at PerCan, ready to take back what was his.

Why did he care—why did she care?

She'd been angry when he left. Distraught, heartbroken even, but time and work had a funny way of fixing things. And then there was Rafael…

Connor Beauregard belonged in the past. But, ever since he had appeared again, she'd felt the need to confront him one last time—just one last time—and he could finally stay there. What better time to do so than now, when he was in jail, when there were eyes and ears watching his every move, and he couldn't so much as make a rude gesture without supervision?

It made sense, which did not exactly make this visit any easier. Connor—Barry—wasn't even supposed to have visitors other than legal personnel, but her lawyer had made it possible. All the way through the process, Kayla's mind kept coming back to the phrase, "A lady has no place in a place like this," and felt the depressing atmosphere of the city jail like a heavy mantle pressing down on her shoulders. Never mind the slate-grey suit she wore, or the high-heeled shoes or wide-brimmed hat; she still felt exposed. The officer pawing through the contents of her purse made her skin crawl, and she swore to toss the thing and buy a new one instantly, Vuitton be damned. The place was designed to let you know you were being watched, observed, and examined at all times, and Kayla hated it two seconds into the process.

If not for pride and determination, she would have turned around and said, "Thanks, I changed my mind," but an inborn stubborn streak kept her complying with every request from the officers with her head held high, saying nothing more than yes or no.

The room where she was to meet Connor felt more like an abandoned classroom than a jail visiting room. A couple of beat-up tables and chairs, a whiteboard on the wall, used often enough to leave shadows of figures and words, and a chair by the door. Naturally.

She wouldn't be alone with Connor. An officer would be there the entire time—heavily armed, no doubt. This room had not been designed with comfort in mind. This room, she thought, was made to serve as a warning. *Be careful you don't end up here.*

Kayla shivered and resisted the impulse to hug her arms to her body. She sat on one of the wooden chairs, pin-straight, clutching the strap of her bag. She did not belong here; this much had been established.

Then the door opened, and he wheeled inside. Instantly, the room seemed too small and the air too stifling and suffocating. Even in a wheelchair, owing to his broken legs, Connor was larger than life. The years that had passed shrank down to nothing, and Kayla felt her nails digging into her palms.

"Well, look who the cat dragged in. I thought I wasn't to have any visitors other than legal counsel."

"I know—a few…"

She hated how tight and tense her voice sounded, hated the smug grin on his face, hated that he could affect her like this after all this time. Finally, she rolled her shoulders and straightened her spine. Who here was in jail, locked up?

"I made it happen," she started again and shrugged.

"You know a few people and called in a few favors, that it?"

Barry rolled up to the old table and put his hands on it. He looked tired, as if he had just come off an eight-hour transcontinental flight. They didn't make him wear shackles, and the only guard was the man sitting by the door. Not like Barry could run with his prison-issue wheelchair.

"That's it. You don't look bad for a guy who just crashed a private plane after stealing it."

Now it was Barry's turn to shrug. "Had to get away."

Did you do it? It was the one question on her mind, and yet the one she didn't want to ask and didn't want to hear the answer. *Did you do it, and what exactly was 'it' anyway? Buy an illegal unregistered handgun and carry it around? Shoot Tadeo Ivers, illegally grow marijuana at PerCan, or…*

"I didn't do it, if that's what you're wanting to ask."

"I didn't ask, Barry, and, in any case, there are way too many 'it's' in play here. I assume you mean shooting Ivers when you say you didn't do it."

"Any of it." Barry slapped his hands onto the table hard, eliciting a stern look and a little straighter posture from the guard at the door. *No outbursts or this visit is over.* He didn't have to say it; he just had to look.

"Any of it," Barry repeated a little quieter. "Starting with the time when all of you wanted to railroad me for Roberto's grow op."

"There is no evidence it was Roberto's."

"There's also no evidence that it was mine. Ergo, I am innocent."

"You are many things, Barry…"

Kayla didn't finish the sentence; she didn't have to. Part of her wanted to jump to her feet and run out of this godawful place. Another part of her watched Barry. She knew him, knew the twitchy little movements of his hands that meant he was impatient and felt trapped, the little tic beside his eye that started when he got angry or frustrated. Oh, he wanted out of there badly. But it served him right being in here for everything he had done and then dropping back into her life like the proverbial bad penny.

"Suit yourself. I don't feel like arguing with you. Why are you here anyway, other than to gloat and no doubt spout some politically correct nonsense about wanting to help?"

Even his voice sounded angry, impatient and frustrated. Oh yes, Barry Wentworth was dying to get out of this jail. Kayla leaned back, folded her arms, and smiled.

"I don't want to help you, Barry," she said after a while and shook her head. "That train's so far out of the station it's in another county."

"Gloating it is then. It's your money to waste asking your lawyer to get you in here. Well…"

He tried to get to his feet, hampered by miscellaneous bandages and stiff limbs, and Kayla pointed at his chair with both index fingers to make him sit back down.

"Not so fast. If I merely wanted to gloat, I would have written a nasty article in the paper and made sure everyone in here got to read it. I so don't care to gloat about you. No. I am here because of Rafael."

"Rafael?"

"Yes. Remember, your friend? Your best friend—the one you started this company with, the one you left holding the bag when you ran out of the old office just because things got a little hot?"

"I was being framed."

"And if you were as innocent as you would have me believe, then that would have come out in the end. You would have hung around to prove it. Give me a break. Things got hot, so you ran. Rafael is the one who stayed around, who looked after the company and made it work. He is the one who built something of value."

"He seems to have done a good job comforting you, didn't he?"

"I make no apologies for our relationship, Barry, so you'd best not even go there. You don't have that right."

Barry shrugged and gave her that long, stony glare that meant he didn't want to talk about something, and there was no use even starting.

"Presumably, you started this company because you wanted to create something good and run it."

A shrug. Still no answer.

"Fine—you created it because of the money, no other reason. I don't care. When Rafael and Al took over, they wanted to build a company. A functioning company that would make a positive impact on people's lives. They wanted to create jobs. They wanted to build something. It has by no means been easy, but they've done it. PerCan is... Heck, you know what PerCan is. You wanted to take it over."

"For the money, honey. I am no do-gooder. You should know that."

"Fine, for the money, Barry. You wanted the company as badly as Rafa did."

"So?"

"So…" She paused and looked down at her hands for a moment, finally took a deep breath, and squared her shoulders. "Believe me, this isn't easy to say, but this company needs either you or him—preferably both."

The bomb dropped, and for a moment, the room became so quiet the ticking of the clock on the wall became almost unbearable.

"Come again?" Barry said, shaking his head, spreading his hands. "What the… I thought Al was now the big man on campus."

"Al is a good man, and he is fighting a good fight, but he is losing, Barry. The media are tearing him to shreds on a daily basis, for doing or not doing something. The stock price is so low you need a magnifying glass, and the short sellers are gathering, betting on this thing dying."

"Not my problem." Barry shrugged. "He wanted it—his father…"

"Can you leave Tadeo out of this for just 10 minutes?" she asked and splayed her fingers.

"No, I cannot leave him out of this." His raised voice garnered them another glare from the guard, and a pointed look at his watch, and Barry continued, a little quieter.

"The man was a joke! When I met him, he was holed up in that dingy diner of his, pretending to be some old-timey gangster boss so no one would challenge him or question his authority. Meanwhile, his son ran around trying to steal my company. My company!"

"Yes, Tadeo was a…"

"An ass."

"As you will. He was difficult. But he is gone. And right now Per-Can needs somebody who can speak to the investors, institutional investors—big money. Somebody to cement a number of deals to get investor confidence up again. Some type of a signal that this company is on a solid road to success. Something to make the shorters back off."

"They are a fact of life. You don't make them back off. You handle them, and don't even try Al on that one. He doesn't have what it takes.

He's just like his father. He'd make a great gangster on TV, but nobody is going to buy a serious investment off him."

"I know he is struggling. And Rafael—Rafael could try, but he still has that investigation hanging over him."

"Well, if you hadn't noticed, Kayla, I am sitting in jail too, waiting for the cops to find the real shooter, doing physical therapy so I can get out of this thing." Barry struck the arms of the wheelchair and swept a finger around the room. "So, darling—thank you for the visit, but I don't see how I can help you."

Kayla put her palms together and brought them to her chest, as if she were praying. For a moment, she merely sat like this. Then she lifted her head.

"Barry—somebody spent a lot of time making up a video that made it look as if Rafael had been at that damned diner the night Tadeo was shot."

"Welcome to the club of suspects. I went out and bought a gun that night. I will admit to that. But I never loaded that gun, and I definitely did not kill Tadeo. So?"

"Is there any possibility you were set up as well?"

"Kayla..." Barry shook his head and slouched, hiding the lower part of his face behind a balled fist. Tight, closed—not giving anything away. The way he sat there he reminded her of nothing so much as a coiled snake. At rest, waiting to strike.

"I know you desperately want Rafael to be innocent—but where did that come from?"

"I am just asking, Barry."

"So, you finally believe that I'm innocent?"

Barry cocked his head and smirked broadly. She wanted to slap him for it.

"Not a chance, but I am finally coming around to this silly belief of Rafael's that you had nothing to do with shooting Ivers. And I am trying to figure out who did."

"Fine—fine," Barry said and made a fist, holding it to his face. He burned to get up and pace. She could see it in every fiber of his tense body, but one look at the guard by the door convinced him to stay put and stick to fidgeting.

"I still don't understand what you want from me. Why you are here? If you think somebody framed Rafael—and me…"

"Then I need to find out who that is. Al has a private investigator on standby, and the man is digging as best as he can, but he is coming up dry—everywhere."

"Why does that not surprise me? And where are our friends and helpers, the police? I appreciate your visit and your time, but I don't have the answers for you."

"Try a bit harder, Barry. Who could have done this and, most importantly—why? The whole thing doesn't make any sense."

"No shit." Barry sat back a little, shuffling in his chair, and folded his arms before his chest. "It doesn't make any sense at all. That's why I'm still sitting here."

"You've lost me."

Kayla shook her head and searched his face, his eyes, the eyes she had looked into with love so long ago. Nothing.

"Barry!"

"Look, I'm not saying I'm 100 percent sure—but pretty sure. One person who loves to see Rafael and me rot in jail is Roberto."

"Roberto? As in Tadeo's older son."

Barry shrugged. "He has the means and the funds, and the time. And he sure as hell doesn't have any loyalties to me, never mind Rafael."

"You forgot motive—why, Barry? Tell me why before you throw out names." Kayla folded over the flap of her huge purse and rose about an inch out of her chair, before a shake of his head brought her back down to sit.

"He wants PerCan, Kayla. Isn't that obvious? He has always wanted the company. He was a small-time drug dealer who did time for his misdeeds. Then Daddy up and buys a marijuana manufacturer? It's a dream come true for the little… The guy. He wants the company for all of the malfeasance he dreams of getting up to while he is in charge."

"Nobody in their right mind would issue or renew a license while a man with a criminal record is in charge. He has to know that."

Another shrug from Barry. "Maybe, but Roberto probably doesn't see that as a big problem. He thinks he can hide behind shell companies and managers and persons in charge, and remain invisible. Invisible—except for what he gets up to behind the scenes."

"That is just…"

"Insane?"

"Improbable. And that he would shoot his own father and frame you and Rafael for this?"

"I don't think he shot Tadeo. And I didn't have to be framed into buying a gun. I did it, period. I didn't use it—but I bought it. It all conveniently plays into Roberto's plan, and, if I were him, I would assume that once Rafael and I were out of the way, and hopefully in jail, I would be able to pull Al over to my side. Family and all. The brothers in charge."

"You're reaching."

"Believe it. I dealt with him back in Singapore, when we were setting up Turner. This is exactly the kind of thing he would do to get his hands on PerCan. But shooting Tadeo, no—that's one size too big for him. He doesn't have the guts or the hatred to shoot his own father."

"Wait, back up a mile." Kayla raised both her hands and closed her eyes, scooting her chair back from the table almost forcefully to put a few extra inches between her and the man she had loved at one time. "Wait, just… What the hell do you mean, when we were setting up Turner?'"

"Nothing—forget it."

"Oh, no, I won't. You will tell me, right now."

"Really? It does not work that way, honey. You are here visiting. You are here until I say to that man by the door, 'Take me out of here.'"

This time, it was Barry's turn to rise out of his chair, and Kayla stopped him with a raised hand.

"You're right, and I am sorry. Barry, I am sorry. I shouldn't have… What you said just now—Turner? Are you talking about Greg Turner?"

Barry merely shrugged and looked down at his hands on the table.

"And you—framed him? Al and an entire pack of lawyers are just about to beat the million good-faith payment back out of him."

"Good luck with that one. He is broker than broke. He needs somebody to pay for his tab at Starbucks—not give back a million he long since pissed away."

"But what are you talking about? You framed him? I need to understand. Barry…"

This time, the raised voices had become too much for the guard at the door. He rose to his feet, came over with slow and deliberate steps, and rapped on the table a few times.

"All right, folks. That's it. This—visit—is highly unusual anyway. I'm going to have to shut this down right now. That's enough. Madam."

He nodded to Kayla and indicated the door. "If you would please."

"Wait. I understand, just one more minute. I just need to know…"

"Lady, he was not supposed to have any visitors in the first place, except for his own lawyer. We made an exception because apparently you know some very important people in some very high places. But that's it. What I am doing here is asking you nicely to get up and end this visit."

"But…"

"Or I can get a whole lot more uncomfortable. And it would be in all the papers—not just yours, Miss Montecito."

Kayla rose to her feet and gave one last helpless look to Barry, who shrugged. "Go along, then."

"Barry!"

"We gave him just enough information on Tadeo to make him want to blow the deal all by himself so Rafael would have to merge with Mariposa, that's all. No big deal. Now go on along."

Kayla felt a hand on her elbow and tore it away.

"I am coming. I am coming. Just…"

"Now, Miss. It's enough."

"I said I am leaving." Violently, Kayla tore her arm away from the guard and stalked toward the door, high heels clicking needlessly loudly on the concrete floor.

"Well, then, come along if you insist. Lead me out of this building."

The guard doubled for a moment and had to scramble to catch up to her. Just as the door closed, she heard Barry's laughter.

We gave him just enough information on Tadeo. What the heck? What had they done? All of a sudden, she couldn't wait to get out of there and talk to Rafael and Al. It could be just a mere coincidence, sure, but she had been running a magazine long enough to realize that mere coincidences happened rarely, if at all.

TWENTY-SIX

"Thank you—thank you very much for the good news." Al said and leaned back, grinning now at the phone in his hand.

"I don't think that this is going to be easy by any means," his lawyer cautioned, "but…"

"We have made a start, understood."

"Well, I…"

"I will be in touch, Raymond. Please prepare any paperwork that might be needed and leave the worrying to me."

"Admire your positive spirit, Al."

"Thank you, Raymond. You take care now."

Al Ivers put down his phone and settled back in his chair with as much of a smug, contented grin as he was able to muster just then.

Justice.

Justice could be a beautiful thing. Even if he never got to collect a penny, a court of justice had compelled Greg Turner to return $1 million, given as a good-faith payment, to Perfect Cannabis Corporation, including interest from the time the proposed merger was terminated and all of the legal fees.

Step one.

And even though he was painfully aware that obtaining this judgment was a formality and would be the easiest part of the whole transaction, he felt as if he had won a victory. He had gotten what he wanted, and for just one moment, he wanted to sit here and enjoy it.

Al sat at his desk a little while later, digging through the never-declining mountain of paperwork, when someone opened the door and stuck his head in.

"Busy?"

"Always. Hello, Irv." Al nodded toward the two visitor's chairs before his desk, realized they were covered in paperwork, and looked around. "Ah…"

"Never mind."

Irv Moody chuckled, deftly took a stack of paperwork off a chair, deposited it beside him on the floor, and sat.

"You're not kidding with the always."

"Nope." Al raised a sheet of paper by the outmost corner, using thumb and index finger as if it were covered in something disgusting, and let it slide back onto his desk top.

"Right at the moment, if you wish to know, I am trying to avoid license issues with this building. It seems the Ministry of Health would like to see pictures of all of our security setups, detailed descriptions, and copies of video footage."

"Don't you supply all of that with your licensing applications?"

"Usually." Al pushed the papers back together and leaned back. "But since we've just moved to a new building—this one—and we've been through the papers and all over the internet with one nasty issue or another, the ministry is being extra careful. They can make one's life… rather difficult."

"No doubt."

"Basically, they can ask for anything they want to see at any time. And it is my job to jump."

Al sounded bitter and dragged a shaky hand through his hair. Irv leaned back a bit, folding his arms behind his head.

"Not quite yours, Al."

"Come again?" Al asked with a raised eyebrow.

"Ivers." Irv Moody cocked his thumbs left and right of him. "You're the CEO here as far as I can read on the nameplate by the door. I don't know, but there are dozens of folks on your payroll running around down on the production floors whose job it should be to take care of all of these things. Delegate, my man."

"I—yes, the license is just important."

"Everything is important, Al—everything. It's like triage in a hospital. The thing that's actually dying is taken care of first."

"Thanks for the lesson, albeit unnecessary."

"Don't thank me. What's dying around here is your company and your share price. What the heck happened? We were riding a really nice 2.50 after the merger, and suddenly, it's tanked to under a buck? It hasn't been that low since your old—since your father was shot."

"I have a nasty group of short sellers who are betting we will die. My CFO tells me they own nothing—naked short sellers, he calls them, although I can't get friendly with that term. They are aggressive, but I can't manage this company to the share price."

"Neither should you. Who's our IR guy? It's news that sells shares. Good news. And you need some of that, my friend. All people are thinking about when they hear PerCan is murderers, gangsters, and wild conspiracy theories. You need to fix that."

Al forked his fingers through his hair and took a deep breath, letting it out slowly. He knew he looked like crap, he felt like crap, and just at that moment, he really wanted to tell Irv Moody to mind his own bloody business and get out of his office so he could get back to work.

Except for the minor little detail: something in the back of his mind reminded him that Irv was actually damn right. He was getting sidetracked into micromanaging every minute job—usually because the person supposed to be doing it was doing a lousy job, mind you—and some of the big-picture stuff was left by the wayside.

A lot of the big-picture stuff.

"Our IR guy left, right around the time Barry took off with your plane and crashed it. Sorry, by the way."

Irv looked pained. "Barry and I will have a little chat about his handling of my airplane, don't you worry about that. That is not what matters. Why is your HR not on the phone 24-7 hiring a proper Investor Relations person to manage your news, even an interim one? Do you have any idea how many wild rumors are circulating on social media? Have you read any of them?"

"Social media?" Al took off his glasses, and it was painfully obvious he hadn't even thought about, never mind checked, in a long time—if ever. He never had found that website Clint had shown him. "Not really."

"Well, there are theories about any one of you being the shooter. Take your pick."

"Great. I will." He took a pen and searched on his desk for a piece of paper that had not been scribbled on. "Make a note about checking and correcting right after I find a…"

"Wrong." Irv's hand came down on Al's searching fingers, making him jump back from the personal contact. Not that he and Irv didn't consider each other friends. It was just… Al Ivers didn't really do touchy-feely too often these days.

"Wrong, Al. You don't do a thing—except find a capable IR person and give them an order. And if he doesn't perform the way you expect, then you get rid of him and start over. And if that one doesn't work to your satisfaction, repeat."

"Yes, but…"

"There are several men and women out there who look perfectly capable of placing an ad—LinkedIn, Monster, dinosaur—whatever all of these online places are called. I haven't looked for a job in ages."

"OK." Al sat back and carefully put his pen back down, unwilling to admit that he had not either, and only had a vague idea what Irv was talking about.

"Al, you have got to let go of some of this stuff, or it's going to kill you."

"Don't I know it?"

"You and the company. There are investors out there, including me," Irv placed his palm on his chest, "including me, who are looking for a CEO who looks like he is going to lead this company out of this pile of manure it has slipped into."

"Again. Do you think I don't know that?"

"Then do something about it, Al." Irv cocked his finger and swept it around at the various piles of paper in the room. Truly, it looked like a college dorm room at study time: piles of paper, a forgotten pizza carton from an all-nighter, his carelessly discarded shoes.

"This isn't it, my friend. This is not what a CEO looks like who knows what he's doing and how to get us back where we belong—to the top."

"Any time you want to take over, Irv…"

"I'm sure you would like that. But you're not getting off that easy. You're getting mired in this small-time shit while the company is on fire all around you, and you can't bury your head in the sand and tell somebody to go take over. Lead—don't manage."

"You get that from your morning motivational calendar, or do you just make it up as you go along?" Al snapped and sat back a bit. "Apologies—it appears I am a bit on edge."

"Not offended over here—and edge is good. Use it."

"Irv," Al said slowly and brought his palms together, slowly rocking back and forth a bit while he chewed on a thought. "The thing is…"

"You've never really run a company like this one, am I right?"

"Uh… no. How…"

"Because it is obvious. You're struggling. You're trying to get everything right and do everything yourself, all the while you're trying to look like you have all the answers."

"I expect that is what most leaders will do."

"No, they don't. Great leaders let competent people do their job, while they keep a 50,000-foot view of the thing, and they know they fuck up. Regularly and big time. That's what the competent people are for. To prevent it from happening too often, and to clean up when it does happen. Go out there and either promote or hire a bunch of talented people and give them a job. While you—and other talented people—busy yourself plastering the news media with one piece of good news after another."

Al shook his head, took a huge breath, and let it out slowly. "I'm not an idiot, you know—I actually do know that—but the only piece of good news I can see right now is that we've won a judgment against GT and Greg Turner."

"There you go then, good news. A million dollars' worth of good news."

"If we ever collect on it. You yourself said that getting a judgment and depositing a check are about as far apart as the North and South Pole."

"Bah, humbug…" Irv waved his hand through the air. "Bloody pessimist I am, aren't I? There's a potential million to be collected. So go out and announce it. That's the immediate news."

"But I can't…"

"Yes, you can. You got a judgment right there that says you can. And then you will hire all those amazing people and announce their joining the company, and then you will…"

Al spread his hands to stem the tide of Irv's ideas.

"I get it, Irving. I get it, OK? No need to bludgeon me to death. Yes, I will make an effort to dig out the good news and blanket the newswires with it."

"And?"

"And I will hire talented people. You are right. I'm getting slammed with stuff. Stuff I shouldn't have to look after. There's just one thing I want to do myself."

"Turner?"

"Turner," Al confirmed. "The man took something that was mine, and I want it back. And I am going to look after it personally."

"Fair enough." Irv nodded. "Long as I don't find you sweeping the hallways or filing old records again. Now, leave this dump for half an hour and join me for a sociable beverage at The Lighthouse?"

Al checked his watch, then the stacks of papers around his office, and finally shrugged.

"Don't rightly see how half an hour is going to make all that much of a difference in here. Let's go."

He still didn't like the way Irv had put his finger right on the sore spot, his lack of leadership experience. But he knew he was right. Al Ivers had to stop beating his head into this thing all by himself and get some help. At least the collective head-beating would make more of an impact—and lessen the pain.

***

Energized after lunch, he had Connie research potential head-hunters and dig out résumés he had been sent out of the blue. He cleared his desk of everything that sat there and had a junior clerk sort it by responsible department—so others could worry about it—and requested staffing lists from every department. Might as well promote a few good people while he was at it.

Mentally, he ran down a list of all of the well-spoken people within the company.

Somewhere, he'd find himself a good speaker of the house as well, other than Kayla, who had her hands full with her own company. He would get her some help, and perhaps with more hands and more minds at the task, Perfect Cannabis would be able to disseminate good news. For once. It was definitely about time.

TWENTY-SEVEN

A break-and-enter in an office downtown didn't really warrant a detective showing up personally, Sean Robertson thought the next morning.

He, however, who could pride himself on having a near eidetic memory, had recognized the address when the call came in and moved with lightning speed to silence the usual newshounds and grabbed the case personally. A few other officers wondered, but they were happy with their breakfast, while he got himself down to the scene.

It was no big deal, he said to his partner, justifying why he went by himself. Just young kids, probably playing a prank. Youths stupid enough to break into the corporate office of a cannabis company, the one place where there was no product to be found, ever. Either that, or somebody stupid, or desperate—or both, which was a frightening combination. All of it good reason not to make massive headlines with this story and its connection to the world of cannabis.

He'd managed to calm down the few journalists who asked, but even as he drove himself downtown, he chewed on the fact that this was the second time in this many days that Green Technologies and the name Greg Turner had come up—in two different cases no less, both involving cannabis, an industry he considered shady to start with. Since he didn't believe in any type of coincidence, he wanted to get to the bottom, preferably without interference.

Greg Turner, on the other hand, Greg Turner needed everyone within a 10-mile radius to know how much he had suffered, what an insult this break-in had been to him and to his company. Did these thugs have any idea who he was and what he was trying to accomplish with this company? He was making life-changing medicine for the people. Never mind that this company was almost broke, and some considered it already so. No, he was convinced he could get it back up to where it belonged. Of course he could. All he needed were a few investors, powerful investors—some funds that had actually been promised to him a long time ago—before slick operators like this PerCan outfit came along.

On and on he went, how he was doing something important here. And along came some small-time punks to ruin it. Don't get him started.

As if anybody could stop him if they tried.

Greg Turner wanted this story in the news, front-page headlines. He wanted everyone to know Green Technologics. Nothing less would do.

There's no bad news as long as they spell your name right, is there? Detective Robertson thought while he looked around the scene of this break-and-enter. B&E wasn't his beat, not even close. B&E was handled by the new guys, rookies who still had to learn how to tell a true criminal from just a misguided individual, but he had muscled in and grabbed the case because of the cannabis connection, because Al Ivers mentioned Turner, and because he hoped to find the common thread here.

Once he'd gotten here, though, he had to fight a sense of disappointment. Nothing. This was honestly just small-time stuff. He tuned out Turner and his ongoing monologue, letting his eyes travel around the shabby little office, cursing the ungodly hour and his misguided eagerness.

Break-and-enter—nothing taken. If he hadn't been so eager... Waste of time. If he'd had a notebook, he would have snapped it closed and left again, muttering under his breath.

"Smells burned in here," he finally said softly, looking for a source, until he found an ashtray on Turner's desk, with the remains of a smoldering cigar in it. "Anybody ever tell you it is no longer legal to smoke at the workplace and other public places?"

"I had a break-in, here," Turner said stiffly. "The intruder struck me in the head, for crying out loud. I'm sure a cigar to calm my nerves should not be a problem. And really, why is it you are turning this around on me again? Should you not be out in the streets already hunting down the criminal who went and…"

Robertson tuned him out again. Fact one, there indeed had been a break-in at this office, and fact two, Turner had been struck. Could be teenagers hoping to get lucky in a cannabis company. Could be—but that did not explain Turner trying to hustle him and his officers out of the building.

He turned slowly again, fighting down the urge to tell Greg Turner to shut his mouth and quit spouting nonsense—and then the whole case changed. Because he saw it. A tiny spot right there by the door-frame. Small enough to be missed by most.

Blood.

Could have been red paint or ink or anything of that sort, but it wasn't. And he had seen enough blood in his career to know it. He also knew it was fresh, or it would have been worn away by anyone coming or going through that particular door. He held up his hand in a *nobody move* gesture, and, surprisingly enough, everyone in the room froze. Turner still fidgeted on his chair, there behind the massive mahogany desk, droning on how he would make this company great again, given just half a chance. Actually, he would make it great again even if you didn't give him a chance. That was what he did; that was who he was.

Robertson made a gun hand with his finger and pointed. "Shut up, Turner."

Surprisingly, he did, too. Maybe it was just the tone of voice the detective used, that *don't mess with me just now* tone that usually had the desired results.

Smoother now—almost gently—he asked, "I thought you said there was no violence here tonight?"

"Violence! Listen to me, man. Of course there was violence. This—this—thug broke in here violently. He…"

"Physical violence, Mr. Turner—physical!"

"Have you not been listening? Have I been talking to the Great Wall for the last hour? We have been violated. Green Technologies has been violated in the most grievous of ways, and I…"

"Physical violence, I mean."

"And I personally was struck."

"How exactly were you struck?"

"What do you mean, how?"

"I mean how. Explain it to me." Robertson waved his hands in the air. "Fist, open hand, blunt instrument? How? And what did you do once you were struck? Did you leave this office?"

"I already told you that, a number of times as a matter of fact. The man broke in here, I surprised him, he knocked me over, with his hands I suppose, and he left. I've told this story more than once by now. I fell against that credenza over there." He vaguely pointed behind his desk. "And by the time I got back up again, and got my senses together, I called 911."

"You didn't go after him?"

"Are you nuts? No, of course not."

Robertson looked at the office beside him. "Am I crazy, Officer?"

"No, sir, I don't think you are."

"There you have it. So you spent the entire time until the officers arrived right here in this room?"

"Yes. I did. How often do we have to go over this?"

"You will need to tell me as often as I need to hear. Stand up, please."

Turner looked around at the other officers, trying to get some support, some assistance here—anything. Obviously, this so-called detective was badgering him, the victim. But, of the three officers in the room, none of them would look at him. They were all vaguely aware that they had missed something, hoping it wouldn't come back and bite them in a soft place.

"Stand up, Mr. Turner, and turn around slowly."

Turner did, still offended, if just a smidgen intrigued what this detective was up to. "Now you may sit down again. You were not injured?"

"Not injured! I was…"

"Physically injured. In a manner that would cause you to bleed."

"I was frightened half to death, I was struck, and…"

Something furious and wild in Robertson's eyes shut this latest tirade down before it could fully come to bloom.

"No, I was not injured in a manner that would draw blood," he said with a certain amount of indignation, nodding at his executive chair behind the desk. "Although I was knocked out for a short period of time. Over there."

Robertson walked to the doorframe, peered down, and stepped back again, treading softly, almost as if he were on tiptoe, making no noise whatsoever.

"Something," he said, "does not add up here."

He pointed both index fingers. "Let's say the perp broke in here, hoping to find weed, was surprised by you, and took off after knocking you down. How is it there is blood on that doorframe over there? Fresh blood? Anybody care to elaborate? Anyone?"

The stern look was as much for his fellow officers, who had failed to see the tiny smear, as it was for Turner, who squirmed visibly in his seat again.

"Well…" he huffed. "I see—well—maybe I did injure myself." He ran his hands through his hair and looked at them, hoping to come up with a small speck of something.

"Not unless you carried your head under your arm, Mr. Turner, going by the location of the blood on the doorframe. And if you did not leave your chair after coming to and calling 911, then I don't see how this could be your blood. Ergo…"

Turner raised his hands—helpless, confused, wily, all of the above?

"Ergo, you either fought back and got in a good punch—for which I wouldn't blame you—or the perp injured himself somewhere on the premises."

"On his way in, of course!" Turner beamed quite suddenly. "He must have gotten a scratch of one kind or another—marvelous!"

"Marvelous, Mr. Turner?"

"Well of course it is. Now you have his DNA. Now you can, you know—hunt the intruder."

"You watch a lot of TV, don't you, Mr. Turner? DNA, indeed. I doubt the department would agree to elaborate DNA testing in a break-and-enter where nothing was in fact taken. However…"

He turned around to his men pointing at all of them in turn. "However, at least we do have something here, no matter how tiny it may be. Let's get to it. I want to know how the man got in, and I want to know how he injured himself. Be thorough. Show me every single sharp surface and corner where he could have done so. Mr. Turner, you better get checked out. There's an ambulance downstairs waiting for you."

"But I am not leaving my office."

"Afraid you have no choice, sir. You will need to get checked out—thoroughly. You won't be able to come in here to work for a little while anyway, while our men process the scene."

"I cannot and I will not leave my office. There are—documents—here, contracts, confidential information. I will not, you hear me?"

"Unfortunately, sir, the moment you called us, this became our crime scene."

"Somebody broke in—that's all."

"Broke in, injured you, and somehow or other left part of himself behind there on the doorframe. I'm afraid I have to insist. This office is closed down until further notice. Cartwright."

He sent Turner off with the officer who had introduced himself as Cartwright and stood in the center of the room, his palms close together.

"Now I need you to check every inch of this place, and the way the perp took to get here, you got that? Every single inch," he said to the remaining men. "I don't like the way he reacted when I found that blood, and I am almost certain there is more to that story than he is telling me. And I don't like the way he insisted on remaining here. What is it I'm not supposed to see?"

TWENTY-EIGHT

Al slammed into the office like a tornado and came to an abrupt halt when he found Rafael and Tess bent over what looked like a set of blueprints.

"Well, hello to you too," Rafael said raising an eyebrow at Al's appearance and wild facial expression. "Somebody chasing after you or what?"

"Turner, Green Technologies. Have you heard?"

"I want to say heard what, Al, which should make it obvious that I haven't. What is it that you think should have made its way to us by now? Did GT finally go bankrupt?"

"The offices of Green Technologies were broken into last night. And from what I hear, Greg was roughed up personally as well."

"Is that so?" Rafael fought to keep the smirk off his face and didn't quite manage. "I'd say that was a matter of time, with the number of people he screwed."

Al didn't laugh; he didn't even smirk. Instead, he got right into Rafael's face, so close most would have taken a step back. Rafael held his ground, squared his shoulders, and scowled.

"What? What's got you all riled up? Greg Turner is no choirboy, and he messed with a lot of good people, and that was before he scuttled our deal. It might not be the good Christian way to chuckle at his misfortune, but—hey."

"Right now, Rafael, I don't give a goddamn about Christian values. I just want you to look me in the eye and tell me neither you, nor anybody else in this company or in your employ, had even the slightest involvement with that break-in, or ever thought about having anything to do with it."

"Now wait just one goddamned…"

"So help me, Rafael, if this was one of our people, I will personally drag them out of here and you right behind. This is no joke."

Al made a fist and shook it, something Rafael had never seen him do, and he did back up then, found Al's fancy office chair, and dropped into it, heavily. For a moment, no one said anything, and Rafael purposely relaxed his body and took a few even breaths before he spoke again.

"Let me catch up here, will you, Al? You really think I—or someone in my employ—hired some thug to break in over at GT and rough up Greg Turner? What would I have to gain?"

"Our million-dollar good-faith payment perhaps? You've talked about this before. You thought this was a nifty idea."

"I thought it was one thing that could work. You insisted on going the legal route, so I backed off. And moreover, I told everyone else to back off and beware even going near the thought. Happy now?"

"No. And neither should you be. If I jumped to this conclusion, how long do you think before Robertson and his merry band of investigators come on by and ask those same questions? It's not that big of a stretch."

"And you really think I would?" Rafael pushed his hands against the armrests of the chair and sat up a little straighter. "Against your wishes?"

"Don't play the offended party, Rafael Covin. You talk about a very specific crime, and a few weeks later, it is committed? That is a huge coincidence. And I don't believe in coincidences."

"Nice to know where you sit, brother."

Rafael put his hands against the edge of Al's desk and pushed back, putting a bit of distance between himself and Al.

"I have been fighting these ridiculous rumors for months now," Al said, rubbing his temples. "Forgive me if I'm getting intense about it."

"For the last time Al, the very last. When you just barged in here like a runaway steam engine was the first time I ever heard about a break-in at GT, thought about it, or considered it. I did not as much as encourage somebody to walk by that building, never mind break into it. Is that finally good enough for you?"

Al took a step back and rubbed his hands as if he had suddenly caught a chill. Emotions chased over his face one after the other, but still, he remained silent.

"I resent as hell having to mention this, but before you even open your mouth, asking me where I was, if it's last night you're talking about, then might I suggest you check the personnel logs?"

"Why?"

"Because Tessa and I spent half the night trying to troubleshoot the goddamned security cameras on flower room seven—which will not stay on, as you well know. And the Ministry of Health has been after our asses to get it fixed. We personally replaced every yard of wire in the walls to get it done. That ought to be enough, but it galls the hell out of me that you would even ask."

"I had to," Al mumbled, finally found a visitor's chair that wasn't covered in paper, and dropped into it.

"The hell you did. You could have just accepted it the first time I said no."

Al waved his hand through the air.

"When you're done berating me, you know Robertson is going to show up here asking the same thing. And right after that, the Ministry of Health is going to be mighty interested why the police are here—again. I wouldn't be surprised if they took our license, for the final time."

"Why the hell would they? Another licensed producer was broken into, big deal. So what? Doesn't mean we are involved in anything."

"Turner owes us a lot of money."

"He owes everybody money. And some of the people he borrowed from, they're not all that polite. As we know all too well, finding someone willing to lend money to a cannabis company is not as straightforward as it sounds."

"Don't remind me." Al shook his head. "I have nightmares of Barry trying to fob off that fool Mirko with a check when he got behind in his payments."

"Mirko was a dickhead—sorry, Tessa. Who's to say Turner didn't get himself into a similar bind? His lender shows up wanting money, but there is none. Think things might get a bit rough, huh?"

"Probably."

"Now careful you don't break anything saying you're sorry for suspecting me in the first place."

Al flashed him a quick look of irritation. "I had every reason to ask. I'm trying every day to keep this company together and to silence these internet rumors. And everywhere I turn, there's another fire to put out. Firefighting is all I ever do around here. Making sure somebody doesn't get the idea to shut us down or take away our license. I get up in the morning wondering when the next crisis will hit. I do not need this kind of press or attention. Our stock definitely doesn't need it. According to Irv Moody, I'm supposed to leave all of this to run itself and go wine and dine some institutional investors."

"That wouldn't be a bad idea." Rafael nodded. "Worked for Barry."

"And it worked for you. But I cannot do that if everywhere I go, somebody asks me about the most recent crime that magically had our name connected to it."

"I remember." Rafael simmered down a bit and put his hand on Al's shoulder. "People used to ask me if I knew where Barry had run to before I could get one word in. And then he turns out to be some sort of preacher in the middle of nowhere—I wanted to slap him stupid."

"Too late," Al said automatically, answering their standing joke, and at least a bit of color returned to his face.

"The point is, Al, you're worrying about all of this, and it's taken you off your game, and that won't end well."

"I never had a game to begin with."

"Wrong. It's just different from me and Barry."

Rafael answered a slight knock at the door and admitted their new Investor Relations guru, whose name he could never remember. Callan something? He was too young to be anything but fresh out of college, too hip to be anything but here temporarily, and too woke to fall for Rafael's lines.

"I assume you heard about the break-in at GT." He breezed in as if he owned the place.

"Yes, Callan," Al said with a tired wave. "We heard. We just decided there's likely no need for a statement from our side."

"Hmmm." The young man looked down at a sheaf of papers in his hand and frowned. "The investor boards are all lit up this morning with potential connections, and you…"

"That's because the online investor boards are made up of idiots with nothing to do all day long than sit at their computers and spin conspiracy theories."

"Be that as it may, Al, there are quite a few of them who draw a line between the money GT owes us and your father's, um—background and death, and your brother Roberto."

"Roberto?" Rafael and Al asked as one, and Al spread his hands. "Why Roberto? I haven't heard from or seen my brother in months and then only to make sure he stayed as far away from this company as humanly possible."

"Precisely. They paint him as the man who would be CEO and is not beyond criminal activity."

Rafael raised both hands. "Idiots? Conspiracy nuts with too much time on their hands? Need I say more?"

"No. But we need to manage this, Rafael, before the old rumors about a gangster operation start again."

"Nobody in here is a…"

"Hang on, Rafael," Al piped up, shushing Rafael with a hand. "I know you will call me silly, but Callan has a point. I'm going to change my mind and say let's get out in front of this thing."

"How?" Rafael asked. "By saying it wasn't us? Doesn't that sound stupid, even guilty?"

"Also correct." Al frowned. "But it looks like the hounds are sniffing about, and the police soon will be. So, let's get our facts straight and our answers ready. Put some resources on getting the background on what happened at GT, as much as is known. Then find one of those hundreds of online magazines that are always calling wanting to interview me. Find one with a good coverage and reputation. We're going to show them the questions I'm willing to answer, and the GT story will have a minor bit of space in there."

"Will do."

"And we hope it will go away," Al sighed and motioned Rafael out of his chair, which he grudgingly vacated.

Rafael moved the blinds and looked out over the production floor below, following the busy coming-and-going for a few moments.

"Why break into the executive offices?" he finally asked. "Isn't that a dumb move? If you're after product, the chances of finding it there…"

"Are pretty close to zero," Al finished. "True, but it was the industry's worst-kept secret that GT shipped product out of their executive offices recently. Likely to save on warehousing space or transportation or personnel. Bad decision, it turns out—that office building where they hide out is about as safe as the donut shop on the corner."

"So you think somebody was looking for product," Rafael asked and turned back to the office. Tessa had left with the blueprints, leaving the two men alone again. "I mean—I hope so, that or indeed a creditor, but something…"

"Something about this is awfully fishy and convenient," Al said, nodding. "Why do you think I was crawling up your ass about it 10 minutes ago?"

After a long moment, punctuated only by the far-off noises from Production, Rafael pinched the skin of his throat again and again. "I do not have a good feeling about this one," he said softly. "I guarantee you none of my people had anything to do with it…" The sentence trailed off.

"But?"

"But I had this argument about that with your brother yesterday."

"Dante? Our Dante?"

"You got another brother besides Roberto and Dante?"

Al ignored that remark and sighed. "And what did my dearest brother Dante think?"

"He thought of all the good things we could do with a mil in R&D or product development, if you could just convince Turner."

"I get the picture." Al forked his hands through his hair and physically sagged behind his desk. "I'll have a talk with him later. Don't think he would do anything stupid, but…"

"If you don't mind my saying so, Al, you look already done in."

"No shit. There are days…" He straightened a few pieces of paper exactly square to one another, lined them up with the bottom of his desk, and sighed again. "There are days where the best course of action looks to be packing my old briefcase over there, leaving the keys on my desk, and not looking back."

"Give up? Come on Al, what the hell? After everything we've accomplished here? We've dragged this thing out of the muck a number of times. We'll think of something. This is not like you."

"No, that's exactly it, Rafael. We've dragged this thing out of too many tight spots, and there never does seem to be an end in sight. How many more times are we going to have to do this?"

"That's not you talking. You're just exhausted, and pissed off, and discouraged."

"Irv Moody seems to think I'm not CEO material."

"Well, Irv Moody can go and…" Rafael waggled his fingers and took a few steps toward Al. "You get my drift? Unless he is stepping up to help, I don't want to hear what he thinks. We can do this."

Al said nothing, leaving a long, silent moment until someone knocked at the door. He frowned, straightened just a little, and called, "Come."

In the door appeared Crystal from the front reception desk, and one look at her facial expression told them there was more bad news to be had.

"Yes?" Al asked with a resigned sigh. "What is it this time?"

"There's someone down in the reception hall to see you—to see both of you." She looked between Rafael and Al. "But—we didn't know if we should let him up here or not, given… well, given the circumstances."

"The circumstances?" Al asked, shaking his head. "As in?"

"As in—well—" Crystal swallowed once and started again. "Down in the reception area, having a coffee, wanting to see both of you, is Mr. Barry Wentworth, sir."

Time stood still, and something sucked all of the air out of the room. Al raised his hand with the index finger pointed and opened his mouth to speak, but no sound came out. Rafael looked at him, blinking rapidly, just as unable to speak, while Crystal opened her hands and closed them again.

Barry Wentworth.

Of all the people either one of them could have named to walk into their offices today—all the men and women in the world who might have some sort of business with Perfect Cannabis today—he was not one of them.

"How—what?" Al finally said and shook his head, clearing cobwebs. "Never mind. Send him up here, Crystal. Rafael and I will deal with him."

"Will do. Thank you, Mr. Ivers."

She turned to leave, and Al called after her. "And Crystal, have somebody—anybody—from security come up and spend some time in the proximity of these offices. Just in case."

"Yes, sir, of course."

"Is that necessary?" Rafael asked, watching her dart through the door and down the hall, relieved that someone else was dealing with this now.

"Necessary, Rafael? Geez, did they release him from jail, or did he somehow manage to sneak out? Is he being followed by a large division of the local police? Is he coming here for a friendly chat or to do something utterly crazy? Hell, yes, I do think that is necessary. Don't you?"

"I'll say," Rafael said and wiped his hand over his face. "He does know how to keep it interesting now, doesn't he?"

"Never a dull moment with Barry. From your reaction, I'm assuming you did not know anything about this either."

"Last I heard, he was languishing in jail. Flight risk was the term I heard used. Wouldn't Robertson have called us if—I mean, if he'd…" Rafael stumbled, unable to finish the sentence.

"Broken out," Al finished helpfully. "Again, the hell if I know. Why now, why today?" He stepped behind his desk again, straightening paper that did not need straightening, lining the edge of his monitor up precisely with the desk.

"Rafael."

"OK, OK." Rafael started pacing the length of their office, punctuating his words with his index fingers as if he were conducting a large orchestra. "You and I better be on the same page when he gets here. I have as much idea as you do what he actually wants or needs at this time, but it had better not be something illegal because he'll be out that door faster than he can think."

"Agreed."

"Not much I can do while I am only an advisor, but you know I've got your back. On everything that needs to be done about this."

"Should we have someone call Robertson?" Al asked, frowning. "Just in case?"

"No, I'd say wait. We can always bring in the dog-and-pony show when it's needed."

TWENTY-NINE

Al actually held his breath when the door to the executive offices flew open, crashing into the wall with a bang, only to let it out in a massive exhale when he saw Thomas Donnelly.

The man thought he was ruining PerCan, and absolutely unsuited to be CEO of a large company—but at least that was friendly fire.

"Is it true?" Thomas asked, his massive body filling the doorframe, hands left and right of his chest, ready to strangle somebody if need be. "He is here in the building."

"Wentworth?"

"Who the fuck else, Rafael? Whose brilliant idea was it to let him in? Why is he even out of jail?"

"All valid questions, Thomas." Rafael moved ever so slightly to stand between Al and Thomas. "Short answer, we don't know. How did you find out when we have known for all of 30 seconds?"

"That gal at the door—Crystal—she calls down to get one of my security people to guard your office, and you don't think I'll find out?"

Thomas covered the space between the door and Al's desk. For a large man, he actually moved with surprising speed and agility, Al thought pointlessly, gripping the arms of his chair.

"Our security people," he corrected mildly and pushed up, facing Thomas Donnelly. "Until we find out what this is all about, could I ask you to pipe it down? I don't need…"

"The fuck you don't."

"The entire company to hear us swearing at one another in the executive offices. Perhaps we can at least pretend to pull on the same rope."

"I don't give a damn what rope you are pulling on, Ivers. Those are my people working down there, part of my company that's in here, and I'll be damned if I let him come back in ruining everything."

"Well, we agree on one thing already. I have no intentions of letting anything or anybody ruin this company. You should know that. My father died for it."

For once, Thomas did not have an answer, opened his mouth and closed it again like a fish on dry land, and finally pulled back.

"See that you don't, Ivers."

"Of course." Al said back down again and actually managed a weak smile. "I don't have any objections if you want to remain up here to find out what it is Wentworth wants."

"Nothing good, I'm sure."

"If I could just ask you for a modicum of restraint."

Thomas forked his hands through his almost military brush cut and stomped around, much as Rafael had earlier.

"I call a spade a spade, that's all. What about you?" He nodded at Rafael. "You were best buddies when this here all started."

Rafael backed away and raised both hands. "No idea, Thomas, like I said. Last I heard, he was in jail. I still hope that if his departure was—unauthorized—this company would not be the first place he would stop. But…" Another shrug. "Who knows?"

Thomas looked around the executive office, at the papers covering every surface and potential seating area, and frowned.

"Y'all ever clean up in here, or do you have meetings standing up?"

Rafael displaced a few files off a two-seater leather couch and pointed. "Suit yourself."

Thomas sat, and in silence, the three men waited. It should not really take all that long to get from the reception area up to the executive offices, but Barry Wentworth would not have been the master of drama if he couldn't find a way to make them wait.

Making you wait for him, Rafael thought, *one of the many weapons in Barry's mighty arsenal.* If he chose to do so, Rafael was sure Barry could manipulate time to be where he wanted to be, when he wanted to be.

And now—he was at Perfect Cannabis once again.

What did Barry want? If he'd had to take a guess, Rafael would have said Barry wanted the company back. It was the same thing he'd always wanted, the top seat at PerCan—his brainchild, his company, his title, CEO.

Except now there was a merger partner. And Al Ivers, his sworn enemy, owned most of the original PerCan shares. Barry probably had a lock on most of the original Mariposa shares of Perfect Cannabis Consolidated, but that was far from a majority.

And he would need it, because if they put it to a vote today, no one who had read the online papers over the last few years would vote to put Barry Wentworth into the CEO seat.

No matter what they thought of Al and his accomplishments, or lack thereof, he was trying, and he was making progress, despite his own self-doubts.

There are days where the best course of action looks to be packing my old briefcase over there, leaving the keys on my desk, and not looking back. He knew the feeling too well. Many a day, he had wanted to hang it all up and go back to building things. Except every time he tried, he remembered Barry and the fire and enthusiasm he'd had when they created this company.

We'll go be drug dealers—how hard could it be?

Turns out it could be damned difficult. But every now and then, there would be that one day—when the moon was in Aquarius and the stars all aligned, when your numbers came up and kept coming up right—and everything worked out perfectly. Those were the days you lived for. And then you went back to fighting fires and solving problems and hoping such a day would come back, soon.

Just like tech in the nineties and, after that, real estate. Then cannabis had become the flavor of the day, the place where the easy money was to be had, meaning also the place where the fools were to be found.

Thomas had folded his hands between his knees and stared down at a spot somewhere by his feet, following his own train of thought. He had fought for his company, Mariposa, for well over a year, and he was not about to give up.

Al merely sat staring at the screen of his laptop. Perhaps he thought this would make him look as if he were reading emails, but Rafael knew better. His eyes had that glazed-over look that meant he too followed down the rabbit hole of his own memories with this company and with Barry Wentworth.

Just as Thomas raised his head and opened his mouth, probably to let loose some obscenity-laced remark about Barry's tardiness, it came—the knock at the door. Gentle and polite.

Al made a strangled sound, then coughed to clear his throat and said, "Come," again, with a lot less conviction and chutzpah than he would have liked.

And in an instant, Barry was back.

He stepped into the executive offices, without his usual bluster and theatrics, almost—unsure. He had to lean on a walking cane, Rafael noticed, and one leg would not quite move the way it should. Probably hurt like hell too, but not a trace of it showed in his face. Instead, determination, raw sheer determination, to take one step, and then another, to get done the thing he wanted to get done and to succeed. To win.

"Hello, everyone," he said, managing to sound cheerful, despite the hostile atmosphere in the room. "Long time no see."

"Barry," Al said, and Thomas squared his shoulders.

"What do you want here?"

Rafael knew he wouldn't get a word out if he tried, so he merely rose from his chair and pushed it toward Barry with a nod.

"Thanks."

"No problem." Who knew? He could speak after all! "Looks like it hurts like hell."

"I'll manage. Feels like I crashed a plane, that's all."

"By all rights, you shouldn't be alive," Thomas barked. "So if you want to tell us what you want, and how you got here in the first place, perhaps?"

"Thomas." Al finally raised a hand. "Kindly let me handle this?"

Thomas had a whole lot of things he wanted to say, and none of them kind. Words and phrases bubbled just below the surface. If you looked closely, you could see them in the furious working of his jaw and the angry glint of his eyes, but for once, he managed to keep his mouth shut. For once. Rafael would have grinned, had it not been completely inappropriate.

"Now then, Barry—can I offer you something? Coffee, water?"

"Thanks, Al, I appreciate your hospitality, but I'm sure you share Thomas's eagerness to know what brings me here today."

"Indeed."

"Let me assure you." Barry let his gaze travel around from one man to the next. "Let me assure all of you that I did not break out of jail."

"That's one piece of good news," Thomas muttered under his breath, silenced by a sharp look from Al.

Rafael finally did allow himself the grin he'd been holding back. "My sentiments exactly. It means they let you go. What happened?"

"What happened is that I made some spectacularly dumb choices purchasing the gun they'd tried to nail me with. Turns out the thing had never been fired in its life, and, if it had, it likely would have killed its user. Some mechanical malfunction inside—don't ask me what it was. It's enough to know that Tadeo Ivers was not shot with the gun in my possession."

"But you…"

"Made an ill-advised purchase, Thomas, correct. And I will have to face some consequences for possession of an unregistered firearm. Also correct."

Rafael really did want to ask this man who he was and what he had done with Barry Wentworth. Where was the bluster, the knowledge that he was infallible, always right, and if something went wrong, someone else had screwed up? Where was the drama and the show? Instead, this man here had the pained expression of one who had learned a painful and difficult life lesson and came through it a better person. Nah! Rafael blinked a couple of times to make sure it was really Barry sitting there.

"All right, so they let you go," Al said, and Barry picked it up again.

"For the time being, I am a free man. If only for the fact that they didn't have enough real evidence to make something stick, and stick in a way that my very expensive lawyer wouldn't have driven a truck through."

"Same here." Rafael nodded. "We really like you as a suspect, but nothing we have would make it through court, so you can go—but hang around close."

"Rafael, none of us in this room killed Tadeo Ivers."

"And you know this how?" Thomas wanted to know. "Do you by any chance know who did?"

"No, I do not," Barry said. "I wish I did. Then this nightmare would be over. But if there's one thing you have an abundance of in jail, it is time to think, and it doesn't make sense for any of us to shoot him. I could get into it, but we'd still be here tomorrow, and that's not why I am here."

"Yes, let's get back to it and leave the shooting of my father to the police. Why are you here, Barry?"

"It's easy—you need me."

"Wentworth, if you think anyone on this planet needs you—"

"Thomas!"

"Oh, come on, it's true, Al! He's made a mess out of this company the first go-around, and he thinks we need him in here—give me a break! We need him about as much as we need a fungal outbreak in the grow rooms."

Al sat back, put the tips of his fingers together, and lowered his head slightly, and for once, Rafael was glad he wasn't sitting in the CEO seat. What could he say?

Yes, Thomas is right. Get out of here. Nobody needs or wants you. Rough. And as always, Barry was partially right. They did need someone like him. Someone like him, mind you—perhaps not the actual person.

"Barry," Al finally said, "it's a little presumptuous to say you need me." He raised his hand when Barry opened his mouth to speak. "You're right, though. We do need help in this company. We have issues, we don't have enough hands on deck, and we are chronically short of money."

"Nice of you to tell him, Ivers. Why don't you put it in the paper while you're at it?"

"That is not exactly news, Thomas, merely a summary of where we stand, and if I did not say it, you could look it up on numerous investor bulletin boards online. No, those are the facts."

"Still."

"Still," Al said. "You and Irv Moody and quite a few other people have been coming to me off and on telling me I ought to hire a specialist for this area or that subject. I do understand that we need help. But I won't be doing us a favor if that help is named Barry Wentworth."

Barry's eyes blazed resentment at hearing himself referred to as "help." But to Rafael's amazement, he neither bristled nor shouted nor did anything else to show his irritation and frustration. You had to know him pretty well to see it bubble there under the surface. *The help,* the one thing Barry would never, never ever allow himself to be called. Not on his life. But now, he said nothing. He even smiled, and inclined his head a little.

"I understand that, Al—and Thomas. I've been running public companies for too many years, and I do know all about the importance of public impression and opinion as related to fundraising."

"Yet here you are."

"Here I am." Barry spread his arms and stood awkwardly. "Look, a large portion of this company belongs to me anyway." He wobbled, a little unsteady, and sat again, sacrificing his dramatic gesture to his injuries. "If I wanted to drag this company into a long and drawn-out battle for control, I could do so very easily, but that is the furthest thing from my mind. I want all of us to prosper, and I want PerCan to grow into the largest and most respected grower of medical marijuana this country has ever seen. We here in this room," his finger spun around the four men, "we here have the talent, the knowledge, the drive, and the personalities to make it happen. So I say why waste energy and money and fight internally? Why? Let's work together, let's make this happen, let's build something great from the ashes of past experience."

No one said anything for a moment. Rafael coughed into his hand to hide a little grin. Yep, that was the Barry Wentworth he had known for so long. Grand speeches and grand gestures. Worked. Every. Time.

"Yeah, maybe," Tom said, shrugging. "Fact is, though, folks around here still think you're some shady character—if not worse. Why do more harm? Thanks, but no thanks. Am I right or am I right, Ivers?"

"You're not wrong—but you're not right either." Al still had his fingers together and glared at them over the top of his glasses. "But I'm not settling this argument here and now. Fact is, Barry, we could use funds like a wanderer in the desert if you get my drift. If—and mark the word if because I am not making any promises here—if you had a place in this company, fundraising would be the only spot."

"Fine. It is what I do best after all."

"Whoa—wait, you're not..."

"Thomas, one moment please." Al raised his hand and looked directly at Barry. "What makes you so sure you could raise a single dime for us, given your—colorful history? Who in their right mind?"

"You leave that to me, please."

"Who in their right mind would cut you a check?" Thomas sat back and spread his hands. "Never going to happen."

"Again," Barry said, shrugging. "Not your problem. All you would have to do is use the funds properly when they come in."

"Funds you raised," Thomas said bitterly, shaking his head. "Using who knows what kind of means and stories. No thanks."

Al tapped his hands on his desktop and raised his voice just enough. "Thomas! If you're saying you would do without the new drying equipment and bottling line just because Barry raised the required funds, I will want to reexamine your commitment to this company."

"Well—maybe."

"Correct. Maybe." He turned back to Barry and spread his hands. "All I can tell you is thank you for coming in, congratulations on the good news of being released, and I am going to have to take this to the board. As you knew I would."

"As I knew—and that is all I ask for. Thank you for not throwing my ass out the front door."

Both men stood and shook hands. Rafael, who had said nothing during the entire exchange, rose and clapped Barry on the back.

"Good to see you out, man."

"Of course." Barry winked. "I am innocent after all."

Barry Wentworth smiled softly, nodded at Thomas Donnelly, and slowly made his way to the door and out. Rafael let out a breath he didn't realize he had been holding and dropped into his seat again.

"Of all the people."

"Innocent," Thomas scoffed. "Innocent my ass. Of all the people who woke up this morning—if someone is anything but innocent, it's him."

"Thomas, let it go." Al sighed and squeezed the bridge of his nose with his thumb and forefinger. "You do not like the man. You have made that perfectly clear to everyone in this room, and within shouting distance."

"Good. I hope it takes this time. We don't want him around here." He struck an innocent cabinet with his fist and rolled his shoulders.

"Unfortunately, he is right—we need someone like him."

"Like him, Al, yes. Key word—like. Not him personally."

"He owns a lot of shares." Al spread his hands at shoulder height and indicated the entire company around them. "Go there. Fight with him at every turn while he is exercising his voting rights. Lose opportunities and whatever credibility we have left out there while people watch your infighting and write nasty columns about the management at PerCan. How long do you think you can run a company like this? Thankfully, that is neither my nor your decision to make."

"What exactly is that supposed to mean?" Thomas asked, squaring his shoulders, still ready to do battle.

"It means I am going to do exactly what I said I would do. I will make a recommendation to the board, and we will decide as a board of executives. And we will all live with the decision. All of us. Do I make myself clear?"

Thomas grumbled, surreptitiously rubbed his knuckles, and said no more.

"And once that decision has been made, I will not tolerate any backroom intrigue against it. And that goes for you too, Rafael. I don't have to tell you that Kayla might hit the ceiling when she hears about this."

Rafael snapped his head up and shrugged. "No doubt about that."

"This is not the day I was planning to have today, people, or decisions I thought I would have to make."

Al sat back, ran both hands through his hair hard, and finally covered his face. The papers littering his desk reflected him just as he was—a man who had so many things on his plate, he did not know where to put his eyes first.

"Any idea what your recommendation will be yet?" Rafael asked, and Al shook his head.

"I'm going to have to get this straight in my brain first, and I would appreciate it if you helped me analyze all of our options, please. Good and bad."

"You know where I stand," Thomas said stiffly. "There are no options. And with that, I will go and take care of our operations again, as long as we still have some, that is. Gents."

He rose and left the room stiffly, resentment leaking out of every pore, closing the door harder than it strictly needed.

Rafael closed his eyes, took a deep breath, and let it all out again, then made a pistol finger and pointed at Al. "Stick a fork in you," he said, shaking his head.

"Too late. I was done about an hour ago. When I found out about the break-in at Turner's, and people connecting my name to it." He stopped and rolled his eyes for a moment. "Wondering why Clint can't get that damned short seller's website shut down, and what they're going to make of it all."

"These people spend too much time talking about the past," Rafael said. "And your father, and you, and Barry."

Instead of answering, Al got up and looked down at the production floor. Rafael was about to get up and leave him to his own thoughts when he turned around again.

"I wish I know who was constantly feeding them with internal information. They'll have a field day, when they realize Barry wants to come back in."

"I'll warn my people not to go there," Rafael said quickly. "But you have to realize…"

"Yes, I have to realize, Rafael. When I invested the first time around, I had never even heard of medical marijuana, but I watched Barry's presentation, and I couldn't figure it out. He was totally nuts. But—he had the touch."

"Define touch?"

"Some sort of voodoo—mojo, magic—whatever you want to call it. When he spoke, everything else ceased to matter. He promised you the moon and the stars, and by all rights, you should have raised your hand and questioned it. Reason demanded you stand up and ask him to show you those wonderful facts he spoke of so eloquently. But no, Barry wove a spell. He promised. He said everything you wanted and needed to hear, and by the time the presentation was over, you had your checkbook out already. You were buying into the dream."

"That just about sums up Barry in one," Rafael said. "Selling you a dream. Seen him operate a thousand times. Still don't know how he does it. At some point I decided—Covin, it doesn't matter how, as long as he does it and as long as he is on your team. Some of the stuff we ran together—well, it didn't have a snowball's chance in hell, but he raised money. Magic."

Rafael pretended to wave a magic wand.

The silence spread between them as the shadows in the room became longer, and the ambient noise from the production floors beyond piped down just a little. Rafael could gauge the rhythm of the plant like his own heartbeat. Just now the office and clerical staff would go home. The trimmers and cutters and everyone involved in drying and packaging cannabis would call it a day and leave whatever didn't get done today until tomorrow. The security staff would check all areas where no one was supposed to linger and chivvy anyone still there.

The automated lighting systems would take over and dim the corridors while providing the plants in the grow pods with the exact amount of light in the exact perfect spectrum and temperature. Technicians would wander through the connecting accessways, monitoring the work of the lighting and fertigation systems, check and note readings, and, overall, the plant would slowly start to go into a light hibernation until the first shift arrived tomorrow.

He'd built a good manufacturing plant, he knew that, but Rafael rose again and stepped over to the picture window, staring down at the deep shadows that made up the plant.

"Most of this building, this plant… No, call it everything, was made possible by the funds he raised, Al."

He didn't turn around, but sensed that Al nodded quiet assent.

"And we're struggling. There are people betting against us."

"You think people will not remember?" Al asked, coming to stand beside him. "And, if they do, can they get past the history?"

"The new name didn't fool anybody. But, above everything, he is a character. Love him, hate him, but people talk about him. They come around and pay attention to find out what he's going to get up to next."

"Potentially like the famous trainwreck you can't look away from? Gawk before they hose the blood off the sidewalk."

"Ouch." Rafael made a face. "You're not pulling any punches today, are you?"

"I'm trying to work out the worst-case scenario, if we agree to work with him. My recommendation to the board absolutely has to be in the best interest of all of our shareholders."

"You're not God, Al. Let the board decide."

"No." Al cut off Rafael and whatever else he might want to say with a chop of his hand. "You all have been in my ears for weeks to act like a proper CEO. If we are considering letting him back in, I have to be convinced in here." He lightly tapped the area of his heart. "In here—that this is the best thing for those folks out there who have entrusted us with their money."

"I'm not sure anybody can give you odds on that. Nobody would even try."

"You ever notice that we spend a lot of time just winging it around here. Hoping things will work out sort of like we wanted?"

"Maybe that's all we have, Al." Rafael held out his right hand, fingers splayed. "Number one," he ticked it off on his thumb, "we are in dire need of cash. If we don't raise any… Well, you know what happens then. Number two," ticking the index finger now, "Barry is good at this kind of thing—better than anyone I know. Three," middle finger, "Barry has a lot of notoriety going for him. Maybe that will make people listen, maybe not, but worth a try.

"Four, he has racked up one heck of a lot of infractions recently that might reflect on the company. And five, nobody around here trusts him. With the possible exception of you," Al fired back, ticking off on his fingers, just as Rafael had.

"I do not trust Barry whatsoever," Rafael said. "But you know what he hates more than having to answer to the CFO? Being embarrassed. For some reason, he thinks he still has it all going for himself. Well, now that he's opened his mouth that far, he does have something to prove, doesn't he?" Rafael held Al's stare hard and slowly smiled. "He thinks he can just get back out there and do his fundraising thing, and everything will be like it used to be." Rafael stopped, slowly raised his shoulders, and let them fall again. "Not like anybody out there would wait for him to fall flat on his face, now would they?"

Now he'd made Al smile, albeit a wan, tired kind of smile. "That they are."

"There'd be pools going. How long is it going to take Wentworth to fail and admit defeat?"

"Now you're the one who is being downright nasty."

"Yes." Rafael shrugged again. "But let's be honest. We have nothing to lose."

"Wrong, Rafael. We have the entire company to lose if we count on him raising funds we need, and he doesn't come through. You've been fundraising. You know how hard it is. Do you want to try again?"

"If necessary." Rafael straightened a bit and cracked his knuckles to show he was entirely serious, even though his smile had faltered a bit. "I'm not nearly as good at it as Barry is. But if he fails, you can step in, or I can step in, or anybody we choose to hire can step in. In the meantime, he will work his tail off to prove something to all of us, and it will keep him busy."

"Out of our hair, you mean."

"Out of your hair on the board, why not? He'll be too busy traveling all over, seeing people instead of stirring the pot at board meetings, causing dissent with his share votes, blocking decisions that need to be made, criticizing smart deals just because he feels like it."

Al said nothing for a long time, listening to the plant's sounds just as Rafael was, passing the same thought back and forth in his head until he thought it would explode.

"Enough," he finally said. "We're not going to decide this tonight."

"Dream on, didn't think we would."

"It should have been an easy decision."

"Keep dreaming, Ivers. I was running this company way before you, and I've yet to run into a decision that was easy."

Rafael clapped Al on the shoulder, and together they left, past the last security personnel patrolling the halls and a janitor swinging his mop in slow circles.

"Did you ever get that security camera issue fixed?"

"Don't ask." Rafael raised his hands in mock surrender and laughed. "I don't think I've ever seen anybody's fingers move as fast as Tess's when she was rewiring the damned thing. I swear she could make a fortune with that skill."

"Don't put thoughts in her head. She's been rather helpful in the last few weeks."

THIRTY

Across town, Detective Robertson and his assistant Brian Winston still found themselves in Robertson's cubicle office, while everyone else in town was already in front of their TVs, feet up, watching the news. Robertson stared unfocused at an old cup of coffee and the familiar folder before him.

"I still don't get it," he said again. "Guy breaks into a marijuana company, is surprised by the boss, knocks him down, and then leaves without taking anything? All while injuring himself—in some way we haven't figured out yet."

"Panic?" his assistant asked.

"Could be panic." Robertson nodded. "But look at Turner. He's no match for a determined burglar. Besides, he claims he was out cold from the first punch. So where—and how—did our perp injure himself?"

"Could have been anything."

Brian Winston really had wanted to go home an hour ago, but sucking up to the boss by staying rather than heading home to his family seemed like a better career move to make just then. Probably. Secretly, he decided on another half hour. In half an hour, if Robertson hadn't come up with anything solid, he'd go home too.

"Probably just cut himself breaking in."

"Did you see anything that might account for an injury that would cause bleeding?"

Brian shook his head slowly. "Not that I recall. We checked his probable entry route from one end to the other, more than once, and didn't come up with anything. Could be a sharp corner somewhere, I guess."

"Did you find a sharp corner?"

"None that I recall now, but—it's getting a bit late, and my brain's fried."

Not subtle at all. But even the non-subtle clue seemed to be lost on Detective Sergeant Robertson, chewing on this particularly gummy mystery.

"I didn't either." He took off his glasses and dangled them by an ear wire from his fingers, leaning back, focusing on something far away. "Potted plant with a shattered pot out back in the alley, but that could have been tossed out by any of the tenants. You guys check that?"

"Um—let me check." His assistant shuffled though a number of pages on his desk, trying not to curse out loud. A potted plant in the alley behind an old building? Jesus F. Who even noticed, never mind checking?

"Don't think so, sorry."

"Have your guys go back tomorrow and do so—probably has nothing to do with it. But let's be sure because nothing else about this makes sense either."

"Um, OK—yeah, sure," Brian said, desperately counting the minutes.

"I know there's something we are missing. I know it." Robertson now spun the glasses around slowly. "What I want to know is where our perp got injured. That's the key to the whole thing. If it was on the way in, fine. We find out where, we find out how—done. Though that still leaves the question why he didn't take anything, when he'd already knocked out Turner. He left several boxes of cannabis oil behind. And what I really want to know…"

Brian almost held his breath because sure and enough, there'd be another task for him to follow, and just as sure, he'd probably not like it.

"What I really want to know, Winston, is what is Greg Turner hiding from us? Because he is hiding something. A blind man can see that."

His phone chirped with a reminder, and Robertson got to his feet. He checked the screen and forked a hand through his hair.

"Jesus, I was supposed to make that call an hour ago. And you? Why are you still here? Go home, and first thing tomorrow, check that flower pot and get me the answers I'm looking for."

"Yes, sir, of course, just waiting for you."

"Never mind waiting for me. You'll be here half the night. Now get out of here."

"Yes, sir."

"And don't forget that potted plant and my answers."

Winston headed for the exit as fast as propriety would allow, and the last thing he heard while pushing his arms into the sleeves of his jacket was Detective Sergeant Robertson muttering to himself.

"Where the hell did that bastard hurt himself?"

Why his boss would waste this kind of time on a case that amounted to nothing, a case of a break-in where nothing was stolen, he still had not figured out.

THIRTY-ONE

Kayla only shrugged.

When Rafael finally got home and found her in his kitchen, preparing, as she called it, one of the rare home-cooked meals Rafael ever saw, he decided to drop everything and tell her about Barry within his first three sentences.

He'd been prepared for a shitstorm, armored against abuse hurled at him in lieu of Barry and set to proclaim his continued non-involvement. Wasn't his decision to make and he wouldn't make it; he was just the messenger, so don't shoot. At least not with live ammunition. All the bigger was his surprise when Kayla merely shrugged, turned down the stew simmering on his stove, and untied the towel from her waist.

Wait. Perhaps the outrage was only waiting in the wings, so as not to spoil dinner. The shareholders had lost money when Barry took off, the company had lost opportunities, money, and reputation, but Kayla—Kayla had had her heart ripped out of her chest, stomped on it a bit, and the pieces left behind.

"Not the reaction I had expected," he finally said after sorting through all possible scenarios in his mind, settling on the safe bet. "You're taking this with more grace than I thought you would. More than Thomas Donnelly for sure."

"You expected me to throw my hands in the air and go wailing and screaming, proclaiming never-ending revenge perhaps? If you wouldn't mind setting the table and opening the wine, please?"

She'd bought wine? Rafael got to his feet and did as told. "No, not really. But given your—history, I expected you to start a sentence with, 'If that man ever sets foot into this company again.'"

"Then what?" Kayla laughed, an amused soft tinkle in her voice he'd realized he'd missed for too long. "Then I will leave this board immediately? Then I will sell all my shares and retreat in anger? Come, Rafa, when have you ever known me to be melodramatic about business?"

"Anything I say now can and will be used against me. I'm not going there." Rafael smiled back. "I'm—no, I mean, that is kind of the attitude I had toward the whole thing and tried to convey to Al, but your... grace... surprises me."

"Thank you. I accept the compliment. I buried my anger when I went to see him in jail. That was all it took."

She wiped her hands on the towel, as if she wanted to rid herself of the memory, and shuddered a bit.

"You—what?" Rafael sat. The power of coherent speech seemed to have left him for the moment. "I—come again? You went to jail?"

"You know, you're adorable when you're confused."

"I—I am sure." Rafael said, desperately trying to catch up. "Mind explaining it to me so the confused and feebleminded can join you?"

"It's simple." Kayla brought the food to the table and nodded at his chair. "Sit."

Rafael sat.

"PerCan is in dire need of funds, and Barry Wentworth is one of the best fundraisers I have ever met. He has a gift, Rafael."

"Yes, but—"

"And whether I like him or think he's a jerk makes no damn difference at the moment. I will not sit beside him at the company Christmas party. But if it saves the company, I am quite willing to make a deal with the devil right now. You and I, and a lot of shareholders I personally know, have too much invested in this company to allow its downfall because of personal grievances, you understand?"

"Well—OK."

"It remains to be seen if he can overcome the stigma of—recent negative news reports regarding his person and practices."

"That's putting it nicely."

"But I think he will. I've watched him, Rafael. I've watched him take the worst batch of lemons life could throw him and make lemonade out of them and then pass the bucket to raise funds. Who knows what he's going to do? Maybe he'll come out of the gate and proclaim he found Jesus." Kayla raised her arms in a credible parody of Barry when he was preaching. "He has one task, which is to raise funds for PerCan—period. If he does it, he'll get paid. If not…" Kayla shrugged. "Life's a bitch, isn't it? Now eat before it gets cold. I do not make a habit of laboring in the kitchen on a regular basis. The least we could do is eat it when I make the effort."

Rafael put his fork into the stew and ate, mechanically, consciously making an effort to praise the meal at regular intervals while his thoughts tumbled all over one another. He had expected many things, but not this. And where did jail fit into this picture?

"Back up for a second," he finally said. "You actually went to jail to see him?"

"Of course I did. That's where he was at that moment, so that's where I went to see him."

"Didn't think he had visiting hours."

"He didn't. My lawyer can be very persuasive." She pulled her shoulders together and made a face of sheer distaste. "I went in to see him, in that place, and to close off that chapter of my life once and for all, and it worked."

"And Barry? How did he react to seeing you?"

"Oh please. Barry, he was his usual self, full of bluster and conviction. Master of the world, even if it is his own world."

"I am—stunned."

"Well, you shouldn't be. It is all you ever go on about, how much money you need, and what you could do…"

Rafael put his fork down and looked at her for a long moment. They had become obsessed, to the exclusion of everything else. And none of it was healthy.

"I am so sorry and grateful at the same time," he said slowly. "I didn't realize how obsessed I'd become."

"It's all right," she said again, came around the table, and gently massaged his shoulders. "I remember what it was like when you were CEO and how it lit you up."

"I was having a lot of fun," Rafael said and grinned. "But I almost forgot there is more to life, so much more."

He took her hands into both of it and gave them a squeeze. "I almost missed the best part. So why don't you tell me why you went all the way to city jail to see Barry and why you never told me about it?"

"It was my ghost." She leaned over and kissed the top of his head. "And my job to get rid of it, so I did."

THIRTY-TWO

Thomas had told his assistant, and his assistant had told a few other people, and by noon the next day, the entire building hummed with gossip and speculation. Al had noticed people chatting who grew silent and looked away when he came close.

He had put his phone on silent to be able to work, but he could feel a strange kind of tension in the air. The sideways look his secretary gave him, the fellow from Quality Control who brought testing results and put them on his desk without meeting his eyes—all of these incidents spoke a loud and clear language. Something was up.

Al stepped over to the glass wall and looked down to the production floor, and he saw them, groups of people sticking their heads together, looking left and right as if they didn't want to get caught doing something indecent. Something was definitely going around.

It didn't take a genius to put together what had happened and what the gossip was all about. Barry Wentworth was coming back—or was he?

Everybody wanted to know.

He cursed softly and called Connie.

"Can you call both Thomas and Rafael please? I want to see them in my office right now. I don't care what they are doing at the moment. Tell them to drop it."

"Yes, sir."

She raised her eyes and opened her mouth to say something, but Al stopped her, making a slicing motion with his hand.

"Never mind the gossip right now. I have a good idea what's going around the building, and I'm ending it. Now go and call those two."

"Yes, sir."

Conny slunk away, and Al pushed his chair into place with a little kick. Yet another thing to deal with, and now he was yelling at his own people. Something he had promised himself he would never do. Slowly but surely, this thing was getting away from him. A company headed for the abyss, strife and disconnect among the staff, an old nemesis about to return, and, still, the unsolved murder of his father.

Vaguely, he remembered his physician telling him to take some time to come to terms with Tadeo's death and make peace with it. But he didn't have the time to get his shoes polished, never mind having an extended time-out.

Al sat up straight, forking his fingers through his hair, and took a deep breath. Just in time, as the door opened and Rafael and Thomas stepped in together. Literally together, one glaring at the other, demanding priority.

Judging by their faces and the storm clouds in Rafael's eyes, they already knew what was going on and why he, Al, had called them in here.

Thomas stood tall, hands behind his back, a smug little grin on his face, while Rafael dropped into a chair with a weary exhaustion.

"Nice work, Thomas," Al said. "Get the staff riled up against an idea from the get-go, to make sure nothing other than your own opinion has a chance of being considered."

He made a circle with forefinger and thumb and waved it in Thomas's face.

"Forget about the fact that there is a board of directors that will be deciding things. Forget about any kind of confidentiality, chain of command, or decent news releasing protocol. Oh no, Thomas Donnelly will just go out and do as he damn well pleases."

"Are you done, Ivers? Half of this company and staff are still mine."

"Yours, Donnelly? I suggest you check your shareholder list, carefully. Because what you will find is that Barry Wentworth, the man you are fighting against, still owns a massive chunk thereof."

"So what? That doesn't mean we're going to take orders from him. The hell I let him muck around in management."

"Did you hear anybody talk about management? We are talking—no, we are not even talking. We are thinking about fundraising. It is one thought, one option, and we are considering it. Or we were until you…"

"Have you not had enough, Ivers? He cheated you. You and Rafael and Kayla Montecito, and you…"

"Hold, hold, hold." Rafael suddenly stood and stepped between them, his arms out to either side, creating distance between the two combatants. "Wait."

"I'm not done here, Rafael."

"Thomas, shut it for 30 seconds. I have some information that will—well—put you on your ass, because it did me."

Thomas opened his mouth, took a breath, and closed it again. He inclined his head the fraction of an inch and raised an eyebrow. *Nothing will convince me.* He didn't have to say it. It stood in the room. Al had started to say something and abandoned the effort.

"Kayla," Rafael began so softly both men leaned in a bit to hear him. "The Kayla Montecito you are trying so hard to protect, Donnelly. She is quite excited about the idea if it will help the company."

"Come again?"

Al blinked and shook his head.

"You heard right. Kayla Montecito turned a few levers I didn't know could turn and went to see Barry Wentworth in jail. Let that sink in for a second. She wanted some closure, and she found it," he said, still speaking softly in direct opposition to Thomas's bluster. "And when she was done with that, she realized what a big asset he could be right now. You know what she told me? And I quote verbatim. 'If I, the person who was with him, the person Connor left like a bit of spare luggage, if I can put all that aside for the good of the company, then a bunch of grown-ass men should be able to do the same.'"

"Grown-ass men? She said that?"

"And she meant it. Picture it." He spread his hands left and right by his shoulders. "She actually went into city jail to talk to him."

"Well…"

"No, not *well*, Thomas. She put aside everything that man did to her, to look out for this very company." Rafael tapped the desk beside him, emphasizing every word. "I for one went to bed damned ashamed last night. I don't know about you."

He turned on his heel, sat back in his chair in the corner, and folded his arms before his chest. Al looked thunderstruck.

"That—was entirely unexpected," he said.

"Still, I think…"

"Thomas!"

"Cool it—I get it." Thomas looked around the room and finally found a folding chair leaning against the wall. He grabbed it, unfolded it, and straddled it with his elbows on the back.

"Give me two minutes to process. So, you're saying…"

"I am saying I now have a mess on my hands, Thomas Donnelly. Your mess."

He shot a warning glance at Thomas, but got no argument.

"We owe it to the shareholders," he continued, "to try our best, presenting this idea to the board, weighing pros and cons and deciding as a group. Agreed?"

"Most board members will have the same reaction I did, the same as Rafael did by the way," Thomas grumbled.

"So be it. Kayla set a shining example for us all. If she can look past the end of her own nose and make a decision in the interest of the company, why not us?"

"The police?"

"If the board decides in favor of Barry Wentworth, he'll have to figure out how to do his job within the framework of his release. That is not our problem."

"The licensing board? Are they going to give us a hard time?"

"I don't think so. I'll have Raymond check the legalities. But it's a good point. I'll get an answer before the board meeting. You're still wandering around the edge of the real problem, though, Thomas."

"Which is?"

Al pointed toward the glass wall and the production areas beyond it.

"Our own people, Thomas. Your hotheaded reaction has everyone stirred up with rumors and suspicions, and I expect you to handle it—you, personally."

"But—I..."

"I don't care how you do it, just do it," Al said, hitting the table with a flat palm. "Make sure our people know that whatever happens, whatever we do, it is what we—the board—feel is the best possible course of action for the good of the company. Do you understand me?"

Thomas only nodded and looked at the floor beyond his chair.

"Kayla Montecito walked into jail to see a man she despises for the good of the company," Al said, his voice a papery, soft tone Rafael had come to pay attention to. It rarely meant anything good. "So, the least you can do is fix a mess you yourself created, Thomas. Get to it. Now."

Thomas sighed, shrugged, and stood from his chair, putting it back against the wall. "I'll give it a shot."

"I'd suggest you'd do more than just give it a shot."

Thomas slunk off, and Rafael was about to relax and grab the abandoned chair, only to find Al pointing at him.

"And you, I am sure, were not helping at all."

"What? But I just..."

"People listen to you, Rafael. Lord knows how you do it, but the men and women in this company close their mouths and listen when you speak. I suggest you go use that talent, and use it wisely."

"Uh—sure, though I don't know…"

"And Kayla is adored in this company. Knowing that she was at least in favor of this unholy idea ought to calm people a bit. At least until we can have our board meeting and come to a decision."

"I will try." Rafael put his head back and looked at the ceiling, and Al raised his hands beside his head, fingers spread wide.

"If we fail to save this company, I have a future somewhere herding some type of animal, because surely herding all of you into one direction is the more difficult operation."

"Aw, Al."

"Just don't. Go out there, get to work, and try to fix this mess you've made."

THIRTY-THREE

Al knew, without giving it another thought, that mentioning a potential involvement of Barry J. Wentworth in this company would be as far from easy as one could get and still be in the same zip code. For the next few days at least, Thomas appeared to be doing his job, with an assist from Rafael, because he could sense the mood in the building quieting and calming again.

A few workers still gave him a wary side-eye, and he knew they were likely polishing up their résumés, looking at other cannabis producers. For the first time, Al thought he would know what it felt like for people like Greg Turner to face the long, slow, yet inevitable, death of something you had built.

Not happening, he reminded himself regularly. *There's still life in this cannabis company. All we need is a bit of cash to get us past this tight spot right here.*

And right there was the crux of the matter.

THIRTY-FOUR

He didn't have to use a lot of pointless verbiage either to explain the situation at his board meeting a few days later. Firstly, people knew what was happening within their individual departments anyway, and secondly, the rumors were fast and detailed—in house and online.

Al looked down at the old-fashioned paper handout on the table in front of him, flicked it away softly, and straightened up a little, mentally and physically.

"So, for the benefit of anyone who may not have understood this before now, the situation is grave," he said quietly. "We need an immediate influx of cash within the next six weeks or thereabouts or face dire consequences."

Kayla had her hands folded in her lap, looking at her notes, Thomas tried valiantly to keep his mouth shut, and others fidgeted or looked at their phones. Al cleared his throat, looking at them in turn.

"The deafening silence in this room tells me you are all aware of the situation but unable to offer a viable solution at this time."

"Hire a fundraiser," Clint, the CFO who had come over from Mariposa, said, shrugging. "Been done before, hasn't it?"

"Indeed, it has. Thank you for the fitting segue, Clint, because I do have a proposal in my hands that could…"

"You are not really going to go there, are you?"

"Why yes, Clint, for the sake of this company I am willing to go just about anywhere, including this proposal, if it will save us."

He barely bit off the end of his sentence, which he thought should have been, "And so should you if your work, our people, and their well-being means anything to you." He was not doing this out of vanity or to be proved right, for God's sake. What he was suggesting to do only served one purpose: to save their company.

"Somebody care to clue the rest of us in?"

Kayla raised a hand. "If you don't mind, Al, I can certainly do the honors, again, for the benefit of everyone here in the room."

Al indicated he didn't mind, and Kayla rose slowly. "We have a proposal on the table that would see Mr. Barry Wentworth return as a fundraising consultant to PerCan."

A chorus of voices interrupted her, and she raised both hands. "As a consultant only, gentlemen. To raise money—and get paid for this effort. That's all. He knows the company, he knows the players in the industry, he's been there before."

"And last time around, he almost managed to ruin the company in the process. Remember that one, Kayla?"

"Indeed, I do, Clint. It's not something I could easily forget, but I also know that he cares about this company and went through a lot of trouble to get his hands on a large share position. By hook or by crook, he will always have a part, and it is in his own interest to prevent it from going down."

"Is he even out of jail yet?" someone asked, and Al reeled the conversation back into his end of the table.

"He came to see me a few days ago. Apparently, he has been released for the moment, as there really is not enough evidence to tie him to anything."

"No evidence..."

"No evidence, because I really didn't do it."

The door to the conference room opened wide, and in strode the master of the dramatic entry—or exit, as the case may be. Barry J. Wentworth.

Al raised his hands, in a little gesture of helplessness. If the meeting had got away from him earlier, it was gone now, and he'd never get control of it back. Pointless to try. Barry stood for a moment, clearly enjoying the cacophony of voices and arguments that met him like a solid wall.

"I see you all remember me."

Thomas Donnelly finally couldn't hold back any more, jumped to his feet, and waved a finger at Barry. "Wentworth, the last time I heard about you, you were in jail while they investigated Ivers's murder, and the time before that, you were heading there because of an illegal grow op right here in the building."

"Right on both cases, Thomas." Barry smiled his broadest 500-watt charmer. "And in both cases, they had nothing to tie me to either crime, and even though I was their favorite suspect, they had to let me go."

"This is a closed board meeting, Mr. Wentworth," Clint said a bit stiffly, and with a snide look at Al. "I am not sure what you think you are doing here, but you most certainly don't have any business in the room. If you please…"

"I came here because you need me, gentlemen—and lady." He nodded at Kayla. "Some of you already know this, others only suspect, but I have a solution to your dilemma, and I came here to present it to you personally, rather than letting these good folks get torn apart in the discussion. I am all for expediency."

Another smile, another nod at Kayla and Al, and for a moment, Al toyed with the idea of calling a time-out while someone removed Barry from the room—physically, if necessary. He forced himself to relax his tense shoulders and sighed. Even if he did, he could not see any way this meeting would still progress into something useful.

"Then expediate yourself out of the room. What part of 'closed meeting' do I need to explain to you?"

"10 minutes, that's all I ask. 10 minutes of your time. Then make a decision."

"Give me one reason I should waste time listening to you Wentworth," Thomas still stood, shaking his finger at the door. "Leave this meeting. Now."

"I would really like it if you would listen to me, Thomas, because we all—everyone in here…" Barry spun his finger around the room from one to the other. "We truly care about this company, its people and its well-being. And because we care, we have devoted all of our resources, including personal resources, to its success."

Barry looked straight at Thomas at this point. "We have given everything, stopped at nothing to put PerCan where it belongs—at the top. And I count myself among this group. I founded this company from nothing and gave years of my life and my reputation to it. I would most certainly not endanger it by growing illegally in the back room or murdering another shareholder, no matter how much I disliked him. I fight my battles in the boardrooms, not in filthy alleys. And I fight to win."

He let the silence float through the room for a moment and took a step closer to the boardroom table, opening his hands.

You could still see the preacher in him, Al thought, and for a moment, he wished for just an ounce of Wentworth's talent for theatrics and drama. At the same time, he would hate that world. Realistically, he wanted Wentworth to come back, so someone else would have to worry about the performances and the shows and the investors.

Kayla smiled serenely beside him, winking secretly, and he knew she had to be thinking the same thing. Little minx for guiding the CEO of this company exactly where she wanted him. Rafael better watch out for himself, if it wasn't too late already.

"I have a plan," Barry said. "And I can guarantee you that it will not only get you out of this temporary tight spot, but it will allow PerCan to expand, to grow, open new markets, and become the standard by which cannabis companies in the future will be measured."

Barry talked for more than 10 minutes, about his plan, his vision of the future, and his guaranteed road map as to how PerCan would get there, and, as if by a miracle, no one dared to interrupt him. He was only spelling out the very thing they all wanted, what they had worked for, and, in the case of Thomas, what they had sacrificed their personal fortunes for. He promised them victory, and when he stopped speaking, no one said a word for a long moment.

Barry did not sit or make a move for the door; he merely stood still and met their eyes, one after the other, without flinching or looking away. He stood tall, arms relaxed. He was the man who would guide this company to their future.

"Only as a consultant," Thomas finally spoke up. "If I am even going to make my mind go there for one little step, I need a guarantee that you will never sit on this board ever again."

Barry's face revealed nothing but a small smile. "That, gentlemen, is entirely up to you. You guide this company via this board. You make those decisions."

All the right notes with just the right emphasis. Al wanted to hate the man, really, but he couldn't but admire his skill and precision. A preacher indeed, and just then, his congregation would have opened the wallets. Like Father, like son. Last time he'd checked, Beauregard Senior had announced for the third time his retirement from TV preaching, but the networks kept increasing their offers. Shucks, you just couldn't turn down that kind of money for the Lord.

Barry inclined his head just a tiny bit and took a step back. "And with that, I will leave you to do just that. Gentlemen, Kayla…"

He nodded at Al and Kayla with a just a hint of a smile and a cheeky wink and left the boardroom as suddenly as he had entered it, leaning on his cane, limping just the tiniest bit, but holding his head up straight.

"Of all the dad-gummed cheek… To waltz into a closed board meeting. Why the hell didn't you call for security to come up here and…?"

Al held up a hand to stop the verbal onslaught from Thomas and pushed the papers in front of him into a messy little pile.

"It wouldn't have done any good. But it saves me everything I wanted to say before he interrupted. In summation—we need a fundraiser, he's offered to work for an extremely reasonable rate, he thinks he can do it." Al shook his head and looked left and right for moment. "Anything I am missing here?"

"The utter insanity of considering to hire this man, after everything he's done to this company?"

"Clint…"

"He has raised millions for this company," Kayla said softly, and the quarreling stopped. "I was there. No matter what I think of the man on a personal level, if you are looking to hire a fundraiser, there's no one better."

Clint scoffed. "Netflix could make a miniseries just out of the things he has been accused of doing, or maybe has done and nobody ever caught on," he said. "No. I can't possibly sign off on this. It would be suicide."

"That is your opinion, Clint, and I appreciate hearing it. He certainly has something to prove at this point."

"There's something so—seedy about this."

"He is a character for sure." Kayla smiled broadly. "And I for one know exactly of which I speak. But in a sea of MBA clones, the character is the one who is going to stick out, the one they are going to be talking about when he leaves the room, and that's the guy I want on our side. My opinion as well, no more, no less."

She sat back in her chair and smiled at Al, who knew he fully had lost control of this meeting for good. First, Barry waltzed in like he owned the place, then Kayla took center stage—and thank God for that—and now the steady background murmur in the room made it quite clear that no one was really listening to him or paying attention.

"Well then." He rose, as if standing could give him a little extra something. "It seems we have two camps here, for and against. I will add that I've asked Legal to check with the police department and the licensing office, and while they're not thrilled about it, they do not have any real objections to him working or working here, long as he does not work with any controlled substances. I've had an agreement drafted that reflects this—if we do choose to go that route. He would have one task, and that is raising funds. He receives a finder's fee if he is successful, and he does not if he strikes out. We have, in fact, very little to lose if—if we choose to take him up on it."

"It is utterly ludicrous that we are even sitting here discussing it," Thomas said, shaking his head. "It's a deal with the devil... You are right, though. If he signs that, then payment is contingent upon him raising funds, and then we have nothing to lose. Hell, we even look very forgiving, and it might be kinda fun to watch him fall flat on his face and waste a few months doing so."

"You can't possibly consider..."

"Have you ever heard of getting over past mistakes..."

"Folks." Al raised his hands again to stem the tide of opinions. "I know we could sit here and argue for hours, but I would favor voting on this now. Whatever we might say for or against is not going to materially change the way any of us feels. Let's vote on the issue and see if we can solve this."

**

"And just like that," Kayla recounted later to Rafael, "just like that they decided to let him have a go at it and try his luck. It took all of us a while to go from, 'Are you nuts?' to, 'Worth a try.'"

Rafael grinned. "It was always what he was best at, spinning a story and raising funds."

"The preacher, Al called him."

"An apt description." Rafael laughed. "And now, once we finally get some cash in the till, Al can concentrate on running the company instead of putting out fires, and life at PerCan will get a heck of a lot better."

"And when they finally figure out who shot Tadeo Ivers," Kayla reminded him. "That is one thing I'd rather have off our plates and our collective conscience sooner rather than later. And you and Al could run the company together."

"Don't know if I still want that." Rafael looked away and rested his face in his hand, though Kayla wouldn't let him get away with it.

"Look who's talking. You missed the place so much you got downright depressed when you got fired."

"True, but I'm getting old. And PerCan is like a troubled teenager. You love 'em even when the police show up at your door twice a week, but inside, you're just hoping they'll grow up and move out so you can sit back and do nothing but enjoy retirement."

Kayla laughed brightly at his joke, though secretly, he thought she didn't need to laugh quite as hard or as long as she did.

THIRTY-FIVE

Barry J. Wentworth signed the agreement that would put him in charge of raising funds for PerCan Consolidated, claimed some graphic designers, podcast, and short-film producers onto his team, and went to work without missing a step. It didn't bother him that the headlines called him the Fox in Charge of the Henhouse or proclaimed the Second Coming of Wentworth. He let it roll off his back with a nod to the correct spelling of his name.

"Long as they are talking about me," he would say, "at least they are not talking about that fool Greg Turner."

The media had fun with it for a few days and eventually moved on, while the collective workforce at PerCan held their breath, to see if he would deliver. Could he raise the funds to save the company? Every glimpse of him was noteworthy and became subject to lunchroom discussion. True to form, he didn't hang around the offices or even the greenhouses, unless he needed photos and video footage. He always had a smart comeback, and since everyone on staff had discussed his story at some point in their lives, they felt they had a legend in their midst.

***

Rafael held back as much as he could, knowing his opinion would be considered an endorsement one way or another, but once the board had decided to hire Barry, he breathed a huge sigh of relief. Unlike the rest of them, he didn't wonder or guess. He knew Barry would deliver. There really wasn't a question. He had watched it happen.

A week later, the packaging line was kicking up its usual fuss, and after cursing at it, telling Dante to throw it on the trash heap and get on with ordering a new one, Rafael went down there. To swing a hammer himself, as he called it.

He stormed down the hall and into the packaging room on a full head of steam, proclaiming to anyone who wanted to listen that packaging machine goulash was being made here, when he stopped short.

Right there, a group of photographers and a couple of young girls with no discernible direct job clustered around Barry Wentworth. Barry, bent over a script of some sort on a tablet, raised his head and smiled broadly.

"Rafael, my man. In your element fighting the machinery, as I can hear. How the hell are you?"

"Connor—Barry—um, the packaging line… I was, well…"

"Fixing it or throwing it out? And Barry will do just fine. Anything else will just confuse people."

"The original plan was one last chance to fix the damned thing, and then…" He waved a wrench in the general area of the packaging line. "End of the line for you. You hear?"

"Sorry to get in your way. Mind if we take a few pictures first? We're working on a new investor deck."

"Um, sure—whatever. I'll wait."

He watched the phalanx around Barry moving as he directed and couldn't but wonder—who the hell was this now? Apologizing? Asking if he minded? He finally sidled up to the group and to Barry.

"Welcome back," he said softly, and Barry shrugged.

"I founded this place. It was our idea. Only fitting that we should all be back here, don't you think?"

"Yeah, well—lot of stuff happened, you know…" His eyes traveled to a long fine scar along Barry's hairline, a memento from his plane crash, and he grinned. "Did Irv ever forgive you for wrecking his plane?"

"Not really, no. Although his insurance promised him a new one, and I plan on hitting him up for investments the moment that happens. I have a feeling that plane will stand between us forever—but he's a good guy."

"Yeah, I brought him in for a bit already."

"I heard. I also heard you did a bang-up job saving this place after I had to—leave town. Didn't know you had the fundraising game in you." Barry managed a smile and clapped Rafael on the shoulder. "Go, Rafael."

"Wasn't like I had a whole lot of choice." Rafael said and kicked at something invisible by his feet. "It had to be done, and Ivers insisted."

"Ivers!"

Barry's eyes flashed for a moment before he hid it again and looked down on his script. "Boys, make sure you get a good shot of a number of packages of finished product, OK? I want a large shot of just bottles." Turning to Rafael, he said, "That was a dark part of history. We can all count our lucky stars that's over. Not like he's grandly missed or anything."

"I'm sure there are people who would tend to agree with you, but still…"

"Still, we want to know who murdered him. Don't worry—eventually, it will be solved. In the end Tadeo got old and soft, but he screwed a lot of people over in his lifetime. Including Turner. But that's ancient history." He swept the thought and the sentence away with one hand and turned to his photographers again.

"We'll catch up later, Rafael. Let me deal with this. I have to make sure they get what I want. Save some room for drinks at The Lighthouse. It's been too long."

Rafael waited another 10 minutes, realized he was wasting time and getting in everyone's way, and finally decided to give the packaging line another day of grace. He could and would fix it or throw it away another day. It could wait. Except Barry's words kept nagging at him—*he screwed a lot of people, including Turner.* How the heck did Turner suddenly pop up in this conversation about Ivers? He'd not even been aware that Greg Turner and Tadeo Ivers had known one another. Not that it should matter at this point, but it wouldn't leave him.

***

"Hey, did you know your dad and Greg Turner knew one another?" he asked of Al when he got back upstairs to the executive offices, and the question drew a long blank look from Al.

"Not—directly," Al finally said after a two-minute pause. "This is almost… ancient history. I think Greg's father and Tadeo may have had some dealings, but it is seriously ancient stuff. How did this come up?"

"You never mentioned it when we arranged the merger."

"I wasn't consciously aware of it at the time." Al sat back and rolled a kink out of his shoulders. "It wasn't like there was a recent deal on the table. They had some type of acquaintance years ago, when Greg Turner was nothing but a teenager. I honestly never thought of it. What brought up this sudden bout of reminiscence?"

"Something Barry said just now."

"Barry?"

"Yes. I was in packaging—he's down there taking photos for a new investor deck."

"That much at least is good news. Time is ticking. And?"

"Just something he mentioned about Tadeo. How nobody missed him because he screwed a lot of people. Sorry…" He looked at Al and got nothing but a little shrug.

"He would know, I guess. And?"

"Including Turner. He said 'including Turner,'" Rafael said, wrinkling his brow. "And way back at that first board meeting when he came back to take over, another remark, 'once I had got rid of Turner.' It's like there's something about Greg Turner I can't put my fingers on."

"Rafael, might I make a small suggestion?"

"Sure." Rafael sat back and forced a broad smile, if only because he realized how silly he was sounding, even to his own ears. Nothing there, except a couple of offhand remarks.

"You are chewing on a few off-the-cuff remarks. And if it's one thing Barry excels at, it is making dumb remarks. If I were you…?"

"You would mind your own business and get back to the business at hand?"

"Correct," Al said, returning the broad smile. "We have a ton of work ahead of us. That is if Wentworth comes through with funds. So…"

"We should get on with it and not waste time on conspiracy theories," Rafael finished.

"Correct again. Give the man a raise. Now, tell me about the packaging line. Any truth to the rumor that I am going to have to budget for a new one?"

"Perhaps."

Rafael forced any mention of Greg Turner and his odd behavior out of his mind and explained his plans to Al. It was probably nothing, and he had better things to do. Except when he let his mind wander, he still wondered why Tadeo Ivers should have screwed Greg Turner, and if it had anything to do with Turner's odd behavior and him blowing up a merger about to happen.

He stopped thinking about Barry's remarks, as business at hand claimed his attention with a vengeance. They ran into one another now and then, when Barry needed something from the offices, or came to pick up printed matter, or promotional items that suddenly appeared: pens, cell phone chargers and holders, all emblazoned with the PerCan logo. They chatted cordially enough, but for some reason, they never got around to the drinks at The Lighthouse Barry had mentioned, or the extended catching-up.

Rafael thought it might have been the fact that he had straightened up the company after Connor, left town, or the fact that he and Kayla were now an item as his sons called it, or maybe just the fact that they knew all of each other's embarrassing secrets, but their conversations never did move beyond, "Amazing day we're having today." Things came up, in business and personally, and Rafael never came around to asking Barry about the connection between Greg Turner and Tadeo Ivers.

In the end he forgot about it and adopted Al's shoulder-shrug attitude—one of those weird coincidences life sometimes threw at you. Things needed to be done. There was the new packaging line that had to be purchased over Al's loud protests and installed over Thomas's assurance that it couldn't possibly go there without ruining workflow. But it didn't.

Tessa joined them in the graphic and web design department full time and appeared to be settling into the company to everyone's satisfaction. Clint, the CFO who had come over from Mariposa, proved to be a capable man who took more and more projects away from Al without asking, leaving more time for Al to concentrate on the company. Things started to fall into place, and no one could have been happier about it than Rafael. For all his bluster and talk about retiring, he couldn't imagine the day when he would walk away for the last time.

THIRTY-SIX

In the end it only took three months. The first time Barry actually raised funds through a group of institutional investors, everyone wanted to run and hug the man. He, of course, responded with, "Aw, shucks, it's just over a million, no need to get excited," all the while grinning smugly at Thomas Donnelly. Rafael expected him to stick his tongue out, which, thank God, didn't happen, but that moment set the tone. Barry was back, and he was back big time.

After that day, funds trickled in on a steady basis, which allowed them to do what they were good at: growing high-quality cannabis for an increasingly demanding pharmaceutical and recreational market.

Rafael still loved to stand upstairs in the boardroom at the grand window watching the hub of activity below. Sometimes, he thought it looked like a giant anthill, and all the little ants had a specific goal and went on to achieving it. Normalcy finally settled into the life at Perfect Cannabis.

He grinned and turned away from his favorite view, making his way back to the executive office he still shared with Al. Both because the company kept growing, and they never did have an independent space for Rafael before some new hire claimed it, and because the two had become used to sharing and saw no urgency to changing the seating arrangements.

"Who would have thought?" he said to Al. "Hurrah for boredom. For once, there are no fires to put out."

"You can deal with a handful of specific complaints Customer Care sent over for comment if you're bored with your duties, Rafael. I don't mind."

"I didn't mean no fires. I meant no gigantic, ruin-the-entire-place kind of blazes. We are finally running as we should. Little stuff we can manage."

"Yes." Al managed a tiny smile. "I hear you. This—is what you had in mind when you came up with the idea for this company, is that it?"

"Uh—no, we didn't have a clue when we came up with the idea for this company, so this is totally not what we had in mind. I don't think we ever thought past collecting a lot of investor funds, but…" He pointed both index fingers for emphasis. "But this is exactly right. This is how a company such as ours should be run. It's perfect."

"Or it could be," Al answered. "If the police finally gave up on you as a suspect and we could share this CEO seat. That would make my day a lot sweeter."

"Can't have everything." Rafael sat down and idly flipped through a few papers on his desk. "I think I'm just the last one standing. All of their other suspects eventually came up with an alibi or some well-founded reason why they couldn't have done it, and here we are—last man standing."

"It's been well over a year, and they should make up their mind. Last man standing is not an indictable offense, Rafael, even if you were mad as all get-out at Tadeo."

"You know me. I get mad quick and simmer down quick. But the good Detective Robertson checks in with me regularly enough to keep me just this side of comfortable."

"It will go away sooner rather than later. It has to." Al sat back, took off his reading glasses, and screwed the cap on his pen. "The case will go cold, something will capture their interest, and finally, they'll let it go. I'll be giving thanks when that day comes."

"And you personally," Rafael asked. "Don't you want to know who shot Tadeo?"

"I do. In a desire to see justice done kind of way. Do I need to watch someone taken to prison to have final closure? No. I had closure when they told me he was gone and he had left all of his corporate interests to me. That was it."

"Interesting." Rafael toyed with the papers on his desk again when one at the bottom of the pile caught his eye.

"I need to clean my desk," he said, picking it up with two fingers as if it were a soiled handkerchief. "This should have been thrown out before now."

"What is it?"

"Conversation notes from that time when Robertson came in here after the break-in at Green Technologies."

"Yeah, ditch it." Al nodded toward the bin. "Another weird situation at Green Technologies. Guy breaks in, takes nothing, and beats up Turner. And while he does that, he leaves a bit of his blood behind—just weird. Not that Turner didn't deserve a good thrashing."

"Everything about Turner is weird, period," Rafael muttered and fed the offending pages into the shredder.

Talking about Greg Turner made him remember Barry's remarks again, and he had no desire to follow that line of thinking. Turner had felt—off—from the day they had the merger agreement with him, and Rafael had finally run out of steam worrying about it. Maybe some things did not make sense, and you couldn't beat them into making sense either. But it would have been nice to be off Robertson's suspect list or person-of-interest list. At least it would make him sleep better.

***

He said the same thing to Kayla at a late-night dinner at their favorite restaurant.

"You're not the only one," Kayla said, poking at her food long enough for a waiter to fix her with a concerned look. "I know you didn't do it, but as far as Robertson's concerned, there is no other suspect. And for some reason, he is not willing to let it go."

"I still want to know who tried to set me up with those fake videos." Rafael signaled to the same waiter for more wine. "I wish I knew…"

Kayla pushed her wineglass in little circles and finally shook her head. "I know you like things all organized and orderly, but…" She closed her eyes for a moment and sat back, at just the angle where the candlelight made her blonde hair shine and glittered off the diamond at her throat. "But it's time to let it go. They've proven it was a fake, and you were not at the diner that night. That's it. Everything else is not your job. It is in the hands of the police, for better or worse."

"Yes, and I am still a person of interest."

"They'll get over it." She waved her hand in front of her face. "They'll drop it, eventually. Do you know how many cold cases there are in this country? Millions, Rafael—millions. Murders that never were solved, Jane and John Does, robberies… The list is endless. Cases go cold all the time. Once a year, somebody hauls them out of the archives, looks at them, and puts them back."

"That's your advice?" Rafael asked incredulously. "Seriously? Just hope that everybody will forget about it? What about Al? Don't you think he would want to know who killed his father?"

"Of course he should know." The edge in her voice let him know that she was getting irritated with him now. "Of course. But first and foremost, I am concerned with you. For the better part of a year, this has preoccupied our lives now. Please. Let's just think and talk and worry about anything other than Tadeo Ivers and who may or may not have wanted to end his life."

Her voice rose just sharply enough at the end of her sentence to make their waiter give them another concerned look from across the restaurant, and Rafael covered her hand with his own.

"I am sorry. I get—a little intense at times where this topic is concerned."

"Stop right there." She smiled and winked at him and took the hand over hers. "Don't follow it up with a 'but' or a 'therefore.' Just tell me you'll let this go."

"I will try to let this go," Rafael said with his hand over his heart, and he smiled, even though he knew that it would still occupy his thoughts. He knew when it was just him and the work and his tools, and his thoughts wandered, he would always worry. Who killed Tadeo Ivers? Why fake a video to try to blame him? Why Rafael, of all people? As far as he knew, he didn't have any enemies—none that would be willing and able to go this far, anyway.

But a promise was a promise, and he changed the subject, talking about his other favorite obsession: the renovations he was planning on his own house so Kayla could finally sell the luxury downtown condo and work on making it a proper home.

***

Rafael and Al arrived almost at the same time the following morning and walked across the parking lot, joking about it. Al carried his usual beat-up leather briefcase, while Rafael swung a backpack stuffed quite full.

"Beat you by 35 seconds." Rafael grinned.

"I was not aware that we were keeping score," Al said.

"We were not. Until I made it up just now—but I know, starting tomorrow, you'll start doing it, and it will piss you off." He laughed and elbowed Al in the side.

"You are being extremely childish." Al raised an eyebrow and shook his head; then he held out a hand and stopped Rafael. "Wait."

"What?"

Rafael shifted his backpack and searched his friend's face. "What did I miss? Meeting today? Inspection?"

"No—not at all." Al grinned broadly. "When was the last time you and I walked into the PerCan building kidding around without expecting some sort of disaster on the other side of that door?" He nodded toward the broad double doors and started to walk again. "Perhaps we finally have a handle on this thing."

"True." Rafael fell in step beside him. "It helps that Barry has been doing well with his fundraising, and we can do some of the things that have been waiting for too long."

Al put his hand on the palm reader by the doors and let the great glass doors slide apart for him and Rafael. They crossed the reception area, nodding at the ladies there, and took the stairs to the executive offices. Another nod to a minor challenge between them—who would get tired of it and head for the elevator first? Rafael was convinced his years of walking construction sites put him in better shape effortlessly, while Al paid exorbitant fees for a gym membership.

"I heard him say he's not raising funds as fast as he would like to," Al said. "I guess his past is giving him a bit more of a challenge to overcome than he had counted on."

"A little humility is not entirely bad for him," Rafael said in a lowered voice and turned back to Al when he heard him chuckle.

"What? The man lives to save the world, all day, every day? A little bite of humble pie never did anyone harm."

"Indeed," said Al, still with that amused smile on his face. "No argument there. I'm just grateful he does raise funds for us—independent of any life lessons he may or may not learn while he is doing it."

"Well," Rafael powered up his laptop and pulled up the automation logs from the previous night, "I still say it's healthy for him. Make him a lot easier to be around, too."

Al tilted his head a bit and watched Rafael for a long moment. "So, I gather the two of you did not uptake your erstwhile friendship when he resurfaced as Barry Wentworth?"

"Yeah, we talk friendly enough when we run into one another," he said, shrugging. "But you know how it goes. It's not the same. We mostly talked about his plan to branch out into other companies as a professional fundraiser."

"It would seem that is a career he would be most suited to—agreed. But you still haven't answered my question, Rafael."

"Which was? I forgot—you do keep going on."

"You and Barry, you were close friends at one point. I guess I am just—wondering what happened."

Rafael looked up from his reports and swung an index finger in large circles, indicating the building all around them.

"What happened? This happened. This building, this company, these people. I discovered I rather like building something of value and building it to last rather than... Does that answer your question? Because I really need to get back to these reports."

"By all means." Al fired up his own laptop and scrolled through notices, reports, and emails and did not speak again. But every now and then, he would look up, see Rafael's concentrated stare as he double-checked machine performances from the night before, and he smiled.

***

Thanks to Barry's success raising funds, they were able to ramp up production and sales, and modernize a few things in the packing area, one field that still gave them massive headaches. Rafael had to admit that he rarely went into that area of the building unless they called him down specifically. His pride and joy, his babies, were the cultivation rooms, and he realized, with a guilty conscience, that's where he recommended spending funds, as well.

There was one area, though, that hadn't been touched in a long time: the employee space in the center of the building with the live trees, benches, and quiet areas. With much of his own manual labor and effort, along with their arborists and a few hired construction people, he trimmed it back up to standard. Had the dead trees replaced, other greenery added, and a little coffee and refreshment station on either end of the space. It became popular with employees who needed a break or wanted to have a quiet conversation, and he always remembered planning it that way when he saw it busy with employees, management, and outside vendors.

"They call it a breakout area now," he said, rolling his eyes at Al. "All I wanted was a little quiet place to get away from things. But I like the way it looks and feels, and our people love it, breaking out or not."

Al grinned secretly and congratulated Rafael on his success. It was far too obvious—Rafael's love for the place and all of the people who worked there shone out of every pore.

Overall, the mood at PerCan improved day by day. With every positive news story that was published, every YouTube video and taped interview that ended up on someone's investor blog, they knew things were looking up, and they would get ever better from there on in.

THIRTY-SEVEN

Rafael had snuck away to enjoy a cup of coffee in the atrium area, hidden behind some neatly trimmed trees. He kicked back, let the calming ambience of the place work on him, and smiled. Not far, under another tree, a couple of employees played chess on their break, and another one lounged on a bench, making a phone call. Rafael grinned. This was it. This was what he'd had in mind.

Just then, as if to mock him, his cell phone pinged with an urgent message.

Detective Robertson would like to see both of us in the conference room.

'Both of us.' Since Al never had been a suspect, that could only mean that whatever the detective wanted to discuss with them had something to do with this company, or would impact it in some way.

Go away, he thought. *Go away and don't destroy the way things are—perfect just now. Just go away!*

Maybe it was good news this time? The detective's name always put him on edge. But, for once, couldn't it be something good? Like they had caught the actual murderer? Rafael finished his coffee in a hurry and got to his feet.

You on your way?

His phone again. Damned things, he never did like to be interrupted for every silly little thing, but now Kayla chimed in on another conversation.

Rafael? Did u know Robertson is in building?

OMW, he replied to both of them. And still he didn't move.

He had felt relieved when Tess's discovery of the video fake had taken him off the list of active, viable suspects, but the entire thing had left him with a nasty aftertaste. Robertson was not done with Rafael. What if he'd been involved after all? What if the video was faked for show? What if—what if—what if… He would only feel better once the shooter was behind bars.

However, he'd never find out what today's visit was all about unless he started to move and put one foot in front of the other, in the direction of the conference room. He was reminded of being called to the principal's office during his school days. He'd spent time at Mr. Peabody's office as a teenager—a lot of time. Reluctantly, he took a breath and decided to get it over with.

Was it his imagination, or did a few pitiful glances follow him as he walked out of the atrium and in the direction of the management offices? Nah, he was already acting guilty, and if his time at detention had taught him anything, never act guilty until they showed you the evidence.

The detective stood by the glass window looking down at the production floor and the goings-on between the grow pods.

"Good afternoon, Mr. Covin," he said briskly. "I was beginning to think I would miss you after all."

"Sorry. Got caught up with an issue on the—ah—packing line."

"I thought that was finally fixed," Al spoke up and failed to catch Rafael's twitching eyebrows.

"Never mind, gents. Nice place you have built here." Robertson indicated the space below and kept watching for a moment. "I don't know anything about growing marijuana, but down there, it looks as if everyone knows what they are doing. Also, I've heard some great things about your product. The older one gets, the more applications for it there appear to be."

"That's nice to hear," Al said and joined him at the window, folding his hands behind his back in an expression of *can you get on with this.*

"Indeed. Couple of colleagues were injured on a job—sprains, bruises, that kind of thing—so they tried your topical. Since they knew I was on your case, they told me about it. Seems to work wonders, so I am told."

"Our agronomist is one of the best there is," Rafael said, a bit breathless, forcing some semblance of calm. "Got him all the way out of Colorado to work with us."

"Really. Go figure!"

Robertson finally turned away from the window and nodded at the conference table. "Sit, gentlemen. You probably wonder why I have come to visit you in person."

"A bit." Rafael hated how tiny and squeaky his voice sounded all of a sudden. Al only nodded.

"Well, don't worry. What I have to tell you has almost nothing to do with this amazing company you've built here."

"I am not really in favor of the word 'almost,'" Rafael said, although his heartbeat slowed down quite a bit.

Again, Al nodded and folded his hands on the conference table in front of him.

"Well then. Why don't you tell us what brings you here, Detective? As you can see…" A small nod in the direction of the window. "This amazing company we have built here usually requires our presence and vigilance at this time of day."

Robertson smiled and turned to Rafael with two fingers on his lips. "How is the lovely Miss Montecito?"

"Robertson, I swear, if you were not a detective, I would…"

"Yes, Rafael?"

"Do something that is likely referenced somewhere in a list about insulting police officers," Al put in quickly. "But since you are getting to the point now, he will not have to worry about it."

A stern look in Rafael's direction. Robertson actually laughed.

"My apologies. I am having some fun with you. You looked so intense when you were walking in here, as if you expected me to have handcuffs ready. Something I should know about?"

"Your brand of humor is a little offbeat today, Detective," Rafael said weakly and shook his head.

"All right then, on to business." Robertson straightened up and smiled. "I know you are used to detective shows on TV where lab results and search results are usually available once the commercial break is over."

"Can't say I watch much of that," Al said, earning a stern look from Rafael.

"We're a good-sized police department, but things still take time—too much time. Which is why…" He bent down and dug around for a folder in his portfolio. "This took quite a while to reach me."

A folder landed on the conference table with a soft swish, and Robertson opened it, adjusting his glasses.

"After Tadeo Ivers was found shot to death, we of course obtained search warrants for all of our suspect's homes and devices, including cell phones."

He looked up at Rafael over the rim of his glasses, who grimaced and nodded. "I do remember having to turn everything in—was no fun for a little while."

"Indeed. Now we also obtained such a warrant for your brother, Roberto Ivers." Al blinked a few times, leaned back, and brought his folded hands to his chin.

"I remember," he said. "But I also remember you were a little—cross—with him because much of the contents of his phone appeared to have been wiped before Roberto gave it to you."

"It happens." Robertson poured a glass of water from a carafe on the table. "And when we suspect something like this to have taken place, that's when Plan B kicks in."

Rafael rested his folded hands on his knees and nodded slowly. "Tech guys in bad suits going over the thing restoring everything that was deleted in the last 15 years?"

"That's also a bit of TV lore. Usually, there are easier ways."

Robertson looked from one to the other as if he were teaching a couple of eager students and finally raised a finger to point at the ceiling when neither of them answered.

"The cloud, gents. Our warrant usually includes cloud storage, just in case we discover something there our lovely suspect thought we shouldn't really be looking at. Sometimes you get lucky, you know? They wipe the device and forget about cloud storage. Always worth a try. Now me? I don't even think about it until…"

"And in Roberto's case?" Al brought him back to the subject at hand, and Robertson smiled again.

"In Roberto's case we found a few interesting things. If you remember, he was involved in some nasty illegal business, which, while putting him on our radar to watch, also gave him an alibi. Couldn't have done this crime because I was busy committing another crime over here…"

"Yes, yes, I remember." Now even Al's voice acquired a bit of impatience. "And?"

Instead of answering, Robertson opened the file he had dug up earlier and pulled a handful of 8-by-10 glossy photographs from it. Al and Rafael stared, and it took a moment before they realized what they were looking at.

"The parking lot," Rafael said. "Behind the diner. That looks like…"

"Like material that might be used in the video that framed you. Good," Al said and raised a single eyebrow. "Surely now you are finally convinced that Rafael was set up—by my own brother, it looks like."

"Well… on their own, these pictures would have been pretty thin evidence either way as to whether he had or had not ordered that video made."

"Oh, come on." Al was already half out of his chair when Robertson raised both hands.

"Sit down again, Al. I'm not done yet."

Get on with it then, Rafael could only think, and a desperate look passed between him and Al.

"Yes?"

"As it so happens, Roberto is quite taken with the marijuana business. I'm not sure if you are aware, but he recently acquired a massive share in a much smaller manufacturer."

"I didn't know," Al mumbled. "And I'm not sure if congratulations or condolences are in order."

"You know, we were not either. Either way, when we invited him down to the station to speak to these photos, he was most eager to cooperate and to keep any type of suspicion off his person so as not to endanger this new venture of his."

Another sip of water and Rafael had visions of beating the man to death with the very folder of pictures in front of him. One look at Al and he realized his fingers were clenched into fists so tight his knuckles stood out white and bloodless.

"Well, to conclude—your brother in fact admitted to being the one who ordered this elaborate fake made and explained to us why he had done so. Not a great move on his part, but we thought it credible, and now…"

He smiled at both of them, swept his folder back into the portfolio, and rose to leave.

"We can finally take you off the list of persons of interest for good, Rafael. I thought you would like to hear about this personally."

He took a few steps toward the door before Al had a chance to recover and react.

"Wait, wait. That is fantastic news, and thank you very much. But are you not going to tell us what these—credible reasons were?"

Robertson stopped. "I thought you were in a hurry?"

"Al, this man's sense of humor makes me want to strangle him," Rafael said. "Is that OK?"

"No. But I share the sentiment."

Robertson sat back down. "Never mind, I was just…"

"Kidding, we know."

"Rafael, in another life, I would like you. That is another reason why I wanted to bring you the news personally. This is a good thing."

Rafael nodded, mentally giving up on ever finding up why, but holding the feeling of gratitude that rapidly expanded inside him. Finally. The thing he'd been waiting for since the night Tadeo was shot. He was in the clear.

"Barry Wentworth and your brother had quite the little plan, as he told us," Robertson continued, as if he had never got up. "According to Roberto, they were going to run all of this…" He swung his index finger around the room and ended up pointing at the window. "All of this—together. Barry would run it. Roberto would be in charge of the operations."

"As if," Rafael scoffed. "There is a little more to it than holding a title and standing up here watching over the whole thing."

"Probably. But this is what they had in mind—according to Roberto." Robertson gave a little sideways glance to Al, who shook his head without saying anything. "You, Al, would also be in there somehow as far as I understood, but certainly not CEO. More like…"

"Another token Ivers?"

"Something like that, yes."

"To me, the idea of Roberto running the production floor without supervision is sickening."

"It's all right, Rafa, not bothering me." Al nodded at Robertson. "Continue."

"Well, when he came back and Wentworth didn't follow through, he was a bit—upset about the circumstances. But while he was still trying

340

to figure out how to make Barry stick to their original agreement, your father was shot." He nodded at Al and paused for a moment. "Like a true con man, he thought there had to be a way to make this situation work in his favor, and he found it. He and you…" another nod at Al, "had alibis. You, Rafael, could be framed—at least long enough that by the time you were no longer under suspicion, nobody in this place would remember your name. That was the plan."

Rafael scoffed again, but Al held out a hand, interrupting him. "And Kayla?"

"No plan for her. According to Roberto, they assumed…" he gave a little sideways glance at Rafael, "that she would fall back in line with Barry, since they had been together at one point."

That one elicited a hearty laugh from Rafael. "Oh, the little idiot. I would just have loved to be a fly on the wall when they explained their plan to Kayla. The sparks would not have been just flying. There would have been dead bodies. Sorry, Detective."

"No offense taken."

"So, this was about the company, all along?" Al asked, visibly grappling with the thought. "The company? This entire story framing Rafael, keeping him under suspicion all this time? That video was not a cheap job! And then what? Everybody would just—what? Forget about everything Rafael had done for the company?"

"As far as thinking things through goes, I don't think your brother did a lot of that," Robertson said. "He saw an opportunity, and he took it, figuring he would work everything else out later."

"I can see why he and Barry became friends," Rafael muttered. "Not like I haven't heard that one before."

Al jumped to his feet and paced the conference room in long angry strides. "I fail to understand how you just sit there and joke about this, Rafael."

"It's easy, man. I am no longer a suspect. I'm ready to party."

"They tried to pin my father's murder on you. Murder, Rafael. Not just any little misdemeanor. And what would have happened if Tess hadn't found out the security video was a fake? You might have gone away for something you did not do."

"Eventually, it would have come out, Al," Robertson said and raised his hands, trying, and failing, to calm down Al. "We have our own experts."

"And I would have hired a dream team of lawyers who would have hired a damned expert. Robertson is right, Al. Eventually, it would have come out. It would have just taken a heck of a lot longer."

"And would have bankrupted you with lawyers' fees and potentially ruined your personal relationships."

"True." A little sobered, Rafael sat back. "What'll happen to him now?"

"Oh, there will be a case against him. And everyone who helped him put this little thing together. It'll take time. I'm sure you will eventually have a chance to bring a civil suit against Roberto if you are interested in that."

"Oh, he is interested, all right," Al said before Rafael could open his mouth to reply.

"Al, I really don't know if…"

"Shut up for the moment." Al raised a hand and rounded on Robertson. "And what about our father's murder? Did he have anything to do with that? How does that fit into this twisted scheme?"

"Not according to his own testimony. And you remember he has an alibi for the time of the murder."

"Involved in a different crime across town," Al said. "Forgive me. That is just a bit convenient after what I just heard."

"I understand. No doubt you will have more questions as you go along." This time, Robertson got to his feet in earnest. "I can't promise you to have all the answers, but I will try. I am sorry if this upset you."

"No, you tried." Al waved him off, though his eyes still blazed anger. "I was the one who insisted on being here."

"As I said, I like both of you and what you've put together here. And I thought the news that Rafael is finally in the clear for good would be welcome. That is why I came here to deliver it personally."

"It is most welcome news, Detective. It is I who must apologize for my outburst. Not every day I find out that my brother's little criminal enterprises impact me as they do here. One question I do have, though."

"Which is?" Robertson sat again.

"You refer to the—arrangement—between my brother and Barry Wentworth as a deal. Do you have any information what went down between them to make them strike this little bargain? The Barry Wentworth I knew was rather particular about the people he wanted to sit on the board of directors with him."

"Sorry, I don't. We'll have more questions for your brother, of course, but at the moment, it looks like Wentworth made him a lot of promises because he needed him right then and there."

They shook hands, and Detective Sergeant Robertson finally left PerCan, for what he hoped would be the last time in an official capacity, as he told them when he left the building.

Rafael still sat shaking his head while Al stood at the window, arms folded in front of him, looking down at the production floor.

"Are you going to say something, Al?"

"I feel I should—apologize—for the misdeeds of my brother and the trouble they brought on for you."

"Not your doing." Rafael came to stand beside him. "'Less you helped him make that video."

"Of course not. Don't even joke about this."

"I—uh, it's just weird, man. I mean, if he wanted me gone, well, your father had already fired me. All he needed to do was make that firing stand once you were in charge."

"And you think I would have gone along with this?"

"Probably not. But still… To frame someone for murder to get him out of a company is a bit of an extreme solution."

"Oh, master of understatement," Al said, turning away and continuing his pacing of the conference room. "It is extreme. I don't dare think what would have happened if you'd gone to jail for it. No big deal, as long as Roberto got what he wanted. His whole life…"

"Don't, Al." Rafael touched his friend on the arm. "Don't talk yourself into a rage over it. It's over. We'll deal… We'll move on. We always have."

"Always, he wanted this company," Al continued as if he hadn't heard Rafael. "Always. From the moment our father invested in PerCan. He wanted this company and the criminal possibilities he saw there. And now this. I am personally going to go there and…"

"No, you won't." This time, Rafael physically stopped his pacing and grabbed both of Al's hands.

"No, you won't. Just simmer down. Finally, after months of trying our best to make things work, we are both, at the same time, off the police's radar and out of their sights. We have a company to run, a life to live, and you are not going to fuck it all up again by going after your brother."

The rough language brought Al up short, and he said nothing.

"I mean it, Al. Even if the little bastard deserves it. Heck, I want to go after him and show him just what I can do with a two-by-four and a bucket full of cable ties too. But let it go. Please. Let it go."

Still breathing hard, Al freed his hands from Rafael's grip and sat in his chair again, leaning forward slightly and putting his hands over his head.

"My apologies, Rafael. After all this time of me telling you to let this thing go, this latest revelation appears to have got the better of me for a moment."

His voice just shook a little, and Rafael dropped into the seat beside him. *No problem*, he wanted to say, but the moment seemed fragile somehow. Al's voice actually shook. He'd never heard or seen him like this, not when their business was in danger of going bankrupt, not even when they told him Tadeo had been shot. Rafael held his tongue and sat beside him until Al finally took a deep breath and straightened up.

"My apologies—I needed a moment," he said again, and Rafael shook his head.

"No problem, man. I think I just might have to digest this too, you know. It's over. I'm not a suspect anymore. I can leave town without handing notice to that detective. Jesus…"

"Were you thinking of going anywhere?"

The joke was feeble, but at least somewhere in there, the Al he knew started to resurface.

"Hell yes. Acapulco. You check the weather out there lately?"

Al clapped him on the shoulder and shook his head.

"Acapulco! Forget about it. The first thing we need to do is install you in this company as Director of Facilities. I've been wanting to do this for a very long time."

"No wait. The first thing, the very first thing we have to do, Al, is have a big-ass blowout to celebrate the fact that I am finally off the hook for good. Unless you'd rather not."

He glanced sideways at Al, just in case the mention of a grand blowout to celebrate Roberto's confession didn't sit well with him, but Al already smiled again.

"Go. Tell Kayla what happened here and don't come back for the rest of the day. I'm sure you're going to be celebrating. And on your way out, tell my secretary to call a full board meeting at the first possible opportunity."

"You got it!"

Rafael got to his feet and left the boardroom. At the door he turned around one more time and looked back at his friend sitting there. Al still hadn't moved an inch. In some ways, hearing that your brother tried to frame your friend would take the starch out of any man—and still, they were no closer to solving the mystery of Tadeo's death. Could

Roberto have been involved in some way after all? Did he have it in him to raise his hand against his own father?

From the looks of him, Al had to be wondering the same thing, but neither one of them was going to get those answers just then and there.

THIRTY-EIGHT

Kayla had decided to work at the house that day, to have more peace, and he stormed straight into the house and up to the room they shared as an office, bursting out the news in one long sentence without so much as hello.

Kayla wanted to jump for joy, disconnected her phone call in the middle of a conversation, and came around the desk, wrapping her arms around him.

"Thank God! Finally... Didn't I tell you? Eventually, they would come around to proving you hadn't done it?"

"No, you told me to let it go. It was only because of Roberto's confession they finally came around to saying, OK... I maybe hadn't done it after all."

"No maybe about it, Rafa."

"No." He held her close and tucked her head under his chin. "This is one of the best days in—I don't know how long. Finally."

"We all knew..."

"Yes, you all knew. But you cannot imagine the weight on your chest if there are people out there thinking you just might have killed another man."

"How's Al taking it?" she asked and took his hand, leading him down to the kitchen and the wine rack.

"Not great. Probably about the way you expect, I don't know. I had to talk him off a ledge there for a minute. That's how angry he was. I wouldn't want to be in Roberto's shoes right now."

Kayla scoffed. "He deserves every bit of Al's wrath he'll get. Not that framing somebody for murder is ever OK, but you? After everything you did for his father and to save that company he wanted so badly? It is ridiculous."

Rafael took the offered glass of wine, tipped it to hers, and took a sip. "Barry promised him they'd run PerCan together."

"Barry promised a lot of things to a lot of people. As you are finding out now, it doesn't mean snap."

"I'd kill to know what went down between them. What would make Barry give away a piece of his company?"

"Do we really need to know?" Kayla drank her own wine and smiled broadly at him. "Rafael, this means you have everything you wanted. You're in the clear, you'll be a director, the company is going well…"

"You're here."

"I'm here. I say we don't care why Barry made a promise and didn't keep it. We don't care why Roberto tried to frame you. None of our business anymore. The only one person I feel bad for is Al."

THIRTY-NINE

In the days and weeks to follow, it became obvious that a lot of people felt for Al. His fellow directors carefully congratulated him on Rafael's good news without making any mention of how this information had come to light.

As expected, the vote to install Rafael as Director of Facilities was unanimous—since he'd been doing the job in all but title anyway. Rafael found himself the target of many a shoulder clap and hug, to the point where it was almost embarrassing, but he wore a grin all day long that he couldn't wipe off his face.

The good news spread through the company and made the rounds among their investors. And in turn they had more reasons to celebrate: better results in Production, rising share prices, happy investors.

It was only one of the online investor journalists writing for their favorite website who dared ask the question. If Roberto Ivers had gone as far as framing Rafael, was it a stretch to think that he'd had something to do with his father's death? Rafael tried to dispose of the trash news article as soon as he could, but Al had already seen it. His mood turned dark almost instantly.

With everyone in the clear, the question still remained: who killed Tadeo Ivers?

In the past, Rafael and Al would speak of it now and then, wondering if Tadeo might have had mortal enemies. Al always made light of the club scene he and his father moved in and usually finished with an awkward joke about how he was happy to be rid of the sordid lot.

Now that the truth about Roberto trying to frame him was out there, Rafael didn't dare speculate about Tadeo's murder or Roberto's involvement. A hard glint came into Al's eyes when either name was mentioned, and he would shut down any conversation with a terse, "We'll see."

Once or twice, Rafael tried to pluck up his courage and tell him it was no big deal. But every now and then, when he stepped into their shared office, Al would quickly blank his monitor and greet Rafael with an obviously fake grin.

"What? Are you looking at internet porn over there?" Rafael said one day. "Cause it's OK if you are. No need to hide it. Unless Kayla is behind me."

"Most definitely not." Al bristled. "I was only—checking a few things."

"I see."

"See what?"

"Nothing. I see—you were checking something. That's all." Rafael turned away and fired up his own monitor. "Don't forget to sign those purchase orders for the mechanical engineers. I need those parts to get another grow room up and running."

"Will do."

They went back to their respective tasks, Rafael rubbing his hands over and over while he read his emails and Al pretending to ignore him, until Al finally cracked.

"Fine. If you must know—Green Technologies is officially bankrupt."

"What? Oh. Not entirely unexpected, don't you think? Turner had it coming ever since he torpedoed our merger agreement. He could have an office down the hall and see his people employed down there, but no!"

Al folded his hands before his face and rolled his shoulders. "His loss. His grow operation, along with every last piece of equipment and machinery, is up for sale at auction now. I was—seeing if there was anything interesting."

Rafael laughed and fired up his browser to find the auction notice Al was referring to.

"Oh, you've got to be kidding me. Are you smoking something? You saw their equipment. Old, older, and oldest. Anything we throw out on the junk heap is better than what he had to offer. Please don't insult our operation like this."

Al said nothing and flipped off his PC. "I need to run into a quick meeting. Need anything while I am out?"

"Nah, I'm good," Rafael muttered, running his eyes down the list of equipment and offered bids.

***

"Son of a frigging gun."

Rafael looked up, but Al had already left, and the door swung shut behind him silently. "Frig, you think I wouldn't notice?"

Right there on the list of offers he could see that most equipment had been bid on quite generously by a company called ATI Trading. An innocent enough name, an innocent enough transaction—if you didn't know that ATI Trading was one of the companies Al used infrequently to conduct business. If you didn't have Rafael's memory for such things and circumstances. Rafael printed out the list, swiped it out of the printer tray, and paced the length of the office, up and down, while reading through it. With every line, his steps became snappier, and his hands flipped through the pages with more energy than strictly needed.

Tessa stepped in to show him the mockups of some investor presentations, and he blew her off with a quick *not now* glance.

"Anything you need help with?" she asked anyway.

"Not now, Tessa, OK?"

"O-K. No problem."

Tessa disappeared again, and Rafael dialed the front desk. "When Al comes back into the building, I need to see him immediately, OK? Mind giving him that message?"

"No need for the message. I forgot my portfolio."

Rafael spun around, and there stood Al, just inside the door, a puzzled look on his face.

"Mind explaining this?" Rafael waved the pages in front of Al's face. "With all due respect—what the hell?"

"If I knew what you were waving at me, I would take a stab at explaining—perhaps."

Rafael flung all the pages down on Al's desk so they scattered. The titles and listings were self-explanatory.

"You… Are already buying all of Turner's equipment. What the hell? Am I running facilities or not? Is there something I need to know? Because sure as heck, we do not need any of this junk in here, unless you have a plan for PerCan that is new to me."

"Rafael, take it easy and sit down. We are not buying any of this." Rafael stopped in front of Al and straightened his shoulders.

"Don't bullshit me, OK? You think I would miss it? You think I wouldn't remember? ATI? You don't use it often, but it is one of yours, right?"

"Correct. ATI is one of my companies."

"Then I am right. You are buying this shit. Al…"

Rafael dropped into his chair and raised his hands, letting them fall into his lap again. "What has got into you? This stuff is useless to us. Please back out of this sale. Please."

"No."

"Please, Al. I am telling you we don't…"

"I know." Suddenly, Al's voice had become very soft, amused almost, and Rafael raised his head from where it was buried in his hands. "We are not buying this stuff—I am."

"I don't…"

"Don't try to understand it. Not now. I am buying Turner's throwaway equipment for one reason and one reason only: to keep Roberto from buying it."

That last sentence sent a chill through Rafael because it was said with a cold determination he hadn't seen in Al before.

"I'm sorry. I still don't quite understand."

"Neither should you, Rafael. My dear brother who tried to take this company as well as frame you for murder purchased another little operation to get into the cannabis business. All of this equipment would be quite useful to him." Al flicked a finger at the pages Rafael had scattered on his desk. "But he is not going to get it. He is about to find out just how cutthroat this business can be."

The way he said it made Rafael remember the strange man he had met at his first investment presentation, the dark figure who didn't speak, just dropped off a fat envelope of cash in the late hours. He shivered and licked suddenly dry lips.

"Don't think about it again. It has nothing to do with you or Per-Can. Just some family business being settled."

Al took his portfolio and stepped out of the office, leaving Rafael more confused than ever before. If he'd said it once, he repeated it again to himself—what the hell.

Rafael, who had more than once told anyone who would listen that his constant pacing gave him more exercise than mindless jogging, paced up and down the office as if he were caught there. The look in Al's eyes when he said "family business being settled" gave him the creeps. He thought he had known his friend, know what he would or wouldn't do, but apparently, Roberto had pushed his brother too far.

He is about to find out just how cutthroat this business can be.

He considered Al a friend, but how far would Al go to get his revenge? Making his brother's life difficult in business, sure. But was there more to it? Would he—could he…

"Hey, Al, you got a—oh, sorry. I was looking for Al."

Barry stepped through the door and nodded at Rafael. "Rafael, heard the good news. Congratulations."

"Yeah, thanks."

Rafael dropped into his chair again and forked his hands through his hair, realizing how exhausted he was from his mental ruminations. Barry, who had actually turned to leave, took a step back and stopped in front of his desk.

"You OK? If you don't mind my saying so, you look like shit."

"I don't mind—and I feel like it."

"What's up? You know if I can help…" Barry pulled up a chair and rested his elbows on his knees. "I've been known to have the odd brilliant idea when it comes to getting out of a tight spot."

Rafael scoffed. "Your advice should come with a warning label, Barry. No, I have a few things on my mind."

"Something I should know about?" Barry asked and came a bit closer.

"No, probably not—it may be nothing at all."

"I don't like the way you look, Rafael. This is more than nothing at all."

Barry came closer still, and Rafael waved his hand.

"Just thinking. About revenge, and Roberto—and about you. What was it with you and him anyway? He really thought you would make him a director here. Got right mad about it too when you didn't. And he took revenge."

"You know how it goes, Rafael. He must have misunderstood something." Barry turned to leave again, but Rafael held his gaze with his eyes.

"No, I am having a hard time with that. The effort he put into trying to frame me and trying to get a seat on the board here—that's way more than just misunderstanding something. And last I heard, he had put an illegal grow op into this place and tried to blame you for it, so there must be a piece to the puzzle I am missing, because now he claims the two of you were going to run this place."

"Just let it go, Rafael."

Barry's hand was on the door handle, and Rafael was by his side in a flash, putting his hand on top.

"I'm tired of people telling me to let it go. I've known you for a lot of years, and I can see when there is something fishy. Out with it. He tried to land me in the slammer."

"Jesus." Barry stepped back and took up his own brief pacing. "Fine. He had information on Turner and Ivers, back when you and Al still planned a merger with GT, and I asked him to use that information. The price for that was a seat on the board. Didn't happen, OK? So now he's sore. Stuff goes wrong, plans change. He'll find that out soon enough."

"What information? You mentioned something about it a while ago, and it didn't make sense." Rafael took a breath and screwed up his face. "*Tadeo screwed a lot of people over in his lifetime. Including Turner. But that's old history.* That's exactly what you said, but it never made sense. Ivers and Greg Turner didn't know one another, did they?"

"Not Greg Turner, his father. Who went by a different last name. Rumor has it he drove Turner's father into bankruptcy. Roberto knew about it, and he made sure Turner found out too. And that he would never want to do business with the likes of Tadeo Ivers, that's all. Nothing serious."

"That's what blew up the merger." Rafael sat again and let out a massive breath he had no idea he'd been holding. "I could never figure out why he wanted out of that merger suddenly when we had everything arranged all neat and tidy."

Barry smirked at that. "Well, I owned a hell of a lot more shares in Mariposa, which was your second choice. Listen, I have to run. I'm seeing some investors. When Al gets back, tell him there's an idea I want to run by him."

Rafael didn't answer, and Barry turned around once more at the door.

"And quit worrying about it. Revenge is overrated. It will blow over soon, and they'll make up. They're brothers."

The door closed behind him, and Rafael felt as if he had finally found the last missing piece to the puzzle.

FORTY

Rafael stabbed his dinner with more force than necessary that night, while telling Kayla the latest installment of this drama.

"I never knew why Greg blew up that merger, why he suddenly backed out—now I do. I thought it had something to do with Irv Moody, who was thinking about coming in with an investment at the time."

"Rafael…"

"And then it turns out it was Connor all along—Barry, who digs up some old story to drive him away. For his own purposes, of course."

"Will you calm down, please?"

"Kayla, I'm so tired of people interfering, messing with, obstructing, or otherwise making it difficult to do business around here."

"Enough." Kayla put her wineglass down a little harder this time and shook her head. "You are getting all worked up again. What does it matter?"

"How can you…"

"It was a shady backroom deal—for which Barry is famous—and GT went away to go bankrupt. End of story."

"Maybe."

"Not maybe, Rafael, that's all that happened. First you get angry because Al is taking revenge on his brother too far, and now you're doing the same thing. Stop getting so riled up by this thing."

"I'm sorry." He put down his cutlery, brought his hands together, and brought them to his face. "I'm sorry. I was just…"

"Getting worked up over nothing?"

"Yes."

"Worrying about things that happened years ago and have no impact on business today?"

"Maybe." Rafael looked up again.

"Well? Are you ready to let it be?"

Rafael sighed and blew out a big breath. "It's just that I... I hate it when..."

"You like to have things all slotted into the plan, just like when you are building a big house. Whereas Barry operates by the seat of his pants."

"Literally!"

"And when things don't work out, strange things happen. That is why he is now only a consultant."

"I know." Rafael sighed again. "I know. Thanks for talking me down."

"Anytime. We have more important things to worry about anyway."

"Such as?" Rafael asked warily.

In his experience, when a woman said, *we have important things to worry about*, something he didn't like was about to happen. Something important he didn't have on his radar yet. He looked at Kayla over the rim of his glasses only to find her laughing.

"The five-year anniversary of PerCan? What did you think I was talking about?"

"Nothing, just being distracted. Anniversary? Do you think we should—have an event or something?"

"Yes. What do they teach you about news?"

"News?" Now, he felt downright silly, on the wrong end of this conversation, and looking like an idiot in the process.

"Good news sells shares, Rafa."

"Oh, that..."

"And a five-year anniversary and the perfect state of our facilities and processes is definitely good news. So yes, I think we should have a small event, something all the financial journalists and bloggers can talk about."

Rafael picked up his fork again and continued to poke at his dinner with little enthusiasm.

"One of the reasons you are in charge of publicity and not me," he said and ate without tasting his food. "But I am proud of PerCan, so yes, it is a good idea."

When he floated the thought to Al the next morning, he was met with a blank stare. "Naturally, we'll have an anniversary, any chance to spread good news."

Apparently, he was the only one who had not thought of a large, public event for quite a while, and it didn't serve to put him into a better mood.

"Time I found out about it."

"Rafael, do you not have enough to do?"

"No."

"Facilities are your job. Your only job. But anyway—plans are not final. You'll have a chance to contribute."

"All right," Rafael said and made a face.

"Is that all that is bothering you? Because you appear to be in a terrible mood that has very little to do with a potential anniversary event."

"No—yes—I don't know."

"Well thank you for clarifying," Al said with a smile. "That is very informative."

"I guess your revenge action with the equipment and finding out that Barry drove Greg into backing out of the merger all in the same day was just a bit much."

"Not the way things are done on your construction site?"

"No. And don't use that analogy with me. Kayla already beat you to the punch for that."

"Good. I need your full attention. You'll be happy to know I bought and disposed of that used equipment already, so my brother won't be using any of it. I'm over it—GT is no longer. Let's never talk about it. Nothing about that dreadful chapter in our company history is ever going to impact us again. Ever. Understood?"

"If you are sure…"

"I am absolutely sure." Al smiled again. "Now tell me what you think of Clint's plans for expansion. I know he's a financial wizard, but I could use your opinion."

FORTY-ONE

From one day to the next, Rafael's plate was more than full. Clint produced a list of countries where marijuana had recently become legally available, or was about to. All of them were a good target for a branch of PerCan. Meanwhile, other, smaller manufacturers became interested in their facilities and the way they ran. The business around marijuana suddenly exploded. People wanted to grow it, buy it, sell it, and figure out the best way to do so.

Not a day went by that he didn't field questions about the facility and the possibility of a tour. Equipment manufacturers came knocking at his door to find out why he had designed PerCan's processes the way he did and how they could potentially work together for everyone's benefit. Tessa hounded him to patent his processes and setup and helped him do so, and the past moved away further than ever. He started to forget.

As Barry had predicted, Roberto seemed to have pulled himself up by his bootstraps and made up with Al because one day, Rafael saw him give a tour to his brother. Barry had moved beyond his murky past and became a popular guest on financial newsreels. Rafael noticed he had set up his own company and did quite well for himself raising funds for others, and again, the past slipped away a bit more.

Rafael enjoyed himself and enjoyed what he was doing and the people he was working with. He'd never set out to become an expert at growing marijuana—just applied his experience in building things to the need of growing those temperamental little plants as safely and as quickly as possible, while keeping quality standards that were hard to beat.

He even tolerated it when Kayla included him on the committee working on the anniversary event. After all, they would need to plan and schedule tours carefully, and they needed a rule framework to do so.

He politely sat through endless meetings, most of the time without grumbling and without admitting that his mind wandered when someone spoke at length about catering or invitations.

He was proud of 'his' company, and not shy about saying so. Quite often, the journalists and bloggers of the financial world wanted his take on PerCan as well. Barry, standing nearby and watching the interview, only grinned and elbowed him when it was all done.

"I call you our secret weapon. That's why everybody suddenly wants to know who you are and how you've built such a perfect setup."

"I thank you for the 'perfect setup' bit. But, pray tell, why secret weapon?"

"Because—that's your difference, your advantage. That's why you are going to make it, and the rest of them out there might not. You have perfected the art of growing cannabis, and you do it right, every time."

"I see."

"First rule of raising funds. What makes you different, and why are you better than the next guy who is coming to knock on the door?" Barry winked and spun his finger around at the spotless, stainless-steel and glass grow rooms around them. "I'd say it's working."

Slowly, they walked down the hall side by side, and Rafael noticed that bit by bit, they had fallen into the old familiarity of two friends again.

"Did you ever think this is where we would end up?" he asked, burying his hands in his pockets as he walked. "In a place like this—successful and growing, planning an anniversary, planning expansions?"

"Nah. All I wanted back then was to raise money, to tell you the truth. Running the thing would have frustrated me too much. But you—you found your spot."

"After Old Man Ivers basically beat me into it by threatening he would ruin everything I had if I didn't take over. That's the kind of offer you really don't turn down. As mad as I was back then—I'm not complaining."

At the mention of Tadeo Ivers, they both fell silent and walked companionably down the hall toward the executive offices.

"Tadeo Ivers," Barry finally said. "What a character. Sometimes, I really do wonder who felt the need to walk in and shoot him."

"Really." Rafael raised an eyebrow. "Lot of people still think it was you, you know."

"And then there were some who thought it was you!"

"Over a job? Not likely. I was madder than a wet hen. But I wouldn't kill anybody over it."

Barry chuckled again. "I've seen you mad like that, and it is not a pretty thing."

He didn't, Rafael noticed, give a list of reasons, or even one reason why he himself wouldn't have shot Ivers. Whatever. Mentally, he shrugged. After all this time, he'd become tired of wondering. And he really didn't think Barry had it in him to pull the trigger on someone.

"So, you're beating the drums for the grand anniversary celebration? Inviting investors, journalists, anyone who will listen?"

"Of course." Barry shrugged. "I told Kayla to pull out all the stops and then double down on it."

"Long as you don't show up in a helicopter, Barry. Please, no helicopter this time."

"You know—that is not entirely..." He laughed when he saw Rafael spin around and open his mouth to offer an opinion. "Take it easy, no helicopters. I will be at the celebrations and holding court with all of 'my' people, but I don't need an article somewhere on how I squander the funds I raise."

"Good man." Rafael toed the sterile white paper booties off his feet at the door to the offices and waited for Barry to do the same.

Together, they stepped into the reception area where Kayla was waiting for them.

"Done on another day of interviews and photos?" she asked and stepped beside Rafael in a possessive manner he found rather charming.

"We make believers out of doubters, every time." Barry fell into step beside them. "Your man looks so capable and trustworthy on film. I have to make him do his little spiel in front of the camera. Nobody does it like him."

"Good to hear." Kayla laughed. "I am looking forward to our anniversary event. You will join us, correct?"

"Wouldn't miss it. Last time we had an event..."

"No helicopters," Kayla and Rafael said at the very same time, and Barry waved and went laughing down the hall in search of the supply office and promotional items he had ordered.

FORTY-TWO

The day was to start with a breakfast reception for all of the employees and any of the journalists who felt they needed a bit of extra time and wanted to pick up the printed material about PerCan to include in their stories.

Kayla had hired the city's best caterers to set up breakfast buffet stations in the entrance, little groups of tables and displays with materials about PerCan's history and timeline. Tessa and her graphics department had slaved over every page of the presentation, taking thousands of photos in the grow rooms, and editing the wording over and over until Kayla, Al, and even Barry agreed it was perfect. Around the perimeter of the reception hung life-size photos of the earliest stages of PerCan, and Rafael cringed every time he saw the one with the helicopter in it. After all, he decided it was part of PerCan's history, a part most people even remembered, and he left it there.

If you walked around the perimeter with your coffee, you could follow the exact timeline of PerCan, from the first fundraising events at restaurants downtown, the mostly empty building, to failed attempts at indoor grow rooms, only to end up with an enormous enlargement of the current setup, right by the door into the growing area.

Said door had a large industrial planning board beside it, with the times when there would be tours of the grow areas and 10 slots below them. The idea was for folks to pop their business cards into one of the slots, as Rafael didn't want any more than 10 people plus a narrator down in the grow area at any one time.

As it was, he was paranoid about anyone being even close to the areas where cannabis was grown or being worked on, to the point where he had stuck arrows onto the ground where one was allowed to walk.

No arrow, no walking. He impressed this fact on anyone who would listen and threatened his narrators with unspeakable fates if they didn't head-count their charges on an ongoing basis and make sure no one was walking outside boundaries—absolutely sure.

Kayla had told him people would be too afraid to look for a bathroom and earned a raised eyebrow for that remark. *Hold it, then.*

While all this was going on, he and Al would take turns up in the conference room in front of the glass wall, telling people a bit about PerCan, what it stood for, and how they had come to be here. Anyone who couldn't get into one of the tours would at least be able to look down at the business on the grow floor.

At lunch, there would be a brief break and more food served, while people circulated and asked questions, culminating in a champagne reception late afternoon.

Rafael's narrators would then turn into security guards, chivvying anyone out of the building who didn't belong, while Rafael and his staff got busy putting their precious plants and the building to bed properly.

If all went well, and there was no reason why it shouldn't, the next day, the papers and online blogs would have nothing but wonderful things to say about PerCan and the humble origins they had overcome. The stock price would rise, investors would be happy, and they would all go on to do the same thing another day. And, as Al was fond of saying, those darn short sellers would for once have to eat their own words.

Such was the plan anyway.

***

And now, finally, Al, Rafael, Kayla, and Barry had done all of the planning they could. The anniversary was scheduled for the following day. Nothing could possibly go wrong. Al sent everyone home tasked with getting a good night's sleep, which as much as guaranteed that no one would.

Rafael griped at not being allowed to have one final walkthrough, but, in the end, flanked by Kayla and Al, he went home. Surprising himself, he fell asleep almost instantly and woke at his customary time, which Al had been known to refer to as "before the blasted crack of dawn."

He didn't like it. As if he had opened the paper to a bad horoscope prediction, he instantly felt that something would go wrong.

Had he thought of everything? Yes, he had.

Anything left out? Not to his knowledge.

Then what the heck? They had gone over every possible emergency and made allowances for it, correct? Still…

Rafael jumped when Kayla, still in a nightshirt and silk robe, touched the back of his neck.

"Couldn't sleep?"

"No." He shook his head and drained the cup of strong coffee he'd made for himself. "I just can't shake the feeling that something will go wrong today."

"Nothing will."

Rafael only crossed his fingers.

"We thought of everything, haven't we? Then what…?"

"Heck if I know."

He rinsed his mug and put it in the sink, running some water into it.

"I know we have an emergency plan for absolutely everything…"

"Rafael? You made us have a plan in case someone fainted or had a heart attack down inside one of the grow rooms—where no one is allowed to go."

"It never hurts to be prepared. I just can't shake the feeling."

"Probably just memories from the grand opening." Gently, she massaged his shoulders for a moment and gave him a soft tap on the back. "Nothing like that's going to happen today, OK?"

"From your mouth to God's ears," he muttered, forcing a smile. No sense in getting both of them riled up.

***

They had thought of everything, and he was probably just making a mountain out of—nothing at all. He forced himself to put on the most cheerful face he had in his arsenal, and went through the motions of getting ready, greeted the arriving employees at PerCan when they started to show up, and did his best to shoo away dark thoughts when they came up. Nothing would go wrong today. Nothing.

10 o'clock on the dot, the first guests began arriving for the breakfast meetings, and, from then on, he did not have an opportunity to think about things going wrong. He spoke about their grow room and health concepts, about how he isolated growing plants, how no one but the agronomists even got close to the plants, how to keep out infections and diseases, and how to train and motivate workers. He gave tours, spoke about the health benefits of marijuana and the history of PerCan, and every time he had a chance to come up for air, he grabbed a cup of strong coffee and saw the rest of the board members doing the exact same thing.

Everything was going according to plan—nothing could go wrong.

After noon, the caterers changed their offerings to hot foods, and he found himself standing in a quiet corner beside Al with a plate of appetizers in hand.

"How's it going?"

"I don't think I've spoken this much in a single morning in several years," Al said, wiping the tiredness from his eyes with his fingers.

"But I believe that means it is going fantastic. Everyone wants to know how we do what we do, and they all seem to think we're doing a good job at it."

"Better believe it." Rafael ate most of a chicken wing in one large bite. "This food is great," he said, still chewing. "Kayla outdid herself with the planning."

"I can see that," Al said, raised an eyebrow, and handed him another napkin. "Bless your appetite. I wish I could shake the feeling…"

"Not you too."

Rafael put down his plate, balled up the napkin, and fired it at a convenient nearby bin. "Not you too, Al, please. All morning I've been going around with this feeling…"

"That something will happen?"

"I said don't say it."

Al put his hands together and covered his mouth, his way of saying he didn't know what to say, and Rafael shrugged.

"I've got this—feeling. Kayla says quit it, and we thought of everything."

"We did."

"There you go."

Even to his own ears, he did not sound convincing.

"I think I'm going to step away from the action for a bit and be in my office," Al said, looking out over the throng of people in the reception hall. "Not that anyone would notice."

"Sure—go and leave me to it," Rafael said and grinned suddenly. "What if Mirko shows up?"

"Mirko…? Oh!"

They both remembered the loan shark with the outrageous demand and grinned.

"I assure you he was not on the invite list," Al said with a forced bit of cheer.

Quietly, he took the stairs up to the executive office, and Rafael looked after him. Crowds had never been Al's thing. They were not his thing either, but with being the man who had built all of this came a certain notoriety and pride, and he had decided to enjoy it, Catholic guilt be damned.

He watched over the crowd from his spot in a corner, leaning casually against a support pillar, feeling quite pleased with himself, when a small commotion at the entrance drew his eyes. Nothing big, nothing that screamed *incident*. His security people were too well trained for that. But nevertheless, something out of the ordinary had happened over there at the west entrance. Something other than a guest walking in, showing his invitation code, and being admitted.

Rafael automatically straightened a bit, narrowing his eyes at the scene. All thoughts of pride in his building and processes and accomplishments were instantly forgotten as he zeroed in on what might have happened there to raise his antennae.

Someone was trying to come in. Nay, insisted on coming in. And the man most certainly didn't hold an invitation code, but he held enough authority to make the men at the door question their judgment and orders. No surprise there. The man demanding entry was Detective Sergeant Robertson.

As if summoned by Rafael's watchfulness, Al had appeared at the top of the stairs once again.

Almost as one, they strode toward the entrance and reached the man trying to gain admittance at the same time.

"Carter," Rafael said to the security guard and nodded his head in the direction of other guests coming in.

"Detective." Very gently, Al put his hand on Robertson's elbow and steered him away from the curious group of guests that had gathered behind them. "We have an anniversary celebration going on today. If it is not too much to ask, does this have time later on or tomorrow?"

"You're going to want to hear this."

Robertson had been there often enough to know where he was going and headed upstairs toward the boardroom, leaving Rafael and Al no choice but to follow him.

Rafael swept one last concerned look over the crowd below and texted Kayla what was happening, so she could take care of damage control around the people who had noticed the detective. Within moments, they were out of sight, and Al opened the door to the boardroom.

"I hope that whatever you have to tell us is important enough to disrupt our anniversary celebration, Detective. I really don't need any rumors online tomorrow, 'police at PerCan celebrations.'" His fingers made air quotes around that last bit even as he stepped over to the window and looked down at the production floor.

Everything appeared to be quiet.

"It most likely could have held until tomorrow," Rafael said, pouring himself a glass of water from the carafe on the table. "You did mention last time that both Al and I…"

"Take it easy." Robertson raised a hand, fingers splayed. "I'm going to make this quick and come right out with it. We found the gun that was used to shoot your father."

Rafael and Al dropped into two chairs almost simultaneously, and Rafael thought he could hear Al say a silent *what*, but he couldn't be sure. When he looked over, all of the color seemed to have drained from Al's face, and he visibly fought for composure.

"Where, when, who?" he finally managed to say and forked his hands through his hair. "Do you know anything else—I mean, who did it—why?"

"One thing at a time." Robertson took a chair across from them and, since no one offered, poured a glass of water for himself. "Do you want Rafael to stay?"

"Yes, of course," Al said gruffly and glowered.

"All right. This will hit the news media first thing tomorrow. That's why I decided to disturb your anniversary celebrations."

"Yes, yes, yes. Carry on."

"I don't have all of the information yet, Al, but what we do know is as follows. Two days ago, the boys from Vice picked up a small-time drug dealer downtown."

"Drugs, not Roberto, please."

Al's voice was barely above a whisper, and Rafael ached for him, but the detective already shook his head.

"Nothing to do with your brother. This guy has been on our radar for a while. He's just a small-time runner for a much bigger dealer, and we were hoping he would eventually lead us to that person or group."

Al only nodded.

"We picked him up with enough product on his person to lock him up, but we decided to squeeze him a bit, and we got a search warrant for his house. Bingo, we found a lot more product. Enough in fact to put him away for a nice, long time. And now I know I have a chance to get him to talk."

"And what does all of this have to do with Tadeo Ivers?" Rafael asked, since Al was visibly fighting for composure.

"Up to now—nothing. Until we get down to analyzing everything interesting the boys brought back from this man's house. Turned out he had a very nice nine-millimeter weapon in a duffle bag, right in the same closet where he kept his stash."

"Drugs and guns at a criminal's house. So far, I'm not seeing anything all that unusual," Rafael started and then looked from Al to Robertson. "Oh."

"Standard practice. We did a ballistics check to see if there were any other crimes it linked back to and—bingo."

"My father's murder," Al said tonelessly, and Robertson nodded.

"Yes, the gun is a match to the Smith and Wesson M&P9 used in the shooting of Tadeo Ivers. I am sorry if this brings back bad memories, Al, but I need to know…"

Al waved away the remainder of Robertson's sentence and got to his feet. "I need a moment to process, please."

"Take your time."

Rafael watched him pace up and down the length of the conference room and tried to wrap his own mind around what he had just heard.

A small-time criminal and dealer? That didn't make any sense whatsoever. Tadeo might do business with anyone and everyone, but he didn't get involved with underlings. No, Tadeo Ivers would have dealt with the town's top dealer, if not higher. None of this made sense as of yet.

"This doesn't make any sense." Al echoed his thoughts. "Is this all you have? A drug dealer in possession of that gun?"

"As of right now—yes. Of course, that investigation is..."

"Ongoing, I know, and you came in here to give us a heads-up. I appreciate that, Detective, but I have nothing to offer that would make this make sense."

Al had straightened up, stopped in front of Robertson, and lasered in on him with cold, dark eyes.

"Nothing. My father did many things, but he was not a drug dealer himself, or involved in the milieu. I would know."

"Are you sure? Sometimes we think we know a person, but..."

"I ran his business affairs for years, Detective. If there had been anything even reminiscent of drugs, I would have seen it. I would not have stood for it and left."

"And he respected that—despite the fact that he in fact acquired a major stake in a marijuana manufacturer."

"He respected that." Al nodded. "And after all of the issues he was having with Roberto when he was younger, he had no desire to get involved in drugs. PerCan at the time manufactured medical marijuana."

"All right." Robertson scratched his head thoughtfully. "That was going to be one of my questions. Is there any connection between your father and illegal drugs that you are aware of?"

"There is not."

"Any reason why he would know a small-time criminal?"

Al shook his head again. "Nothing I am aware of—what is this man's name anyway? Perhaps I've heard it before."

"Before I tell you, this must remain confidential, agreed?"

"Agreed."

"Ranker, Bobby Ranker," Robertson said. "Ever heard of him before?"

"No." Al thought for a moment, massaging the palm of his hand with his thumb. "No. Name doesn't ring a bell at all. I mean, he could have had some low-level job at one of the clubs and not necessarily caught my attention—but why would a janitor or a dishwasher either know or want to shoot my father?"

"So, it is possible?"

"Yes, of course it is possible, Detective." Al bristled. "I said I don't remember him. I cannot confirm whether he did or did not work for one of our clubs, and, if so, if he had a disagreement with my father, but had it been an agreement worthy of murder, I do believe I would have been told."

"How so?"

Al sighed and rubbed the bridge of his nose with thumb and forefinger, as if to wipe away a headache building there.

"Rafael, I really don't want to exclude you here—I in fact need you here—but if both of us are missing at the celebrations, there's going to be gossip. Do you mind?"

"No problem." Rafael got to his feet. "If you're fine on your own."

"No, I am not," Al said rather curtly. "The timing of this could have not been worse. But I'm going to put the company first and say please go and take care of our guests."

Rafael nodded, clapped Al on the shoulder on his way out, nodded to Detective Robertson, and left the room. Just outside the closed door, he rolled his shoulders and put on his public face. Al was right in that their sudden exit would have been noticed and would be the subject of chatter. As he came down the stairs, he met Kayla's worried eyes, and, in a second, she was beside him.

"What was that all about?" she whispered. "A few people saw Robertson, and there's a rumor going around."

Rafael winked. "Nothing at all," he said loud enough so the people standing close to them would be sure to hear. "The detective just came around to congratulate us, since he knows both Al and me rather well. Let's just say showing up at a cannabis plant is not really great PR for a police detective."

"No, I wouldn't think so."

Kayla smiled, took his hand, and led him over to the champagne bar and a group of journalists discussing the various merits of indoor versus outdoor grows. Nothing to see here, just keep the anniversary party going.

***

Up in the conference room, Al brought his palms together and to his face, as he did often when deep in thought, although Rafael had told him it made him look as if he were praying.

"Bobby Ranker," he repeated.

"Yes?"

"I don't know him. We may have had an employee by that name, but payroll issues were outsourced. No reason I would have known him unless he committed fraud, theft, or any of the dozen other issues we had with employees."

"And yet?"

"Nothing worth committing murder over," Al repeated. "Worst that would have happened would have been I would have fired him and told him never to come within 10 feet of one of our clubs."

"OK," said the detective, "so we're saying he was likely not working for one of the clubs."

"Likely." Al nodded. "And I was the official representative for Tadeo's organization. I was there to keep an eye on things and to keep hands out of tills. At the same time—those people could be incessantly gos-sipy." He rolled his eyes thinking about those days and smiled a brittle smile. "Not a day went by someone didn't stop me to tell me about another employee's minor infraction, so I would go and punish them."

Detective Robertson only nodded, waiting for Al to continue.

"Meaning, if something had occurred—something big enough to war-rant committing murder, mind you—I likely would have heard about it."

"That's not much."

"No." Al nodded. "Just call it a working theory then. And don't forget that we were constantly being checked on by some of your own departments—Health Department, parole officers. Some days it was revolving doors depending on the club in question."

"That's true too."

"I am sure you have already done this. But once you send off to ADP to get a copy of our payroll records and Ranker's not on there…"

Robertson spread his hands, helpless.

"You're back at square one. What does this Ranker have to say about all of this?"

"We picked him up on a different charge, and he copped to that stuff pretty quickly. The moment he heard about a connection between that gun and Tadeo's murder, he said, 'hell no,' and lawyered up faster than anything. He's now just cooling his heels with his mouth shut. I need something to make him a bit more talkative."

Al spread his hands, a little irritated now. "Detective, I said this before, but this is a bad time for you to burst in here and tell me about this fellow Ranker. I appreciate that you wanted me to find out right away and find out from you rather than—other sources. I also appreciate that you need information on this man, but…"

"But you'd rather I make myself scarce."

"Amongst other things. If all you wanted to get out of me was a reaction to see if I still may have some involvement, you have your reaction. I don't know the man, never met him, am not aware of his history with Tadeo. If you wanted to give me semi-good news—fine. Do pick a better time next time, will you?"

"Understood."

Robertson gathered his things and left Al to his own thoughts in the boardroom. What his thought process had been, Al would never know. There was nothing he could do with the information the man brought him, other than get upset about it, and/or spread it around, neither one of which Al cared to do just now.

A small-time criminal found with the gun that had shot his father. It tore open every single patch he had put over the memory of Tadeo's death—and it brought back everything he thought he had buried.

This man Ranker either had shot his father, or he knew who had. Why? Why would this criminal take a gun to him? All the security guards and silliness at the diner aside, Al couldn't name a single enemy of Tadeo's he would have taken seriously. An old man who owned seedy strip clubs and liked to operate right on the edge of the law, especially where taxes and assorted government rules were involved. He could be cheap with his employees, had a temper and a rude manner of speaking—none of which were reasons to kill a man.

His cell phone chirped, and he swiped to a message of Rafael. *Everything OK? Saw Robertson leave.*

Yes, fine, down in a minute.

He put his hands flat on the table and spent a moment gathering himself, before he put on the CEO face again, opened the door, and walked down the stairs to the reception below. Right now, there were more important things to attend to.

***

Hours later, after the staff had cleaned up, the caterers moved out, and Rafael had checked his precious plants, they sat together in that very same boardroom. Kayla joined them only moments later, having rescued a stray bottle of champagne downstairs, and offered everyone a glass.

"What I wanted to do was toast a successful anniversary, guys, but it looks like that has completely slipped your mind."

"A little," Al said and poured himself a glass of water instead. "My apologies. Did Robertson's appearance cause a disturbance amongst the employees or the press?"

"I took care of it." She shook her head. "A few of the employees were concerned, but I told them the same as everyone else—he just came to congratulate."

"Thank you. Last thing I needed today. A public scandal the day of the anniversary. Shades of the grand opening."

"Don't even go there." Rafael eyed the carafe of water, then the champagne bottle and the water again. "Hell with it," he said and took the glass of champagne. "I had this feeling this morning."

"Tell me again what he wanted," Kayla asked, brows furrowed. "Because all of this sounds rather odd to me. Why would he show up here, today, on the anniversary of PerCan?"

Al sipped his water and stared off into space. Finally, he shook his head and let his shoulders sink back against the soft back of his chair. "I don't know. It seems they picked up a minor criminal on a drug charge, and when they searched his home—they found a gun."

"Not uncommon in that milieu, I presume."

"It is, however, the gun that issued the shot that killed my father."

"What?"

Kayla, who had reached for her glass, brought her hand to her mouth. "I am so sorry. Why didn't you say anything? I have so many questions. Who is this man? What is his relationship to Tadeo? Why would he have that gun? Wait—this is good news, is it not?"

Confused, she stopped, searching Al's face. Al had settled further back in his chair and rubbed the bridge of his nose with thumb and forefinger again.

"Yes—no—maybe. There are no answers, Kayla. Thus far, said criminal just denies having anything to do with my father's shooting and called for a lawyer to back him up. Robertson came here on a fishing expedition to see if I would know the man and give him any sort of ammunition for their questioning."

"And?"

"I'll tell you the same thing I told him. I've never heard of the man. I don't think he worked for us, unless he was some low-level laborer somewhere I never met. As far as I know he has zero connection to my father."

"And yet," Rafael said, reaching for the champagne bottle once again. "He shot him."

"He denies having done so."

"Right—it was not me, Detective." Rafael raised his hands and eyes to the ceiling and scoffed. "Honest, it wasn't me. Tried that one, it didn't work, and I wasn't caught with the gun that killed him."

"Rafael…"

Al rested his face in his palm, and Kayla held out a hand to stop him, shaking her head. "Leave it be."

"Thank you. One the one hand, I am glad Robertson came here and told me. On the other, I wish his sense of timing were not so horrible," Al said. "Plus, this really does not get us anywhere. We are no closer to knowing who shot my father than we were a week ago."

"But he had the gun," Rafael protested.

"Which he could have purchased—wherever these people purchase guns. Or found."

"Found, come on!"

"Al is right, Rafael," Kayla said softly. "They need more, or all they can get him for is whatever they picked him up for originally."

"Which is why Robertson was here in the first place."

"What's this guy's name anyway?" Rafael asked. "Just out of curiosity, if you don't mind."

"Ranker, Bobby Ranker," Al said. "Ring a bell with you at all?"

379

"Wish it did." Rafael shook his head. "You know, after all this time, and all of us wondering whodunit, that's it? A complete unknown, for no good reason?"

"Possibly."

"I don't buy it."

"Gentlemen." Kayla upended the champagne bottle into her glass and finally dropped the empty bottle into a trash bin. "I think we should do what I always tell you to do—move on. We've had a great anniversary. We sent most of the journalists here today home with great stories and wonderful printed material about our facilities."

"Thanks for holding up the fort, Kayla. I appreciate it," Al said and forced a small smile.

"You're welcome. It's why I am here. At the same time, I think we should put this cannabis plant to bed until tomorrow and all go home."

"Seconded." Rafael raised his hand. "My brain is overflowing with everything that happened today."

"It was a good day."

"It was a fantastic day."

They clinked their glasses, finished their drinks, and did just as Kayla had suggested.

***

Somewhere across town, Detective Robertson pored over the employment records to all of Tadeo Ivers's clubs, not coming up with anything.

Irv Moody finished polishing his plane, which the insurance had restored just as new.

Barry Wentworth had taken off for one of the more expensive restaurants downtown and had missed the commotion around the detective, but since he was in the middle of buying drinks for the entire restaurant, he didn't much care.

It had been a great day.

FORTY-THREE

"Largest cannabis plant in the area celebrates five years in business." In the papers, they barely merited a small sentence, but the online financial bloggers had been out in force, and most of them had something to say about PerCan's milestone.

"The bad boys of cannabis have finally made good," Rafael read out loud while Kayla poured coffee. "After years of scandals and irregularities, the boys at PerCan finally seem to have seen the light—they know what they are doing, and they do it well."

"I like that one." She put a mug in front of him.

"There are a few others in the same vein. I think the stock exchanges are going to be busy today and the shorters crying."

"Are you happy with the way it turned out?"

"Hell yes," Rafael said, taking a sip of his coffee. "This guy has it right." He nodded at the screen of his laptop. "After years of battling one emergency after another, it is nice to have it right finally."

Kayla scrolled through her own news blasts on her phone and grinned. "There are a few online videos of you explaining the grows and the facilities."

"But I didn't want…" He reached, but she swiped at his hand, pulling her phone just out of reach.

"They got your good side too. Very cute."

Rafael blushed and looked away. "Dear God…"

"No mention of a detective there. Looks like my quick excuse worked."

Instantly, Rafael's demeanor sobered. "Not sure what he was thinking, coming in the day of the anniversary."

"He needed to get the job done and went looking for anything that would work. Sound familiar?"

"It does. But what are you still searching for so intently?"

Kayla searched through page after page of some type of information on her phone, her brow furrowing more and more as she went on.

"Crime. Didn't Robertson say they picked up Ranker during the commission of some sort of drug-related crime?"

"Don't know—likely. And you think you're going to find that on there?" He nodded toward her phone. "Really?"

"Apparently not." Frustrated, she turned off her phone and all but flung it on the table. "I'm not good at research. I'll ask my crime reporter at the publishing house to do a bit of digging."

"Don't you always tell Al and me to let it go?"

"I just want to see where he was picked up and why. Maybe there's a clue. Something that would help Al."

"In the crime stats?" Rafael sipped his coffee and looked back at his own phone. "You know, if you're bored, there are other things I could use help on, but OK. Go ahead."

"A clue could be anywhere, Rafael."

Rafael wasn't interested in crime and small-town criminals. He knew he would only get angry if he looked at the statistics of some young punk shoving a gun into a shop clerk's face just to get a hundred bucks out of the till. He could talk at length about that one, but Kayla didn't let up.

"Even though I run a gossip rag, as you like to call it, we do have a local crime section, and it's well done. I think you've met our reporter—lovely lady. She has a true-crime podcast as well, which is fantastic. One day, I will get you to listen to a few episodes. Anyway, she…"

"Taught you everything she knew? I think it's great that you're trying to help Al, but if recent experience is anything to go by, none of us should be calling ourselves detectives. To tell you the truth, most crime doesn't make any sense. My opinion, for what it's worth."

"Noted." Kayla winked at him and started to type at her phone furiously. "You'll see, my dear—you will see…"

Rafael rolled his eyes and went back to business. And there was lots of business left to do. The news had been wonderful, the shareholders, brokers, and investors were happy, and he'd received a great number of messages from Barry's clients, but he still had to grow marijuana. And in order to do that, he had to attend to hundreds of everyday little details about watering, feeding, temperature, lighting, and everything else the moneymen didn't really understand.

He sent Kayla off to her publishing empire with a kiss and went back to PerCan.

The mood couldn't have been better that day. Al had sent out for coffee and pastries and put out a spread in the entrance area to thank everyone for their contributions. The cleaners had been through, and every last cup, fork, and crumpled paper had been removed, and PerCan all but sparkled.

Whistling, Rafael took the stairs two at a time and walked into their shared office.

"Kayla is on a crime-solving spree about this Ranker," he announced to Al, who sat bent over the screen of his laptop. "She is going to find the evidence that will convict him—or at least that is what she is planning."

"Give her my best," Al said, looking up from the email he was reading. "I'm not personally convinced Ranker did it, but detect away. Where did this sudden interest in crime-solving come from?"

"Don't ask." Rafael flung himself into a chair and fired up his own laptop. "I think she's listened to one too many podcasts about criminals, but heck. How are you doing with all of this if you don't mind my asking?"

"I would prefer if everybody would stop asking," Al said, a little too short, but Rafael let it slide. "Have a look at this. Online comments about last night."

"I saw—fantastic."

"Barry called half an hour ago. Told me he had eight requests this morning already. Large investor groups, looking for more information."

Rafael whistled. "Go, Barry. Looks like he's still got it."

"He does. One of the better decisions we made while still being totally unsure if we should even be making it."

Rafael sat back in his chair and pumped his fist into the air.

"I'm all for it. Picture it, I can finally get to work on that extension at the back, start getting a license for more grow space. Heck, the land behind this building is going to…"

"Easy." Al raised his hands, tamping the enthusiasm a little bit. "Let's have the funds in first, shall we? But you know what that means?"

Both men looked at each other, broad, stupid grins on their faces, and finally fist-bumped.

"We made it," Rafael said. "We pulled this thing out of the muck it was in after Connor's original departure, cleaned it up, dusted it off, and made something great out of it. We did it."

"We did it," Al said, and the broad grin on his face was all the reward Rafael needed just then.

"But… I have something else for you here, and you may not really like it all that much."

"Oh, Al. Could you have let me enjoy the victory a bit longer?" Rafael slumped on his desk and raised a forefinger. "What now? Who's been arrested, what machine has blown up, which grow room has an infection?"

"None of the above." Al slipped a sheaf of papers in front of him. "It appears the world of growing medical-grade marijuana successfully on a large scale is a relatively small one, and our fame has—let's say—spread."

"Oh?"

Rafael had no idea what to expect and pulled the papers a little closer, squinting at the headlines. "Malta? As in the country of?"

"As in the country of, my friend. Medical marijuana has just become legal over there, and they would like to know if PerCan would be interested in a joint venture to put a state-of-the-art growing plant there."

"Holy…"

"You said it. And in fact, I've had some general how-about-it inquiries from Spain and Italy as well. There's likely going to be more."

"But, but… Al, we're just a couple of guys. Where is all of this coming from?"

"Don't look now, Rafael, but it stopped being just a couple of guys a long time ago. While you were down on the floor fighting the packing line probably. Our product is amongst the best and purest. Our setup is considered one of the best in the business."

"Yeah, but…"

"This is just further proof." Al nodded at the screen with all the comments about the anniversary. "We know what we are doing, and people are eager to work with us."

"Wow."

"We could, if you like, work on a few of these expansions. Go into other countries, do the same thing. It would mean a lot of travel for you—but it might be exciting, fun, and rewarding. What do you think? Would you be up for it?"

Rafael sat stunned, blinking a few times. His earlier complacency and just all-around great feeling about the anniversary had been blown away. They. Wanted. Him.

His designs—his inventions—his setups…

"But…" He said, groping for words. "This—here—is ours…"

"Nope. It's yours, Rafael," Al said, still smiling like a 10-year-old at Christmas.

"But, wait, I designed all of this for PerCan—for this plant, for our setup…"

"My friend, what I am about to tell you is entirely personal, OK? So, don't go carrying this off into the boardroom where it doesn't belong. When you sat down and figured out how to best set up this plant down there, when you came up with designs how to isolate the grow rooms to minimize infections, make the workflow more efficient, to minimize human contact, and all those things that make this plant work, you did not have a contract with PerCan."

"But Tadeo—your father…"

"Threatened you into saving his company and didn't worry about agreements or contracts. Yes, that was Tadeo."

"I was paid," Rafael protested, even if he knew what was coming.

"Sometimes. Not on a regular basis and certainly not on a contract. So, if I were you, I would head down to a patent lawyer the moment you finish that coffee there." Al nodded at the cup beside Rafael. "Or maybe even before that, depending on how much you need the caffeine, and then we'll talk about licensing your work for PerCan and for anybody else in the rest of the world who seems to want a piece of it."

"Well, I'll be… Son of a…"

Rafael's hands dropped to the armrests of his chair, and for a few moments, he was unable to grasp anything. His brain flat-out refused to take any idea or thought and make coherent sense of it.

"So, you're telling me," he finally said, "that there are people out there who are so convinced that I have the secret recipe to run a cannabis plant, they are willing to pay me for that knowledge?"

"Yep."

"Actual money?"

"A lot of actual money, my friend, and you better believe it." Al grinned as broadly as he had ever seen him do.

"But this—everything down there…" Rafael swept his hands around the room and toward the window into the production floor. "I just did what made sense, what was needed at the time, and put it all together into… You know—a neat little package."

"Rafael." Al brought his hands together to his face and looked over his glasses at him. "You've been tinkering with the grow setup at PerCan since the day Connor said, 'You do it.' You figured it out. You perfected it."

"Well, I wouldn't say…"

"You did. I've compared our yields, our efficiency, the health of our plants, the rate at which we get infections or disturbances—everything. And nobody gets our rates. Not even close."

"I—am still floored."

"You should be proud. Get it together, Rafael. And put your notes together, and patent this stuff—just to be on the safe side. And go talk to Kayla. I can see some international travel in your near future, so please make her aware of that possibility."

"I—I guess…"

"And for God's sake, stop stammering, Rafael. You're the man who spoke up to my father at every turn when he was being difficult. And he was being difficult a lot. Now that the time has come to earn your just rewards, you need to enjoy it."

"Yes, sir, enjoying it, sir." Rafael grinned and mock-saluted to Al. "I'm glad. I'm happy I was able to work it all out that way, to make it happen. Shit. I'm ecstatic."

He ran his hand over his head and around his neck and shook his head, grinning from ear to ear now.

"Who would have thought I would invent something worth having someday? Guess I better put all of this in a portfolio."

"Why don't you? And when you're done with that, come back and help me with all of those requests here, will you?"

Al had to call after him because Rafael had got to his feet and was half out the door already. True to form, when good news like this hit him, he was most comfortable down on the production floor, with his people. Tinkering with processes and machinery, and checking mechanical logs and readouts. He'd be lost to the world for a few hours, Al rationalized, while he communed with his invention down there.

The last few months had been amazing for them. Had it not been for his father's death and the unanswered questions around it, he might have said they ranked among the best of his life.

***

Barry found that his job of raising funds and finding investors became a lot easier after the anniversary.

Everybody wanted a piece of PerCan, no matter how small. In the meantime, he didn't raise funds for ongoing operations, but for expansion, branches nearby, and licensed facilities overseas. Might as well throw it in there.

He still didn't have a lot of friends on the board, but meanwhile, all of them had come around to realizing that he was doing what he should always have done, what he was best at—telling the story of PerCan. Telling the world how much they had done already and what they were about to do next. People wanted to hear it, and they wanted to be part of that story.

Competition amongst cannabis companies had become somewhat cutthroat.

Roberto's little outfit still hung in, although many people suspected that was because Al supported him with funds now and then. He never did see any of Green Technology's equipment. Al had had it scrapped almost as soon as he bought it. In a way, it had forced Roberto to knuckle down, do the hard work, and pull his little operation out of the muck on his own, and for the moment, at least, it seemed to be working, and he was happy doing what he was doing.

FORTY-FOUR

Al walked into his office one afternoon a few months later only to find Kayla sitting at Rafael's desk skimming through a sheaf of papers.

"Good afternoon, Kayla. I'm sorry. Did I miss a meeting of some type?"

Automatically, he reached for his old-fashioned calendar, but Kayla already waved him off.

"No, of course not. That's a bad sign when people think you only show up for the meetings, is it not?"

"Not necessarily. You have your own company to run after all."

"You're being kind, Al." Kayla smiled broadly at him, which always seemed to make Al blush a little, and she enjoyed that.

"No, I was going to meet Rafael here to take him to a late lunch, but he's busy for a few more minutes on the production floor."

"Oh, dear." Al dropped into his own chair and reached for his laptop automatically. "If Rafael is tinkering with his processes down there, I am afraid you might be in for a bit of a wait."

"I figured. I brought some material I want to read anyway." Kayla waved the sheaf of papers he had seen her studying earlier. "Don't mind me. No need to entertain me in the meantime."

"It would not have been a hardship."

Al glanced at the papers in her hand, dying to know what had her wrinkling her brow and chewing her lower lip compulsively, but too polite to ask. She finally took off her reading glasses and smiled at him.

"You really want to know what this is, don't you?"

"It never occurred… Is it that obvious?"

"A bit. But only if you look really close." Kayla smiled that broad, winning smile again and tapped her papers. "These—are the old arrest records for Bobby Ranker for the past few years."

"Oh, Kayla." Al's face visibly fell. "Rafa told me you were doing all of this research, but you know you don't have to."

"I know. Don't let it get around, but I am actually old enough I don't have to do anything I don't want to. But I really wanted to."

Al sighed slowly, but Kayla raised a hand in his direction, not allowing any kind of discussion.

"This man was picked up in possession of the very gun that was used to shoot your father. I want to know why he had it, if he in fact shot Tadeo, and, if so, why."

"But, Kayla, shouldn't Detective Robertson worry about that? He is the one in charge there, no?"

"Yes, Al, he is." Kayla rose and began to pace a bit, twirling her reading glasses between thumb and forefinger.

"You really don't know this guy?"

"No," Al sighed. "I already…"

"And it stands to reason, that if he was a serious enemy of Tadeo's, you would know him?"

"Probably, but Kayla…" At this point, Al rose, stopped her, and gently took her shoulder. "I went over this with Robertson—ad nauseam, as they say."

"I am aware of that, Al." A little annoyed note had crept into her voice, and she shook off his hands. "Pardon me while I'm trying to help figure out why your own father was shot, will you?"

Al sighed and threw up his hands.

"You will do as you wish, Kayla. I'm only telling you not to waste your time."

"It is my time to waste. Now this Ranker here." She tapped her notes with her fingertips. "He's your typical small-time crook.

With the exception of one incident, it's all small-time hustler stuff. B&E, possession, solicitation." She rolled her eyes. "Just a common, streetwise, sleazy guy. The kind of guy who would be an enforcer perhaps?"

"My father didn't have any enforcers. There was nothing to enforce. He just liked to make believe there was."

"So how did they connect? That's what I want to know."

"You're assuming Ranker is the one who committed the shooting?" Al turned away.

"Aren't you?" Kayla stopped in front of him and brought her finger to her lips. "You're not, are you? You're still believing someone else shot him, and Ranker just ended up with this gun."

"It's a possibility," Al said curtly and began scrolling through his computer again. "There is an assumption that a smart criminal would rid himself of the weapon that might tie him to a capital crime."

Kayla had stepped up to the edge of his desk as close as she could and looked down at him.

"You have thought about it—but you don't want to believe he was shot by a small-time hustler?"

"Your description, not mine. A minute ago, you called Ranker sleazy because all but one of his offenses were such."

"Yeah." Kayla picked up her printout again. "Small cons and hustles—and one hit-and-run."

"Hit-and-run?" Al asked. "Weird." He shook his head. "Now if I can get back to this please? I still have a company to run."

"Not an actual hit-and-run," Kayla said, reading the printout. "Peeled out of a parking spot on Beale Street and damaged another car. He took off, but someone saw it and put down his license number. Yay for alert pedestrians. Al?"

Most of the color had suddenly drained from Al's face, and he dropped the pen he was holding, letting it clatter to the ground, while his free hand automatically made a fist.

"Are you all right? What happened?" Kayla came beside him and put a hand on his shoulder. "Al! For a second there, you looked like you'd seen a ghost."

"For a second there, I did, my dear." He managed a pained smile. "Beale Street is around the corner from where the old Green Technologies offices used to be located, and it's where I had to drop off a check when I bought their equipment after the bankruptcy."

Kayla dropped back into her chair and put her palms together, thinking. For a long time, she didn't speak until she finally lined all of the pages of her printout up side by side and looked at them.

"Green Technologies, PerCan, Tadeo Ivers. There is something tying all of these together, don't you think?"

"Two cannabis companies, that's all. You're seeing things."

"Maybe."

She was still staring at her printouts when Rafael walked into the room.

"My apologies, I got held up down in Production." He looked from Al to Kayla, saw her deep in thought about something, and cocked his head. "Did I walk in on something embarrassing?"

"Not at all, Rafael," Al said. "Kayla is trying to figure out why Ranker may or may not have shot Tadeo, and she's wondering if a hit-and-run on Beale Street might be the answer."

"Beale Street!"

Rafael's response came as if shot out of a gun. "He ran somebody down on Beale? What the…"

"No, no—not that kind of hit-and-run," Kayla said quickly. "Damaging a parked vehicle, that's all. And you don't have to make it sound so silly, Al. I just thought it odd that two different cannabis companies were involved here." She handed Rafael the page with the arrest reports and got up from his chair rather abruptly. The chair rolled back and smacked into the wall behind with a soft thud. "I was only trying to help, thinking that we all might have some peace around this thing. But if you would rather I did not, then I will give up."

"Holy fuck!"

Rafael was known to swear around the workers down on the floor or if something irritated him immensely, but in front of Kayla, and even with Al, he tried to clean up his language. Hearing him swear, they stopped and gave him a wide look.

"Rafael?"

"Holy—pardon my language. Honey, you just cracked this thing wide open."

"What are you talking about?"

Kayla and Al were both beside him in giant steps and looked over his shoulder. Rafael's finger hovered just an inch above the hit-and-run arrest notice.

"There."

"Yes? Damage to a vehicle, called in by a pedestrian. They picked up Ranker, he paid for the damages, said he did not notice, but it was still considered a hit-and-run. So?"

"So—everything. Look at the date."

"August second. Again, so?"

Kayla shrugged and spread her hands, but once again, the color had drained out of Al's face.

"August second. It couldn't be."

"Says right here. 589 Beale."

"But that's, like, down the road."

"Right around the corner. If a guy wanted to make a quick getaway, that is."

"Holy…" Al clapped his hand to his mouth. "Holy… I wonder if Robertson has seen this."

"I'm happy to see that the two of you agree on whatever it is you have discovered, but would somebody care to let me know?" Kayla asked, looking between the men and the report in Rafael's hand. "Because I've been staring at that thing for a while, and nothing jumps out."

"That's because we didn't really bother you with this one," Rafael said and put his hand on her shoulder. "It was a sore point with the two of us."

"OK, so?"

"You see, August second." Al picked up the thread. "That was the day someone broke into the offices of Green Technologies."

"No kidding."

"Oddly, nothing was actually taken, but Greg Turner was a bit—roughed up, and he had a cockamamie story. Some yarn about a guy breaking in, and Turner caught him and chased him out of the building. Except, supposedly, he was still out cold when they found him."

"Meaning Ranker might be the man who broke in—that fits with his MO. But why do the two of you look like lightning has struck?"

"Because that story is just weird," Rafael said slowly, still tapping her reports. "None of it made sense. Guy walks in, beats up Turner, leaves him lying there, but takes off again without stealing anything?"

Kayla thought for a moment and shook her head.

"If this in fact hangs together somehow," she said, "then I can't see how."

"I'll be damned," Rafael said with a certain amount of admiration in his voice and stroked his chin.

"I wouldn't go quite that far," Kayla said. "We can put him there, so maybe he had something to do with it, but that's it."

Al took the printout and studied it. "I wonder how Robertson never twigged on this one," he said softly. "They could have had him much earlier."

"B&E without anything stolen, a hit-and-run without any personal injuries—not the kind of stuff you waste time on," Rafael said. "Even in a police department that isn't busy. And ours is. Somebody typed up a report and filed it and done."

"That's despicable."

"That's reality," Rafael said. "Wasn't it you who told me how many unsolved cold cases there are? And this was not even unsolved. Just—weird."

"Be that as it may." Al finally took the printout with Ranker's rap sheet off Rafael and smoothed out the pages. "We should show this to the good detective. I dare say he'll be a little bit embarrassed. On the other hand, it still doesn't give us the slightest hint on how Ranker came into possession of that gun."

"There's that," Rafael said, and worried a little cut on the side of his index finger with his thumb. Something was nagging at him. Something he had heard a while ago, something he had wanted to remember at the time, something to fit exactly into this weird situation. If he could just remember what it was.

"Are you coming for lunch, Rafael? This thing can wait for a bit, I believe."

"What—yeah, sure, give me a minute." He looked up and smiled at Kayla.

Just then, he remembered that she had likely been waiting for him in his office and checked the time.

"I made you wait already—I am so sorry."

"Don't be. It was well worth it."

It would be worth it if there had been anything definitive—even the slightest bit of evidence that Bobby Ranker had actually pulled the trigger, or that he knew who had. Rafael rolled the situation over in his mind, all through lunch. No matter how much Kayla tried to start a conversation, he couldn't follow anything she told him.

He poked at his food and managed to say something about the taste or quality. Most of it seemed to satisfy her because she did not nag him about being preoccupied. If he could just remember.

"This thing is really bothering you, isn't it?" she finally asked, and he nodded.

"Yes, and I am trying to figure it out, but…"

"What? What are you trying to figure out?"

"I wish I knew, Kayla! I know somebody said something to me a little while ago that fit exactly in with this scenario. It's right here."

He tapped the left side of his head. "I just can't put my finger on it. I know the solution is there. I know it is."

"Give yourself a break before you go insane. You will think about it sooner or later. Meanwhile, Al said he would inform the detective of what we found."

"What you found. We only stumbled on this because you buckled down and did the research."

"Doesn't matter," Kayla said and winked. "I only hope they can use it to get more out of Ranker."

"He was on Beale Street the night of a burglary, big deal. He paid for the damages to the other car, and they haven't got anything on him for the thing at GT. If I were him, I would tell them to go fly a kite."

"Well, you're not him!"

"Thank God."

FORTY-FIVE

When they returned to PerCan, Al had done just as promised and shown his findings to Detective Robertson.

"He was embarrassed, yes, but less than enthused," Al told Kayla and Rafael. "It is something they missed, but not really a big deal in his book."

Rafael shrugged his shoulders in a *told ya* gesture and took off his jacket to go back down to the production floor. If nothing else happened, he still had cannabis to grow, harvest, package, and sell, and everything but the *sell* part depended on his setup working properly. This—this was where he needed to concentrate his energy and his mental powers.

For the hundredth time that day, he checked a temperature log and tried to concentrate on possible reasons for a temperature fluctuation in pod five, which was preventing his plants from thriving as they should. Again, he went all over the grow room with temperature probes, checked the access hallway between the pods, and rebooted the controller software. He grilled Dante Ivers and his crew about anything and everything that had been done in or near that grow pod, and eventually, he forgot about Bobby Ranker and his activities the night of the break-in at Green Technologies.

***

Al, in the meantime, tried to do the same thing with his financial forecasts, although after an hour and three different interruptions, he had to admit he was not really getting anywhere.

What an odd coincidence it was, though.

With an effort, Al tore his thoughts away once again and focused on the screen before him, where little numbers were doing a merry hula dance. It was no use; he was not going to get this done today. Being the boss had its perks, he finally thought, shrugged into his jacket, and decided to go for an extended walk. Maybe the fresh air would do him some good.

***

Over at the police headquarters, Detective Robertson rested his chin in his hand and stared down at the pages Al Ivers had just faxed him.

"Anything interesting?" his assistant Brian asked, merely because he thought anything concerning Ivers was definitely interesting, this being the first-ever murder case he had come across in his short career.

"I doubt it." Robertson shook his head. "Hit-and-run, no personal injuries, debt promptly settled."

"Oh, well." Brian made a face, knowing that he would likely be asked to file those papers away with the old case the boss mentioned, and he hated the archives.

"Except. The one odd thing is it happened the night of the Green Tech break-in."

"OK."

"On the same block."

"Getting warmer, but why did we catch this one? Did Traffic send it up?"

"No, somebody sent it to me, thought there was something there." Robertson picked up the pages and tapped the edge of them against his palm. "Probably nothing—but then again, we have nothing useful anyway."

He sighed again, worried his lower lip with this thumb and forefinger, and wrote something on a piece of paper.

"Tell you what, Brian? Why don't you go and get me that file out of the archives. Least I could do is read through it, even if it comes to nothing."

"I knew you were going to ask that, sir."

Brian Winston got to his feet and went to the door, dragging his feet as if he were being led to a dentist's appointment.

"What? You like the archives," Robertson cackled, but he never saw the middle finger Winston was extending out of sight.

He pretended not to see Brian Winston's pinched face and dusty clothes when the young man returned and put the file on his desk without another word.

Just as Robertson had expected, there was nothing of note there. Bobby Ranker had apparently dinged another car while moving out of a parking spot and decided it was better to take off without worrying about the damage. Unfortunately for him, an alert pedestrian walking his dog late at night had seen the incident, snapped a picture with his phone, and sent it to the police. By the time the owner of the damaged car even got up the next morning, it was all sorted, and Ranker had been charged.

Naturally, he swore he had not noticed the scratch—how often had they heard that one?—and offered to pay for all the damages. End of case.

Robertson was not really interested in the hit-and-run anyway, except for the timing it provided. It put Ranker squarely on Beale Street, just a hair after the break-in at Green Technologies. Coincidence? Could be, but Robertson liked to believe that coincidences did not really exist. Things happened for a reason, and people acted for a reason. And once he found that reason, he usually found the key to the case.

Being a jerk and a creep aside, what would Ranker even be doing on Beale in the middle of the night? There were no bars around, no shops, and very few residential developments. That dog walker spotting the accident was a pure fluke. So, what was he doing there? Visiting someone? Who—and why?

Robertson sat back and chewed on his thumbnail. And what were the odds that he would end up with two cases involving Bobby Ranker? He took the file on the GT break-in and the thin folder on the accident and put them side by side. The only thing connecting them was Ranker. Ranker, who was a sleazeball and had been caught in possession of a gun that had killed Tadeo Ivers.

A gun he had apparently 'found' somewhere along the river.

"Tell me something I don't know," he muttered and stared at his files, willing them to give up the connection.

What if he hadn't just stumbled about that gun? What if that gun had some sort of connection to the Green Technologies incident? Greg Turner had specifically mentioned that the burglar had a knife, not a gun. A knife. Could Turner be giving him the runaround? He had no reason to…

Robertson rose and brushed his hands on his pant legs. Ranker's bail had come through, and they would have to let him go the next morning. Unless they could nail him on something. Finding a gun was not technically illegal. Best he could do at this point was unlawful possession, and Ranker, possessed of that peculiar charm all conmen have, would convince a sitting judge he'd truly meant to turn it in, but a few personal issues got in the way.

"One shot, Robertson," he told himself and pressed a buzzer for his assistant.

"Come along then, Winston, I have a few questions for our friend Ranker," he said, already on his way down to the holding cells.

"Shouldn't we call his lawyer to be present?"

"We're not questioning him on the gun he found." He drew vivid air quotes around that last word. "I'm going to ask him if he saw something the night of the GT break-in. As a witness, you know."

"You can do that?"

"I can do that." He nodded. "And we'll just see if anything shakes loose. It's the only shot we have before we have to turn the man loose again tomorrow, and the least I can do is give him a hard time about that night on Beale."

FORTY-SIX

As if by mutual agreement, Rafael, Kayla, and Al did not discuss their discovery again that night. They enjoyed dinner out together and spoke of anything but Bobby Ranker, the gun that killed Tadeo, or any kind of incident on Beale Street.

Al explained their expansion plans to Kayla, the different countries they might go into and what it meant to PerCan.

The fate of a small-time crook was of no interest just then.

The next morning, Al arrived at PerCan whistling, which he hadn't done in a long time. He noticed that Rafael's car had not arrived yet, and he grinned with barely hidden glee.

For once, he had beaten the man who prided himself on being first down on the production floor. He'd barely had time to push the button on the cappuccino maker in their office when Rafael came running in.

"Beat you by about…" Al checked his watch. "Five minutes."

"Stuff it, Ivers."

"I hate to add to your pain," Al said, tasting his coffee, "but we have a conference call in 10. Are you ready?"

Rafael said nothing, but fired up his laptop and the presentation he'd been working on. "Good to go."

Rafael impressed the group looking for a cannabis grow five minutes into the call, and they didn't let their attention stray from there. When he spoke, they could tell that he knew what he was doing, that he spent most of the day down where the production actually took place, and if there was a problem, there was a chance he had encountered and solved it before.

Rafael had barely moved through the first part of his presentation when Al's cell phone chirped with a new text.

Al silenced it quickly, but when he looked down at it, he saw Detective Robertson's name. He didn't mind the man, but he still couldn't help the little spike in his blood pressure every time he saw the name.

Rafael went through his presentation and finished with a flourish. Usually, he expected Al to add a few more details, but today, Al wanted to end the call in a hurry. Even as they signed off, he had already reached for his cell phone and stared at the screen.

"Bad news?" Rafael asked, closing his presentation.

"I don't know," Al said and stroked his chin. "It's from Robertson."

"Oh, what's up?"

"Doesn't say." Al frowned. "Just *there's a development. Stand by.*"

"Weird." Rafael shrugged. "Maybe he sent it to you by accident."

"What makes you say that?"

"Because it doesn't tell you anything. 'There's a development.' Sounds to me like it's meant for somebody else."

Al didn't answer, and Rafael got to his feet.

"Gotta go down into Production, check on the temperature issue in pod five. I hope I finally nailed the sucker. There are a few pipe seals I don't like... Ah, never mind."

Al checked the message again and toyed with the idea of calling the detective back to find out what happened, but halfway into dialing his number, he changed his mind and pocketed his phone again. Not his problem, right? They would get in touch if there was something he needed to know or do something about. Meanwhile, he had an agreement to work out with that group in Malta.

Instead of Robertson, he called Raymond in Legal and set up a meeting to hammer out a joint venture agreement.

***

Every now and then, as the morning went on and he and Raymond went over minor details of the contract, he glanced at his phone. Still nothing from Robertson.

Kayla dropped in around lunch just to say hi and she was in the area, and as if by mutual agreement, neither Rafael nor Al told her about Robertson's odd message. Maybe it had been a misdirect after all.

Still, the nagging feeling wouldn't leave his mind though. Midafternoon, when he realized he had read page one of Raymond's contract for the fifth time and had no recollection of the terms and conditions, he finally gave up and dialed Robertson's number. Rafael was still busy down in Production, or he would have given him a hard time about this one!

"Robertson."

"Detective, good day to you. It's Al—Al Ivers here. Have you got a minute?"

"One, if that's all you need. I'm a little busy here."

"I was calling to ask about your message from this morning?"

"My what? Oh—that? My apologies, that was meant for my assistant Brian. Must have dialed a wrong number."

A misdirect after all. Al sighed, disappointed, ready to sign off with an apology, when he heard someone call out in the background, "765 Beale. Tell him to bring the full forensics team, techs, and the K9 unit if they're available."

"Detective? 765 Beale is the old offices of Green Technologies. What on Earth?" Robertson sighed audibly.

"Al, that wasn't meant for you. I would appreciate it if you…"

"Forgot what I heard? Not likely. Not after everything we discovered about Bobby Ranker. The man who was found with the gun that shot my father, might I remind you, the man who was involved in an accident at that address."

"I guess you're right." Robertson sighed again, and Al could almost see him glowering at whoever had spoken in the background, forking his fingers through his hair. "All right."

"So?"

"I will update you later—shortly. Al… really."

It was weak. Robertson knew it, Al knew it, and he made a fist with his right hand. "Fine," he said softly. "You do that."

He hung up the phone, knowing that this was far from the last word spoken on this subject.

He began pacing his office, up and down, and for once, he didn't see the busy production floor down below. His eyes were fixed on his feet as he walked and the thoughts tumbled one over the other.

Bobby Ranker—the gun that killed his father—the break-in at Green Technologies—*there's a development*—Bobby Ranker—the gun—his father… He struck the palm of his left hand with the fist of his right and tried to begin again, but it did not make any sense. None of the puzzle pieces fit together. He sat back at his desk again and pressed his fingers into his temples.

The door to the office opened, and Rafael walked in with his usual quick stride and let the door swing shut behind him.

"Hey, I think it is the temperature sensor after all. I still don't like what's going on in pod five… What the heck?"

He stared at Al, sitting hunched in his chair, deep furrows on his face. "Al, are you all right? Did something happen?"

Two strides brought him to Al's side, and he touched his shoulder with a hand. "What happened? You look like…"

Al shook his head, visibly struggling.

"I know it's obsessive, but I called Robertson back."

"Yeah, well, I figured you would. So?"

"Just like you said. The text was not for me—it was for his assistant."

Rafael spread his hands and sat at his own desk, all the while keeping a careful eye on Al, who had gone white as the notepad in front of him.

"He was just about to fob me off," Al said, forking his hand through his hair, "when I heard someone yell in the background. 765 Beale. Bring the full forensics, techs, and the K9 unit."

He raised his head, and their eyes met as the same recognition of the address happened for Rafael.

"Holy shit," Rafael said. "Beale, Green Tech—they've been out of that place since the bankruptcy. Is there another case?"

"And if Robertson had said, 'Hey, we're on another case,' I would have hung up and walked away," Al said softly. "Instead, he acted… Odd."

"Odd? Odd how? Don't make me pull this out of you one piece at the time."

"He stuttered about for a bit and said, 'I will update you later.'"

"Meaning…"

"Meaning this has to have to something to do with my father's shooting, or he would never have any reason to update me later." Al made heavy air quotes around the past phrase. "And that's probably why he sent that text to me. He was thinking he would need to update me, to tell me about what had happened—albeit later."

"Holy shit," Rafael said again, and he folded his hands and brought them to his mouth, thinking. "Well…" He fished his keychain from the corner of his desk and nodded toward the door. "Cancel the rest of your day. We're going there."

"Into the middle of a police investigation? Rafael, I appreciate your support, but I don't think this would be wise."

"Wise? Wise, Al? No it would not be wise at all, but we are going to get some answers here. If Ranker or Green Technologies or somebody there had anything to do with your father's death, we are going to find out. You have nothing less than a right to that. Let's go."

Al rose and shrugged into his jacket, even though he still shook his head.

"I don't want to disturb any investigation they might have going on at the moment…"

"We are not going to be disturbing anything. We're going to find Robertson, and we are going to make him tell us what he knows. Unless you want to sit around here, imagining what it might be, waiting for this guy to update you at his leisure. Let's go. Now."

Rafael pressed hard. He had finally remembered the thought that had been bothering him for days now, the little harmless fact, the tiny circumstance that had been going around his head, just out of reach, elusive and teasing with little flashes here and there, and he hoped to God he was wrong about it. If there was one thing that needed to come out of this fool's errand, he had to be wrong.

He all but dragged Al past the folks at the front desk, waved someone away who had an urgent question for them, and called over his shoulder.

"We need to take care of something urgently. Anyone shows up, my apologies—we'll be back in a while."

Hopefully. If all went well, they would be back on the inside of a couple of hours, and this would all be a weird coincidence. It could be, right? Weirder things had happened. Or maybe there was really another incident on Beale Street, and they would end up embarrassed. It could happen.

Rafael drove fast without speaking and left the car in a no-parking zone at the end of Beale and Lennox Street. The hell with a ticket. Around them, a half dozen police squad cars and police vans were parked rather haphazardly, and a uniformed officer leading two beautiful large Belgian Malinois on long leads passed them.

"Police dogs," Al said faintly, and Rafael nodded.

"Yup, could be just a drug thing, you know."

Al nodded, but without any conviction. He obviously didn't think it was just a drug thing either.

Uniformed policemen milled around the lobby of 765 Beale, checking people who had business in the building and those who did not, and Rafael nodded to the side of the building, where a back alley promised a service entrance.

"Always pays to know where the maintenance people go in. Follow me."

Al was just one step behind him. They climbed the maintenance stairs floor after floor and hardly noticed the effort until they finally emerged on the fifth floor.

Rafael pulled the door to the hallway open and was immediately stopped by a uniformed policeman.

"Sir, there's an ongoing investigation on this floor. You cannot be here right now. I'm afraid I will have to ask you to leave."

"We have business with Detective Sergeant Robertson," Rafael bluffed while Al turned a shade paler if that was possible. "He's expecting us. Covin and Ivers."

Did the officer blink when Rafael said Ivers? Did he recognize that name, perhaps in connection with whatever the heck was going on here?

"Wait here," he said curtly. "I will check with the detective. Do not move, understand?"

"Not moving, sir," Rafael said sarcastically. "Yes, sir."

It took only a few moments until Detective Robertson appeared around the bend of the hall, disheveled, serious, and not at all happy to see them.

"I should have expected the two of you," he said. "You can't be here. You know that. This is…"

"An active investigation—we know, skip over all that, will you?" Rafael said and spun his finger in little circles in the air. "Instead, tell us what this has to do with his father's death."

"Rafael—I don't… Where do you get the idea…?" Robertson stopped, sighed, and looked at Al. "Are you all right? You look like… You don't look well."

"I would appreciate finding out what all of this has to do with my father's death," Al said tightly, and Robertson looked around.

"Who says it has anything…"

"Detective…" Rafael advanced a step on Robertson.

"Fine, I will give you 10 minutes and update you on everything we know. But not up here. This is a potential crime scene. You do not want to compromise this investigation for anything, do you hear me?"

He fixed Al in a hard stare, and Al shook his head. "No, of course not. I just need answers."

"Fine. There's a coffee shop in the food court on the lowest level. Wait there for me."

He turned away from them, and Rafael thought he could hear him cuss out the officer who had fallen for his line, as Al tugged on his jacket.

"Out—move. He's right. If this does have something to do with Tadeo's shooting, we can't chance contaminating something."

This time it was Al who took a hold of Rafael's sleeve and tugged him back down the stairs. Rafael hardly put up a fight. He was still wishing they were wrong, and all of this would turn out to be a strange coincidence.

They would laugh about this—sure, in about a year. They would sit here and laugh about this. They'd be somewhere in Malta or Italy or Spain or wherever they were planning on expanding and chat over a beer. *Remember when we stormed in at the abandoned Green Technologies offices? We were so excited. We thought we'd solved a crime.* Except the offices of Green Tech were anything but abandoned right now, and Rafael—Rafael thought he knew exactly what had gone down.

He dropped into a chair at a charred wooden table in the food court and nodded when Al made a suggestion, hardly caring what he drank or ate for that matter. Al returned with three paper cups, fished sugar and creamers out of his pocket, and dropped into another chair. He pushed a cup toward Rafael and dumped sugar into his own.

"It's you who doesn't look well now," he said, searching Rafael's face. "Too many memories of police officers?"

"What? No." Rafael ran his finger around the rim of his coffee cup lid. "It's just..."

Al waited, finally shrugged, and took a sip of his coffee, making a face. "Something is up," he said. "Something about all of this is connected to my father's death."

"Suddenly, you call him 'my father,'" Rafael said, tried his own coffee, and pushed it away again, making a face. "It used to be just Tadeo."

"I know," Al said back and stared at the cup in front of him. "I guess it took him dying, and dying in a violent way, to break me of that habit."

"Any regrets?"

"Jesus, Rafael, I can't have this conversation here and now. I just want to know what happened—I'll deal with everything else once I have that."

"I guess. I'm sorry." Rafael abandoned his coffee and pulled out his cell phone. "I'm going to make a quick call. Have to tell Kayla where we are and what happened."

"Do that." Al nodded, but his thoughts were elsewhere—far away by the look on his face.

Rafael called Kayla and gave her the Cliffs Notes version of what was going on. He couldn't yet tell her what he suspected in his heart to be true, but she should know where they were and what they were doing. By the time he hung up the phone, Detective Robertson came clipping through the food court toward them, and without waiting for a hello, he started to speak, pointing an angry index finger at Rafael and Al in turn.

"Al, I know I accidentally sent you a text, but you showing up here at a crime scene is unacceptable, do you hear me? Unacceptable. You could compromise the entire investigation if anyone feels like sharing the news that bystanders were trampling on my crime scene."

"We're not mere bystanders," Al said calmly. "If this is about my father's murder, I am not a bystander. I am a victim, and if this was about an unrelated case, you wouldn't be down here giving us a hard time. You would have booted us out of the building and threatened to arrest us."

Robertson sat, took the coffee cup, glanced at it, and put it down again.

"So, Detective?"

Outwardly, Al appeared to be as calm as could be. If you hadn't seen him half an hour ago, white as a sheet, unable to form complete sentences, Rafael thought, you would believe the mere bystander story.

Robertson sighed, took his glasses off his nose, and folded and unfolded them several times. The frames looked like he did this kind of damage on a regular basis. Finally, he opened his mouth and gestured with the glasses in his hand.

"What I am about to tell you needs to stay in strict confidence between the three of us, is that clear? I cannot repeat often enough how much this investigation could be damaged if anyone…"

"Understood." Al nodded. "As far as we are concerned, this meeting never happened, OK? Good with you, Rafael?"

Rafael nodded, unable to speak around the massive lump in his throat. This was bad.

"Carry on, then."

It was rather obvious that Robertson wanted to be anywhere but in that dingy food court sitting between them, a cup of horrid, tepid coffee in front of him, but finally, he spoke.

"Bobby Ranker, the fellow we picked up on a minor drug charge…"

"Yes, and you searched his home and found that gun…"

"The gun that fired the shot that killed your father—yes. I asked him any which way I could phrase it if he knew anything about this crime. If he had heard anything about it at all. He kept insisting no, he'd never heard about it, he only found this gun down by the river somewhere and kept it around for a few days."

"I bet he just had not had a chance to turn it in to the police," Rafael said sarcastically.

"Something like that, yes. Soon as he sees this is getting serious, he lawyers up, and I can't get anything useful out of him. His lawyer knew that, of course, and told me to come back when I had actual evidence to tie his client to the crime."

"But the gun that was used in a murder," Al insisted, "you had to be able to take that somewhere, no?"

"No evidence, Al." Robertson shook his head. "Said he found it, he even took us to the spot by the river where he found it, and that was the end. I couldn't make any kind of connection between him and your father because there was none. You know that."

Al only nodded, remembering quite well the days he had racked his brain to remember if he'd come across the name Ranker. He'd even phoned ADP personally to see if Ranker had ever been in their payroll files.

"Nothing," Robertson echoed. "There was an off chance that maybe your dad paid him cash, but here's the thing about cash…"

"Untraceable," Al muttered. "Go on."

"He made bail on the original drug charge late this afternoon, and I could only hold him for so long before I'd have to let him go. No evidence on the shooting—end of story. And just as I am writing out the order to do that, you called."

"Kayla's sleuthing," Rafael muttered.

"That lady of yours is a force to be reckoned with," Robertson said, eliciting a small grin from Rafael. "The one thing all of my cops missed—she digs it up on the inside of a few hours."

"She's something, all right."

"But here's the thing. I'm looking at it and looking at it, and it is just property damage, a ding in a car, nothing else. The location is nowhere near your dad's diner or home, or anyplace he frequents regularly. It's nothing right? No connection."

Al only nodded, having thought the same thing over and over and from all different angles.

"So, I know he's going to walk out of the station, no way around it. But the guy is a criminal, a conman, and I don't like him. This may be a shocker, but I really dislike that little weasel. So, I decide, yeah, I am going to let him go, but first, I am going to give him a bit of a hard time, right? I'm going to rag on him about this hit-and-run and how dumb he is, just to make sure he knows I have my eye on him from now on."

Robertson pointed at his own eyes with two fingers, and at Rafael and Al in turn.

"You're rattling his chain," Rafael said. "But there's more to this story."

He spun his finger in circles, *get on with it,* and Robertson raised an eyebrow.

"In a hurry, are you? Fine. I went down to Holding, and I brought Kayla's research with me—stuffed a whole bunch of empty pages into a folder to make it look like the city phone book. I get down there, and all I do is ask him about the night of August second, that little incident on Beale Street, and he goes all white and shifty on me."

"White and shifty," Al repeated slowly, nodding as if it meant anything to him. "And?"

"There's something there. I know there's something there," Robertson continued, "Innocent guy would have said, 'I paid for the damages—everything was cleared up.' But he didn't. He's muttering and talking around this thing in little circles. And suddenly, I'm sure he's lying."

"Which does appear to be his default mode," Al said. He still didn't know where this was leading, while a heavy feeling of dread spread through Rafael, slowly but surely.

"So, I kept asking him," Robertson said, "kept at it. What about that night, what happened there, did you see something? And I kept waiting for him to call for his lawyer, but he didn't. He's too rattled about the whole thing, and finally, I asked him, 'What did you do, Bobby?'"

Robertson leaned back, brought his palms together before his face, and looked at Rafael and Al and back to Rafael. They sat leaning forward, hardly even breathing, waiting.

"And suddenly, Ranker says, 'I didn't shoot—it was all him.'"

Silence settled over the table punctuated by a sudden crash, as Rafael dropped his coffee cup. Cussing, he cleaned it up, while Al and Robertson never took their eyes off one another.

"I always knew there was more to that break-in than Turner ever told us," Robertson continued. "Always. This was no ordinary break-in. And now I knew I was getting close. I was sweating that he'd clam up and call his lawyer, but once he said, 'I didn't shoot,' once he started talking, it's like it's all coming out of him in one long story. He'd been carrying this around, and he wanted to tell it."

Rafael dropped back into his chair, kneading his hands, but neither Al nor Robertson paid him any mind. Both men still had their eyes locked on another, the coffee long forgotten and cold between them. Al didn't speak.

"Go back to the beginning, I told him," Robertson said. "Tell me what happened, and if you're honest with me, I'll figure out a way to help you, but you need to tell me what happened. So…" Robertson swallowed and brought his fist to his mouth for a second. "Apparently, Ranker was prowling around downtown that night. He needed to score some drugs, and in order to do that, he needed cash—fast. He's looking for somewhere to break in. He is walking around when he sees a sign, Green Technologies, and he remembers, hey, those guys grow marijuana in there. Why don't I go and score some?"

"There was never any product in that location—that was their administration office," Rafael said. "They'd never have gotten permission to have product there."

"Ranker was desperate, Rafael, and he was not too bright. Sure, you and I would have figured that out. Him? He thinks, oh, cannabis, cool. I'm going to go get me some."

"Dumbass," Rafael muttered under his breath, earning a stern glance from Al.

"So," Robertson continued, "he sneaks around back, finds a service entrance…" He paused for a moment and glared from Al to Rafael and back. "The same one the two of you gentlemen used, I am sure. He sneaks in and goes up the staircase until he finds Green Technologies."

"Fifth floor, it's a long climb."

Again, Rafael earned a glare from Al. *Will you let him finish before wisecracking?* he seemed to think, and Rafael raised his hands.

"He jimmies open the door, goes in, and—surprise—there is Greg Turner sitting in his office. Maybe he worked late, fell asleep, who knows? According to Ranker, they struggle, he is trying to knock out Turner so he can get out of there, when Turner grabs a gun and shoots."

Robertson paused for dramatic effect, but Al already spun his finger—*keep going.*

"It's dark in that office, cramped quarters, what have you. The shot misses, goes wide, hits a potted plant, and splinters the pot. One of those shards hits Ranker—which is how his blood came to be on the doorframe."

Robertson looked from Al to Rafael, but both men sat completely still, hands folded in front of them, hardly even breathing. Neither of them looked particularly well, but perhaps that was to be expected.

"Ranker says he panicked," Robertson said softly. "Turner was stunned the shot had missed, so he knocked him out, grabbed the gun and that stupid plant, and got out of there. I guess he thought if his break-in was a bust, at least he could sell the gun to one of his cronies. The plant—who the heck knows why he took that stupid thing? I even saw it sitting there outside the back door, but it's long gone now. And that, gentlemen, is where our investigation is at. We're combing through the old office space up there to find any kind of evidence or connection…"

"It was Turner, all along," Rafael said with a grave voice, finally giving words to the dread he'd had ever since finding out Robertson was investigating at Beale Street, ever since he had remembered that nagging comment in the back of his mind. "It was Turner."

"Come again?" Robertson asked, finally cluing in that there was something passing between Rafael and Al, something he definitely was not party to. Neither of the men spoke.

"Rafael? We are still all over that office space up there, trying to connect that gun to anything. If you have any information, now is the time to tell me. I can have you back at the station just as quick as you can say no comment."

"My father and Turner had a history," Al said, so softly they had to strain to hear him.

"History? What kind of history? My guys didn't find anything—and we looked a few years back."

"It goes back a long, long time." Al shook his head.

"Well, what is it all about? Speak, man, or the same I promised your friend here goes for you."

"I don't know the details," Al said wearily. "We were in merger talks with Green Tech, and suddenly, he tried to get out, tried to grab our biggest investor, bankrupt Green Tech, and start over elsewhere."

"I didn't know that," Robertson said. Now he was the one spinning his finger. "But that is still thin for homicide."

"That was not it." Rafael took up the story. "Barry Wentworth, still Connor back then, had a—vested interest—in PerCan merging with Mariposa, not Green Technologies, so he unearthed some old story, something that went on between Turner and Ivers way back when, and he reminded him that he should never do business with an Ivers again. Ever."

Rafael looked sideways at Al, who still sat rooted to his chair, refusing to move, but Al did not even acknowledge him.

"That's it, folks? That's all you've got? Some old story from the dark ages that made him think twice about going into business with you? That's all?"

"Some old story that made him not want to go into business with Tadeo Ivers," Al said softly. "The man who then turned up dead, and he is in possession of the gun."

Robertson was already on his feet, pulling out his radio and issuing staccato orders into it.

"I'm going to go talk to Turner," he said quickly, his mind now a mask of stone. "You two are going to go back to your office and do not move. Do you understand me? Do not move. Keep yourself available, while I decide if I can find any kind of charge to bring against you."

He all but ran through the food court, eliciting a number of curious stares, no more so than the two men who sat at the table, unmoving, staring at two cups and some spilled sugar on the table.

"You think he meant it with the not moving?" Rafael asked after a few minutes, and Al attempted a weak smile.

"I don't understand how you can manage to wisecrack at a time like this, Rafael, but keep on going. I have a feeling we will need all the good humor we can get."

They rose, dropped the untouched coffee into the nearest trash bin, and made their way out the building and into the street, where they found Rafael's car. *No parking ticket*, he thought, *look at that. Got lucky for once.* But if it was one thing neither one of them felt just then, it was lucky.

They barely spoke on the way back to the office, nodded at the ladies in Reception, and when he finally closed their office door behind them, Rafael thought he could breathe again.

"Turner," he finally said. "Of all people—Turner."

Al didn't answer, shook his head, and sat at his laptop.

"I mean, I knew there had to be a reason for him to walk out of the merger, after all this time we put into it, but—murder?"

"Forgive me for saying this, Rafael." Al ran a pointed finger around the outside of his laptop. "But I lay this squarely at Barry's door."

"Barry?"

"Yes, Barry. If he had not dug up some ancient story just to make sure we ended up merging with Mariposa instead of GT, then…"

"Then your father would still be alive."

"Correct."

Al flipped open the laptop and hit the on button with more force than strictly necessary. He rested his face on a clenched fist, and for the first time in many, many months, Rafael didn't know what to say to his friend.

Barry and he had been friends. They had set up this operation. They had done everything together until—well, until Barry walked out. Then he and Al had taken over. And now?

"I'm…"

"Don't say I'm sorry—please, Rafael. For one thing, you do know that I am not blaming you for any of this. For the other, I don't want you to talk me out of being angry at Barry. He caused this, with the same reckless disregard for rules and convention that got the company into hot water in the first place. The first time, he walked away. What's he going to do now? Say, 'Sorry, not my fault,' and walk away again?"

Rafael only shrugged.

"I want him to take responsibility for once in his miserable life."

"You and many others," Rafael said so softly he could barely even hear himself. He remembered a similar conversation with Irv Moody, after Barry had crashed his plane, attempting to flee, or indeed Tadeo Ivers after they had caught Barry with an illegal grow op, down in the far end of the building.

"I hear you," he finally said. "And I know this is not going to make one damn bit of difference to the way you feel, but if there's anything I can do for you—don't even ask. It's done."

"I know."

He sat back and stared off at the wall opposite his desk, deep in thought. Rafael considered how long he'd have to wait politely before being able to pretend that something needed his attention down in the grow area. There was nothing he could think of to say that would have made Al feel better, nothing he could have brought up in defense of Barry or even against him. Al was right. Barry had not pulled the trigger, but he sure enough had teed up Turner to make the shot. Was that illegal in some way? The last thing they needed now was for Barry to be in the headlines once again. Jesus! Almost immediately, he felt ashamed for thinking of the company at a time like this, and again, he groped for something to say, when their door opened quite suddenly.

"Rafael—Al? What happened? I couldn't wait any longer, and your reception ladies told me you'd got back half an hour ago. What's going on?"

Kayla stepped into the office and looked from one man to the other, sensing that something was terribly wrong. Rafael nodded at another chair by his desk, and without a word, she sat, and reached out to cover his hand with hers.

"What happened?"

"Barry Wentworth," Al said slowly, pushing his fingertips into his forehead and letting out a deep sigh. "Or, more simply speaking, another great mess."

"That's not new, sorry, Rafael. I know he's your friend, but…"

She shook her head at Rafael, who still tried and failed to find something to say that wouldn't sound awful. Finally, he just decided on telling her the entire story, from Al getting a text that wasn't meant for him to driving down to Green Technologies, to finally putting the pieces all together only an hour ago. An hour? Somehow it felt more like ages.

"Turner," Kayla said with the same disbelief in her voice. "Turner shot Tadeo? Jesus, Al, I don't know what to say right now, other than I am so, so sorry."

"Welcome to the club." Al shook his head. "Rafael has been struggling with the same thing for the past hour, and he was there when it happened."

"But why would Turner want to shoot Tadeo?"

"Some old story which only Barry will be able to explain to us, except he is the very last person I want to see right now."

"Well, you may not, but I certainly do." Kayla straightened a bit in her chair. "If only to give him a piece of my mind."

"I knew he had done something to get Turner to walk away," Rafael said. "It slipped out in conversation a few months ago already. He told me Turner and Ivers Senior had some type of history. That was all he said, and at that point, I just didn't want to know any more."

"He did," Kayla said softly. "When I went to see him in jail, he mentioned something similar. Except I thought it was all BS, so I didn't think about it again."

Someone knocked at their door, and Rafael looked at Al, who only shrugged. Might as well.

"Come," he said softly, then cleared his throat and spoke a little louder. "Come in."

"Good afternoon, wonderful people, I come bearing excellent news which will make you grateful that I am here."

"Speak of the devil and in he walks," Kayla said and stood toe to toe with Barry J. Wentworth.

"The devil? Dear Kayla, I bring good news. I have another institutional investor lined up. The money is just rolling in since the anniversary, and your expansion plans are now all but guaranteed, Rafael. Why's everybody looking so downtrodden? Did someone die?"

"Good question Barry," Rafael said. "Sit down, close the door behind you, and grab a chair. This is going to take a moment."

"Sorry, folks, any other time, but I have an appointment I really should not…"

"Cancel it," Al barked, and for a moment, Rafael could see an image of the old Al, dark, angry, and just a bit dangerous. Even Barry didn't think it a good idea to argue just then.

"OK." He sat. "Anybody care to fill me in?"

Rafael did while Al paced up and down in front of the window, pausing to look down at Production at regular intervals.

"Shit," Barry finally said. "Turner? Well, what did that fool have to go get a gun and shoot someone for?"

"Indeed, Barry." Al stood before him and glowered down at a slouching Barry. "Why don't you fill us in? Go on. Tell us what you dug up that would get Turner angry enough to shoot my father?"

"Hey, hey, easy, Ivers. All I wanted was for him to walk away from the merger, and he did."

"And then he shot my father." Al was shouting now, making the silence that followed all the more oppressive. He pressed his lips together in a thin line and finally continued in a lowered voice, soft enough to give Rafael the shivers. "I want to know what you told him, so please cut the bullshit."

"It was just a business deal between Turner's old man and yours—your father."

"A business deal? What kind of business deal?"

"I guess Turner Senior, whose name was actually Hughes, owned a club somewhere close to one of Ivers's. Ivers wanted to combine the two into one giant thing, Hughes said no, and Ivers ruined him."

"A club," Al snorted and rolled his eyes to the ceiling. "A club. Barry, nobody commits murder because of a club that goes under. You open a new one around the corner, trust me—I worked the business a whole lot longer than you have."

"Well, maybe you should talk to your brother then. He's the one who dug up the story."

"Remind me again how the two of you even came to work together?"

"Roberto." Barry said the name as if it were filthy. "Running away from your old man and his latest ideas for Roberto's life. He thought what we were doing was cool, and Tadeo had no intentions of letting him into this business after the stunt he pulled with the secret grow op," Barry said. "I should know—I was blamed for it."

"And?"

"I told him we could partner in this business—long as he found something that would make Turner walk away from that merger.

He's the one who dug up that story and served it to Turner on a silver platter. Merger? Boom."

Barry spread his hands outward and shrugged. "I didn't need to or want to know any more about it."

"And you didn't hold up your end of the bargain either," Al said and walked to the window, staring down onto the production floor.

"After everything that happened when I got back? No, of course not. Not my fault if Turner went crazy."

Al still kept his back turned, his hands tensed in the pockets of his jacket, and Rafael decided to step in.

"Nobody is blaming anybody, Barry. Just trying to make it make sense. If you think about it, that really is not a reason to go out and shoot somebody."

Barry looked down at his hands and picked at something on his right thumbnail. There was more, Rafael thought. With Barry, you never got the whole story unless you went digging for it. Barry shook his head.

"I don't know, Rafael. Maybe he just went nuts when he realized he was losing his own business."

"Nah, doesn't ring."

"Listen, guys." Barry got to his feet again and tugged his blazer down properly. "There." He pointed at an envelope he had brought, which now lay abandoned on Al's desk. "Commitment letters for several million dollars of investments. That's what I brought you today. That is what you hired me for. Let me know how your expansion plans turn out, will you? I have a client to see just now. You have yourselves a great day."

He walked out without looking back, and Rafael still stood bent over the chair he'd been sitting in, wondering what just happened.

He dropped into his own chair and forked his hand through his hair. He looked at Kayla, who had pulled out her phone and furiously typed away at it.

"The world of news never stops, does it," he said weakly only to fill the silence in the room, and Kayla shook her head.

"You got it. But I am messaging with my researcher. Nothing on Turner né Hughes yet, but she is digging."

"I think my head is exploding."

Rafael went to the espresso machine in the corner and pushed buttons. "Al? You look like you could use something."

"Sure."

Al turned around and came to take a cup off Rafael. "His casual disregard for anything but his own purposes has the ability of driving me insane."

"Yup. And he's still the best fundraiser there ever was."

"And a major shareholder."

"And that." Rafael took another cup and put it down in front of Kayla, who was still typing so fast his eyes couldn't follow.

"So where do we go from here?"

"Take a step back," Al said, cupping his cappuccino with both hands. "Turner will go to jail, no doubt, Barry will continue being Barry, and I may just have to live with a set of strange and unsatisfying facts about the death of my father."

Can you do that, Rafael meant to say, when Kayla interrupted him.

"Oliver Hughes," she said, reading off the screen of her phone. "Successful businessman, entrepreneur, and club owner about 35 years ago."

"So, it was all about another club then," Al said, taking a sip, sounding just a bit disappointed.

"Not just any club, though." Kayla swiped up on the phone and continued reading. "The Golden Pearl, an upscale social club with an integrated dining room which became wildly successful due to its imaginative cuisine and exclusive musical entertainment."

Al nodded, drinking his coffee. "Tadeo would have wanted that. A step up from the seedier places he owned, his chance to become respected. What happened?"

"Still trying to figure that out."

"It would still not be worth committing murder over," Rafael muttered, finally bringing his own cup to the desk.

Kayla shot him a pointed glare, and he took a sip of his coffee, promptly burning his tongue, cussing softly.

"I wonder where Robertson is," he said, blowing gently on his cup.

"Likely out taking in Turner, asking him a few direct questions about murdering Tadeo," she suggested. "You can hardly expect him to keep you up to date on the ongoing investigation you interrupted this morning."

"While giving him a suspect he wouldn't have had otherwise."

"Aw, poor Rafael, are you feeling unappreciated?"

She grinned at him and Al and opened her mouth to say something. Just then, Kayla's phone chimed with another message from her researcher. She looked down, reading, and covered her mouth with a hand.

"Oh no."

"What? What did she find?"

Two steps brought Al to Kayla's side, and he read over her shoulder.

"38-year-old business man, Oliver Hughes, committed suicide today in the storeroom of his upscale social club, The Golden Pearl. Hughes is said to have been distraught over the bankruptcy of his business and his personal bankruptcy and hanged himself with his own belt. Hughes leaves behind a wife and five-year-old son."

"Turner," Rafael said softly. "Barry was not kidding when he said Tadeo ruined Turner's father."

Kayla still sat with her hand covering her mouth, and Al closed his eyes, took a step back, and all but dropped into his chair.

"So, Turner," he said, "grew up without a father."

"And probably not under the greatest of circumstances either," Kayla added, looking down at her screen. "Considering he left behind business and personal bankruptcies. And years later, he finds himself contemplating a merger with the man who was responsible for it all. What are the chances? No wonder..."

She bit off the rest of her sentence. *No wonder he committed murder.*

"But why did he even go there?" Rafael asked. "Why start it all only to walk away?"

"He may not have known," Kayla said. "At five years of age, probably didn't fully grasp what was going on and, if I were a mother, I may not tell my son either. Better to make up some tidy story that lets him grow up without the pain of the past."

She walked up to Al and hugged him, sitting in his chair. "I am so sorry, Al. I don't know what to say right now."

"It's all right." He forced a tight smile and ordered papers on his desk that didn't need ordering. "Long time ago—I myself was only a wee lad back then."

"That doesn't really make it..."

"I know, OK? I know that doesn't really make a difference, but stop, please. Right at the moment, I cannot use any sympathy. I was wrong. I was dead wrong, in case you were wondering. Solving the mystery around my father's death does not make it any easier to handle."

He took a deep breath and looked up at Rafael.

"Can we get back to work now please? I need to work out the plans for our expansion. That money Barry brought in will be helpful for that. Speaking of which, I need someone to have those papers taken down to Finance, scanned in, and taken care of properly."

"You got it." Rafael took the envelope and took Kayla by the arm, pointing her toward the door.

She pulled away to come back to Al, but Rafael shook his head gently. Right now, his friend needed to be alone.

FORTY-SEVEN

Al stayed buried in work for the rest of the day, and Rafael spread word he was occupied and to leave him alone unless the matter was of utmost urgency. He stopped himself just in time from using the old phrase, "matter of life or death." How quickly perspectives could change.

He found harmless reasons all through the day to drop by their office for a coffee, or to drop some harmless-looking paperwork on his own desk, and, every time, Al barely looked up, acknowledged him with a nod, and bent to his work again.

Perhaps time would reconcile him to what happened; Rafael most certainly hoped so. Right then, he resolved to phone his mother on the weekend, who lived in a home a few hours away, just to find out how she was doing.

Every now and then, he would stop and allow himself to think about Detective Sergeant Robertson arresting Turner. They would have gone to his house by now, right? They would have arrested him or at least taken him in for questioning.

Rafael thought of that dark, featureless interview room with the cameras and the microphones and shuddered. It was nothing like chats on *Law & Order*—it was hours upon hours upon hours of having to answer the same damn questions over and over until you got tired of saying, *I already answered that*. That alone, he figured, should really stop people from committing any kind of crime, but then again, he was a builder, not a criminal.

He considered giving Dante the heads-up because he liked the guy, and he figured Dante should know what was going on, but in the end decided against it. Not his place. Dante would find out when Turner was arrested.

Turner would certainly confess, now that all the pieces lined up.

"You got something on your mind, Rafael?"

Rafael looked up and straight into the eyes of Dante.

"Uh—no, not really, why do you ask?"

"Because you've been staring at that readout for the last 20 minutes. For what it's worth, I've come around to your thinking. One of the wall seals must be leaking, messing with the temperature sensor in there." He nodded at pod five. "But unless we take everything down and reseal the walls, I don't see as how you can fix it."

Rafael stared at the readouts on the panel and through the window into the grow pod, then back at the readouts. 20 minutes? He'd been standing there for 20 minutes.

"It shouldn't really make that massive of a difference," he said, dragging his mind back with an effort. "There is something else going on, maybe in the environmental controls. For now..." He rolled his shoulders and scrolled through the readout history on his panel. "For now, move all of the plants in there into pod six as soon as it is cleaned and sterilized. They finished the harvest in there just this morning."

"I was part of that, Rafael," Dante reminded him, but Rafael only nodded.

"Good, then get an extra crew to get a move on, sterilize the space, and move these plants. I don't want to lose the entire harvest because the electronics kick up a fuss."

He nodded again and walked away before Dante could tell him they were his electronics, and he had told them all of it functioned fully automated. He really did need to run a full test panel on all environmental controls and elements for that particular pod, and that would take him several days.

"Goddammit," he muttered as he walked and eventually ran into Kayla.

"Bad news?"

"No more than usual. Damn plants are finicky little suckers."

"I thought you were going to work on your language."

"I was. But what can I tell you? I'm a…"

"A builder, not a poet," Kayla finished. "I heard it—just keep trying. Have you checked on Al lately?"

"Couple of hours ago, I don't want him to think I'm hovering."

"I also don't want him to think that this is his problem and he'll just have to deal with it. Which is why I invited him to dinner."

"And he in fact said yes?"

That would have surprised Rafael, since usually he had to drag things out of Al, especially things of a more personal nature, but Kayla had her ways.

"He said he would think about it."

"Ah."

"I need you to make sure he shows up."

"I—don't really think…" Rafael began, trying to put into words that, if Al went into possum-mode, there was no way he could manage to drag him out, when his phone saved him by chirping.

"Hang on…"

He flicked on the screen and read a text from Al.

I would presume Kayla is at this moment trying to convince you to drag me to dinner with you.

You would presume correct.

I don't have time for that.

She won't like it.

No doubt, but Robertson just asked me to see him at the station.

???

I don't know. If you have the time, I would appreciate your company.

You got it.

428

Rafael slipped his phone back into his pocket and put his palms together. "Don't kill me, OK?"

"I'm not going to like it, am I?"

"No. Robertson asked Al to come in. He likely has a few more questions. And Al asked if I had the time to accompany him."

"Of course. I want to help Al through—if possible, without strangling Barry, although that is still an option. If this helps, I'm all for it."

"Wonder what Robertson wants?" Rafael mused. "I thought he'd be questioning Turner by now. What's he want with Al?"

"Turner may have confessed." Kayla shook her head. "Or not. They may need details from Al. Go with him. I'll see you later."

Rafael nodded, but again, his mind was on something else. Details? Why would they need Al now? When they surely had arrested Turner. They had to have. Or at least brought him in for questioning.

***

"The man probably has a good attorney," he said to Al as they drove out to the station.

"Probably."

"You see, if I'm Turner, and I've done it, then I've probably already thought about what to do if it ever comes out, right?"

"You're not Turner. And I can't see you shooting somebody."

"Well, I wouldn't, but…"

"Rafael." Al held up his hand, stopping any speculation. "For one, please keep your eye on the road or let me drive. For another, these speculations are neither helpful nor entertaining. I have no idea what Robertson wants with me. He did not say. So, I will find out when I get there. I asked you to come along, but only…"

"To keep you from spiraling into the insane?" Rafael asked with a guilty grin and slowed down their speed.

"Amongst other things, yes."

And that, Rafael figured, was as close as Al Ivers would ever come to saying, *I just needed a friend.* He would take it. He stopped talking about Turner and his arrest and the shooting, and speculated instead about the dinner Kayla probably had been planning—a dinner they now missed.

To their surprise, the moment Al announced his name to the officer at the front desk, they were led into a comfortable but cluttered office and found seats.

"Robertson's office?" Rafael ventured.

"Possibly."

Rafael wanted to speculate again—perhaps Turner had confessed, perhaps they needed one more statement, and Al could give it, perhaps Turner was blaming someone else entirely… Wisely, he kept his mouth shut.

"This is killing you, isn't it?" Al asked.

"I don't know what you are talking about."

"You are naturally curious, Rafael. That's what makes you so good at discovering and tailoring solutions to problems. But not speculating about the solution must be driving you insane by now."

"A little."

Al smiled, and Rafael realized, gratefully, that he had missed that wry little smile. "You are also a dreadful liar."

"Well, there, you see…"

Rafael was all ready to defend himself and his lack of prevarication skills when the door opened and Detective Sergeant Robertson swept in, slammed the door, and dropped into his chair, all in one fluid motion.

"Al." He nodded. "You brought Rafael for moral support?"

"If it is all right?"

Robertson forked both hands through his hair, and Rafael noticed for the first time that he actually looked pretty bad. Disheveled, tired, angry—old. He had not had a great day.

And he and Al had contributed to his bad day. The look on Robertson's face could only be described as… What? Grave? Rafael shifted uncomfortably in his chair.

They sat, and for a moment, all he could hear was a far-off conversation out in the hallway and then a deep sigh from Robertson.

"As you know," he began, rubbing his hands together, "we had certain suspicions about Greg Turner and his involvement in your father's death."

Al only nodded, hands folded primly in his lap, but the fingers clenched tight and the knuckles almost white.

"I went to his house earlier to pick him up for a little chat—not an outright arrest, although we could have—but just a chat, to get his take on everything that happened."

"And?" Rafael asked eagerly, earning a stern glare from Robertson. Finally, the detective shook his head.

"Gone," he said after a moment.

"What do you mean gone?"

"Gone, Al. As in flown the coop, left town, disappeared. Withdrew himself from the consequences of his actions."

Rafael heard a great rushing in his ears. Beside him, Al audibly fought for breath, and the knuckles on his clenched hands cracked.

"Here," Robertson said. "We found this in his desk at his house. I probably should not be showing you this, but there may be—consequences."

He placed what looked like a clear cellophane sleeve on the desk between them. Inside it was a single white sheet of paper with a few handwritten lines. Al still fought to breathe, so Rafael pulled the plastic sleeve closer, almost afraid to touch it, and read.

"As you are reading this," he said out loud, "I can assume you have made the connection between that common little robber breaking in at Green Technologies and the gun in my desk and its history. The moment I heard you arrested him, I knew my time was up.

"I didn't know what Tadeo Ivers had done to our family until Roberto came to rub my nose in it. Oh, how he enjoyed it! What a typical Ivers. Perhaps Tadeo himself didn't know who I was, since my mother took on her maiden name after my father hanged himself.

"It killed him, not only his own bankruptcy, but taking with him all the other small suppliers he couldn't pay—it literally killed him.

"And Ivers, who had driven him into ruin for the sake of the property and the club on it, stood by and walked away scot-free.

"He deserved to die, for everything he had done—if there's any justice in this world, he deserved it.

"If I am taking the coward's way out, so be it. I tried to avenge my father's death with his shooting, but it was not enough, not even close.

"Rest assured, I will not stop until the Ivers family, who drove him into suicide, is gone."

Rafael put the paper in its plastic sleeve back down on the table and licked his suddenly dry lips. Al sat perfectly still, barely breathing.

"So, it is as you assumed," Robertson said, breaking the silence. "He tried to avenge his father."

"Do you have any idea where he—may have gone?" Rafael tried, and Robertson shook his head.

"Heck, Rafael, I don't even know when he left. It was impossible to tell from the state of his house, and he left everything behind—everything. Phone, credit cards, bank cards."

"Anything you could use to trace him."

"Exactly. As we speak, we are covering major airports, freeways, and the like because, if he's smart, he'll try to get out of the country. Other than that, we'll have to wait for a lucky break to catch him."

"And until then…" Al broke the silence, his voice raspy and painful.

"That is why I called you in here, Al. Read his last sentence again—*until the Ivers family is gone. The Ivers family.* All of you. I have a very strong suspicion he will target the rest of your family."

"But…"

"Don't argue with me, Al. We are going to have to talk protection here. Until Greg Turner has been caught, I cannot guarantee your safety. Matter of fact, I can almost guarantee you he will come after you and your brothers. He's already killed once. What's another life sentence on top of that, when we finally catch him?"

ACKNOWLEDGEMENTS

I am immensely thankful as I write the acknowledgments for Book 3 in this series. The "Cannabis Preacher" series has been such an incredible journey of creativity and imagination. Without the support and contributions of numerous individuals, this book would not have been possible.

First and foremost, I want to express my deepest appreciation to my loyal readers. Your enthusiasm and unwavering support have been the driving force behind my determination to continue this series. Your kind words and encouragement have touched my heart, and I am eternally grateful for your continued belief in my storytelling.

I would like to extend my heartfelt thanks to my editor, whose keen eye and insightful feedback have been instrumental in shaping this book. Your dedication to perfection has pushed me to improve and refine my writing, and I am sincerely grateful for your guidance and expertise.

To the entire publishing team at PRB who worked tirelessly to bring this book to life, I am profoundly indebted to you. From the designers and illustrators who crafted the captivating cover and interior elements to the project team that meticulously ensured every detail was in place, your professionalism and commitment to excellence have exceeded my expectations. It has been an honor collaborating with such talented individuals.

A special mention goes to my family (human and canine alike 🐾) and friends for their unwavering support throughout this series. Your love, encouragement, and belief in my abilities have been a constant source of inspiration. I am incredibly lucky to have you all in my corner, cheering me on every step of the way.

I am also grateful to the writing community, both online and offline, for fostering an environment of camaraderie and shared passion. The friendships and connections I have made within this community have been invaluable, providing me with a network of like-minded individuals who have uplifted and motivated me during challenging times.

Lastly, I would like to express my deepest appreciation to the characters themselves—the vibrant, multidimensional beings who have taken on a life of their own. Their stories have resonated with readers, and it is humbling to witness their impact. Without their voices echoing in my mind, this series would never have come to life.

To all those who have contributed in big and small ways, I offer my sincerest thanks. You have all played an indispensable role in bringing Book 3 of this series to fruition. May this book captivate and transport readers, just as it has captivated and transported me throughout its creation.

With heartfelt gratitude,

Sabine